TRACING
the
SHADOW

Also by Sarah Ash

LORD OF SNOW AND SHADOWS
Book One of the Tears of Artamon

PRISONER OF THE IRON TOWER
Book Two of the Tears of Artamon

CHILDREN OF THE SERPENT GATE
Book Three of the Tears of Artamon

TRACING
the
SHADOW

Book One of the Alchymist's Legacy

Sarah Ash

BANTAM BOOKS

TRACING THE SHADOW
A Bantam Spectra Book / February 2008

Published by Bantam Dell
A Division of Random House, Inc.
New York, New York

Library of Congress Cataloging-in-Publication Data

Ash, Sarah.
Tracing the shadow / Sarah Ash.
p. cm. — (The alchymist's legacy ; bk. 1)
"A Bantam Spectra book."
ISBN 978-0-553-80519-2
I. Title.
PS3601.S523T73 2008
813'.6—dc22
2007036284

Printed in the United States of America
Published simultaneously in Canada

www.bantamdell.com

10 9 8 7 6 5 4 3 2 1
BVG

For Joan, *ma belle-mère*

ACKNOWLEDGMENTS

My warmest thanks go to:

My editor, Anne Groell, for her expertise, patience, and encouragement

My agents, Merrilee Heifetz and John Richard Parker, for getting this project off the ground

Two very talented artists: Phil Heffernan for the cover art and Neil Gower for the map

Josh Pasternak for his care in helping *Tracing* evolve from typescript to printed book

Ariel, my ever-resourceful webmaster

Alain Nevant and Stéphane Marsan and all their fellow Mousquetaires for welcoming me to Bragelonne

Michael for reminding me to "Go upstairs and write!"

Blessed Azilia, let thy light shine through the darkness and show us the way to paradise.

—Vesper Prayer of the Knights of the Commanderie

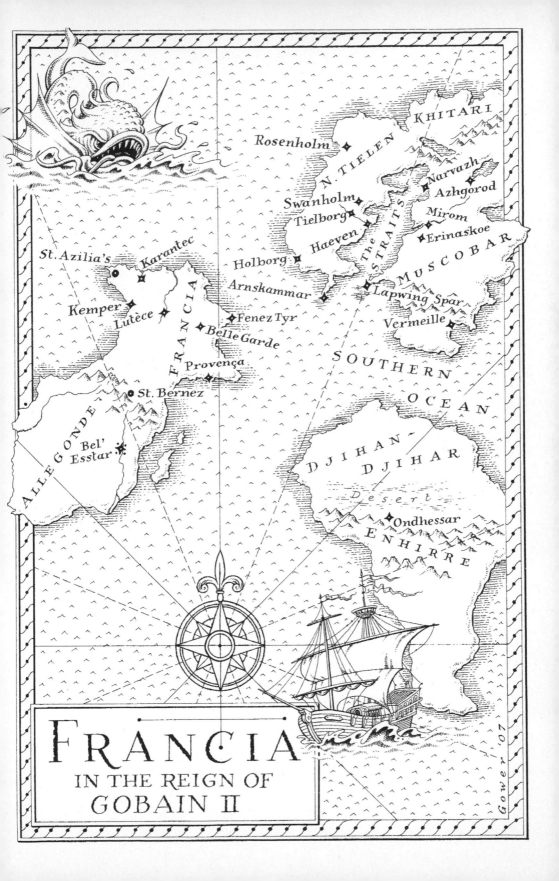

Rosenholm

KHITARI

N. TIELEN

Narvazh

Azhgorod

Swanholm

Mirom

Tielborg

Haeven

Erinaskoe

St. Azilia's

Karantec

MUSCOBAR

Holborg

Kemper

Arnskammar

Lapwing Spar

Lutèce

FRANCIA

Fenez Tyr

Vermeille

Belle Garde

SOUTHERN

Provença

St. Bernez

OCEAN

ALLEGONDE

Bel' Esstar

DJIHAN-
DJIHAR
Desert

Ondhessar

ENHIRRE

FRANCIA
IN THE REIGN OF
GOBAIN II

Gower '07

PROLOGUE

Ruaud de Lanvaux staggered as he passed beneath the archway into fabled Ondhessar. He was exhausted. Blood dripped into one eye from a scimitar slash he had received in the final assault on the citadel, and he wiped it away on the back of his hand.

"Fly our standard from the highest tower," he ordered. "Let all Enhirre see that the Francian Commanderie is here to stay."

The courtyard in front of him was strewn with bodies. The Enhirrans had fought like cornered dogs, desperately refusing to admit defeat. Even a hardened soldier like Ruaud was shaken by the sight; the night air stank of death. Even as his triumphant Guerriers took possession of the citadel, meticulously checking out every tower, every passageway on his orders, he heard the occasional pistol shot and stifled cry.

Ruaud walked slowly on across the bloodstained courtyard. His men were checking the dead, turning them over one by one, stripping them of their weapons.

And then he caught a low, rasping groan close by.

"This one's still alive, Captain," called Lieutenant Konan, holding his knife blade to the Enhirran's throat. Ruaud went over. By the torchlight, he saw that the wounded man was young, hardly more than a boy. From the glistening blood seeping out from beneath his body and trickling from the side of his mouth, it was obvious that he wasn't likely to last long. "Shall I put him out of his misery?" growled Konan.

The Enhirran murmured something and Ruaud saw a flicker of

defiant fire in his dulled eyes. "Is he asking for water?" He went down on one knee beside him. "At least give the lad a drink."

"You . . . defile . . . the holy place," whispered the Enhirran in the common tongue. "You . . . have no right . . . to be here . . ."

"No right?" Konan grabbed the boy by the hair as if he was about to slit his throat. "You insolent—"

"Konan." Ruaud placed a restraining hand on his lieutenant's arm. "Let him be."

"In Azilis's name . . . I curse you . . . and all Francia . . ." The young warrior's voice became more indistinct. "They will avenge us. They will come after you, the hawks that fly in the night . . ." The threat ended in a choking cough as blood gushed from his mouth. When Konan laid him down, his eyes had slid upward, staring sightlessly at the stars.

"Look, Captain." Lieutenant Konan pointed. "See this? Is it some kind of tribal marking? Every man I've found has it."

There was a tattoo, in indigo ink, on the boy's left hand and another identical mark on his forehead

"It looks like a character in Old Enhirran," Ruaud said. "The letter 'A.' "

"A? For Azilia?" Konan said, a tremble of emotion in his deep voice. "The Eternal Singer? Have we found the place at last?"

"But at such a high cost." Ruaud drew his hand over the boy's staring eyes, closing the lids. "Hundreds of Enhirrans have died here over the past days."

"We have as much right as they to come on pilgrimage!" Konan said indignantly.

Ruaud let out a sigh that issued from the depths of his soul. "I fear they will not be quick to forgive us for taking Ondhessar."

She had many names. To the Francians, she was Saint Azilia; to the Allegondans, she was Elesstar, the Beloved, patron saint and protectress of their capital city, Bel'Esstar. To the people of Enhirre, her birthplace, she was Azilis, the Eternal Singer. For hundreds of years, the Enhirrans had kept this place a secret from the rest of the quadrant, constructing the fortress-citadel of Ondhessar to protect Azilis's Shrine.

A faint, high, eerie voice drifted over the scene of carnage, as clear as if spun from starlight . . .

"D'you hear that, Captain?" said Konan, wiping his bloodied knife clean.

Ruaud's rational mind told him that the singing was just a natural phenomenon, the cold wind of the desert night whistling between the towers . . .

Until Alain Friard appeared at the doorway of one of the towers, beckoning excitedly.

"We've found her, Captain."

Ruaud followed Friard. The fragile thread of sound grew clearer, more intense as he entered the shadowed doorway. A gleam of light faintly illuminated a dark passageway that wound down deep into the earth.

The atmosphere grew colder as he descended, one hand against the rough rock wall to guide him. The eerie song made the air tingle. They must be drawing nearer.

A pale figure glimmered in the shadows. Ruaud stopped, heart beating too fast—until he realized it was only a marble statue. Ancient, yet radiant with a bewitching, androgynous beauty, Azilia stood with both hands cupped, holding a lotus flower, symbol of the immortal soul. White light emanated from the crystal petals. And at the heart of the lotus lay the source of the sound: a white crystal of glittering purity. The high, unearthly strain was emanating from the stone.

"How can it be that the stone is singing?" Père Laorans, the regiment's priest, stood gazing up at the statue, his bearded face bathed in the white light. "Is it a natural phenomenon or the miraculous influence of the saint?"

Ruaud, entranced, extended one hand to touch the crystal lotus petals. As his fingers made contact, a loud grinding startled him; the other Guerriers whirled around, grasping their sword hilts, fearing a surprise attack. But an opening had appeared in the wall behind the statue, slowly gaping to reveal a cavity. Père Laorans thrust his hands into the cavity before Ruaud could stop him and let out a shout of excitement.

"Look!" he cried, pulling out his discovery. "Manuscripts. Scrolls. Ancient writings."

Ruaud looked at the ancient parchments, so discolored with age and dust that it was hard to see any writing on them until Père Laorans held them close to the crystals. Faint characters began to appear on the faded vellum, almost as if the silvery light had brought them to life.

"Old Enhirran," said Père Laorans triumphantly. "*The Book of Azilis,*" he translated. " 'The Eternal . . . Singer.' " He looked up at Ruaud. "This is one of the Sacred Texts," he said in hushed tones.

"So this is a significant find?" Ruaud forgot his exhaustion; even his wound seemed to have stopped stinging since he entered the cavern.

"It must date back to Saint Sergius's time . . . or even earlier. Maybe even to the time that Azilia herself was still alive."

The great citadel of Ondhessar dominated the ridge, towering high above the hidden valley. Armed sentries constantly patrolled its battlements, where the crimson banners of the Commanderie fluttered in the wind. Cannons protruded from its battlements, ready to repel attackers.

But the trespasser had infiltrated the citadel by a secret way. With the setting of the sun came the faint, high, eerie voice he had been waiting to hear, as clear as if spun from starlight . . .

The trespasser flitted from tower to tower, gazing up at the worn carvings that surrounded each gaping doorway. He kept glancing uneasily over his shoulder, aware that he could be discovered at any moment. He had entered forbidden ground, and the price for discovery was death.

No time to linger.

The fragile voice grew clearer, more intense. He entered the shadowed doorway and followed the thread of sound down a dark stair. If he was caught in the act of trespass, there would be no possible escape; he would be trapped deep belowground. The Guerriers of the Commanderie had dedicated their lives to the annihilation of all who practiced the Forbidden Arts. It had taken him many months of delicate investigation and deception to discover the location of this mystery. He was not going to let a few fanatical Francians stand in his way.

"And here you are," he said softly. The statue of Azilis stood before him, holding the lotus flower in which nestled the source of the unearthly sound. "An aethyr crystal."

The trespasser gazed down at his prize in amazement, the soft radiance illuminating his face. Then he moved swiftly, purposefully, taking a sharp chisel from his pocket, working to pry the rare stone from the lotus within the statue's curved fingers.

Just as it came loose, the sound stopped abruptly. Hastily, he thrust his prize into his inner pocket, took out another stone, a clear crystal, and put it in the lotus gem's place.

"Someone's in the Shrine!" Booted feet clattered overhead, coming nearer.

He had been discovered.

"Give yourself up! You're surrounded."

He made for the winding stair and started to climb.

"The tower! Cut him off at the entrance!" There was still a chance he might get away, but his knees were aching as he stumbled on upward, each worn step seeming steeper than the last.

The arched doorway lay ahead. The moon had risen while he was underground. He hurried onward, hearing his own painful wheezing echoing in the lofty vault of the tower.

I'm getting too old for this kind of venture.

Outside, the citadel towers loomed above him, silvered by the rising moon. If he could just make it to his craft . . .

A Guerrier appeared out of the shadows. "Stop, or we shoot." He leveled a pistol at him. "You won't get away." The voice was young and earnest.

Yet the trespasser ran on, ignoring the warning.

"Fire!"

Tiny bursts of flame lit the darkness as the powder in the pans ignited and shots rang out. Musket balls whizzed past him, grazing off chips of stone as he ran.

"After him—don't let him escape!"

He reached his craft, little bigger than a rowboat, and crawled inside, shaking loose the sail.

Must find enough strength to get away.

He closed his eyes, seeking the path of the winds. Streaking like crystal dragons, they scored interweaving tracks through the night, high above. He reached out to them and felt a sudden shudder in the air as one tore across the desert toward the fort.

Clouds of dust and sand arose, blotting out the stars. And as the sail filled, the wind began to lift the craft into the air.

The first Guerrier, swifter than the rest, caught up with him. He made a grab for the craft, clinging on to the side.

Damn you, you won't stop me now.

The trespasser twisted his fingers together, making the hand signs to control the wind beneath his craft.

Dust, grit, and sand, sucked up from below, showered down, peppering the Guerrier, laceratingly sharp as tiny shards of glass. Half-blinded, he loosed his hold and fell. The craft rose and went spinning away. The last the trespasser saw as the fast-gusting wind bore him swiftly upward toward the stars was the young Guerrier lying sprawled on the ground.

CHAPTER 1

The Aethyr Vox stood on Magister Linnaius's desk, collecting dust. It had stood there for many weeks, awaiting its inventor's return. And Rieuk Mordiern, Linnaius's apprentice, had been assigned to cleaning duties again. With a feather duster, he began to clean the delicate mechanism.

"Apprentice alchymist? Unpaid servant, more like," he muttered to the empty laboratory.

In his master's absence, Rieuk had been kept busy assisting Magister de Maunoir, but he was still charged with keeping Linnaius's laboratory spotless, in readiness for his return.

The Aethyr Vox had been developed by two alchymists, Linnaius and Hervé de Maunoir. The device was designed to convey the voice through the aethyr by setting up resonances, using crystals that had been alchymically charged. A second Vox had been installed in Magister de Maunoir's cottage beyond the college walls, and the two magisters had spent many long hours trying to communicate with each other. But to their frustration, it still did not work.

Next to the Vox stood a tray glittering with quartz crystals of varying shapes and types; each one had already been tested in the Vox as a conductor and discarded. Rieuk set down the duster and lifted one, balancing it in the palm of his hand.

He could sense a faint resonance emanating from the heart of the crystal. This natural connection between his flesh and blood and the rock was intoxicating. It was as if he were listening to the heartbeat of the earth itself. He had begun of late to realize that the other students did not share this ability. If he closed his eyes and let his mind become fully attuned to the pulse, he could sometimes glimpse the aethyr stream: a fast-flowing current moving between worlds and dimensions.

The crystal vibrations flowed through Rieuk's body. This one sang like a high, reedy flute, emitting little pulses of citrine light. Entranced by the purity of its cleansing tone, he stood there, his tasks forgotten, listening intently.

The door burst open. Startled, Rieuk almost dropped the crystal. But it was only Deniel, Magister de Rhuys's apprentice.

"Magister Gonery needs you. It's urgent."

Rieuk slipped the crystal into his jacket pocket for safekeeping. "What's so urgent it can't wait till I've done my chores?" he asked as he followed Deniel out into the corridor.

"Important visitors from the capital. Asking for your master. Hurry!"

The Vox. It must be about the Vox.

Rieuk ran all the way from Magister Linnaius's tower to the principal's study, almost sliding down the spiral stair. He arrived out of breath.

"Ah, here is Rieuk Mordiern, Magister Linnaius's apprentice," said Magister Gonery, beckoning him inside. "Close the door, Rieuk. We don't want to be interrupted."

Two strangers turned to stare at him. Both wore long and travel-stained coats, yet there was something about their haughty bearing that spoke of power and influence. These must be the government officials, come to check on the invention that they had funded. One had a grizzled, neatly trimmed beard; the other, smooth-shaven, hovered behind, holding a dispatch case.

"Well?" asked the elder of the two, seating himself opposite Magister Gonery. "Is the device ready?"

Rieuk shot an anguished look at the old alchymist.

"There have been a few . . . minor problems," said Gonery in level tones.

"Unfortunate for my masters . . . but rather more unfortunate for you and the college." The government official's voice was smooth and pleasantly modulated but Rieuk heard an unmistakable hint of warning and shivered. "Magister Linnaius made us a promise. He assured us that the Vox would be finished by early summer. And now, when Francia has its greatest need, you tell me that he's encountered a 'few problems'?"

"Where is he?" demanded the other. "Why is he not here, as we arranged? Does he intend to insult us by sending a mere apprentice in his stead? Or is he too ashamed to show his face?"

A *mere* apprentice. That stung.

"Rieuk, tell our visitors where your master has gone."

Rieuk felt as if a hand had tightened around his vocal cords. "My—my master has gone overseas to find a special kind of crystal for the Vox."

The elder of the two let out an impatient sigh. "This is unacceptable. The Ministry has paid the college a considerable sum of money to finance this project."

"Exactly when was your master planning on returning?" said the other, rounding on Rieuk. Rieuk took a step back.

"If the Admiralty could just grant us another week or so . . ." put in Magister Gonery. Rieuk had never heard Magister Gonery speak so deferentially before.

"In my opinion, too much is riding on the success of Magister Linnaius's invention," said the elder official to his colleague. He leaned on Magister Gonery's desk, confronting the old alchymist. "Have you *any* idea what's happening outside the peaceful confines of your little college, Magister?"

Gonery shook his head.

"Francia is under threat. War with Tielen is almost inevitable. We need the Vox *now.*"

War? Rieuk's eyes widened at the thought. Were the Tielens about to launch an invasion?

"Heaven knows, it's been hard enough trying to keep the Inquisition away from your doors. And now there's a new Inquisitor, who is more than eager to prove himself to the king."

"A new Inquisitor?" Magister Gonery repeated slowly, as though digesting this information.

"Alois Visant. And he has his eye on this college. It seems that there have been complaints in the town. Accusations. At the first whisper of forbidden practices, he will shut you down and put you all on trial."

"We have nothing to hide," said Gonery mildly.

This news only increased Rieuk's apprehension; if the Admiralty officials went away empty-handed, they would withdraw their protection and the college would be in danger from the religious fanatics running the Inquisition. They were suspicious of alchymy, regarding it as little different from the forbidden Dark Arts.

"We're busy men, Magister. We can't waste any more time here," said the elder.

"If you were to return tomorrow, gentlemen, I'm sure that —"

"We're on our way to the naval dockyards at Fenez-Tyr. If there's a breakthrough, send word to us there, at the manager's house." The younger official placed a paper on Gonery's desk and snapped his case shut.

"If we hear nothing from you by the end of the week, then your funding will be stopped and the project canceled." The elder official stopped at the door, then turned back as if a thought had just occurred to him. "And if that happens, we can no longer protect you from investigation by the Inquisition."

Magister Gonery nodded.

"We'll show ourselves out. Good-day to you, Magister Gonery."

When the visitors had gone, Magister Gonery sank back down into his chair. Rieuk glanced at the elderly alchymist, uncertain what to do. The official's ominous last words kept repeating in his head. An Inquisition investigation.

"This is serious, isn't it, Magister?"

"What?" Gonery looked up, blinking, as if he had forgotten Rieuk was there. "Events have overtaken us, Rieuk. It seems that the Tielens have taken our ministers by surprise."

"But if we could make the Vox work, it would save the college from closure." Rieuk's hand slid into his pocket where the citrine crystal lay and felt a little tingle of energy tickle his fingertips. "Magister, let me try. You know I have some skill with crystals. If it's to save the college—"

"And has Magister Linnaius given you permission to work on his invention?"

Rieuk hesitated. "Well, not exactly . . ."

"If I were you, I would not attempt anything that would make Magister Linnaius angry," said Gonery, regarding him severely over the top of his spectacles.

"So what was all that about?" Deniel met Rieuk as he approached the laboratory. "Oh, come on, you can tell me. I won't blab. Was it about the Vox?"

Rieuk recovered enough to nod.

"Can't you ask to be transferred to Maistre de Rhuys? He's much more easygoing."

"But he already has you and Madoc."

"And we split the work between us. Which leaves time for fun." Deniel reached out and tousled Rieuk's hair. "When was the last time you came out into Karantec with us?"

Rieuk gave a little shrug.

"Madoc and I are off to the tavern after dinner. There's a new girl working there, Jenovefa." Deniel outlined a voluptuous silhouette with both hands.

"I've got to work."

"Poor Rieuk. Nearly eighteen and never been kissed. I'm getting worried about you." Rieuk winced and ducked out of Deniel's range. "Always studying. There's more to life than alchymy."

But Rieuk had sensed a breath of winter's wind shiver along the passageway. Deniel must have felt it too because he turned instinctively, just as Magister Linnaius appeared behind him.

"M—Magister!" stammered Rieuk. "You've just missed the Admiralty officials."

"Unfortunate." Linnaius loomed over Rieuk, his eyes burning cold as ice. "Where is Magister de Maunoir?"

"I—I heard that his wife was sick," offered Deniel. "He's looking after little Klervie."

Magister Linnaius let out a short sigh of exasperation. "I have urgent news for Maistre Gonery. Rieuk, take this down to Magister de Maunoir." He thrust a small wooden box into Rieuk's hands.

"N—now?" It was nearly six in the evening and the dinner bell would soon be ringing out over the college towers.

"Must I repeat myself?" Magister Linnaius gave him a look of such chill disdain that Rieuk abandoned any hope of eating. "And Deniel, what are you doing idling outside my laboratory? Magister de Rhuys is looking for you." With that, Magister Linnaius swept on down the passageway.

"So no dinner for you tonight?" Deniel called back over his shoulder. "Shall I ask the kitchen to save some for you? It's fish stew—with mussels."

"Why couldn't you have got back a quarter hour earlier?" Rieuk muttered. But at least he had the chance to put the citrine crystal back before Magister Linnaius noticed it was missing. He reached into his pocket and drew it out, feeling again the pulse of its crystalline heartbeat.

But now he could sense another faint pulsation nearby. The crystal that nestled in his cupped hands must have set off a sympathetic resonance in another. And wasn't that precisely what Magister Linnaius had been trying to do, find two crystals that were "in tune" with each other?

Rieuk cast around for the source of the answering vibrations. The sound grew stronger as he moved toward the plain wooden box that his master had told him to take to Magister de Maunoir. With shaking fingers, Rieuk undid the metal catch and opened the lid.

Inside, cushioned on midnight-black silk, lay a crystal. It was clear, except for a single vein of milky white at its heart. "So beautiful," Rieuk murmured, hardly daring to touch it for fear of sullying its purity. "Like a fallen star."

Surely it wouldn't hurt to try? He lifted the glass cover and carefully inserted the still-vibrating citrine quartz in the Vox on the desk and adjusted the voice receptor. Then he closed the box lid on the crystal and set out. He could just imagine the magister's astonished comments when the Vox Aethyria began to transmit his voice. "*So young Rieuk Mordiern solved the problem that had you foxed, Kaspar!*"

Clutching the box, Rieuk ran down the winding lane that led toward the river and Magister de Maunoir's cottage. A fair-haired little girl was teasing an indolent grey tabby cat on the doorstep, waving an aspen twig over its whiskers and giggling delightedly whenever the cat opened one sleepy eye to bat the twig away.

"Hallo, m'sieur Rieuk!"

The little girl was smiling up at him, her eyes blue as the summer sky. He recognized the sweet face of Klervie, Hervé's daughter.

"Klervie, is your father at home?"

Klervie banged on the front door. "Papa!"

Magister de Maunoir appeared on the step with one finger pressed to his lips. "Ssh, Klervie. Maman still has a bad headache. Play quietly with Mewen." The cat rolled off the step and made a sudden dash toward the back garden with Klervie dancing after it. "I'm sorry, Rieuk." Magister de Maunoir looked even more careworn and bemused than usual. "Have you brought a message from the college?"

"It's about the Vox," Rieuk said in a loud whisper. "I think I've found two crystals with a sympathetic resonance."

Hervé de Maunoir's tired expression vanished. "You'd better come in!"

He led Rieuk to his study which, unlike Magister Linnaius's spotless laboratory, was crammed with precariously piled stacks of books, jars of gruesome specimens pickled in cloudy alcohol, and cases of dried insects. On the desk, amid all the clutter, gleamed the second Vox, twin to the one in college.

"I don't recall ever seeing a stone like this before," said de Maunoir in puzzled tones. He picked it up and examined it. "Where did you find it?"

Rieuk hesitated a moment. "Magister Linnaius brought it back with him."

"So he's returned at last! And he told you to use it in the Vox?"

Rieuk made a vague gesture. "He told me to bring it to you . . ."

"Well, I don't suppose it can hurt to try."

"It worked in the laboratory." Rieuk refused to let himself be defeated. Yet the crystal remained silent, and every attempt to make it sing as it had before failed.

"Perhaps we should try again tomorrow."

"Hervé," called a woman's voice weakly. "Has Klervie had her supper?"

Hervé leaped up. "Is that the time already?" he called back. "I'm on my way, dear." He returned a minute or so later. "She's not in the garden. She must have gone to her friend Youna's." Rieuk did not miss the flustered look in his eyes. "I'll be back soon."

"Let me try once more, Magister." His future as an alchymist might rest on this one act. If he succeeded, the Admiralty would get their invention and the college would be saved from closure.

"By all means . . ." Hervé was already hurrying out of the door.

Rieuk took the crystal out of the Vox and pressed it to his forehead, seeking again for that elusive voice. For a second he felt a tremor of energy, like a distant flicker of lightning. Hastily, he replaced it, and waited.

And waited.

Tired and dejected, Rieuk leaned forward on the desk beside the Vox and let his head rest on his outstretched arms. He closed his eyes. So close to success and yet still so far . . .

"So you really think this will lead to war?"

War? Who was talking of war? The voice had been faint, but utterly distinct.

"Francia laid claim to the islands first. Yet the Arkhan of Enhirre has just signed a trade treaty with Prince Karl of Tielen." That dry tone sounded just like his master's. But how could it be? *"He's granted Tielen exclusive rights to the spice trade. And now it's stalemate . . ."* The voice faded out. Rieuk raised his head, wondering if he had caught fragments of a conversation drifting in as people passed by the cottage.

"Are you being entirely frank with me, Kaspar?"

Rieuk sat bolt upright. Few people were permitted to call Magister Linnaius by his first name.

"You've a distracted look about you." The voice was issuing from the receiver of the Aethyr Vox. *"You haven't been doing any meddling yourself, have you?"*

"I may have stirred up a little trouble, yes, but nothing that I can't take care of."

Rieuk gripped the edge of the desk, rigid with concentration. The voices faded in and out, almost as if the two speakers were pacing to and fro in front of the Vox.

"Yes, but trouble may follow you here to Karantec and bring misfortune on us all," came Gonery's voice, suddenly clear, as though he were bending close to the speaker, making Rieuk jump.

"What's this?" demanded Magister Linnaius. *"Who placed this crystal in the transmitter, Gonery? Has Hervé been working on*

the Vox?" Rieuk shrank back. Even though logic told him that neither alchymist could see him, he felt as if he had been caught red-handed.

"I haven't seen Hervé today."

"Then who's been in my rooms?" The question was asked in such a menacing tone that Rieuk felt a sick, sinking sensation in his stomach. Magister Linnaius did not sound in the least pleased.

"Only your apprentice."

"Rieuk? Could he have tampered with—"

A thin, high whining sound began to emanate from the Vox.

"What is that infernal racket?"

The sound set Rieuk's teeth on edge. It was like chalk rasped over a blackboard, a knife blade scraped against glass. And it went on and on, growing ever more piercing.

"It's coming from the Vox!"

"I'll remove the cryst—" The voices ceased abruptly as the connection was broken. But the excruciating sound continued, drilling through all the cavities of his skull. Pressing a hand to one aching ear, Rieuk reached out to prise out the throbbing stone from its setting.

But the excruciating sound did not stop. The crystal lay in his sweating palms, still emitting its shrill vibrating cry, almost as if it were alive. His whole body began to judder in sympathy. And now the crystal began to glow with a cloudy white light, so that its brightness made his flesh seem transparent.

The door was flung open and Hervé de Maunoir ran in. "What's happening?" he shouted, his voice barely audible above the din.

"The Vox works. But it's—tearing me apart!" Someone—something—was trapped inside. Its agony possessed Rieuk until he felt himself sucked helplessly into its frenzy of despair.

"Where are you?" he cried, his voice barely audible above the wailing cry.

A slender, translucent figure appeared, sealed within a column of milky-white light. The light was so dazzling that he could not see the figure clearly, he could only hear its anguished cry—a cry that seared all thoughts from his brain but one: *Set me free.*

CHAPTER 2

A deliciously creamy perfume wafts through Klervie's dream: she runs through dew-soaked grass, the cool wetness dampening her bare feet. The pale shadow of the unicorn flits in front of her as she pursues it, eager to stroke its silky flanks. It will lead her to the hidden grove where the Faie dance in the moonlight. And if you catch a Faie, it must grant you a wish. White flowers open their petals as the unicorn passes and a delicious scent breathes out. Mmm . . . vanilla cream . . .

A faint, thin cry shudders through the starlit night . . .

And Klervie awoke. She lay still, clutching the sheet to her. It had been such a beautiful dream until—

There it was again! And it was coming from the kitchen, she was sure of it. It was the desolate, desperate cry of a trapped creature.

"Mewen, you *bad* cat!' she whispered. The family's sleek grey tabby had taken to bringing in his prey half-dead, delighting in tormenting it until it expired of exhaustion, or he grew bored. Klervie slipped out of her truckle bed and padded across the moonlit flagstones, wondering if it were a field mouse or a baby rabbit. Could she rescue it in time from Mewen's cruel claws?

Yet again the cry whispered through the cottage. Klervie stopped. It made her feel cold and shivery, even though the summer night was close and airless. And it was not coming from the kitchen; it had issued from Papa's study. And the light she had taken for moonlight was seeping from beneath Papa's study door. Was he working late?

Klervie went up on tiptoe to raise the latch. The door slowly opened, revealing a strange radiance that flickered like silver firelight burning from a tray of translucent coals on the desk. The light sharply outlined in shadow-silhouette the two men bending over the tray. They were so engrossed that they did not see her. She just stood staring, bewitched. A little voice nagged at the back of her mind, warning, "*Go back to bed. Papa will be angry if you disturb his work.*"

And yet she lingered.

"What *is* it?" She recognized the voice of Rieuk Mordiern, hoarse with excitement.

"I believe it may be an aethyrial spirit," said Papa. Both men spoke softly, amazedly.

"But how did I —"

"In working with aethyr, it is always possible to encounter forces invisible to mortal man. Even to entrap them. It seems you may have done just that."

Klervie heard the words but did not understand them. She must still be dreaming. For there, fading in and out of clarity like a reflection seen in a wind-rippled lake, she glimpsed a face, its features twisted into an expression of such agony that it pained her to look at it. And as she gazed, she saw it fix on her for a second with its anguish-riven eyes.

Was it a Faie? So translucent was its form, it could have been scratched on glass. And it seemed to be begging her to help it.

"It's changing," warned Papa. "Don't let go, Rieuk. If it gets loose, God knows what damage it'll do."

The dazzle of light emanating from the Faie was increasing, until it was so bright that Klervie's eyes ached to look at it. It began to spin, particles of brightness flying off like scattered raindrops.

"It's resisting."

Its high-pitched scream of defiance shattered glass and made Klervie press her hands to her ears.

"Help me," gasped Rieuk. "I can't hold it for much longer."

Papa raised his hands high above the wavering spirit. "By the power of my blood, I bind you! Transmute," he commanded, "and contain." Klervie could not see what they were doing as both leaned over the desk, their shadows blotting out the silvered light. There came a last faint, wailing shriek—and suddenly all the brilliance was sucked out of the air.

"What have you done, Rieuk?" a voice asked exhaustedly in the darkness. "What have you done?"

"You damned fool!" A stinging blow caught Rieuk across the cheek and chin; he reeled, toppling backward, knocking over a laboratory stool. He had no idea that the magister could muster so much physical strength. "What were you thinking of, risking something so dangerous?" Magister Linnaius's silver eyes glinted with fury in the gloom, cold as winter lightning. "You let out an aethyr spirit. You could have killed us all!"

Rieuk cowered, terrified. He had never seen his master so angry before. "B—but I made the Vox Aethyria work—"

"You deserve to be expelled. Meddling with elemental forces far too strong for you to contain."

"Expelled?" That single word shocked Rieuk to silence. Not one student had been expelled in all his seven years at the college. To be expelled before completing his apprenticeship was the worst possible punishment the magister could inflict.

"And look at this Vox, it's damaged beyond repair." Linnaius picked up a piece of twisted metal and let it drop again with a clang. "Hervé and I will have to start over." He examined the crystal. "And just when the Admiralty are breathing down our necks, threatening us with the Inquisition—"

"Please, Magister." Rieuk struggled to his knees. He could taste blood; the stone in Linnaius's signet ring had cut his lip open. "I was only trying to help. Please don't have me expelled."

The Magister's eyes gleamed cold as winter ice in the early dawnlight. Rieuk shivered. He knew that implacable look. "Now I'll have to order new parts for the Vox from Maistre Guirec to replace those that were ruined by your foolish tampering. And as for you—you will go to your study and stay there until you're sent for."

Kaspar Linnaius stared down at the twisted pieces of his Vox Aethyria. That arrogant fool of a green-eyed boy had undone all his plans. Why had he ever agreed to take him on as his apprentice? He should have known the boy would cause trouble. Was it because he had seen something of his younger self in that wan face? When the waif had arrived drenched at the college door one wet, windy autumn night, his unkempt brown hair plastered to his head by the driving rain, his thin face dominated by those huge, pleading eyes of green, he had remembered from over a hundred years ago what it felt like to trudge for weeks on end, always hungry, shunned and rejected for being "different" . . .

Linnaius brought his clenched fist down on his desk. What was he doing, allowing sentimental memories to cloud his judgment? *Am I turning into Gonery?* He had finally run out of patience with his headstrong, ambitious apprentice.

Yet Rieuk Mordiern made the Vox work.

The delicate metal spindles, cogs, and shafts wavered, blurring together as he stared at them. A mist was obscuring his vision. The tightness in his chest increased and he felt himself fighting for breath.

I'm spent. I used too much of my power in Enhirre and I'm fading . . .

With great effort, he rose to his feet, the laboratory jars swimming before his eyes as he struggled toward the door. He caught sight of himself in the mirror and saw that his hair had turned as white as thistledown.

In the echoing hallway he passed Goustan de Rhuys, who gazed at him with concern.

"Kaspar, are you all right? You look . . ."

"Old?" Linnaius managed a wry grimace. "Tell Gonery I'm off to Maistre Guirec. Nothing can be done to repair the Vox till he's made new parts . . ."

"This stone is no ordinary crystal, is it, Kaspar?" Magister Gonery held the jewel up to the light, turning it round and round.

Kaspar Linnaius let out a grunt. "Damn it, Gonery, did you think I'd forgotten that the Vox is all that's keeping the Inquisition at bay? But every crystal Hervé and I tried just didn't work. I had to go a long way to find one that was a little . . . different." Exhaustion overcame him; he sank down into a chair.

"A little *too* different, as it turned out. What in the name of the five elements is it?"

"It's an aethyr crystal."

Gonery raised one wispy eyebrow. "And how exactly did you come by it?"

"It's better you don't know." Linnaius had expended too much of his remaining strength. Weakened by the long, wind-tossed flight from Ondhessar, he wasn't sure how long he would last.

"Kaspar?" said Gonery warningly. He put the stone down. "What have you done to yourself? You look so ill."

"Don't worry," said Linnaius lightly, "I made certain it would be very hard for anyone to follow me." The daylight seemed to fade from the room; when he blinked, he found he was lying on the floor of the study, with Gonery hovering anxiously over him.

"You need rest, Kaspar. Let Hervé and Rieuk repair the Vox."

"Don't—let—that—damned apprentice anywhere near my Vox," Linnaius managed to grit out the words.

"But you said yourself that Rieuk made it work."

"He's an elemental. I suspected as much, but now we've proof absolute. He doesn't know his own strength. He's a danger to himself and everyone else."

"Rather like you, many years ago, hm?" Gonery reminded him mildly.

Linnaius allowed Gonery to help him to sit up but ignored the last remark. "I may be away for a while," he said, rising unsteadily to his feet. He felt as if a thin transparent veil had unfurled between him and the world around him, muffling sounds, dampening the brightness of the light of day. "My faculties are failing. If I leave it much longer, I won't even have the strength to reach the Jade Springs."

"So even the Elixir has its limits?"

"I hear that the waters of Lake Taigal are exceptionally good for the health. Quite rejuvenating, in fact," said Linnaius, slowly making his way to the door.

———

Rieuk's attic room was situated at the top of the student wing of the college, looking out over the little town of Karantec below, its central street winding down the hill to the sleepy green waters of the River Faou. The younger students slept in a dormitory on the first floor, but the older apprentices—Deniel, Madoc, and Rieuk—were each allotted his own study, on the top attic floor of the ancient building. Swallows nested under the eaves and he could hear their incessant twittering as they skimmed in on swift-scissoring wings to feed their young.

Rieuk threw himself down on the bed and lay there, hands behind his head, glowering at the dawn sky. He had been up half the night cleaning Magister de Maunoir's study. He was past exhaustion now, trembling with self-righteous anger.

"The spirit should be mine. I divined it. I drew it out. So what if I didn't have the power to hold it, to bend it to my will? They could have taught me how. But no! A mere apprentice can't be trusted with an aethyrial spirit."

At the very moment when he had sensed the spirit's life energy, he had also glimpsed what it could be like to wield such power. It was as if a charge of lightning had coursed through his body. And then, when he saw it . . . Pale as the crystal that had birthed it, its unearthly beauty had taken his breath away. He had never encountered any creature like this before—nor heard such a terrible raw keening, that tore through his whole being until he felt as if he were being ripped apart, vein by vein, sinew by sinew. That was when he had lost control, when he had dropped to his knees, hands clutched to his throbbing ears.

At the very moment when he should have used his skills to bind the spirit, he had failed. He had not realized how powerful it would be. And that was when Hervé de Maunoir had stepped in. Somewhere at the back of his mind, a reasoning voice reminded Rieuk that had he not done so, the spirit would have disappeared back inside the aethyr—or, worse still, have wreaked mindless devastation within the cottage, attacking the one who had dared to drag it into the mortal world.

"If we hadn't sealed it within that book, it would have rent you in bloody fragments," Hervé de Maunoir had said in his habitual matter-of-fact way.

So you sealed it, Magister de Maunoir. My aethyrial spirit is trapped in your book.

Rieuk could not stop thinking of it. He hated the way the magisters had reminded him of his lack of experience, his need to gain the wisdom and knowledge that would make him strong enough to control such a power. He hated the fact that they had made him feel gauche and inadequate.

And why was a spirit trapped in that crystal, anyway? Where exactly did my master find it?

Suddenly he became aware that the swallows had fallen silent. The air felt heavy, as if a storm was looming. Rieuk, puzzled, rolled off his bed and went to the window to look out. High above in the cloudy sky, he spotted the faint silhouette of a hawk slowly circling the college. Even as he gazed up at it, the hawk wheeled around and lazily winged away. Within moments, the swallow chicks began to chirp again and the parents returned, darting in, swift and accurate as arrows to their target.

"You're talented, Rieuk. But it doesn't take talent alone to make an alchymist." Magister Gonery leaned forward over his cluttered desk and gazed earnestly into Rieuk's eyes. And although the elderly alchymist's mild expression appeared solicitous, Rieuk was not fooled. "You want too much too soon. You cut corners, take risks. You leave yourself vulnerable to unscrupulous influences."

"But I have a gift with crystals," Rieuk blurted out. "*I* made the Vox work. Why doesn't my master let me use my gift? Why doesn't he trust me?"

"Your gift drew you here. But it also draws you to the attention of *others*. Others who would use you and your gift for their own selfish ends."

Rieuk felt a muscle twitch involuntarily in his cheek and hoped Magister Gonery had not noticed. His uncanny ability to read even the most well-guarded thoughts never failed to unnerve his students.

"They will promise you the things you most desire. And then, before you know what you have done, you will find yourself in thrall. Sealed into a contract that binds you until death—and beyond."

Rieuk had heard this lecture many times before. But this time he feared it was the prelude to his expulsion.

Magister Gonery let out a sigh. "As I said—had you been paying attention—we all recognize that you have the gift. And a gift such as yours is all too rare these days. But it is still raw and ill controlled. If Magister de Maunoir had not been there to contain that aethyrial spirit, it would have escaped and wreaked havoc." He removed his spectacles and began to polish a lens on his sleeve. "And worst of all, I've had to contend with a stream of complaints from the good citizens of Karantec. Even the mayor." He picked up a sheaf of letters on his desk and waved them in front of Rieuk. "I can't let the irresponsible act of one of my students tarnish the college's reputation. Especially in these troubled times."

Rieuk swallowed down the lump in his throat. *Here it comes. The end of my career.*

"Magister Linnaius is adamant that you should be expelled. But I'm putting you on probation until I've consulted with the other magisters. If—and I repeat, *if*—any one of them is willing to take you on as his apprentice, I'll grant you a second chance. Of course, you'll have to repeat the final year's work."

"But Magister Linnaius will influence them. No one will want to—"

A stern look from Magister Gonery silenced him. "And you're banned from all the college laboratories until I've met with the others to discuss your case."

"Banned?"

"You will make yourself useful in other ways, running errands and repairing the damage at Magister de Maunoir's house. And to start with, I'm sending you on an errand."

Rieuk was not listening with full attention; he was seething with self-righteous indignation. So now he was to be used as an errand boy?

"It will give you the chance to reflect upon the foolishness of your actions. And it will put a little distance between you and your master."

"Where are you sending me?" Rieuk said sullenly.

"Magister Linnaius has an arrangement with a skilled horloger in Kemper, one Maistre Guirec."

Rieuk remembered the name. "The one who made the parts for the Vox?"

"The very same. Your master has already ordered new parts. You are to collect them from Sieur Guirec. He's bringing them to Karantec."

"And my master trusts *me* with this errand?" Rieuk muttered.

"*I* trust you." Gonery's rheumy eyes suddenly gleamed with a clear light that pierced Rieuk to the core; caught off guard, he staggered and took a step back. "Your master has other matters on his mind at present. Don't let me down, Rieuk. This is your last chance."

Inquisitor Visant gazed around the interior of the chapel of Saint Argantel's Seminary with a coldly critical eye. He noted an ancient polychrome statue of the patron saint, lit by the uncertain daylight, but nothing else of architectural distinction.

"So this is where you spent your school days, Maistre Donatien? I understand your affection for the place," he added dryly, "but I'm a busy man; was it really necessary to drag me along on your nostalgic journey?"

Grand Maistre Donatien rose from his knees and turned around from the altar, smiling. "Touché, Inquisitor. But there's much more to this chapel than schoolboy memories. I'd never have brought you and your men here if it were not on a matter of the utmost importance."

"And the utmost confidentiality?"

"I've received an urgent request for help from our Guerriers in Enhirre. It seems that a certain Kaspar Linnaius, citizen of Francia, violated the Shrine at Ondhessar, stealing a sacred stone. But at last we have proof positive that Linnaius is a magus: He escaped in a flying craft. We have *witnesses*, Alois."

Visant regarded Donatien without commenting; there had been many bizarre rumors about Linnaius before but never evidence such as this.

"Captain de Lanvaux was injured trying to hold the craft down; he was dragged several feet into the air before the Magus forced him to let go."

"So you want me to arrest Linnaius?"

"Not just Linnaius, but all of his colleagues at the College of Thaumaturgy. They call themselves 'alchymists.' They claim that they're working on scientific experiments. And now," he said triumphantly, "we have proof that they're practicing the Forbidden Arts."

"But if the magi at Karantec are practicing the Forbidden Arts, we'll need more than a company of Guerriers to arrest them."

Donatien beckoned him toward the altar. "Have you ever heard of Argantel's Angelstones?"

Visant shook his head.

"We've gone to great lengths to keep them a well-guarded secret, even within the Commanderie. Until today, only the Grand Maistres have known their hiding place. But I think I can trust you, Inquisitor," Donatien said, with a knowing little smile, "not to divulge their whereabouts to another living soul, can't I?"

He knelt before the altar and took a golden key from a chain around his neck. Visant saw him press in turn a sequence of carved images on the altar: Sergius's crook; Mhir's rose; seven stars for the Seven Heavenly Guardians. With a creak, a little aperture opened below the seven stars, revealing a second, concealed door. Donatien inserted the key, turning it left, then right, then left again. From within the cavity behind the second door, he drew out a wooden box, which he placed on the altar, using the key to unlock it.

Fascinated, Visant drew closer. "Angelstones?" Clear as polished drops of ice, the stones glittered in their plain wooden setting.

"Seven crystals . . . but not of this world. They were given to Saint Argantel by the Angel Lord Galizur as protection against daemons. If a daemon is close by, a streak of darkness sullies the clarity of the crystal."

"But how will this protect *us* against Kaspar Linnaius and the other magi?"

"If Linnaius is a true magus, his powers are daemonic in origin. The Angelstones will counteract those powers and render him helpless."

Visant looked at the crystals. It was difficult to imagine that such pretty gems could subdue a magus wielding the Forbidden Arts. "You said there were seven. I see only five."

"Nothing escapes you, does it?" Donatien said with a little

laugh. "We were forced to employ two to defeat the magi of Ondhessar. And even now we can't be certain that some didn't escape."

"But how can I be sure that they will protect my men?" Skeptical by nature, Visant could not help but feel reluctant to put his trust in Donatien's angelic legacy.

"Each stone was imbued with angelic power by one of the Heavenly Guardians." A faint luminescence from the crystals illuminated Donatien's face as his fingers hovered above the precious stones, as if pondering which one to select. "But once used, that power is exhausted. The crystals of Cassiel and Dahariel are empty now. But one should be sufficient to quell the magi of Karantec. I think this one should serve your purposes well enough; the stone of Ardarel, Lord of Heavenly Fire."

Visant took the stone from Donatien. For a moment, he thought he caught a faint shimmer of flame at its heart—or could it have been a trick of the light? "In Sergius's name, this Angelstone had better work, Maistre," he said dryly. "For if the magi fight back using the Forbidden Arts, my men and I are as good as dead."

CHAPTER 3

Rieuk set out into the town, head down, scowling.

So this is how Gonery means to punish me, treating me as an errand boy, forcing me to fetch and carry like a common servant? And what character-improving lesson am I supposed to learn from this humiliation?

It was all very well for Magister Gonery to warn him of the unscrupulous who lurked in dark corners, waiting to rape him of his talent. Wasn't that precisely what Kaspar Linnaius had done?

It was my gift that divined the spirit imprisoned in the crystal, it was my "raw talent" that drew it out into the mortal world. I made the Vox Aethyria work—and yet Linnaius will take all the glory. He kicked angrily at a loose stone, sending it ricocheting down the cobbled lane.

The sun was sinking as he crossed the old stone bridge that spanned the meandering River Faou, turning the water to violet and gold. The darkening air was still heavy with the day's heat, and swallows swooped low over the shallows, feasting on midges. A serving girl was standing on tiptoe to light the lanterns that hung outside the ivied door of the tavern. As each flame glowed to life, Rieuk saw velvety white moths flitting through the soft twilight, drawn to the brightness. He stopped beneath one of the lanterns to look again at his instructions:

"Ask for Anselm Guirec the Horloger."

A lively babble of voices issued from inside. Rieuk disliked meeting new people, and he especially disliked being forced to seek out a complete stranger. The stink of ale and wine fumes made him wrinkle his nose in disgust, and the fug of the smoky air tickled the back of his throat.

A group of drinkers broke into roars of laughter as he walked past. *Are they laughing at me? And how, in God's name, am I supposed to find Guirec in this throng?*

"You are looking for Sieur Guirec?"

Rieuk started, caught off guard. A man had appeared beside him out of the gloom. He was tall, dressed in a long traveling coat of charcoal grey, his straight black hair loosely tied back at the nape of his neck with a slender bronze ribbon of silk. He wore gold-rimmed spectacles whose cloudy lenses seemed to hide rather than reveal the dark eyes behind. Rieuk's first impression was that he had more the air of a lawyer or a priest than a clockmaker.

"You're not Sieur Guirec."

An enigmatic smile appeared on the stranger's face; he nodded. "Very good. Our predictions were accurate: I see there is no deceiving you, Rieuk Mordiern."

Rieuk took a step back, fearing a trap. "How do you know my name?"

"Your contact was obliged to leave on urgent business; I offered to make the delivery in his stead." He held out a casket. "I believe this is what you came to collect." Rieuk noticed how long and slender the man's fingers were, not gnarled and stained with chymicals like Magister Linnaius's.

"How do I know that you haven't tampered with the contents?" Rieuk stared suspiciously at the casket, then at the smiling stranger.

"Check the seal. You'll find it's unbroken."

To his relief Rieuk saw that it was true. The horloger's mark was intact; the contents must be undamaged.

"We've been watching you, Rieuk."

Alarmed, Rieuk began to back away.

"You're nearly at the end of your apprenticeship, aren't you? Your seven years will be up by summer's end. And then what will you do?"

Rieuk shrugged.

"You're dissatisfied. Frustrated by Magister Gonery's restrictions. Disappointed when others take the credit for the fruits of your hard work."

Even though Rieuk's head was lowered, he was listening now with ardent attention.

"And if I were to tell you that I belong to another order, one which welcomes gifted young magi like yourself and encourages them to develop their talents? We know that you have been investigating certain . . . skills forbidden to Gonery's students."

Rieuk's face began to burn. "Who *are* you? And why all the secrecy?"

The stranger smiled at him again, a frank, winning smile that made Rieuk want to trust him, even though he knew he dared not. "At least tell me who you are," he said warily.

"My name is Imri. Imri Boldiszar."

"Imri," repeated Rieuk softly. "Not a Francian name." That explained the hint of a foreign accent.

"I've risked a great deal in coming here to see you, Rieuk Mordiern. Your masters are very powerful and they would not treat me kindly if they discovered me so close to the heart of their mysteries."

"So why risk discovery just to see me, a mere apprentice?"

"Have you never wondered where your gift came from? Have you never longed to discover your true parentage?"

"My true parentage?" This was getting far too personal, and Rieuk began to wish he had taken the Vox parts and run. "What's that to you?"

"It can make for a lonely childhood. Rejected by the other children because you're different. Cornered one day, driven too far by the other children's goading—and discovering your gift in one moment of sheer, transcendent rage . . ."

Rieuk slowly raised his head to stare into the stranger's face. "How did you know?" he whispered. But Imri Boldiszar just raised one hand and removed his spectacles, revealing dark brown eyes that glimmered with an unnatural golden radiance.

"That's how it is for all of us born with the gift." And Rieuk caught the briefest shadow of pain tainting the warmth of Boldiszar's gaze. "Destined to be misunderstood, rejected by our own flesh and blood, we seek out those rare individuals who understand us . . . because they share the same heritage."

"*You* are—" began Rieuk, then stopped. If this man was indeed another magus, then he was not one of the college's alumni. He had never seen the name "Boldiszar" inscribed in any of the college records. Which must mean . . .

"We want you, Rieuk. Join us."

"You w—want me?" stammered Rieuk.

"I've been sent to find you. To bring you to us . . . if you wish to come."

"But who *are* you?" Rieuk knew that he should have terminated this conversation long ago. He was straying into treacherous waters, but the stranger was speaking the very words he had longed to hear all his life.

Suddenly, Boldiszar reached out, hands cupping Rieuk's face, drawing it closer to his own. Rieuk found himself staring into black-lashed brown eyes, flecked with dark gold, like tortoiseshell. Terrified, he tried to break free but found he could not move. The magus's power held him helpless. And then his terror slowly began to melt into another, quite different feeling.

"Oh Rieuk," whispered Boldiszar, "don't fight me. I can give you everything you've ever dreamed of. I can initiate you into our mysteries. I can even help you awaken your true power." The magus's breath was warm, like a caress, aromatic, with a hint of bittersweet spice.

"My true power?"

"Your masters fear you. Why else would they have held you back, confining you to menial tasks? But I can sense your potential." Imri Boldiszar's mouth touched his in a brief kiss, light as the brush of a bee's wings, yet Rieuk felt a current of dark energy reverberate through his whole body. "I can *taste* your potential," Boldiszar murmured. "There is so much I can teach you, Rieuk. So many secrets that Gonery and Linnaius will never let you share." The dark, tortoiseshell gaze held his until he felt as if he were floating in a star-studded sky. Rieuk closed his eyes, surrendering. Fear and excitement were pulsing through him. He knew he was being seduced—and he wanted it more than anything he had ever wanted in his whole life.

The moon is rising, casting its clear, verdant radiance over dark forests. A tower looms high above them, its jagged turret stark against the pale disc of the emerald moon. Faint, keening cries echo high above the trees. Shadows soar across the moon's brilliance, winged creatures, graceful and swift as hawks. Rieuk is suddenly overwhelmed by a yearning so strong that it makes his whole being burn with longing . . .

Rieuk opened his eyes to find that they were standing beneath the willows on the riverbank in the warm darkness of the summer night, the plashing of the gently flowing water almost drowned by the shrill chorus of frogs. He had no recollection of how they had come to be there. The moon was rising but its chill light was silvered white, like the pure flame of burning magnesium, not the emerald green of his vision.

Imri Boldiszar let his hands travel slowly down from Rieuk's face to rest on his shoulders. And Rieuk, who for so long had hated to be touched, no longer shied away.

"Do you plan to stay at the college all your life? Or would you rather break free and take your chance with me?"

Rieuk had not wanted the dream to end. He craved more. "The emerald moon. The tower." The words came spilling out of his mouth like fast-flowing water. "Where was that place? And the winged ones? What were they?" Nothing else mattered to him anymore. Since Imri had touched his lips to his, Rieuk had been in a daze, unable to think of anything but that eerie moonlit landscape. It had awakened an aching hunger, and he knew he could not rest until it was assuaged.

The church clock rang out, chiming midnight. Rieuk blinked. Where had the last four hours gone?

"You must be thirsty," said Imri casually. "Why not share a bottle of wine with me before you go back to the college? I can have the landlord bring it up to my rooms." His smile was so open, so friendly, that Rieuk found himself following without a second thought.

Imri's rooms were on the top floor of the old riverside inn, up three flights of creaking stairs. Rieuk carefully placed the casket containing the Vox parts on the table. A pale wash of moonlight shone in through the casement window.

"There's a tinderbox on the table," said Imri. "Unless you know some mage-trick to light the lamps?"

There were two oil lamps; Rieuk lifted the glass bowls and struck a flame, coaxing each wick in turn to a gentle glow. When he looked up, he saw that Imri was unfastening his coat, shrugging it off his shoulders, casually draping it over the corner of the bed. He had his back to him so that all Rieuk could see was the silky sheen of his long black hair against the white of his shirt . . . until Imri slowly let slip the thin linen of the shirt, turning around to face him.

Rieuk took a step backward toward the door. What did Imri intend? And then a soft, wondering gasp broke from his throat. "What *is* that?" For painted or tattooed in intricate detail into Imri's honey-brown skin was a bird of prey. Its serrated wings were spread wide open across Imri's breast, its proud head nestling at the base of the magus's throat.

"This," said Imri quietly, "is an Emissary. My Emissary."

Rieuk's fingers were reaching out before he was aware of it. The ink that had etched the feathers was black as shadow, and each feather looked so real that Rieuk was certain that it would feel like stroking the glossy wing of a living creature. As the tips of his fingers connected with the warmth of Imri's skin, he sensed a faint crackle of energy.

"It's . . . *alive?*"

He had been about to snatch his hand away but Imri moved the more swiftly, grasping it, pressing it against his ink-mottled breast.

"B—but how? It's only a tattoo." Rieuk's natural skepticism refused to allow him to accept the physical evidence. But now, touching the etched skin, he could feel not only the strong pulse of Imri's heart but another throbbing heartbeat, wild and fast, as if striving to break free.

Imri murmured into his ear, "Can you sense it? It's one with me . . . and yet I can also send it to do my bidding."

"Show me." Rieuk was surprised at his own boldness. A slow, enigmatic smile spread over Imri's face and Rieuk felt his own heart begin to thud faster, too. This was raw magic, the kind he had always secretly craved, and it was acting like a drug, awakening his senses.

"Tabris," Imri commanded. "Tabris, come forth."

The air shuddered, and a gust of wind whipped Rieuk's hair

across his eyes. Blinking, he looked again and saw the fierce flame of amber eyes staring haughtily back into his. Perched on Imri's forearm was a great hawk, its inky feathers dully shimmering, trembling like shifting moonlit shadows.

"It's—it's real." Rieuk's mouth had gone dry and his voice was husky. "It's . . . beautiful." He could still just make out the pearlescent outline on Imri's skin where the hawk had been etched.

"Show Rieuk what you can do." Imri raised his arm. "Fly, Tabris."

Rieuk ducked instinctively as the hawk lifted off Imri's arm and flew straight toward the window. Rieuk let out a cry of warning, certain that the hawk would crash into the glass and injure itself. But it passed straight through the pane and flew on into the moonlit sky outside.

"Tabris is a shadow hawk, not of this world," Imri said gently, placing a hand on Rieuk's shoulder and steering him toward the casement so that he could watch the hawk's graceful flight across the silver disc of the moon, skimming above the ramshackle roofs of Karantec.

"Tabris," repeated Rieuk mechanically.

"And now I can see what Tabris sees." Imri's eyes had become clouded as he scanned the streets of the town and the roads beyond. "That's far enough. Return."

The air rippled like fast-flowing water and Tabris flew back through the glass, melting like a fading shadow into Imri's body. Rieuk stood transfixed. He had never wanted anything so much in his life before. He looked at Imri with awed respect. "Tell me," he said, finding his voice at last. "Tell me how I can get an Emissary of my own. I'll do anything. *Anything.*"

"We practice a different form of apprenticeship in my order," Imri said, his voice low, intense. "The bond between us will be far closer, far more intimate than that sterile vow of obedience you made to Kaspar Linnaius. A bond that is strongest when two with the gift are drawn together."

A wave of heat seared through Rieuk's body. Even though he stood apart from Imri, it felt as if he were drowning in the warm depths of those golden-brown eyes. "You mean . . ." And then his innate skepticism reasserted itself, and he said dryly, "Do you really expect me to believe that?"

Imri smiled. "No one has fully awakened you. What were your masters thinking of, letting such incredible latent power as yours stagnate?"

"Is it too late, then?"

"Come here," said Imri, "and let's see what I can do."

Long black hair, silkily soft, brushed across Rieuk's chest. Slowly, lazily, Rieuk gave a sigh and opened his eyes and saw that Imri Boldiszar was bending close over him, holding a clear phial to his lips. All the previous night's golden warmth had faded from the magus's eyes, to be replaced by a look of such ruthlessness that Rieuk felt his heart stop with fear. He tried to move and found that his limbs were paralyzed.

Tabris, hovering overhead, alighted on his chest. Rieuk felt as if a dark weight was pressing down on him, forcing the life from his body.

"*Imri? What are you doing to me?*" He tried to speak but his tongue was frozen and no sound came out. His eyes filled with tears. *I trusted you. For the first time in my life, I trusted someone.* The tears spilled down his cheeks and he could not even lift his hand to wipe them away.

Imri stared at him. Through the blur of his tears, Rieuk stared back, hurt and uncomprehending. And then Imri turned away. "It's no use," Rieuk heard him say in an anguished whisper. "I can't do it. I just can't do it. There must be another way. Tabris, return."

The crushing weight lifted as the Emissary faded into his master's body. Rieuk took a breath . . . and heard his own voice faintly asking, "The phial . . . what did it contain? Poison?"

"It's called a soul-glass." Imri sat, shoulders hunched, head lowered. "It is used to contain a stolen soul, so that the stealer may use the empty body for his own purposes."

"Soul-stealing?" Now Rieuk realized the extent of his own gullibility. "You wanted my soul? Or my body? But *why*?"

He heard Imri sigh. "I need to be the semblance of Rieuk Mordiern to get close to Kaspar Linnaius."

"To learn his secrets?"

There was another pause. Eventually Imri said, in a flat tone,

"To get my revenge." He turned around and Rieuk saw again the ruthless fire in his eyes that had so terrified him.

"But if you took my body, what would happen to your own? Wouldn't it just lie here, wasting away, without you inhabiting it?"

"If the soul is parted from its original body for too long, the soulless body dies. But my soul stays within me, and my Emissary enters the victim's body to do my will."

"And *my* soul?" Rieuk had to know everything that Imri had intended to do to him.

"When the soul-glass is crushed, the imprisoned soul is set free . . . but, unable to rejoin its body, it becomes one of the Lost Souls that wander the Ways Beyond, preying on others for all eternity . . ."

Rieuk gazed at Imri. "You'd do that . . . to me?"

Imri gazed back at Rieuk. No one had ever looked at him in that way before. "I had my orders. I was ready to do it. But that was before I met you." Imri bent over him, a curtain of black hair falling on either side of Rieuk's face, and lightly kissed Rieuk's eyelids. Rieuk felt sensation flood back into his paralyzed body. He sat up slowly, dizzy with the thought of how close he had come to annihilation.

"Go. Go before I change my mind. I can't imagine that you would want to stay with me now."

Rieuk pulled his shirt on; but when he tried to do up the buttons, his hands were shaking so much that he could not manage it.

"Here. Let me." Imri's deft fingers took over, as if Rieuk were a child. This small, intimate gesture brought back sensual shivers of how Imri had undone those same buttons the night before.

"You spared my life."

"Huh. The more fool me."

Rieuk was struggling with violently conflicting feelings. Somewhere deep inside him, he was aware that he had gone from being the victim to the victor. "What did my master do to you, Imri?"

"He stole something from my order. Something that was not his to take. And I was charged with getting it back." Imri's voice had become very quiet but Rieuk could hear an intense anger charging every word. "I must return it—or suffer the consequences."

"What will they do to you if you fail?"

Imri Boldiszar gazed steadily at Rieuk, a darkness shadowing his tortoiseshell eyes. "They will strip away my Emissary. And as we are bonded, body and soul, we will both be destroyed."

Imri was telling him plainly that he would be executed by his fellow magi. *He's only saying this to make me feel beholden to him. If I fail, he'll die—and horribly. What better way to persuade me to do his will?*

In the silence that had fallen between them he could sense that Imri was still looking searchingly at him.

"It's called the Lodestar. The sacred Lodestar of Ondhessar. It's a crystal unlike any other in this world."

"A crystal? And my master stole it?"

"You've *seen* the Lodestar?"

Rieuk nodded. It pained him to hear that raw eagerness in Imri's voice. How could he tell him that he had not only seen it, he had let loose the power it contained? "It was—it was my fault." Rieuk turned his head away; he could not look Imri directly in the eyes. "Don't hate me, Imri. My master was working on an invention to carry voices through the aethyr. He went searching for crystals that were in tune with each other to use in the machine. I—I used the crystal and—"

"You set Azilis free?"

"Azilis?" Rieuk repeated, his thoughts in confusion. "You mean the aethyrial spirit? I heard it calling to me. I thought it was trapped. So I—"

"Aethyrial spirit? Is that what Linnaius called her?" Imri spoke slowly, bleakly, as though not able to come to terms with what had happened. Rieuk sensed a dangerous change in Imri's mood. Only a little while ago, the magus had been on the point of stealing his soul. How would he deal with him now? "So the crystal is empty and the spirit is at large?"

"No, no, Magister de Maunoir bound it. It's in a book."

"A book? Where is this book?"

"At the college, most like."

"Then all is not lost." There was a reckless glint in Imri's eyes. He smiled suddenly at Rieuk, and Rieuk felt himself helplessly drawn back, entranced. Imri Boldiszar was a powerful magus and Rieuk would protect him.

CHAPTER 4

"Open up! In the name of the Commanderie!"

Klervie woke to the sound of shouting, men's voices loud in the dark of the night. She heard the thud of fists pounding against the cottage door. Terrified, she lay still, not daring to move.

"Hervé de Maunoir! Open up!"

She heard her mother, Maela, whispering frantically to her father. "Slip out by the pantry window. Go!"

"And leave you to face them alone?"

"I'll stall them. Just go!"

"Break down the door." The brusque order outside was swiftly followed by juddering blows that made the whole cottage tremble. Klervie clapped her hands over her ears.

Suddenly the loudest blow was followed by the splintering rending of timber. The door burst open and men came running in. Klervie shrieked in terror and, snatching up her book, ran to her mother's side.

"What do you think you're doing?" Maela's challenge rang out. "How dare you disturb my child's rest? By what right do you break into my home in the middle of the night?"

At the same time, the sounds of a violent scuffle erupted in the cottage garden, punctuated by shouts. Then came a sudden cry of pain that made Klervie flinch as if she had taken the blow herself. "Papa!" she whispered.

"I have a warrant from the king." A burly officer in a plain black uniform loomed over them, a folded paper in hand; Klervie noticed that it was secured with a scarlet seal.

"A warrant? We are not criminals—" began Maela, but her voice trailed away as more soldiers appeared in the doorway, dragging a man by the arms. "Hervé!" she cried.

Klervie flinched. Her father's head drooped; drops of red dripped from a gash on the side of his skull, staining the clean flagstones. A horrible sick feeling gushed through her whole body; she wanted to run away, but her legs had begun to tremble and she could only stand and stare.

"So you thought you could escape us?" The officer gazed impassively down at her father. "By order of his majesty, King Gobain, I arrest you, Hervé de Maunoir."

"On—what grounds?" Papa seemed to be having difficulty speaking. Klervie felt Maela's hands tighten on her shoulders.

The officer gave a grim laugh. "Heresy. Practicing the Forbidden Arts. Summoning daemons—"

"What?" Maela interrupted him. "My husband is a reputable alchymist. He has never dared to practice the Forbidden Arts. He has more sense!"

"Seize everything. Every book, every piece of writing, down to the smallest scrap," ordered the officer, ignoring her.

Bright gouts of lanternlight illuminated the darkness as the soldiers ransacked the cottage, piling Papa's books into chests, taking away boxes of papers. Klervie held tight to her beloved storybook, determined that no one should take it from her.

"The wards," Maela was murmuring. "Why did the wards fail?"

Though Klervie did not understand what the wards were, she knew that they were there to protect them. And now Maman was saying they had let in these harsh-voiced and brutish men who were turning their home upside down. There came the crash of breaking crockery in the kitchen and Maela winced.

"What have you got there?" The officer loomed over Klervie. His eyes radiated such stern disapproval that she shrank close to her mother, arms crossed, both hands clutching the precious book to her breast.

"You wouldn't begrudge a little child her book of tales?"

"Fairy tales are a dangerous and corrupting influence on young, impressionable minds." The officer snatched the book from Klervie and stared at it with suspicion. Then his stern expression softened. "*Lives of the Holy Saints,*" he read aloud, nodding. He thrust the book back at Klervie. "Not a title I had thought to find in the house of a filthy magus." He turned away, striding into Papa's study, barking out orders.

Klervie gazed at the book in astonishment. In the harsh torchlight she noticed that the picture engraved on the front had changed; instead of the Faie with hair silver as starshine, her arms wound around the neck of a unicorn, she saw a haloed saint, eyes piously upraised, hands fervently clasped together in prayer. But before she could ask Maman why the picture had changed, the officer reappeared.

"We're all done here, Lieutenant. Take him away."

The soldiers began to drag Papa out of the door, his toes bumping over the flagstones, leaving a bloody trail behind.

Maela ran into the lane in her nightgown. She caught hold of one of the men by the arm. "Where are you taking him?"

Klervie had stood watching, mute with fear. Now she ran after her mother, only to see the man throw Maela to the muddy ground.

Klervie stopped, shocked to see how brutally he had treated her mother.

"I'll follow you, Hervé!" Maela cried, her voice shrill, close to breaking. "I won't let them keep us apart! I'll—"

The sky turned white. Klervie shut her eyes, dazzled as an ear-bruising explosion shook the night.

"Oh, *no,*" she heard her mother whisper. Jagged flames leaped high into the misty darkness, coloring the trees and houses a lurid orange.

High on the hill that overlooked the village, the College of Thaumaturgy was burning.

"Stay back!" Imri hissed, tugging Rieuk into the shadows as a troop of soldiers tramped along the lane. They were dragging a prisoner.

"Who are they?"

"Inquisitors."

"But I must warn the others—"

"It's too late." There was such urgency in Imri's voice that the protest died on Rieuk's tongue. "Don't you understand? There's nothing you can do now. I've seen the Commanderie Inquisition in action before. They hate our kind. All you can do is hope we get away without being seen."

At that moment, Rieuk sensed a faint yet familiar electric tingle. Two officers of the Inquisition had stopped close by. One pulled what looked like a fob watch from his breast pocket. A *crystal* watch? As he held it aloft, Rieuk felt a wave of dizziness wash over him. He sagged against a wall, suddenly weak and disoriented.

"Ugh." Beside him, Imri staggered as if he had been kicked in the chest.

"Look, there's a streak of darkness in the stone," said the officer.

"It must sense more mage blood close by," said his companion, raising his pistol. "Could Maunoir's apprentice be hiding out here?"

Rieuk's instinctive reaction was to run like hell. But his limbs were trembling and would not respond to his will. He was helpless.

"Maistre Visant!" came the call. "We've breached the college walls. Come quick!"

The Inquisitors hurried away, and Rieuk saw not the dial of a watch face but the sparkle of a quartz on a golden chain as the officer tucked it back in his pocket.

The instant they had gone, Imri grabbed Rieuk's hand, pulling him along the unlit lane.

"Can't—run—anymore." Rieuk dropped to his knees, trying to gulp in lungfuls of air. His throat was taut and dry and his ribs ached. "What happened back there? I felt so weak."

"Angelstone," Imri rasped. "It—has to be. It negates our power."

"I never knew—" Rieuk broke off as the night sky flared with the lurid brilliance of the burning college. He gazed in dismay as the flames roared toward the stars. All the rare and ancient books would be incinerated in that inferno. All that precious knowledge accumulated over centuries would be lost forever.

"We can't stay here." Imri's hand pressed on his shoulder, firm yet insistent. "They'll scour the lanes. They'll put blocks on the roads."

Rieuk looked up at Imri's face in the fire-streaked darkness and saw nothing but the flames reflected in the lenses of his spectacles. There was no way of reading the expression in the dark eyes behind those blank lenses.

"We must get out of Francia—and as soon as possible."

"So Azilis is free at last." Imri leaned on the rail of the barque, gazing out across the sunlit dazzle of the waves.

Rieuk was fighting to stay in control of his seasickness. The salty wind had freshened, gusting in fierce bursts, stirring up huge waves.

"You saw the conflagration at the college. Maunoir's book could never have survived such a blaze. And as the pages burned, so she would have returned to the aethyr."

"Is that . . . a good thing?" The barque crested another rolling breaker and Rieuk slipped to his knees, clutching his stomach.

Through the rising surges of nausea he heard Imri's voice suddenly quirked with amusement. "Seasick? Silly boy. Why didn't you say so?" Rieuk felt Imri's hand on his head, tousling his hair. He flinched, fearing he was about to puke. And then a swift, bright current of cleansing heat passed through his body from his head to his toes. He opened his eyes and saw Imri kneeling beside him on the damp boards.

"Better?" Imri inquired.

Rieuk drew in a tentative breath. He could feel the barque's timbers shuddering as it cut through the breakers, he could hear the waves slapping against the hull, but the nausea had gone. "What did you do?"

Imri helped him to his feet. "What use is an apprentice to his master if he's lying groaning in the bilges?"

The master of the barque was shouting orders to the crew; the wind changed as they rounded the headland and the sailors began to climb up into the rigging to unfurl more sails. In spite of the sun's bright sparkle on the burnished blue of the summer sea, Rieuk felt as if distant storm clouds were looming, darkening the hours yet to come.

CHAPTER 5

A little crowd of villagers had gathered outside the cottage door. Among them Klervie recognized Hugues the baker and his wife, Gwenna, holding their daughter, Youna, her best friend, by the hand. The mayor, Messieur Brandin, stepped forward.

They've come to help us. Overwhelmed by a rush of warm feelings, Klervie knelt on the window seat to wave to Youna. But Youna turned her head away.

Above them on the hill, Klervie saw the smoking and blackened ruins of the college. The acrid smell of burning tainted the freshness of the morning air.

"What can I do for you?" Maela stood beneath the broken timbers of the doorway, broom in hand.

Mayor Brandin cleared his throat. "We're a peace-loving community, as you know, Madame de Maunoir. But in the light of last night's events—"

"What the mayor is trying to say," interrupted the butcher rudely, "is we don't want you here anymore." Murmurs of assent accompanied his words.

"We had no idea that your husband was involved in such horrible practices," added Demoiselle Nazaire, the schoolteacher.

"We think it better that you and Klervie leave," said the mayor, embarrassedly rubbing his chain of office with his handkerchief. "As soon as possible."

"I see," said Maela. Klervie recognized the stiff tone of voice that her mother used when she was annoyed. "And I don't suppose it has occurred to a single one of you that Hervé might be innocent of these charges?"

"That's irrelevant," said Gwenna, her usual placid smile replaced by a pinched, disapproving look. "Heaven knows what foul and unnatural experiments your husband was conducting up at the college. You heard the explosion. Whatever he and the others were doing up there, it shouldn't have been allowed."

"The others?" Maela echoed. "What happened to the others?"

"All arrested and taken away to the capital, thank God," said Demoiselle Nazaire primly. "All except one wretched soul, who burned to death in the fire. They say the body was so badly charred that—"

"They've taken Hervé to Lutèce? Then that's where Klervie and I are going," said Maela, jutting her chin high as she stared back at the schoolmistress. "I thought we had friends here. But now I see I was mistaken. Come, Klervie; we must pack our belongings."

"Mewen?" Klervie scoured the cottage garden, calling in vain. "You bad cat! Why don't you come?" She looked in all his favorite places: behind the geranium pots, in the herb patch, on the broken wall . . .

"Hurry up, Klervie." Maman hurried toward her and grabbed her by the hand.

"I can't find Mewen. I'm not leaving without Mewen." Klervie stamped her foot.

"The carter's waiting." Maman dragged her up the garden path and lifted her onto the cart, climbing up beside her. The carter shook the reins and his horse ambled off down the lane toward the bridge across the Faou.

"Where are we going?"

Maman looked at her. Klervie saw that her eyes were red-rimmed and she hesitated before she spoke. "We're following Papa. All the way to Lutèce. We're going to see my sister, Lavéna."

"Tante Lavéna?" Klervie could not remember her aunt. She had never left the village before, and everything she knew was receding far too fast as the cart jogged on along the tree-lined lane. Soon all she could see was the hill with the jagged, smoky ruins of the college.

"Why can't Mewen come with us?" Klervie began to fidget. "Who will feed him? Who will give him his milk?"

"Lutèce is a big city," Maman said. "Mewen is a country cat. He would hate the bustle and noise. He can't come with us."

But Klervie could not understand. "I want Mewen," she said, and burst into tears.

"Maela," said Tante Lavéna coldly. Klervie shrank close to Maman. "What are you doing here?"

Maman swallowed hard before she spoke. "We have nowhere else to go."

"I can't let you stay. I can't risk it."

"But why not? I'm your sister." Maman sounded on the verge of tears again, and Klervie squeezed her hand sympathetically. She felt like crying herself; her feet ached from walking over the hard cobblestones and her throat was dry and tickly from breathing in the city dust.

"My sister, who married against our father's wishes," Tante Lavéna said. "Did you think we hadn't heard the news of the arrest?" She was looking up and down the street, over their heads, as though afraid they were being observed. "If I'm seen letting you in, I'm sure to be reported. And I can't risk tarnishing my husband's reputation. He's standing for councilor for our *quartier.*"

"The little one's exhausted. Could you just give her a drink?"

"You don't understand, do you, Maela?" said Tante Lavéna in vexed tones. "Your husband is accused of the most heinous of crimes. You're the wife of a criminal." And she shut the door in Maman's face.

"Tante Lavéna?" Klervie piped up. Why had her auntie not asked them inside?

"There's nothing for us here. Come, Klervie." Maman picked up their case, slowly turned away from Tante Lavéna's doorstep, and began to trudge back along the dusty street the way they had come. The afternoon sun burned hot onto the backs of their heads. Flies buzzed over a pile of stinking refuse lying in the gutter. Klervie was so weary now that she could hardly put one foot in front of the other.

"It smells bad," Klervie said, trying not to cry. "I want to go home, Maman. I want Mewen."

"My very own sister," whispered Maman. She seemed not to have heard what Klervie had said. "Now what shall we do? What *shall* we do?" Klervie heard the despair in her mother's voice and bit back her tears. They reached the end of the street and Maman's pace almost slowed to a stop.

"Madame!"

Maela wearily raised her head. A pigtailed servant girl in a drab grey dress was hurrying toward them over the cobbles, waving frantically to attract their attention.

"You dropped this by our doorstep." Breathless, the girl thrust a cloth purse at Maela. "My mistress told me to return it."

"Your mistress?"

"Madame Lavéna Malestroit." The girl bent over, touching her toes. "Ooh—I've got a stitch in my side."

"That's not your pur —" began Klervie, confused.

"Your mistress is very kind. Please send her my thanks." Maela closed her fingers around the purse.

"You're welcome, I'm sure." The girl straightened up and ran back the way she had come. Maela stood gazing after her in silence.

"Maman?" Klervie tugged at her sleeve. "Maman, what's wrong?"

But all Maman said, her voice choked, was, "Thank you, Lavéna."

Day after day, Maman left Klervie in the care of the sour-faced concierge of their rented room. Klervie hated the old woman, who made her scour the battered, greasy pots and pans until the skin on her fingers was shriveled and sore. In return, she fed Klervie a bowl of watery soup for lunch with a few shreds of leek or mushy carrot tops floating in it, and a hunk of dry bread. The concierge's apartment was dark and smelled of stale soup and mothballs. Klervie bore all this without complaining because Maman had told her she must be a good girl. Yet all the time she was aware of a nagging ache inside her that was not hunger.

She missed playing with Mewen. She missed stroking his soft fur and hearing him purr. But most of all she missed Papa.

Every day Maman returned looking more pale and exhausted than the day before. Klervie came to dread Maman's going.

"Please don't leave me." She clung on to Maman's dress, winding her fingers into the soft cloth.

"Klervie, I must go. It's for your papa. You can't come with me."

"Why can't I come with you? I want to see Papa." The indefinable ache inside her found words. "More than *anything*."

"He's . . ." Maman hesitated. "He's in prison, Klervie. He and the other magisters are all in prison."

"But Papa is not a bad man!" Klervie burst out. "He's not a thief."

A sad smile briefly lit Maman's dulled eyes. She smoothed Klervie's hair with one gentle hand. "*Chérie,* your papa is a brilliant man. But he has made enemies. Powerful enemies. And I fear—" She broke off, biting her lip. "Well, we must stay strong. For Papa's sake."

"Wake up, Klervie."

"Not yet," murmured Klervie, burrowing under the blanket. But Maman gently pulled the blanket away, leaving Klervie blinking sleepily in the milky light of dawn.

"My darling child . . . this may be the last time you see your dearest papa. The last chance you have to say farewell to him."

Klervie gazed into Maman's tear-filled eyes, uncomprehending. "Farewell?" she echoed. "Are they sending him away again? To another prison?"

"No." Maela drew Klervie tight, almost crushing her, so that Klervie could feel her mother's whole body trembling with suppressed sobs. "To a place where he will finally be free."

"Why are all these people here?" Klervie asked, clinging to Maman's hand in the press as they were swept along in the cresting tide. But Maman did not answer, forcing her way grimly on.

Soldiers lined the street. All were garbed in the same plain black uniforms as those worn by the men who had raided the cottage and dragged Papa away. Pikes in hand, they formed a barrier between the surging crowd and the center of the street.

And then Klervie thought she could make out the distant thud of drums—a slow, solemn beat, coming steadily nearer.

The crowd suddenly began to shout and jeer. The roar of their voices terrified Klervie; she felt as if she were surrounded by wild beasts. "Why are they all so angry?"

"Pay them no heed." Maela tugged at Klervie's hand, pulling her onward through the press of people, toward the soldiers.

A wooden cart, drawn by four strong dray horses, was lumbering toward them, its wheels rattling over the cobbles. Soldiers armed with muskets marched in front, matching their slow pace to the ominous beat of the drummers.

Now Klervie could see that there were men on the cart, caged like animals behind metal bars. She heard Maela give a soft gasp.

"Hervé," she whispered. "Oh Hervé, what have they done to you?"

Klervie screwed her eyes to a squint against the watery morning light. She could count five men on the cart and each one was slumped against the bars, as if barely able to stand.

Jostled to and fro by the crowd as it pressed forward to see the prisoners, Klervie almost lost hold of Maela.

Her mother was staring at one of the men. Bruises and blood-crusted cuts marred his face; one eye was half-closed with a swollen, purpled lid. And there seemed to be something wrong with his legs; he was supporting himself by pulling himself up by the bars.

"Maela," he called, his voice gratingly hoarse. "Maela, what are you doing here? For God's sake, take the child away."

Only then did Klervie recognize this gaunt, haggard man as her own father. She reached out, trying to clutch the grimy, blood-streaked hand between her own.

"Papa?"

For a moment, the gaunt face softened. "Klervie, look after your mother. For my sake." The fingers tried to extend farther to touch her hair but the effort seemed too great and she saw a grimace of pain twist his features.

"No communication with the prisoners." A soldier grabbed Maela by the arm and tried to pull her away.

"A few minutes with my husband. I was promised. I sold my ring—my wedding ring—to pay for it." Klervie heard Maela's voice break as though her heart were breaking too. The soldier tugged at her arm, less gently this time.

"Let her go!" shrieked Klervie.

"We were betrayed," said Papa. "Look, Maela. Everyone is here—all save one. Where is Kaspar Linnaius?"

"I can't believe Magister Linnaius would do such a thing." As the cart moved slowly on, Maela hurried alongside, Klervie following.

"We created a great invention together." Papa's bruised, swollen mouth twisted and contorted as he tried to enunciate the words. "An invention that would have made our fortunes. Yet here I am, condemned to die—and *where is Linnaius?*"

"He will come for us," cried another magister in a faint, cracked voice. "He can twist the winds to his will. He will come. You'll see."

One by one, the learned scholars ascended the pyre: lean-faced, kindly Madoc, gazing bemusedly around as if walking in his sleep; softly spoken Goustan de Rhuys, who used to make Klervie laugh by mysteriously plucking little treasures from behind her ear or under her chin—a tiny finch, a spotted butterfly, a barley sugar; venerable, white-haired Magister Gonery, so frail and broken that he had to be carried by the soldiers.

"That one's nothing but a boy," a woman said as Deniel was dragged up by four Guerriers. "You'd think they'd have spared the lad. Look at him; he's trembling so much he can hardly stand."

"Call yourselves mages!" jeered a man in the crowd. "Why don't you save yourselves?"

"Show us your magic tricks," called out another mockingly.

"Magisters of Karantec." A harsh voice rang out across the crowded square. A tall man in flowing robes had climbed up onto a platform. "You have been tried before God by His inquisitors and found guilty of practicing the Forbidden Arts."

"Who is that man?" Klervie quavered.

"His name is Alois Visant." Maman's voice had dwindled to a whisper. "Never forget that name, Klervie. He is a cruel, vindictive man."

"You are all condemned to burn at the stake. May God have mercy on your souls."

"Come away, child. This is no place for you." Maman caught Klervie up in her arms and began to carry her away as the crowd surged forward. Klervie saw the avid looks in their eyes. And then she smelled smoke. Maela battled on against the tide of people; Klervie clung to her, afraid they would both be crushed in the throng.

Maman was sick. She lay on the bed, sometimes plucking feebly at the dirty sheet, sometimes murmuring disjointed words or phrases that Klervie could not understand.

"The wards . . . why did the wards fail?"

Klervie anxiously patted Maman's sweat-damp hand.

"Thirsty," Maman whispered. There was still a little cold camomile tisane in the teapot from the night before. Klervie poured some into a bowl and brought it to Maman, biting her lower lip as she tried not to spill.

Maman drank a sip or two and then sank back, as if the effort had drained her.

"Does that make you feel better, Maman?" Klervie asked earnestly. Papa had told her to look after Maman and she was doing her best to obey his wishes.

Maman tried to stroke Klervie's cheek but her hand dropped back limply onto the threadbare blanket. "You're a good girl, Klervie," she said, her voice so faint that Klervie had to lean in close to hear her. Her eyes closed. Klervie climbed up on the bed and snuggled up to her mother, seeking comfort. But soon she rolled away, seared by the fever heat that was burning through her mother's body.

"What will become of us?" she heard Maman murmur.

———

Klervie awoke with a gnawing pain in her belly. A cloudy daylight lit the attic chamber. Klervie jumped off the bed and went to search in their bag of food. There was only a stale crust of bread left. The fire in the grate had burned itself out, and the scale-encrusted kettle had only a trickle of water inside.

"Maman, I'm hungry," Klervie said.

There came no answer. Klervie went back to the bed and began to tug at Maman's hand, which was lying limply over the side. Maman gave a dry little moan.

"I'm *hungry,*" Klervie insisted. "My tummy hurts."

"Go . . . and ask . . . downstairs . . ."

Klervie shook her head. She was afraid of the old woman who had so grudgingly given them shelter. Her jaundiced eyes were cold and disapproving.

"What d'you mean, your mother's sick?" The concierge dropped her broom. "I'm not having anyone sick in this hostelry; it's bad for business. You'll have to leave." She clapped a handkerchief over her nose and mouth. "Keep your distance, girl. And tell your mother to pack your bags."

"I don't think she's well enough," said Klervie in a small voice.

"Then I'll call the carrier," said the concierge, backing away. "Haven't you got any family to go to? Didn't your mother mention a sister?"

"Tante Lavéna?" Klervie shook her head doubtfully. "I d—don't remember where she lives."

"Then go out and find where. Go on." She took up her broom and began to jab it at Klervie's toes. "Be off with you. And don't come back until you've found your auntie."

Klervie hesitated, not wanting to leave Maman, yet frightened of the old woman and her broom.

She backed away. Then she turned and fled.

It was growing dark and Klervie was lost. She had wandered up and down the tree-lined avenues for hours, searching for Tante Lavéna's house. She had asked but no one knew her aunt's name. Now it was starting to rain. She crept into a doorway for shelter, sliding down with her back to the door, hugging her knees to her chest.

She was so sleepy . . .

When Klervie awoke, cold and stiff, it was night. The wet street gleamed in the light of a lantern.

The scent of cooking meat drifted on the damp breeze. Her empty stomach growled. She could not remember the last time she had eaten. The scent drew her, enticing her out of her hiding place and down a winding alley.

A man was sitting in an archway, hunched over a small brazier, slowly turning a spit on which were skewered two plump chickens, their skins a crisp golden brown. He looked up and saw her.

"You're hungry, aren't you?"

Klervie nodded. The unbearably mouthwatering smell of the roasting fowl, the dripping juices sizzling into the fire, drew her closer. The aching hollow in her empty belly made her want to moan. But there was something about the man's eyes as he watched her that made her skin crawl.

"Come closer, little girl." He beckoned, smiling at her. "I'll bet you'd like to share a slice or two of this with me." He produced a long loaf of fresh-baked crusty bread, and broke off a hunk. "Here!" He tossed it to her and she caught it. "Go on. Eat."

Klervie could not help herself. She started to tear at the bread with her teeth, gulping it down. And oh, it tasted so good that it brought tears to her eyes.

"You're a pretty one. What's your mother doing, letting you roam around here so late?"

"Maman is sick."

He touched her hair, running a curl between his greasy fingertips, and his touch made her shudder. "Hair like gold. This would fetch a good price at the wigmaker's."

Klervie shied abruptly away and he began to laugh. "Did I scare you, sweetheart? Don't worry. I won't cut your hair. You're worth so much more to me *intact.*" Wrapping his hand in a filthy cloth, he took the skewer from over the glowing brazier and slid one of the roast fowl onto a battered metal dish. Then, a dull flash of steel in the gathering dusk, and he had begun to carve into the crackling brown skin with a keen-bladed knife. He stabbed the tip into a slice of white breast meat and offered it to Klervie. Klervie wavered.

"Take it," he said, grinning. "It's yours."

"I have no money," Klervie said in a small voice. The delicious smell of the roast fowl tormented her sore stomach.

"Tender breast meat . . . for a tender child."

Klervie suddenly snatched at the meat and crammed it into her mouth, furiously chewing, swallowing as fast as she could, squeezing her eyes shut with the sheer pleasure of eating.

"How'd you like to stay with old Papa, then?" the man said. "You could snuggle up, nice and cozy, with me here." He patted the sacks on which he was sitting. She saw that greedy glint in his eyes again.

"You're not my papa."

He shrugged and tore a leg off the fowl he'd been carving, chewing on it while the fat trickled down his chin.

"My papa's dead." Klervie took a step back.

"Where d'you think you're off to? Aren't you going to give old Papa a kiss?"

Klervie saw the firelight glinting on his greasy lips and stubbled cheeks. She took another step back. He leaned forward suddenly and grabbed her. "Oh no, you don't! You owe me!" The grease-smeared mouth pressed against hers, while his hand groped beneath her skirts.

Struggling and kicking, Klervie cast around with one hand for something, anything, to help her get away. Her fingers closed on the skewer, hot and slimy with fat and she jabbed it with all her strength into the man's arm.

With a howl, he let go and she hurtled away as fast as she could, heart hammering in her chest as he came lumbering after her. "You've stabbed me, you ungrateful little bitch! Come back here! I'll make you wish you'd never been born . . ."

Maman will be worried. Maman will fret. Maman will cry if I don't get back to her soon . . .

It was not until afternoon the following day that Klervie at last found her way back to their lodgings. She had lost a shoe running to escape the horrible man. But she dared not stop to rest, for fear he'd find her, so she kept limping doggedly on through unfamiliar streets until dawn broke.

"*Klervie . . . Klervie . . .*"

She glanced up, certain that someone was calling her name. Shops were opening their shutters, water carts were clattering over the cobbles.

"*Come quick, Klervie . . .*" The faint, urgent voice drew her onward, one stumbling step at a time. Was it Maman's voice guiding her home? It sounded so familiar . . .

Weary and footsore, she tramped up the rickety stairs and opened the door to see the old woman rifling through their few possessions.

"Where's Maman?" Klervie stared at the empty bed in disbelief. "What have you done with her?"

"Everything costs money, you know. Even a pauper's grave. I had to pay the carter too. I'm not a charitable institution. Aha . . . what's this?" Her fingers closed around Klervie's book, hidden beneath the threadbare blanket, and tugged it out.

Klervie still did not, could not, understand what she was saying.

"Now, this . . . why ever didn't your mother sell this?" She held it up to the light trickling in through the filthy panes, an avaricious gleam in her eyes. "It'd have fetched a good sum."

"My book."

Klervie started forward but the old woman turned on her, her yellowing teeth bared in a snarl. "*My* book now."

Klervie took a step back.

"I'm owed. For the shroud, if nothing else."

"Shroud?" Klervie repeated, still not understanding.

"Your mother's dead, child. Dead and buried—by now." She gave a harsh laugh. "If the body snatchers haven't got hold of her first."

"Dead?" Klervie felt as if all the air had been knocked from her body. Her head spun. She felt herself falling.

"God help us. Don't say you've taken the sickness as well." The concierge, clutching Klervie's book, got to her feet and began to hurry toward the doorway.

The dust motes in the room shivered, caught in a sudden ray of light. Klervie blinked. The concierge stopped in midflight. The shadow of a woman shimmered in the dimness, pale as starlight.

"Maman . . . ?" Klervie murmured. For it seemed to her as she crumpled to the dusty floor that her mother was at her side, standing protectively over her.

The concierge gave a screech of terror. The book dropped from her fingers as she made the sign against evil. Then she ran, with a strange hobbling, stumbling gait, as though all the daemons from the abyss were chasing her.

CHAPTER 6

Tinidor clip-clopped slowly over the cobbles. Captain Ruaud de Lanvaux noticed how passersby hastily made way for him, scrambling out of his path, as if one glance at his black uniform and the golden insignia of the Staff was enough to instill fear and respect. Even carters pulled their wagons to one side and the barouche-drivers stopped to let him pass.

Something must have happened in Lutèce while he was overseas, to provoke this deference. Had Grand Maistre Donatien instigated a purge of heretics? He was so absorbed in his thoughts that he did not notice the fleeing child—or her pursuers—until she was almost under Tinidor's hooves.

He tugged hard on the reins and Tinidor reared up, iron-shod hooves pawing the air.

He saw the child glance up at the huge horse looming above her. Her knees buckled and she toppled into the gutter. Ruaud leaned forward to whisper soothing words in Tinidor's ears. The warhorse gave a snort and, responding at last to his master's voice, brought his front hooves down onto the cobblestones, narrowly missing the child's emaciated body.

Ruaud swung hastily down from the saddle and glared at the cringing gutter thieves. One look at his face—and his hand gripping the hilt of his sword—and they took to their heels, abandoning their prey. Ruaud knelt beside the little girl, lifting her out of the foul-smelling water. His heart pained him to see how thin and frail the body was; he could feel her bones protruding through her filthy rags.

"Little sparrow," he said softly, "are you hurt?"

The child's fair lashes fluttered and eyes dull with hunger gazed at him from a dirt-smeared face. A soft moan issued from cracked lips.

He had encountered many such starving street children on campaign in the dry heat of Enhirre; they clustered around his men, begging for food and water. Their skins might have been darker, but that look of desperate hunger was the same. Ignoring the gathering curious crowd, he took out a little metal flask from his uniform jacket and, supporting the child's head against his knee, poured a few drops into her mouth. All Guerriers carried a flask of well-watered wine in the desert. She spluttered.

"Sour," she whispered.

What had the thieves been so keen to steal from her? Whatever was wrapped in the shreds of sacking, she still clung to it as if her life depended upon it.

"What have you there, child?" he asked, forcing gentleness into a voice more accustomed to shouting orders.

"My book."

Ruaud caught a glimpse of the cover and saw to his surprise that it was a *Lives of the Holy Saints*. Had she stolen it? Or was the child from a devout family?

"What's your name?" he asked.

"Klervie." Her eyes focused on his for a moment. They were startlingly blue and clear, like a rain-washed sky.

"And why are you out on your own, Klervie? Where's your mother?"

The blue dulled again. She turned her head away. "Dead."

"And your father?"

"Dead . . ."

"So who's caring for you?" But he guessed the answer already. She was just another of the teeming city's unnumbered orphans, cast out to fend for herself. She could hardly be more than five or six years in age.

"Come, little one." He caught her up in his arms and settled her on Tinidor's back, placing her little hands on the pommel. "Cling tight or you'll fall off." He climbed up behind her, taking Tinidor's reins in one hand and gripping the drooping child firmly with the other.

What am I doing? I have duties to attend to at the Forteresse.

But wasn't this a part of his calling? He had chosen to become a warrior in God's cause, and that must surely involve defending the weak as well as protecting the shrines and holy places from desecration by unbelievers.

The child's head, her fair hair twisted into dirty rat's tails, drooped back against his chest. An odd and unfamiliar sensation flooded through him as he gazed down at her. In spite of her filthy state and unwashed smell, he felt he must protect this vulnerable child as if she were his own. When he became a Guerrier of the Commanderie, he had taken a vow of celibacy, abjuring all family ties and earthly distractions to dedicate his life to following the way of Saint Sergius. But for a moment, he knew what it was to cherish a little daughter.

Abbess Ermengarde looked at the sleeping waif in Captain de Lanvaux's arms, then glanced briefly into his eyes before modestly lowering her gaze. But inside her breast, her heart had begun to flutter quite immodestly. Ruaud de Lanvaux had returned from the Holy Land with his skin tanned copper by the merciless desert sun, which only served to emphasize the piercing blue of his fair-lashed eyes. Tall and lean, the captain's fine-chiseled features reminded her irresistibly of the warrior angels depicted in the jeweled stained glass of the convent chapel.

"Can you and your good sisters take this child, Abbess?" Ruaud was asking.

The Abbess blinked. Another orphan to care for? And one that looked so sickly . . .

"We are already full, I'm afraid—" she began.

"Would you take her in as a special favor for me?" The radiant blue eyes pierced hers. She wanted so much to say, "Yes, I'll do anything for you, dear Captain," except a mischievous little voice had begun to whisper at the back of her mind, *"Why does this urchin mean so much to him? Surely she couldn't be his . . ."* But she felt herself blushing at such a scandalous and ignoble thought. Ruaud de Lanvaux's reputation was blameless.

"And look." He pointed to the book the child was clutching. "*Lives of the Holy Saints.* She's from a devout family, that's for sure."

Or she's filched it, thought the Abbess. But then she was foolish enough to look up at the captain once more and found herself spellbound by his dazzling gaze. She felt as if the golden sunlight that warmed the white dome of the Holy Shrine in distant Enhirre was reflected in his eyes. "I'm sure that—for you—we can squeeze another one in," she heard herself saying. For surely, if Captain de Lanvaux was so interested in the child, he would come often to the convent to visit her. And that idea appealed to the Abbess more than she could have possibly imagined.

A grave smile spread across his handsome features and the Abbess's heart almost melted. Flustered, she forced herself to look back at the neglected child. "I don't suppose she has a name . . ."

"She called herself Klervie."

The Abbess tutted. "What kind of a name is that? Perhaps you would like to choose another name for her, Captain? One more suitable for a little acolyte of our dear Saint Azilia?" She could not help smiling coyly back at him, unable to restrain herself.

"She has blue eyes of a most remarkable color," said the captain distantly.

"Not unlike yours, dear Captain . . ."

"I think 'Celestine' would make an excellent name for her."

"Then I shall write that name down on our orphanage roll. Celestine. A heavenly name."

"And I shall return to see how she is progressing."

"Oh yes, Captain, please do," said the Abbess, smiling even more warmly. "Please call whenever you wish."

Captain de Lanvaux knelt beside the child and gently placed his hand on her fair head. "Till we meet again, little Celestine."

Klervie could hear angels singing. Their clear, high voices spiraled around her like threads of silver light.

She opened her eyes. She could still hear the angels . . . although now they sounded much farther away.

"Am I dead?"

"Good gracious me, no." A woman's face appeared above hers,

wrinkled and red-cheeked like a cherry. "In fact, you're very much alive." The woman leaned over her and felt her forehead. "The fever's left you at last."

"But I can hear angels singing . . ."

"That?" The woman straightened up, listening. Then she laughed. "That's the Novices' choir practicing their scales. Sister Noyale would be most amused to hear them called angels."

"Novices?" echoed Klervie sleepily, not understanding.

"We have two choirs here. The Novices are the older girls, aged twelve to sixteen. The younger ones are called the Skylarks."

"Where's Maman?" Klervie asked, then remembered. The distant singing seemed to recede even farther as she recalled staring in shock at the empty bed, the concierge's heartless words ringing in her ears. *Your mother's dead, child. Dead and buried.* Tears welled in her eyes, tears of loss and rage at the unjustness of it all. Why had Maman abandoned her? She tried to hold the tears in until her shoulders shook with the effort.

"Whatever's the matter, *ma petite*?" said the woman. Klervie heard kindness and exasperation mingled in her voice. How could she explain? She turned her face away. "Were you dreaming of your mother? Don't grieve for her anymore; you're part of a new family now, one with many sisters, young and old, like me. My name's Kinnie, Sister Kinnie."

Klervie gazed at her through her tears, uncomprehending.

"You're so lucky to have such a good-hearted benefactor. Captain de Lanvaux brought you to us. Otherwise you would have starved on the streets, little one. Now you're under good Saint Azilia's protection. So dry your eyes." Klervie took the handkerchief that Sister Kinnie gave her and mopped her face. "You're still weak after the fever. We'll have to build up your strength, Celestine."

"Celestine?" echoed Klervie. She looked around to see who Sister Kinnie was speaking to.

"Every child who enters our convent is given a new name. Your benefactor named you Celestine. You will soon forget your old name."

In the dusky moonlight, the picture engraved on the front of the book wavered, and in silvery, sinuous lines began to rise from the cover until a tall, slender female form hovered over Klervie, its hands clasped together as though in prayer, its luminous eyes gazing down on her.

"Who are you?" quavered Klervie who was now called Celestine. "Are you a h—holy saint?" She stumbled over the words she had heard the good sisters use.

"*I am the one your father bound to protect you.*"

"Papa?"

"*I am bound to this book, Klervie. I cannot break free. I can only help you through the book.*"

"You mustn't call me Klervie anymore. They've changed my name to Celestine." It was a pretty name, even if it felt like wearing borrowed clothes.

"*Celestine,*" echoed the spirit in a voice like a shimmer of clear raindrops.

"Are you really a Faie?" Celestine asked wonderingly. Faies could grant wishes, or so the tales Maman used to tell her said. And Celestine felt her heart swelling with the desire to make a wish. A wish so strong that her whole body trembled at the very thought of it.

Bring them back. Bring back my papa and maman.

"*I do not know the word 'Faie.' I know only that your father charged me to look after you.*"

"You cannot grant wishes?" The words were barely a whisper; her throat had tightened with the strain of trying not to cry. "Not even one?"

"*I am bound to the book,*" repeated the Faie, and its translucent eyes seemed to brim with tears, mirroring Celestine's disappointment.

"Is this the new girl?"

"What a pale little mite she is."

"What's your name, mite?"

Celestine stared, mute with apprehension, at the gaggle of curious girls surrounding her bed. She wanted to pull the sheet up to cover her face but it was too late to hide.

"Give the poor child room to breathe!" called a woman, and

Celestine recognized Sister Kinnie's voice with relief. "She's still recuperating." Out of breath, Sister Kinnie came bustling up, shooing the girls away from Celestine's bed so that she could sit next to her. "Now, girls, this is Celestine, our new little sister. I want you to teach her about our daily tasks. She's well enough to move out of the Infirmary into Skylarks. So, Angelique, you will help her with her things; Rozenne and Katell, you will take her by the hand and bring her to the dormitory."

"I'm Rozenne," announced a brown-eyed girl, seizing Celestine's right hand in a firm grip and marching her toward the door.

"Wait," wailed a thin-faced girl with dark plaits. "Sister said me, too."

"You're too slow, Katell," said Rozenne, laughing. "Keep up!" The other girls laughed too as Katell hastened after them, plaits flying like streamers.

But Celestine kept looking over her shoulder, anguished that she had been separated from her book.

"What's the matter?" demanded Rozenne.

"My book."

"*Your* book?" echoed Katell punctiliously. "Our book now. We share everything at Saint Azilia's."

"This old tome?" Angelique, tall and willowy, with curling hair the color of spring catkins, cast a disparaging glance at Celestine's most prized possession. "It's just a boring *Lives of the Holy Saints.*"

"My papa gave it to me." Celestine was on the verge of tears again, yet felt ashamed to weep in front of the older girls.

"Don't worry. We won't take it if it means so much to you."

The staircase wound endlessly upward and Celestine, still weak from fever, began to imagine that she would never reach the top. At last, breathless, her legs wobbling from the effort, she stumbled into the dormitory. Though the room was sparsely furnished with two rows of beds, light poured in through tall arched windows set beneath a high, sloping ceiling supported by thick wooden beams.

"The sisters call us the Skylarks, because we're at the very top of the convent," said Rozenne.

"Only the youngest novices sleep up here," Angelique said.

"When you're twelve, you move to the Novices' dormitory on the floor below." She tossed her fair curls. "We Novices sing in the evenings as well as the mornings, so we're not supposed to wake you little ones when we return. You need your sleep to grow."

"This will be your bed," said Rozenne kindly, "next to mine." She took Celestine's book from Angelique and laid it on the little bed. "Katell, fetch a sheet for Celestine's bed."

"How old are you?" Katell asked, suddenly swinging round on her heel to stick her face into Celestine's. Startled, Celestine took a step back, screwing up her eyes, for Katell's breath smelled strongly of licorice comfits.

"I'll be six when the snows come," Celestine said.

"You're only a baby." Rozenne stroked her hair. "I was six when I came here, two years ago."

"I'm seven, but I'm half a head taller than Rozenne." Katell fished in the pocket of her smock and brought out a couple of dusty comfits. "Here. You can have one. Sister Kinnie keeps a jar in the Infirmary. Sometimes she gives them as a reward."

Celestine nodded her thanks and put the comfit in her mouth. The strong flavor made her tongue sting, but she hadn't the heart to spit the gift out into her palm.

Katell twirled away down the dormitory toward a great armoire of dark-stained wood. Celestine trailed after her. As Katell tugged the door open, a faint odor of lavender and starch wafted out. Clean, folded sheets were piled high inside.

"Catch!" Katell tossed her one. Celestine reached up and caught it. Then she saw the painting on the wall. A lady gazed down on the dormitory with eyes of soft violet blue, her golden tresses falling about her shoulders, her slender fingers caressing the keys of a gilded portative organ.

"Oh," breathed Celestine, gazing back. "She's so pretty. Who is she?"

"Don't you know? She's Saint Azilia, silly," said Katell scornfully.

"How could she know?" Rozenne put her hands protectively on Celestine's shoulders, bending down to whisper in her ear. "She's the saint of music. Our patron saint."

Celestine nodded, still staring at the smiling lady.

"And here's a clean smock for you." Katell thrust a folded garment at her.

The smock was made of brown linen, like the ones Rozenne and Katell were wearing. Celestine stared at it in bewilderment, not knowing how to put it on over her shift.

"I'll help you." Rozenne pulled it over Celestine's head and showed her how to tie the fastenings. "Oh dear. It's rather too large for you, isn't it? But you'll grow."

"Now you're a Skylark too." Katell grinned at her. "Don't look so sad! You're not going to cry, are you?"

A bell began to ring, a rapid succession of clangs that echoed around the white convent walls.

"Choir practice!" The girls scampered off, leaving Celestine standing, bemused, in the middle of the dormitory.

"Come on, Celestine!" Rozenne ran back and grabbed her by the hand. "Sister Noyale will scold us if we're late."

The high, vaulted ceiling of the chapel vanished into dim greyness far above Celestine's head. She trotted along at Rozenne's side, hearing the patter of their light footfalls magnified, echoing far into the shadows.

"You're late," said a stern female voice.

"Here's the new Skylark, Sister Noyale."

Celestine shuffled forward, trying not to trip over her smock. Sister Noyale towered above her.

"Sweet Azilia, she's an infant! I'm not running a nursery here." Celestine registered a strong yet handsome face, brown-skinned, with arching dark brows and eyes that flashed with annoyance. She also noticed a round mole like a beauty spot above Sister's Noyale's upper lip—and, fascinated, could not keep her eyes from straying back to it. "Whatever is the Abbess thinking of?"

Celestine shrank back. Sister Noyale scared her. She could sense that all the Skylarks were staring at her. She felt for the warmth of Rozenne's hand and clutched it tightly.

"Sister Kinnie said—" began Rozenne.

"I don't give a fig for what Sister Kinnie said. This choir is not for babes in arms."

What the Skylarks dreaded the most, Celestine soon learned, was the moment when Sister Noyale would abandon her lectern to pace up and down along the rows of singers, hands clasped behind her back, coiffed head down, listening intently for wrong notes. Every time this happened, Celestine would feel her voice begin to dry from terror and her thin piping fade to a whisper.

Please don't let it be me, she prayed silently to Saint Azilia. For before long, the choirmistress would clap her hands and in the ensuing silence sharply call out one of the girls' names. The offender would then be made to sing the last phrase on her own, her faults exposed for all to hear, her cheeks hot red with embarrassment. And when she had finished, if Sister Noyale was displeased, she would be made to repeat it until it was correct—or her fast-dripping tears made it impossible to continue. The thought of having to endure such public humiliation terrified Celestine. She knew Sister Noyale resented her presence in the choir. She suspected that she was waiting for the opportunity to catch her out.

There was so much music to learn by heart. There were chants for worship at daybreak, noontide devotions, twilight hymns, and solemn hymns for the watchnight services. Celestine was bewildered by the complexity of the words and often resorted to merely moving her lips, miming the verses that she could not begin to remember.

"The new girl is not ready, Kinnie," she overheard Sister Noyale complaining. "Her voice is too thin, too underdeveloped to train yet. It will stand out from the rest, like a false coin jingled in with the gold."

"As some of you are aware, Saint Azilia's Day is approaching," said Sister Noyale, eyeing each girl sternly in turn. "And to honor our patron saint, we invite guests to hear us sing. It's the most important day of the year, so we must be note-perfect."

A summer storm was brewing outside and little slivers of distant lightning lit the darkening chapel. Celestine was distracted. She hated storms. Rain and hail began to rattle on the chapel roof. As the rumble of thunder growled, the girls darted nervous glances at each other.

"I expect every Skylark to give me her full attention," said Sister Noyale. She rapped on her lectern with her baton. "It's just a heavy downpour, nothing more. Be thankful that you're not working out in the kitchen gardens this afternoon. Back to 'Protect Us, Blessed Azilia.' " She hummed a pitch. "Here's your note. One, two, and . . ." The first note was almost drowned by a loud crack of thunder. Startled, Celestine looked around. The other girls had begun to sing, evidently more afraid of their choirmistress than the breaking storm.

She was acutely aware that Sister Noyale was on the prowl again and yet every time the thunder rumbled, panic overwhelmed her and the notes she was singing went wrong.

"Celestine!" Sister Noyale's voice was sharp as a slap. "Stand out from the line, where I can see you. Repeat that last phrase."

Celestine froze. She was paralyzed with fear. She felt Rozenne nudge her.

"Hurry up, child. Don't keep me waiting!" Sister Noyale's dark eyes reflected the flash of lightning that suddenly lit the aisle of the chapel.

Celestine stumbled forward onto the blue-and-ochre tiles. She opened her mouth . . . and thunder cracked right overhead. Several girls shrieked, clutching each other. The panes of stained glass rattled in their lead frames. Sister Noyale raised her eyes to heaven.

"Repeat it after me, Celestine." Her voice was less harsh now, but Celestine heard the vexation in it. And as the choirmistress's rich alto voice slowly demonstrated the melody, Celestine felt the tears well up. She hiccuped as she tried to sing, willing the tears away. She could feel a lump swelling in her throat, strangling the notes of the simple phrase so that all that came from her lips was a weak whisper that made her cringe with shame.

Sister Noyale let out an exasperated sigh. "How can I produce anything resembling a performance with such poor material? The Abbess expects me to work miracles. And the festival is only six days away."

Celestine hung her head and her tears dripped onto the tiles. "I'm sorry," she whispered.

"Sorry is not good enough." Sister Noyale's hand cupped her chin, tipping her face up to hers. "Many important and noble visitors will come here on Saint Azilia's Day. They expect to hear perfection. You may be the youngest Skylark, but I will treat you no differently than the rest. Go. And don't come back until you are in control of yourself. I have no room for little crybabies in this choir."

As Celestine fled into the torrential rain, the thunder still grumbled menacingly as the storm clouds moved away over the bay.

CHAPTER 7

"*Celestine.*" A pearl-white light began to glow in the empty dormitory. Celestine raised her head from the damp blanket and blinked. Her eyes felt raw and swollen from weeping. She had not wept so much since . . . but no, she could not even bear to think of that. It made her feel as if she were tumbling off the edge of a vertiginous cliff into a dark pit of shadows . . .

"*Celestine,*" said the soft, solicitous voice once more and Celestine saw the Faie slowly issuing from the book, rising to lean over her with eyes the tender blue of forget-me-nots. "*How can I help you?*"

Celestine shook her head and a hiccuping sob issued from her, the tight knot constricting her throat. "I c—can't sing."

The light radiating from the Faie's gentle blue eyes felt like a caress. Celestine's sobs stilled as she gazed uncertainly back. The Faie had taken the form of the Blessed Saint Azilia, with long tresses of pale gold.

"*Would you like to sing?*" asked the sweet, low voice.

Celestine nodded. To be able to sing as well as the other Skylarks was her heart's desire. She wanted to make Sister Noyale gasp with admiration when she opened her lips. She wanted to make the other girls stare at her with envy. She wanted to be the best.

"*Then I will grant your wish.*"

Translucent fingers reached out to touch Celestine's forehead, tracing the contours of her face and mouth, sliding downward to her throat. Celestine, kneeling up on her blanket, closed her eyes, feeling a soft tingling begin to pass through her body.

Celestine opened her eyes again and saw the Faie bending over her as Maman used to when she kissed her good night. Closer leaned the face until she felt the faint brush of Faie lips upon her own. Her tongue, mouth, and throat began to glow with a silvery warmth that slowly seeped through her whole body. She looked at herself in astonishment, seeing for a moment every limb, every finger softly glowing with the same cloudy radiance as the hovering Faie.

Then, as the glow began to dim, she saw the Faie slowly nod as though approving what it had done.

"*Use my gift well, Celestine.*"

Celestine could only nod in reply. She still felt as though she were filled with light. As the Faie faded back into the book, Celestine heard the sound of footsteps hastening up the stairs.

"Celestine!" Katell rushed in, plaits whirling wildly about her head, closely followed by Rozenne, then Koulmia, who had to stop to catch her breath. "Are you all right?"

"We—came as soon as we—could," puffed Koulmia.

"You should take off your wet smock." Rozenne fussed around her like a mother hen. "You'll catch cold, and then you'll have no voice at all for Saint Azilia's Day."

Celestine let Rozenne drag the damp smock over her head and rub her hair dry with a towel. She was still dazed by her encounter with the Faie, her throat and mouth still glowed with the warmth of the Faie's kiss.

"That Sister Noyale is a horrid old woman." Katell paced the dormitory, thin shoulders hunched, kicking angrily at anything in her path: discarded clogs, water jugs. "She should be punished for making our Celestine cry. We should put toads in her bed. We should sprinkle pepper in her porridge. We should . . ."

The thought of Sister Noyale lifting back the bedcovers to find slimy toads on the mattress, croaking and goggling at her, was irresistible. Celestine felt a little smile pushing at the corners of her mouth.

"Hush, Katell!" Rozenne placed a warning finger over her lips. "She might hear. And then she'd punish you."

"I don't care," declared Katell, hands on her hips. She came over and grinned at Celestine. "That's better." She ruffled Celestine's hair. "We'll help you. We'll teach you ourselves."

Celestine smiled shyly back. Katell might seem a little rough-and-ready, but she had a good heart.

"Skylarks!" Angelique appeared in the dormitory and clapped her hands smartly. "What are you doing up here? You're on kitchen duty today. Sister Kinnie is getting impatient. Put your aprons on—and run."

The faint, sweet sound of singing drifted out across the courtyard from the chapel's open door. In the scullery, Celestine lifted her head from the carrots she was scraping and listened.

Quietly she began to hum the notes of the chant to herself. And then Sister Noyale's hurtful words returned to remind her of her inadequacy.

"*Her voice is too thin, too underdeveloped to train yet. It will stand out from the rest . . .*"

Yet the sound that was issuing from her lips was quite different from before. Although her voice was still soft, the notes flowed sweetly, her tone small but crystal-pure.

"So here you are!"

Celestine stopped and saw Katell, Rozenne, and Koulmia gawking at her.

Then Katell let out a whistle. "Who'd have thought that our teaching could make you into a songbird, Celestine? Sister Noyale—it's time for you to retire!"

"Well done, little songbird." Rozenne rushed forward to smother Celestine in a warm hug. "Have you been practicing down here, all by yourself?"

Celestine nodded.

"It's just as I said," went on Katell, developing her theme. "Sister Noyale terrified her so much that she could hardly produce a single note. How can we prove to her that Celestine can sing as well as the rest of us?"

"Sister Noyale still scares me." Koulmia began to nibble at a peeled carrot. "But every time she starts to glare at me, I think of things I like. Honey cake on Saint Azilia's Day," she said dreamily, "and those rose petal creams that Sister Kinnie makes . . ."

Celestine looked inquiringly up at Rozenne.

"There's always a special feast with treats for the singers after the service," Rozenne said. "And the noble guests give gifts to the convent. If we're lucky, they bring little treats for us, too . . ."

"Sugared almonds," said Katell.

"Barley sugar," added Rozenne.

"Marzipan." Koulmia let out a sigh of longing.

Celestine had a sudden memory of Maman making marzipan in the little cottage kitchen, letting her mix the ground almonds into a thick sticky paste, then cut out little shapes. The recollection was so vivid that the sound of the girls' chatter receded and she lost the sense of their conversation until she heard Koulmia saying, "And she has to perform to the noble guests. Do you think Celestine might be chosen?"

"Chosen?" echoed Celestine.

"Every year one of us is chosen to sing solo. And—"

"It has to be Angelique," Rozenne said, her eyes softening as she clasped her hands together.

"Yes, we all know you have a crush on Angelique," said Katell dryly. "But remember that she's nearly sixteen. If she sings well enough, she'll be sent away to join the convent choir in Lutèce. And then she'll be gone for good."

Rozenne's dreamy expression changed to one of alarm. Then she hugged Celestine tightly again. "Don't worry, Celestine. We won't let them send you away."

"They won't choose any of us Skylarks," Katell said scornfully. "Our voices aren't 'fully developed.' "

"Are those carrots ready yet?" called Sister Elena, bustling into the scullery, balancing an armful of cabbages. On seeing the half-scraped pile, she let out a cry of vexation. "Idle girls! There's soup to be made and here you are, gossiping." She snatched a half-eaten carrot out of Koulmia's hand, tutting. "You'd better help little Celestine. And don't you dare take another bite, Koulmia!"

The sound of the flowing water, echoing around the washhouse, made Celestine feel less self-conscious. She began to sing softly as she spread the wet aprons out on the worn stone slab and scrubbed away with the brush Sister Elena had given her. And the more vigorously she scrubbed, the louder she sang, forgetting that anyone might be passing by.

Wringing the surplus water from the linen just as Sister Elena had taught her, she put the clean apron in the wooden bucket and turned to fish in the water for the next. Then she saw the nuns standing on the opposite side of the washtub and watching her: Sister Kinnie, Sister Elena—and Sister Noyale, arms folded, all regarding her intently.

"I—I'm sorry." Celestine hastily bowed her head, certain she had done something wrong, waiting for the inevitable reprimand.

"You've been hiding something from us, Celestine," said Sister Noyale severely. "You have a voice."

"M—me?"

"Sing for us again. Here is your starting note."

Celestine felt her knees begin to tremble. When she tried to take in a breath, it was as if a cord had tightened around her throat. She opened her mouth and a sad, whispering sound emerged. She tried to avoid Sister Noyale's stern brown eyes, not wanting to see the disapproval and disappointment she sensed was there. And then, as she struggled to sing the first phrase of the hymn, the lapping echo of the water began to soothe her nerves. She breathed more easily and one phrase flowed smoothly into the next. Before she knew it, she had completed the final verse. She looked over the washtub to see Sister Noyale looking back at her, her lips pursed in a strange, unreadable expression.

"Our little Celestine can sing as sweetly as a nightingale!" said Sister Kinnie, beaming. "You must reinstate her, Sister Noyale."

Prince Karl seated himself at Linnaius's desk and examined the invention with keen attention, twiddling the knobs like an excited schoolboy. "So this is the finished Vox Aethyria, eh?"

Linnaius nodded, praying that the prince would not break anything.

"It looks too damned pretty to be part of a scientific experiment."

"If you would be so good as to speak a few words into the voice receptor, highness . . ."

Karl cleared his throat, then said, a little awkwardly, "Eugene, this is your father. Can you hear me?" He waited. Linnaius waited. And then a faint but distinct voice replied, "I hear you, Father. Is the Magus there?"

"He's standing right beside me."

"Is he pleased? Is he smiling?" came back the young man's reply. "He should be. This experiment is a success!"

Prince Karl glanced up at Linnaius. "My son is right; this Vox of yours is going to give us a significant advantage over our enemies." He seized Linnaius's hand and shook it enthusiastically. "Congratulations, Magus. How'd you feel about moving out of the university science faculty and establishing a laboratory all of your own?"

"Y—your highness is too kind." Linnaius was not yet used to Karl's spontaneous gestures of generosity; he had spent so much of his life fending for himself.

"It's in Tielen's interests to keep you working for us," Karl said, laughing heartily. He cast a roll of papers down on Linnaius's desk. "Take a look at these. They're preliminary drawings by the architects I've commissioned to develop a little project of mine. I'd like your thoughts about the laboratory."

An hour or so later, Linnaius was still sitting at his desk, studying the plans, when he heard a voice calling his name. The door opened and a tall young man appeared.

"That was so *exciting*!" His eyes sparkled with an infectious fervor. "Thank you so much, Magus, for letting me be the first to use the Vox!"

Linnaius looked at Karl's son and could not help smiling back, in spite of himself. The young man's passion for science was inspiring. Eugene was a frequent visitor at the faculty, always eager to learn. He was equally passionate about military history, and Linnaius noticed that he was wearing the grey uniform of a cadet at the Tielen Military Academy.

"So your highness has enrolled at the academy?"

"Today. So I won't be able to call in quite so often while I complete my training. They're sending us off into the wilds in the north on a survival exercise. It's to toughen us up for future campaigns."

"Take care, highness," Linnaius heard himself saying. With surprise he realized that, in spite of his best resolve, he had come to care for the boy as if he were his own. Ambitious, cultured, with a keen intellect and an insatiable hunger for knowledge, Eugene resembled his father in many ways, not least in his ability to inspire those around him. *But I must not let myself grow too fond. Personal attachments are risky for a magus. Better to stay aloof, detached . . .*

"Sleds, the frozen sea, making shelters out of compacted snow—I can't wait!" Eugene stopped in front of the Vox, staring down at the glittering device. "But I've been meaning to ask you about these crystals, Magus. They're unlike any gem I've ever seen before. What's the secret?"

Linnaius hesitated. To tell Eugene the truth would be to admit that he was deficient in the skills it took to energize the aethyr crystals. But there was something in Eugene's frank, open expression that required an honest answer. "I have to admit that I 'borrowed' these crystals from the Francian Commanderie. They're aethyr crystals of a rare kind, only found in Enhirre."

"No wonder you're a wanted man in Francia!" said Eugene, breaking into delighted laughter. But then he reached for Linnaius's hand and pressed it between his own. "You do realize that you must never go back to Francia? The Inquisition is hungry for your blood."

"Why would I want to return, highness?" Linnaius said with a frankness that surprised even himself. "Everyone I knew in Francia is dead. And your highness's family has been more than generous to me; I have everything I need to continue my work in Tielen."

To celebrate their patron saint's day, the Blessed Azilia's orphans wore aprons of starched white linen over their smocks and covered their heads with lace-trimmed kerchiefs. Every girl pinned a little bunch of violets to the bib of her apron. Celestine let Rozenne fuss over her, biting her lip as the brisk comb-strokes snagged her hair and hurt her scalp, trying to concentrate on the older girls' gossip.

"Let's take bets on who can collect the most treats," said Katell.

"Betting is very wicked," Koulmia said piously.

"I think Celestine will win," and Katell stuck her face close to

Celestine's, almost rubbing noses. "And then she'll share them with us, *won't you?*"

Her pockets filled with pink-and-white sugared almonds and butter biscuits, Celestine walked away from the guests' table, hearing the admiring voices still murmuring compliments.

"Such a sweet tone."

"And such a sweet-faced child, too."

"How could anyone abandon such a pretty little girl?"

"There was sickness in the city." The Abbess was dominating the conversation now. "One shudders to think what might have happened if the captain hadn't rescued her . . ."

Sugared almonds, glossy barley sugars, and golden sablés were being shared out in the Skylarks' dormitory in a midnight feast. Celestine was so sleepy she kept nodding off, her head against Rozenne's shoulder, as the older girls chattered.

"So Angelique is really going to join the sisters in Lutèce?"

"Well, I wouldn't want to go," declared Katell. "They make you shave your head." She tossed her dark plaits defiantly.

Celestine looked at her in horror. "But Angelique has such pretty hair . . ." The thought of Angelique's honey-blond curls being callously snipped off made her shudder.

"Only if she takes her vows," countered Rozenne. "Only if she dedicates her life to Saint Azilia. They don't make you shave your head if you join the chapel choir. Do they?" she added uncertainly.

"But what else will she do with her life? What can any of us do? We're orphans. No one will want us as wives. Aren't we supposed to show our gratitude to the order for raising us by devoting our lives to the saint?"

"Don't think I'm going to treat you any differently, Celestine," said Sister Noyale sternly. "You may have charmed everyone yesterday, but your voice will need careful nurturing if your gift is not to be frittered away. I've seen it happen so many times before. Early success goes to a Skylark's head and she neglects her technique."

Celestine nodded. She was still terrified of Sister Noyale and had no idea what the choirmistress was talking about. Her head was ringing with the glorious sound of the choir. When she sang, her sadness receded and she thought only of the music. It was the only time that she did not grieve for Maman . . . or Papa.

"Do you really have to leave us, Angelique?" wept Katell.

An autumn gale was blowing, whirling dry leaves and dust around the yard. Overhead, the clouds scudded wildly across the bleak sky. Celestine stood shivering, watching as the older girl's trunk was loaded into the waiting cart. Angelique had been accorded a great honor: She had been selected to join the choir of Saint Meriadec in Lutèce.

"Don't go. We shall miss you so much," Rozenne said in a voice stifled by tears, seizing Angelique's hand as if to hold her back.

"Please stay!" chorused all the Skylarks, running out into the courtyard to surround Angelique.

"And I shall miss you all." Angelique sounded close to tears, too. The errant wind whipped stray locks of her golden hair into her eyes as she bent to hug the Skylarks, each in turn. "Practice your singing, work hard—and then you may be chosen to join me."

Rozenne began to sob.

Celestine hung back, overwhelmed by conflicting feelings. She had not known Angelique as long as the others, but she had come to love the girl as if she were an older sister. There had already been so many painful partings in her life, she could not bear to endure another so soon.

"Aren't you going to say good-bye, Celestine?"

Celestine looked round to see that Angelique had come after her. She gazed up at the older girl and wondered why she could only see a blur where her face should be. Angelique dropped to her knees beside her. "What's this?" she said softly. "Tears?"

"It's the wind," muttered Celestine.

Angelique hugged Celestine to her and Celestine felt the

unbidden tears dampening Angelique's honeyed curls. She did not want the others to see her cry. "But we shan't be parted for long. With a voice as sweet as yours, you'll soon be on your way to Lutèce to join me."

Celestine stared at her. She would not reach sixteen for another nine years. So much could happen in that time.

Would Angelique even remember her?

CHAPTER 8

Plaisaunces was in an uproar. Courtiers huddled together in alcoves, speaking in urgent whispers. Messengers hurtled past, clutching dispatches. Ruaud could sense the growing tension as he made his way through the palace. At every stair and doorway, he was challenged by King Gobain's household guards and obliged to show his papers, as well as the letter from Maistre Donatien requesting—no, demanding—his presence. Ruaud's lieutenant, Alain Friard, followed him, his face a mask of bewilderment as he gazed at the chaotic activity.

"Something's happened, Captain. Is it the Tielens?"

Ruaud nodded. "This doesn't bode well." In his opinion, the king's decision to send the fleet to challenge Prince Karl was ill judged.

"Here we are." He stopped at a great door of gilt-encrusted wood, guarded by halberdiers of the King's House, resplendent in their coats of royal blue and gold.

"Captain de Lanvaux, Lieutenant Friard," announced one of the guards as he opened the door to admit them.

Ruaud noticed Alain Friard's eyes widen as they entered the chamber; the room was hung with martial tapestries and every wall bristled with crossed swords, spears and scimitars, delicate chain mail and plumed helmets, all trophies from the Holy Wars in Djihan-Djihar and Enhirre. A magnificent table dominated the center of the chamber, its surface polished to a mirror sheen.

Grand Maistre Donatien entered, imposing in his black robes.

The golden Order of Saint Sergius hung on an emerald ribbon across his breast. The color of the ribbon did not escape Ruaud's keen eye; it was the same green as the insignia of the Francian Inquisition. This obvious declaration of a new allegiance disturbed Ruaud, yet the benign expression on Donatien's face as he greeted him was like a mask, giving nothing away.

"Maistre," said Ruaud respectfully, dropping to one knee to kiss Donatien's ring of office. "May I present my new lieutenant, Alain Friard?"

"Congratulations on your promotion, Lieutenant," said Donatien, extending his hand. "You served us bravely in Ondhessar."

Blushing, Friard knelt in his turn and touched the Maistre's ring with his lips.

The formalities completed, Ruaud rose. "Do you know why the king summoned us, Maistre?"

As he spoke, the door opened again and another black-garbed priest entered, followed by a young secretary clutching a fat folder of documents. As the priest turned to nod them a curt acknowledgment, Ruaud recognized the hooded, watchful eyes of Inquisitor Visant. But before he could ask why the Inquisition had been invited to this meeting, the inner doors were drawn open and King Gobain strode in. One glance at his face was enough to tell Ruaud that his majesty was in a furious temper.

"Sit, gentlemen!" It was a command and the priests and Guerriers swiftly obeyed. "I won't waste words. By now you'll have heard of our humiliating defeat. By God, the whole quadrant will have heard!" His strong, strident voice boiled with barely restrained fury. "The flagship's sunk, along with nine other warships. My wife's brother, Aimery, is missing. Every remaining ship in the fleet is damaged—we'll be lucky if half of them limp back to Fenez-Tyr."

This was a comprehensive defeat. Ruaud, dumbstruck, stared at his reflection in the glassy tabletop. The thought of so many sailors lost in the sea battle, so many families bereaved and grieving, bruised his heart. Even the king had fallen silent, his chin sunk on his chest. No one spoke until Donatien cleared his throat and said, "Prayers will be said for the admiral and his men throughout Francia; I'll send word to all the parishes directly. And would your majesty like me to conduct a service here at Plaisaunces?"

Gobain slowly raised his head. His eyes burned. "I want you to find me the man who caused this conflagration, Donatien."

"Me, majesty?" Donatien said in tones of mild surprise. "But what can I do against Prince Karl?"

Gobain leaned across the table toward Donatien and spoke in a low, grinding voice. "Not that upstart Karl, but his damned Royal Artificier or whatever fancy name he's known by."

A slight frown furrowed Donatien's smooth brow. "I beg your pardon, majesty, but I don't quite follow—"

Gobain let out a snort of frustration. "Visant! Tell the Grand Maistre what your men have uncovered."

Visant beckoned the secretary to open the bulging folder. He removed a file of papers and smoothed them out with neat, precise hand movements. "Alchymy," he said. "The first reports from the survivors bear out my worst suspicions. Shells that exploded, letting off a pale, choking gas that caused confusion, blindness, and debilitating nausea among the sailors. Mortars that burst, setting fire to sails and rigging with flames that could not be extinguished with water. Sophisticated weapons that gave the Tielens an extraordinary advantage over our fleet."

"And your point, Inquisitor?" said Ruaud.

"Alchymical weapons, without a doubt, Captain," Visant said coldly. "Manufactured by one Kaspar Linnaius, late of the College of Thaumaturgy in Francia."

"You told me all the magi were dead, Visant." Gobain's voice was quiet now, ominously quiet.

"Indeed, I believed so myself," said Visant. "We tried Gonery, Maunoir, and Rhuys, with all their apprentices. Every man was found guilty and burned at the stake. But it seems that one escaped our raid . . ."

"Seems?" echoed the king scornfully. "D'you mean you don't know?"

"What the Inquisitor is saying, majesty," intervened Donatien, "is that when his men raided the college, there was an almighty explosion followed by a conflagration. When the Guerriers sifted through the rubble, they found some charred human remains in the West Tower. We assumed that both Kaspar Linnaius and his apprentice, Rieuk Mordiern, were killed in the blast."

"An almighty explosion, hm?" the king repeated. "The very

same alchymical firepowder that the Tielens have just used against our ships with such devastating effects."

"Powder that can reduce a tower to rubble," said Visant, a little defensively, Ruaud noted, "leaves very little behind of a body that can be positively identified. We're talking fragments of charred bone."

"Indeed," added Donatien, coming to his rescue, "the magisters evinced some considerable distress when confronted with the evidence, leading us to construe that Linnaius had destroyed himself and his apprentice rather than be taken alive. However . . ."

"He played you all for fools," said Gobain, sitting back in his chair and crossing his arms. "He faked his own suicide—and went off to Tielen, to sell his services to Prince Karl."

"He's still alive?" Ruaud and the other officers gazed at one another in consternation.

"Very much so, and enjoying the protection of his royal patron. It seems it pleases Karl to encourage the pursuit of such heretical sciences. He's even created a special position at court for Linnaius."

"So even though his wretched apprentice perished, he escaped?"

"My agents were a little more diligent than yours, Inquisitor." Ruaud saw a triumphant gleam in Gobain's eyes. "You assumed Linnaius was dead. But it seems that a certain Sieur Guirec, a clockmaker from Kemper, made a trip to the college to deliver parts to Linnaius. He never returned home. He must have been waiting to meet with the magus in the West Tower when your men stormed the college—and the explosion took place. Poor devil."

An embarrassed silence followed. Ruaud studied the tabletop, aware that Visant and Donatien must be furious at being humiliated by the king in front of their inferior officers.

"How can we make up for this grievous oversight, majesty?" Donatien's smooth tones were at their most placating.

"I want Linnaius. The man's a traitor. Betraying his own countrymen—it's outrageous! Burning's too good for him. I want him to suffer!"

"With respect, majesty," said Visant, reading from the open file,

"Linnaius is not, technically speaking, a Francian, although it seems he has resided here for well over one hundred years."

Alain Friard stared at Ruaud. "How can he be so old?" he whispered.

"By foul and unholy practices," said Donatien, overhearing. "By use of the Forbidden Arts."

"We have no record of his true nationality. Although some say he may be Tielen by birth, others say Allegondan, and others still have even suggested that he was born in Khendye—"

"What matters," interrupted the king impatiently, "is that we stop him. Before he teaches all the Tielen scientists his deadly alchymy and Prince Karl invades Francia."

"Perhaps such a situation could be avoided," said Donatien, "if your majesty were to agree to talks with Prince Karl—"

The king's clenched fist came down with a loud thud on the table, making the silver inkwells jump. "I will *not* parley with Karl or his ministers."

"Very well," said Donatien.

"Captain de Lanvaux—you're due to return to Enhirre next week, I believe. I want you to stay here in Francia."

"Me, sire?" Ruaud had not been expecting this and he could see from Donatien's look of surprise that neither had the Grand Maistre.

"Now that the rebels have been brought under our control, a man of your ability is wasted on guard duty."

Ruaud tried not to wince at the king's lack of tact. To make a pilgrimage to protect the holy shrines was a task that all Guerriers of the Commanderie viewed as an honor, not a duty. But then, Gobain had never shown himself interested in matters of faith.

"Surely the Inquisition is better equipped to deal with this matter, majesty," said Visant.

"But the point, Visant," said the king, leaning across the table to stare bullishly into his face, "is that the Inquisition has failed. A powerful alchymist escaped your net. And now he harbors a grudge against us because we executed his colleagues. We have made a formidable enemy for Francia."

"And while he remains in Tielen under Prince Karl's protection, there's very little we can do about it," said Visant dryly.

"Which is why I'm choosing you, de Lanvaux, to set up a new detachment within the Commanderie," Gobain continued, ignoring Visant. "I want you to choose and train agents. Agents clever and committed enough to outwit a magus."

"Sire—" began Visant but Gobain held up a hand to silence him.

"Your agents will liaise with Inquisitor Visant's men, of course," he continued, "but you will train them to work undercover. Abroad, if need be."

Ruaud was trying to digest this information. The appointment was an honor—but in favoring him, the king was snubbing both Visant and Donatien, his superiors. "And how will I select these agents, majesty?"

"Whatever way you please." Gobain rose. "I leave the details to you. Funds have already been allocated to cover your expenses." As his guardsmen opened the inner doors, ready to escort him to his private apartments, he called back over his shoulder, "You will base your operations at the Forteresse, but you will also have an office here, at Plaisaunces. I shall expect a weekly report on—"

"Gobain!" Queen Aliénor appeared in the doorway, a letter clutched in her hand, her face streaked with tears. "Aimery's lost. He's gone down with his ship."

She ran up to the king, thrusting the letter into his hands. The king cast a quick glance over it. "This confirms what I feared from the first dispatches."

"Why did you send him, Gobain? You sent him to his death!"

The king flushed an angry red. "*I* sent him? The navy was his own choice, Aliénor."

"But if you knew we were going to war, you could have ordered him to stay behind—"

"The Tielens got the better of us! God knows I didn't want to lose so many men and ships. We've been thoroughly humiliated."

Aliénor took a little step backward as though she was about to faint. "Aimery," she whispered. "Oh Aimery, why did it have to be you?"

"A chair for her majesty!" Ruaud hurried over to her side but she gave him a look so forbidding that it stopped him in his tracks.

"Dear majesty," said Donatien, his voice suddenly warm and compassionate, "I am here whenever you wish to discuss arrangements for your brother's funeral. But if you need time to grieve alone, my private chapel is at your disposal. I can ensure that you are left undisturbed for as long as you wish."

"Thank you, Maistre Donatien," said the queen, placing her hand on his. "You have always been so understanding."

The king gave a grunt of exasperation at this, turned on his heel, and left the chamber without another word to his wife. She gave a sad little shake of her head. "Will you accompany me, Grand Maistre? Let us pray for Aimery's soul together."

Ruaud and the others bowed as the queen left, supported by Donatien. He was aware that Visant was looking sidelong at him, as though assessing his new partner. "What did you make of that?" he asked casually.

"A sad loss for Francia and for the queen." Ruaud said, unwilling to speak his thoughts aloud where they might be overheard.

"You defeated the magi in Ondhessar; I defeated their Francian brothers at Karantec. But in Kaspar Linnaius we are dealing with a very powerful adversary. There was more to this attack on our fleet than the king was prepared to tell us. A fierce storm blew up out of nowhere and drove several of our ships onto the rocks."

"The magus who stole Azilia's crystal used the power of the wind to escape from Ondhessar." Ruaud felt his shoulder begin to ache again at the memory; the bones damaged in his fall had taken a long time to mend. "I did all I could to stop him but . . ." His hand had moved involuntarily to touch the old injury. "And now he dares to destroy our fleet by such underhanded means?" He was more determined now than ever to take on the king's mission.

"You've been matched against a formidable opponent, Captain. Your bravery is not in question. But are you sure that you're ready for this task?" Visant gave him a hard, questioning look. "Don't be in such a hurry to throw your life away. You have much to learn." And before Ruaud could reply, the Inquisitor turned and left the council chamber.

"Why do you want to train as an exorcist, Captain?" The old priest stared at him through pebble-thick lenses. "What makes you think you're suitable for such a challenging role?" In spite of Père Judicael's calm manner, Ruaud was not deceived. The elderly father had a formidable reputation as a most rigorous and tenacious fighter of evil.

"It's not the path I had seen myself following when I joined the Commanderie. But his majesty has requested me, so . . ."

"You served with great distinction at Ondhessar. You were awarded the Order of the Golden Staff."

Ruaud, not certain what Père Judicael was implying, acknowledged the compliment with a nod.

"And you never encountered anything strange or inexplicable in the Holy Lands?"

Ruaud blinked. "Strange?" For days, he had been studying arcane and esoteric manuscripts kept locked away in the vaults of the Commanderie Library.

Père Judicael pushed himself to his feet with the aid of an ivory-handled cane and limped over to Ruaud. "To defeat a magus, you must learn to think like a magus. Do you really want to look into the depths of your soul? Aren't you afraid what you might find there?"

"But the magi are born with the taint of evil in their blood. A taint that gives them unique powers. They're *different* from us."

"Are they, indeed?" A strange little smile appeared on the exorcist's lips. "Ask yourself, Captain, what drives them to act as they do? Love, greed, hate, fear . . . all mortal emotions. They are not so different from us. And we can use those emotions to bring them down. Follow me."

Père Judicael led Ruaud into a black chamber, lit only by a single high, barred window. The instant the door was shut, the old priest pulled a lever and the light from the window was extinguished as a shutter came down. Ruaud, cast into pitch-darkness, felt as if he were falling into a lightless pit. The sensation was disturbing, stirring up memories of long-forgotten childhood nightmares.

"What can you see?" asked Père Judicael's dry voice.

Slowly, as Ruaud's eyes became accustomed to the lack of light, he saw that he was standing at the center of a circle that had been painted on the black boards with a luminescent silvery substance. Unfamiliar sigils were painted in different sectors of the circle.

"What does this mean?" he asked warily.

"Don't worry, Captain. If you were possessed by an evil spirit, it would have reacted quite violently to those signs by now. You are standing in the Circle of Galizur, one of the Seven Heavenly Guardians." Père Judicael operated the lever again, letting a wan daylight back into the room.

"Ah." Ruaud was still not entirely convinced by the theatricality of this effect. "So you practice exorcism by angelography. Can you actually *communicate* with the angels?"

Père Judicael pursed his thin lips as if Ruaud had suggested something blasphemous. "Only the Blessed Sergius was pure enough in heart to summon the Heavenly Guardians to his aid. The rest of us blemished mortals must manage as best we can."

"But you can invoke their protective powers?"

Père Judicael only answered his question with another. "Are you prepared to undergo the ordeals that a trainee exorcist must endure?"

"The king has given me an order; I'm duty-bound to obey." Ruaud wondered exactly what the old priest meant by "ordeals." "Besides, how can I expect my Guerriers to respect me as a leader if I haven't undertaken the same training?"

"Even though you may not emerge the same man that you are now?" The old man's cormorant stare unsettled Ruaud even more than his ominous words.

"I place my trust in God," he answered simply. "He will guide me; He always has."

"You may be wondering why I've summoned you all here in secret," said Grand Maistre Donatien. Ruaud took in a swift glance at the other members of the Commanderie assembled in Donatien's rooms in the Forteresse: Inquisitor Visant; Lieutenant Konan; and Père Laorans. As they seated themselves around the table, he sensed that Donatien's mood was far from welcoming.

"It has been brought to my attention, Laorans," continued Donatien, "that you made a singularly disturbing discovery in Ondhessar."

"Disturbing, Grand Maistre?" said Laorans, looking puzzled.

Donatien let out a little sigh. "The Codex—or, indeed, codices, for I understand that there are more than one."

"Indeed, Maistre, this is the most significant collection of writings to fall into our hands in many centuries!" Laorans's face lit up with a scholar's enthusiasm, and Ruaud felt a sudden pang of alarm, sensing that Donatien was laying a trap.

"How would you assess yourself as a scholar of Old Enhirran?" asked Inquisitor Visant smoothly.

"I am accounted one of the best in the field," said Laorans, modestly lowering his gaze.

"Then how do you explain this?" Donatien pushed a folder into the center of the table.

"Surely my translation is self-explanatory?"

Ruaud saw Donatien exchange a glance with Visant. Then he leaned forward and said quietly, "Do I have to remind you of the Sacred Texts, as translated by the Blessed Sergius? 'In the beginning, the Winged Guardians who watch over our world walked among mortals and taught us to obey Divine Law.' "

"I take exception to your implication, Grand Maistre!" Laorans's eyes lit with that same obstinate, obsessed expression Ruaud remembered from Ondhessar. "I learned the Sergian Texts by heart at Saint Argantel's Seminary when I was ten years old."

" 'But some of the Guardians were proud and disobedient,' " continued Donatien relentlessly. " 'Their sin was to disobey Divine Will, the Will that forbade any union between them and the mortals in their care. Children were born of this union, mortal children with unnatural powers.' "

"Yes, yes, I know the passage as well as you," interrupted Laorans impatiently. " 'So the Divine Will spoke to Galizur, charging him to seek out these accursed children and destroy them. For if they are not stopped, they will use their powers to unravel the natural forces that bind the worlds together and become instruments of destruction.' "

Visant opened an ancient illuminated copy of the Holy Texts, one of the Commanderie's treasures, and pointed to a passage scribed in ink as red as fresh blood. " 'Great then was the woe of the transgressors as they were cast into that place of dust and shadows, there to repent their sin throughout all eternity.' "

"So by your own admission you know that this Codex from Ondhessar is heretical!" declared Donatien triumphantly. "And yet you still continued with your translation?"

"I considered it my duty as a scholar to do so."

"What if it got into the wrong hands? It could seed dissension throughout the whole quadrant!"

"Forgive me, Grand Maistre," broke in Konan's deep rumble of a voice, "but you've lost me completely. Are you saying that the manuscript we found in the Shrine at Ondhessar is a fake? A forgery? Or worse?"

Ruaud looked at his lieutenant, grateful that he had voiced one of the many questions that someone needed to ask.

"This Codex undermines our most fundamental beliefs." Donatien's habitual amiable expression had gone, replaced by a look of grim determination.

"Magic is forbidden, because the Divine Will forbade it," said Visant. "Mortal man was never meant to wield magic."

"Why else does it tell us of the terrible punishments inflicted on the Guardians who transgressed? Yet this Ondhessar Codex says that those Fallen Guardians not only had forbidden congress with mortals, but they taught their children how to use their magical powers. It even asserts that the magi are none other than the children of the Fallen Guardians!" Donatien's face had turned an angry red and he brought his fist down on the table. "This Codex is blasphemous! It goes against everything we believe. It goes against the Sacred Texts." He turned on Laorans. "Your translation must be at fault."

"I agree, it *is* an obscure variant of Old Enhirran. Some of the characters are ambiguous. But the names—the names are undoubtedly the same."

"Then what we have here is nothing but an apocryphal text, written by an obscure, heretical sect. A sect that has been wiped from mortal memory because they practiced the Forbidden Arts."

"But, Maistre—," began Laorans.

"Didn't you hear me? It's not the true Word! We are faced with an impossible decision." Donatien began to pace the narrow chamber, his hands behind his back. "Do we destroy it? Or, since you've blabbed the news to half the scholars in the quadrant that you've found an ancient sacred scripture dating from before Artamon's reign, do we have to lie? Do we announce that it disintegrated before you could complete your translation?"

"But is it truly blasphemous?"

"Listen to yourself!" Donatien stopped and stared into

Laorans's face with a look so chilling that Laorans shrank away. "Already it's made you begin to question your own faith. If these dangerous words were read by our congregations . . ."

"I would never d—dare to question," stammered Laorans. "But suppose—just suppose for one moment—that *this* is right, and the Sergian translation is the heretical version?"

Laorans, you idiot. In the ensuing astonished silence, Ruaud felt as if the temperature in the room had plummeted.

Visant recovered the first. "You may give thanks to God that only the four of us heard you say such a sinful thing. Men have gone to the stake for less. On what possible grounds, Laorans, do you base such a suggestion?"

"I—I was merely hypothesizing. I never intended—"

"We are carrying out Divine Will in eradicating the magi, the last few survivors of that accursed bloodline."

Laorans would not give in so easily. "Yet suppose that the children with angel blood in their veins were not accursed, but gifted? And that they were meant to use their gifts to help us, as this Codex suggests?"

"Gifts?" Visant pulled out a thick leather-bound folder and began to read aloud from it. " 'Nine years ago, incident reported in Vasconie—a young boy is said to have caused a rockslide, burying several of his companions. One pulled dead from the rubble; two others crippled for life. Villagers said that the boy was often shunned and taunted by his peers because of his "weird eyes." Mother reported to have died in childbirth, "screaming in agony."' Or this one. 'Forty-one years ago, province of Armel. Devastating flood washes away crops and livestock; little girl drowned. Older brother found weeping near local lake. "I was only trying to help end the drought. I never meant for anyone to be hurt." Grieving father described son Goustan as, "different from my other children, especially his strange blue eyes."' And 'Earthquake in Allegonde, twenty-two years back.' Shall I go on?" He thrust the folder toward Père Laorans. "These are just some of the children born with 'angel blood.' How can you possibly suggest that such gifts are of benefit to mankind?"

Donatien placed a gilded casket on the table and opened it. Inside, cushioned on ivory silk, lay fragments of wood, charred and ancient.

"Sergius's Staff?" said Ruaud, staring in wonder. This priceless relic of their patron saint was so fragile that it was kept hidden away and was rarely brought out, even by the senior members of the Commanderie.

"Before you leave this chamber, I'm afraid I must ask you to take a vow on the Staff, gentlemen. A vow never to reveal—on pain of death—what we have discussed today."

"So you are suppressing my translation?" Laorans stared challengingly at Donatien.

"When you became a Guerrier, you promised to obey me, as representative of Divine Will here on earth."

Ruaud caught Konan's eye; the big man looked distinctly uncomfortable.

"Believe me, Laorans, this grieves me almost beyond words." Donatien's tone had become softer, almost appeasing. "I've never had to impose my will on any of my fellow Guerriers before."

Laorans placed his hand on the casket. "I swear to you, Maistre, by Sergius's Staff, never to reveal the results of my researches and translations." The vow was made, but Ruaud had heard the suppressed rage in Laorans's voice.

"Now you, Captain."

Ruaud closed his eyes a moment in silent prayer. In making this vow, he was betraying the trust of one of his own men. Yet Donatien was his spiritual leader and commanding officer; he must obey him or face ignominious court-martial. He stretched out his hand and began, "I swear, by Sergius's Staff . . ."

"And now that I have your vow, Laorans, I have exciting news. I'm sending you to set up a new mission in Serindher."

"Serindher?" repeated Père Laorans dazedly.

"You will leave Saint Argantel's Seminary and lead a group of ten priests to spread our missionary work far beyond the western quadrant."

"And far enough away," murmured Konan in Ruaud's ear, "to cause no further trouble."

CHAPTER 9

A chill wind gusted across the red sands as the sun sank and darkness sucked the vivid colors from the many towers—cream, rose pink, and orange by day, and now grey in night's fast-creeping shadow. Nature had formed these strange slender cones and pillars from the living volcanic rock on the barren plain.

Rieuk gazed at the valley below him.

"Is this the place?" he said to Imri. "It's so . . . desolate."

"The local tribesmen call them the Towers of the Ghaouls," said Imri. "They believe that they're inhabited by the wayward spirits of the desert. They say that as the sun sets, you can hear the song of the spirits that haunt the valley. They sing so sweetly to lure you inside, then they suck out your soul."

"Soul stealers?" said Rieuk. He shivered. The journey to Enhirre had taken many months, complicated by the hostilities between Francia and Tielen. But Rieuk had never been happier. He had never found anyone in Karantec who understood him as intimately as Imri. Every moment that he spent in his company, he learned of new wonders.

"Watch your step," Imri cautioned, setting off down the stony track. Rieuk followed, treading carefully in the twilight; it was a sheer drop to jumbled rocks and spiny bushes far below the winding path.

Night had fallen by the time he reached the valley. He looked around. "Imri?" he called into the gloom.

Suddenly he heard a rustle of movement. He turned, but too

late. Someone threw a sack over his head; another tackled him, bringing him to the ground. Brigands! He struggled and kicked, shouting for Imri until a gag was thrust into his mouth and his cries were silenced.

Rieuk stood, bound and blindfolded, listening helplessly as distant voices echoed about him. They seemed to be arguing.

"Where is Kaspar Linnaius? You were sent to bring the wind mage back to answer for his crime."

"I ask your forgiveness, Lord Estael." Rieuk recognized Imri's soft, persuasive tones. "I was forced to cut short my mission. The Commanderie struck again, sending the Inquisition against the college at Karantec."

All the voices began to talk at once.

"Imri." This speaker was authoritative and stern; the others fell silent. "Was Linnaius taken?"

"No, my lord. But we suspect that they used another Angelstone; we saw—and felt—its power."

"And where is Linnaius now?" demanded another. "With so few of the true blood left, we may even need his support. Not some pretty boy who caught your eye . . ."

"This 'pretty boy' is a crystal mage." Imri's voice was tinged with quiet amusement. "He was Linnaius's apprentice."

"A true-blood crystal mage?" said the first speaker, and Rieuk heard the others murmuring excitedly together. "Remove his blindfold. Cut his bonds."

A burnished gleam of torch flames smeared Rieuk's vision; he blinked, trying to focus. As his eyes became accustomed to the light, he saw that he was in the center of an ancient circular hall beneath a high dome. Around the walls, half in shadow, stood his interrogators, their features hidden beneath hawk masks of beaten metal.

"He wishes to become one of us," continued Imri. "With his powers, I believe he would be a great asset to the order. Look at his eyes. He's a true elemental, like Linnaius. But his training has been neglected and he sorely needs our guidance."

One wearing a gilded mask approached Rieuk and, placing his hands on his shoulders, gazed deep into his eyes. "How do we know that you won't betray us once you've learned our mysteries?" This scrutiny was so intense and invasive that Rieuk felt as if his mind had been stripped bare.

"I'd give my life to protect Imri."

"I see." The magus in the gilded mask went back to consult the others.

"He wishes to become an Emissary." Imri placed a protective arm around Rieuk's shoulders.

"Let the boy speak for himself."

"And I want to learn how to control my powers." Rieuk heard a tremor in his voice and tried to steady it. He wished to show the magi that he was not afraid of them.

Rieuk saw the magi silently consulting one another. *What shall I do if they reject me? My life will be over.* He felt Imri's fingers tightening around his shoulder. *Will they kill me now that I've witnessed their secret sanctuary? Or will they scour away the memories, and leave me wandering witless in the desert?*

The magus in the gilded mask brought out a crystal and placed it in Rieuk's hands. "Show us what you can do."

Rieuk's fingers were still numb from his bonds. He looked down at the crystal and saw that it was of the same delicate clarity as the one Linnaius had stolen from Ondhessar. "Is this . . . an aethyr crystal?" He held it to his forehead. "It's so beautiful." A faint, clear pulse throbbed from deep within him, matching the vibrations of the crystal. Slowly he lowered it, willing the single pulse to become two. A shudder ran through the crystal . . . and it split in half.

Rieuk held out the divided crystal in his outstretched hands.

One by one, the magi began to remove their masks. Last of all, the magus with the gilded hawk mask revealed his features, and Rieuk saw a face that could have been sculpted out of rock by the harsh desert winds. Beneath strong iron-grey brows, the eyes of a fellow elemental magus stared piercingly at him, lighter than Imri's, yet glinting with a faint sheen of fire. Imri gave Rieuk a little push forward and Rieuk went down on one knee before the magus.

"Lord Estael, I commend Rieuk Mordiern to you."

"So now my protégé has taken on an apprentice of his own?"

Rieuk glanced in surprise at Imri, who was looking at Lord Estael with an expression of gentle respect. "If I can teach Rieuk half as well as you taught me, dear lord, then I will truly have cause to feel content."

An hour ago, Rieuk had been tied and blindfolded, a prisoner of the magi of Ondhessar. Now he sat with them at supper, too dazed to eat or drink. They had removed their masks and he saw, around the table, eight other magi, some as venerable as Magister Gonery. Yet every magus had eyes that glittered with the same unnatural light as his own. He glimpsed the limpid blue of water, the rich golden brown of earth, and the flicker of fire. The only element absent was the strange, clear silver of a wind master; was Linnaius the only air magus still alive?

"The news of the Commanderie's attack on our brothers in Karantec is most disquieting," said Lord Estael. "Did Imri tell you of the massacre here?"

Rieuk shook his head. His mouth was still parched with fear and the burn of the harsh desert air. Imri filled Rieuk's glass with wine. "Drink," he whispered.

"Enhirre suffered a crushing defeat at the hands of your countrymen. Many of our fellow magi were destroyed defending the citadel. We few survived the attack on Ondhessar. The Commanderie used their Angelstones against us—the one weapon in their defense that renders our own powers useless. Our stronghold is still under their control. But if you are truly a crystal mage, you may be able to help us take it back."

Rieuk took a mouthful of red wine. It was dry on his tongue, with a musky aftertaste. "I will do all I can, my lord." He knew he would promise them anything to earn his Emissary.

Rieuk slowly followed Imri up an endlessly winding stair, taking care not to tread on Imri's ceremonial robes. He had unfastened Imri's hair and combed it until it hung, dully glistening, about his shoulders. He liked the silky feel of Imri's hair beneath his fingers, and the repetitive act of passing the comb through the strands had made him forget the ordeal he was about to endure.

At the top of the tower they came out into the last blaze of the setting sun. A breeze had arisen. Rieuk had expected to see the other towers of the desolate, dry valley below and the distant gleam of snow on the peak of Mount Makhon. Instead, he heard the whisper of wind in tree branches.

"Imri, where *are* we? I don't remember any trees . . ."

"I've brought you to the place where the smoke hawks gather at night. Where better to lure your Emissary to you?"

"I know nothing of hawks, or any kind of hunting birds." Rieuk was baffled by this information. "How am I expected to lure one? Dangle a dead rabbit on a string? And then when it comes, what do I do? Grab hold? They can peck out a man's eyes."

Imri laughed. "I thought you had more imagination!"

Rieuk did not like to be laughed at, even by Imri. He moved away and leaned on the high parapet wall, gazing down at the wind-stirred branches of the forest below. "This is impossible. I don't even know where to start."

In truth, he was feeling increasingly jittery as the moment for the ceremony approached. He knew it was going to be painful and protracted. He knew that, once it started, there was no going back. Above all, he knew that there was no way he could emerge from it unchanged. Suppose he was not strong enough to bear the pain? Suppose he cried out like a scared child and begged them to stop? Or worse, suppose the pain was so great that he lost control of his bodily functions? He did not want to be humiliated in front of Imri and these austere and powerful magi.

"Remember. This is no ordinary hawk." Imri came up behind him and wrapped his arms around him, as if understanding his unspoken fears. "This is a shadow hawk, a spirit bird that crosses the rift between worlds."

But Rieuk was in no mood to be consoled. He pushed himself free from Imri's embrace and backed away.

The last fiery traces of sunset were fading and darkness was covering the forest like a cloak of shadows.

"How, then, do I lure it to me?"

"With your blood. Just as Hervé de Maunoir bound the spirit to serve him, so you will draw one to you with a drop of your blood."

"Is it so simple?"

"We are standing at a portal that opens both ways, Rieuk. That is why, if you watch the moon rising from this side of the tower, you will notice a difference . . ."

"Why did I never learn about the Emissaries till I met you?" Rieuk still could not rid himself of his innate skepticism. "There was not one single reference in any of the treatises in the library at Karantec."

"The Emissaries are the most closely guarded secret of my order. Do you think I would have brought you here unless you had sworn your life to our cause? To tell anyone about this place means the most shameful of deaths: the stripping away of your Emissary."

Stripping away. Those words provoked a shudder of disgust and fear. It would be painful enough to be bonded with a shadow hawk . . . but how much more painful to suffer it being plucked out of your living tissue!

"There's no turning back now, is there?" he said. "You're telling me that unless I go through with the ceremony, there's no way you can let me walk away from here alive, knowing your secret."

"Why would you want to walk away?" He never saw or heard Imri move but suddenly the magus was standing before him in the gloom. Imri's hands touched his face, gently raising it toward his own. "Look into my eyes, Rieuk, and tell me the truth. Could you leave me now?"

A glimmer of light touched the tops of the trees. Rieuk gazed into Imri's moonlit eyes and felt himself drowning in a confusion of love, desire, and terror. He was bound to Imri—though whether by sorcery, ambition, or sheer hunger for affection, he no longer knew.

"No," he said helplessly.

Imri leaned forward and brushed Rieuk's forehead with his lips.

"Look. The moon is rising," he said softly. "When the emerald moon appears above the tower, then we know that the Rift is opening."

A rift to where? All manner of unsettling questions crowded into Rieuk's mind. Could he fall into this rift and find himself in another world? Or was it only possible for the eerie light of this other moon to shine through the Rift, bringing a flock of elusive shadow-winged hawks drifting on the lunar wind just long enough for him to try to summon the hawk who would be his Emissary?

Shadows soared across the pale disc of the emerald moon—winged creatures, graceful and swift as hawks. Faint, keening cries echoed high above the tower. Rieuk realized that he was seeing the light of a moon shining in from another world, as Imri had shown him in Karantec. That knowledge filled him with a sense of excitement so powerful that he felt as light-headed as if he had been drinking sparkling wine.

Imri gazed up into the sky, and his features were bathed in the eerie iridescence. "The hawks come to feed from the sap of the Haoma trees that grow beyond the Rift."

Rieuk was so absorbed, he never saw Imri take out the knife until he caught the glint of a slender silver blade in the emerald moonlight and felt its razor-keen edge bite as Imri made a swift incision in his wrist.

Drops of warm red blood splashed onto the stones of the parapet; the sight of it made him feel faint. "What are you doing? Do you mean to let me bleed to death?"

Imri smiled at him and lifted the gash to his mouth, sealing the edges with the warmth of his lips.

Rieuk heard a skirling cry that shivered through his body with the same precision as the blade had sliced through his flesh. A shadow fell across them. Glancing up, he saw that the hawks were circling right overhead.

"They've come." Imri's hand rested on his shoulder, a firm, strong pressure, lending him a confidence he badly needed. The proud-eyed hawks came swooping down toward him out of the darkness. Rieuk clutched at the rim of the parapet to keep from falling. The wind from their wings brought a gust of air from another world; it wafted an elusive breath of alien scents and tastes into his gaping mouth.

"Stand your ground. The Emissary will seek you out. It will know you by the scent of your blood."

Stand my ground? Easily said! Rieuk felt his hair blown hither and thither as the great hawks skimmed the top of his head, darting so close that he could hear the whispering beat of their wings.

Then he became aware that, in the swirling maelstrom of smoke-flecked feathers passing above him, one alone had fixed him with piercing topaz eyes. That topaz glare burned like a flare in the darkness. Serrated wing tips brushed his face, his eyelids. The hawk alighted on the parapet and dipped its silvered beak in his blood, all the time keeping its eyes fixed on his. Rieuk, fascinated, could not look away.

"It looks as though it has chosen you." As Imri spoke, the hawk lifted its crimson-stained beak and let out a shivering cry. "Offer your arm, the elbow crooked, so—"

The hawk lifted into the air and, claws extended, settled on Rieuk's forearm. He had braced himself to take the bird's weight but to his surprise it landed gently.

This is what I was born for. Rieuk, enchanted and amazed, could still not quite believe what was happening to him. And yet it felt so right. This was the exhilaration he had been longing for all his life, a heady taste of the real magic that Gonery and Linnaius had kept from him. He looked at Imri, his eyes filling with tears of gratitude. *If you had not come to find me, I would never have had the chance to experience this wonder.*

The other hawks began to keen as they fluttered overhead, as though aware that they were losing one of their number.

"The Rift is closing," Imri said, gazing up at them. "Let's go down before your Emissary changes its mind and tries to follow its kin." As he held the door open for Rieuk, the gleam of the emerald moon began to fade and the cries of the hawks grew fainter.

As Rieuk followed Imri slowly down the narrow spiral stair, the weight of the hawk grew greater, until his arm ached with the strain.

"It's so heavy," he gasped, leaning against the dusty stones to support himself.

"In the Rift between worlds he weighed less than a shadow. But now in our world, he has taken on physical substance. Once he has become a part of you . . ." It seemed to Rieuk that Imri was going farther away from him and he was left behind in darkness, unable to see his way. He stumbled, almost losing his footing. The hawk turned its stern gaze on him and spread its dusky wings as if to fly away. Rieuk reeled backward, hitting the curved wall of the tower.

Rising out of the darkness was a smoke-winged figure, as tall as he was, gazing at him through wild eyes of topaz and jet.

Rieuk drew in a gasping breath.

"Who—who are you?"

"*I am your Emissary.*" Although the creature had not spoken aloud, he heard the voice within his head, each word as precise and clear as a plucked string. "*My name is Ormas.*"

"Ormas?" repeated Rieuk dazedly.

"*Your blood called to mine. Now my blood will be yours. My eyes will be your eyes.*"

The smoky air swirled and once again Rieuk felt the weight of the hawk on his forearm.

"Ormas," he said again. "My Emissary." He lifted his hand and dared to stroke the soft, speckled feathers on the hawk's breast.

Torchlight flared in the dark stairwell below. When Rieuk reached the foot of the tower stair, he found Imri waiting for him, his eyes shadowed, unreadable.

"I—I know its name," Rieuk stammered. Imri nodded. There was something in his manner that was so remote, so inaccessible, that it made Rieuk ask, "What's wrong, Imri?" And then, as his eyes grew accustomed to the torchlight, he saw the others waiting for him. Their faces masked, they moved silently, purposefully toward him.

"Imri!" cried Rieuk, instinctively taking a step back toward his master. "Has this all been a trap? Have you just been using me to get what you wanted?"

"I'm sorry, Rieuk," said Imri, his voice expressionless.

Hands clamped on Rieuk's shoulders, steering him away from Imri. Were they going to dispose of him? And what would they do with Ormas?

Maistre Gonery's warnings ran through his panicking brain as they dragged him into a nearby chamber.

"*They will promise you the things you most desire. And then, before you know what you have done, you will find yourself in thrall. Sealed into a contract that binds you until death—and beyond.*"

A narrow table stood in the center of the chamber. Beneath it Rieuk could see that thin channels had been cut into the stone floor, leading to a drain in the far corner. It reminded him suddenly and horribly of the dissection room in the college. Those channels were to sluice away blood and other leaking fluids. Two smaller tables had been placed on either side of the bed; on each stood small bottles of dark inks. Alongside lay metal bowls and a glittering array of needles, sharp-nibbed pens, and slender scalpels. When Rieuk saw these, he began to back away but the restraining hands gripped him more tightly. There was no possibility of escape.

One of the masked men approached, and held a cup of beaten metal to Rieuk's lips. "Drink."

"What is it?" said Rieuk, catching a hint of bitterness beneath the strong, honeyed smell rising from the liquid. Poison.

"An opiate. To help you bear the pain. Drink."

The pain. Where was Imri? Rieuk turned his head from side to side, seeking in vain. Imri had not once left his side since the day they met in Karantec. He felt suddenly abandoned and utterly alone.

"You must remain conscious throughout the ceremony. If you faint, it will fail. So—*drink.*"

Rieuk reluctantly opened his lips and the bitter liquid slid down his throat, making him cough convulsively. When the wheezing and coughing stopped, he saw that Ormas had lifted from his arm and was now perched on the table, regarding him curiously, its head to one side.

Was the opiate working so soon? Rieuk felt a strange sense of detachment as the hawk-masked magi began to strip off his clothes. Next they rubbed his body with a clear, sharp-smelling liquid that made his skin tingle. When they strapped him, face upward, to the table, he was aware of the hard grain of the wood pressing into his spine, the tight restraints of leather and metal holding his arms and legs secure. And most of all, he was aware of Ormas's bright eye burning like an unwavering candleflame.

He was unprepared for the efficient brutality of what followed. As he lay helpless, one of the hawk-masked magi seized Ormas and, with one swift slash of a knife, cut the hawk's throat.

"No!" Rieuk heard a scream of fury tear from his own throat. Black blood spurted out, spattering him and the officiating magi, who held bowls out to catch it. But Rieuk could only watch as Ormas's body went limp in the bloodstained hands of the magus and the bright gaze dimmed.

Then they pried open the drooping wings, until they could pin them to a board, outspread, as if the hawk were caught soaring upward in flight. Too late, he felt tears leaking from his eyes, that his overweening ambition and desire for power had brought about the bloody destruction of such a beautiful and noble creature.

"*Master. I am still here.*" Rieuk heard Ormas's voice and thought he glimpsed the hawk's shadow hovering high above him. Before his drugged brain had time to acknowledge Ormas's presence, the magi were bending over him. He caught the glint of steel—and then the torment began.

At first the opiate dulled the sensation as the tattooing needles pierced his skin and the magi set about their intricate work. But then as his own blood slowly trickled out, he began to feel each sharp cut as the blade went in, followed by the aching sting of Ormas's black blood as it seeped into his flesh. Each needle-prick burned like fire. He gritted his teeth, trying not to cry out, knowing it was more than he could do to bite back his agony. If they had wanted to extract the most intimate secrets about Kaspar Linnaius and the college, now would have been the ideal time.

How long is this going to last? How long will it take to imprint each one of Ormas's mottled feathers into my body? How much longer can I endure it?

As each feather was painstakingly copied, the distinctive markings faded on Ormas's limp body until nothing was left but a pale shadow. Ormas's physical body was slowly fading, and as Ormas faded, so Rieuk felt himself slowly sliding down into a dark place of slow-searing agony. Memories that were not his own etched themselves into his mind as the magi imprinted the hawk into his lacerated flesh. He felt as if he were lifting out of himself to stare down at a young man's bleeding body, twisting and arching as if desperate to burst the bonds that bound him. And then he crashed back down again into the reality of that tortured body. Whose eyes had he been looking through?

He felt the sudden, feverish beat of shadowy wings and saw many Emissaries hovering above him, their wild eyes burning like golden stars . . .

Rieuk felt gentle hands lifting his head. Someone held a glass to his lips.

"Drink," said a voice. Cool water flowed into his mouth and he swallowed obediently. There seemed to be a medicinal tang to the liquid, for it left a faintly astringent aftertaste at the back of his throat. Someone gently wiped his face with a warm, damp cloth.

"The opiate is wearing off. How do you feel?"

"Imri?" Rieuk slowly forced his heavy lids open and saw Imri gazing down at him. He tried to sit up but felt Imri's restraining hand on his shoulder.

"Don't try to move. Not yet."

Rieuk gazed down at his body and saw that his chest and neck were swathed in bandages, concealing the marks where they had scored the Emissary into his flesh. "D—did it work?"

"Is your Emissary awake?"

Rieuk's hand moved automatically to rest on the place above his heart where the hawk had been engraved. "Ormas?" he said tentatively.

"*What is your will, master?*" He recognized the shadow hawk's keen voice as it vibrated through his mind.

"Imri, he's there! I can hear him speaking to me!" In his excitement, Rieuk forgot Imri's warning and tried to shift his position. The slight movement set off a jarring throb of pain.

"Yes, it will hurt like hell at first," Imri said, smiling. "But the pain will pass. And then you'll be ready to start training for your first mission."

"My first mission? Already?" When even the slightest movement caused him pain, it seemed far too soon to be talking of training.

"You made a vow, remember? In exchange for Ormas, you promised to serve the order. We've received a summons to attend on our most illustrious patron. He's most interested in meeting you."

The vast pillared hall of the Arkhan's palace was filled with tiered lamps burning sweet-scented oils whose cloudy vapors swirled, trailing a faint haze of bronze smoke in the warm evening air. The scents they gave off were subtle, tinged with hints of damask rose and cinnamon.

Rieuk rubbed his eyes. Was this some drug-induced dream? As he followed Imri across the marble floor of the great hall, their footfall echoing into the distant recesses, he noticed white-robed guards standing between the pillars, each one holding an unsheathed scimitar across his breast, each one watching them as they passed.

At the end of the hall were two massive doors inlaid with beaten metals that gleamed dully in the lamplight. Guards barred their way, crossing spears across the doors. Imri spoke quietly with them in a tongue Rieuk had never heard before. They nodded and, lowering their spears, opened one of the heavy doors so that the two magi could enter.

The room beyond was smaller, more intimate in scale; Rieuk noticed a desk covered in stellar charts. Candleflames bloomed in exquisitely carved lotus flowers of crystal on the desk and in alcoves in the wall.

"Aethyr crystals," he whispered to Imri.

A breath of cooler air stirred gold-spangled gauze curtains. Behind, a balcony opened onto the night, where a man was training a telescope on the stars.

"My lord Arkhan?" said Imri respectfully.

The astronomer left his stargazing and came into the room. He was plainly dressed in a linen robe draped over a loose tunic and trousers—an unconventional blend of Western and Eastern fashions.

Imri knelt on the marble floor, bowing low until his forehead touched the tiles, and Rieuk copied him.

"This is Rieuk Mordiern," said Imri in the common tongue. "He was apprenticed to Kaspar Linnaius. He is now an Emissary."

"Rise, Emissary Mordiern." Arkhan Sardion's voice was smooth and even-toned.

Rieuk slowly raised his head and sat back on his heels. He still felt dizzy. The Arkhan's hawklike features swam in and out of focus. He saw eyes that burned surprisingly blue in a tawny face. Sardion was of middle years, sparely built, with dark hair faintly streaked with silver.

"Are you prepared to pay the price?" The Arkhan stretched out his hand to touch Rieuk's face, tipping his chin upward till Rieuk was dazzled by the blue blaze of his eyes. "Can you prove to us that you have earned your Emissary?"

Rieuk nodded.

"Even if it means killing your own countrymen?"

There had been no talk of killing before.

"We share a common enemy, Rieuk Mordiern: the Commanderie. Their Guerriers have invaded Enhirre and massacred my people." Although Sardion's voice was quiet, Rieuk sensed a fierce anger simmering within him. "They have taken control of the sacred treasures that the magi have watched over since before the time of Artamon. They have violated the sanctity of the hidden valley with the shedding of Enhirran blood."

"What do you want me to do, my lord?"

"You're a crystal mage. I want you to use your gift to track down the last remaining Angelstones and shatter them."

Rieuk blinked. Had he heard correctly? "But the Angelstones negate our powers." This was too great a task to imagine, let alone accomplish. "I've felt their force, my lord; so has Imri."

"According to my intelligence, the Francians have already exhausted the angelic powers contained in three of the stones; two here at Ondhessar, and one at Karantec."

That single Angelstone at Karantec had left him so weak that he could hardly find the strength to stagger away.

"Which leaves only four. A small price to pay, for a crystal mage, for becoming an Emissary."

Only four. The task was daunting. Rieuk could no longer sustain the Arkhan's penetrating gaze; he hoped Sardion would not interpret it as a sign of weakness.

"And when you've destroyed their Angelstones," continued Sardion, "we will drive the Francians out of Ondhessar."

"You won't be alone, Rieuk," said Imri. Rieuk felt Imri's hand on his shoulder, a firm, comforting pressure. *Imri.* His own hand rose to cover Imri's in silent gratitude. "You'll have Ormas to help you. And I'll be at your side."

"Hold still," ordered Imri as he snipped at Rieuk's bandages. "How can I remove these dressings if you keep jerking about?"

Rieuk gritted his teeth. "Are you sure I'm healed? It feels as if you're skinning me alive."

"There's a little dried blood stuck to the fabric." Imri patiently continued to unwind the last, stained linen strips. "I'll just wipe it clean . . ." The cloth was impregnated with the same clear, cold spirit the magi had used before the tattooing ceremony; the medicinal smell made Rieuk's eyes water. Imri stepped back to examine his handiwork and slowly nodded his approval. "It's a good transference. Take a look for yourself." He held up an oval mirror in front of Rieuk.

The image of the shadow hawk shimmered before Rieuk's eyes, painstakingly inked in smoky blood into his skin, each mottled feather, each sharp talon perfectly reproduced.

"It's . . . *beautiful*," said Rieuk. There seemed to be a knot in his throat, for his voice was faint and hoarse. Days had passed in which he had sensed Ormas drowsing within him, not yet ready to awake. He had even begun to worry that the transference had failed.

"Get dressed." Imri said, tossing Rieuk's shirt to him. "It's time to begin your training."

In the hour before twilight, as the light of the setting sun dyed the saffron stone of the twisted Towers of the Ghaouls to a reddened ochre, Imri led Rieuk to the top of the arid ridge above the hidden valley.

"Your control of your Emissary is much improved," he said. "So this evening, we're going to try a little reconnaissance. At the head of the next valley lies the Fort of Ondhessar. I want you to send Ormas to spy out the land. Report to me everything that you see."

Rieuk closed his eyes, centering all his concentration on his Emissary. "Ormas, awake."

"*Ready, master.*" The hawk's voice still sent a thrill of excitement through him.

"Fly across the valley to the fort, Ormas."

Ormas darted from Rieuk's breast and soared into the pale violet sky. Rieuk kept his own eyes closed, looking through Ormas's as he sped across the darkening sands. Soon the imposing walls of a great fortress loomed on the horizon, silhouetted against the scarlet-streaked sky.

"Go closer in, Ormas."

As Ormas used the last of the day's warm air currents to glide soundlessly above the high walls of the citadel, Rieuk saw

Commanderie sentries patrolling, muskets on their shoulders. Their standard, a golden crook on a black background, fluttered in the evening breeze alongside the rich royal blue of the Francian flag.

"What can you see?" Imri asked suddenly, making Rieuk start.

"There are at least ten sentries keeping watch on the ramparts. Guerriers are lighting lanterns at the top of each tower . . ."

"How many towers?"

"Eight . . . no, ten. Go farther in, Ormas." Ormas flew lower still in the gathering dark, so close that Rieuk could see the sentries' features, lit by the watch fires they were kindling against the chill of the desert night.

"And how are the Francians armed?"

"Cannon in each tower."

As Ormas circled lower, Rieuk saw one of the Guerriers glance up. He reached for his musket.

"Get out fast!" Rieuk cried as the Guerrier primed his pan and aimed. Ormas darted up toward the first stars. Rieuk heard the crack and whistle of a fired musket ball that had passed too close.

He felt Imri's hand on his shoulder. "Mortal weapons cannot harm the shadow hawks."

Rieuk anxiously scanned the darkening horizon for a sight of his hawk returning. He had lost his connection with his Emissary. He began to panic. The sky was red as blood where the sun was setting far beyond the rim of the desert, and he could see no trace of Ormas.

"Go, Tabris," said Imri and loosed his shadow hawk into the dusk. Rieuk sensed the flicker of feathered wings on the edge of his mind's seeing. He realized that he was looking through Ormas at Tabris flying fast toward him on powerful wings.

"There you are," he whispered, glad that he had not lost mastery of his hawk. Tabris flew close, closer still to Ormas, until the two hawks were darting around each other in a skillful, daring aerial dance.

A distant roar, as if of a far-off wind, disturbed the silence.

"What's that?" Imri looked at Rieuk as the shadows of night flowed through the valley like a night tide. "A sandstorm?"

CHAPTER 10

"The wind mage has returned." Lord Estael's hawk, Almiras, perched on his master's shoulder, regarding Rieuk and Imri with fierce, jasper eyes. "He has already infiltrated the Arkhan's palace. He's on the hunt for aethyr crystals."

"For the Vox," whispered Rieuk.

"He may be rash enough to come here. You must stop him at all costs."

Rieuk and Imri had kept vigil all night, their Emissaries circling overhead. At dawn an old man emerged from one of the towers, peering up into the sky, shading his eyes as if the daylight were too bright. Rieuk caught a glint of ice as the man scanned the sky.

"Don't go too close, Ormas," he warned. It must be Kaspar Linnaius, for those cold, silver-grey eyes could only belong to one of true mage blood. But the Magus had aged almost beyond recognition; his brown hair had thinned and faded to a whitish grey and he stood stooping, like an elderly scholar.

Rieuk turned to Imri. "It's him. It has to be." Just the sight of his old master had sent a surge of hatred and fear through his whole body; his hands were shaking. "But he looks so old."

Imri put his hands on Rieuk's shoulders, gazing into his eyes. "Don't be deceived, Rieuk. His body may be weak—which will work to our advantage—but I sense no diminishing of his powers. This may be the most dangerous task I've ever had to undertake. Leave him to me. I don't want you hurt."

"This is as much my responsibility as yours." Rieuk gazed back staunchly. "Besides, we're partners, aren't we? I vowed to be at your side, no matter what dangers there were to be faced."

"Stop, Kaspar Linnaius." Imri barred his way as he left the tower. "My master, Lord Estael, wants to talk with you."

"I have nothing to say to him, Imri Boldiszar." Linnaius continued on his way.

"Wait!" Rieuk cried.

"Rieuk Mordiern?" Linnaius quavered. For a moment he seemed genuinely shaken. "Didn't you die in the fire at the college? They found your body."

"They found some remains. They assumed it was me."

To Rieuk's surprise, Linnaius suddenly began to laugh, a dry, mirthless sound. "So Lord Estael has loosed his hawks." The Magus's laughter sent a warning shiver through Rieuk's body. Suddenly uncertain, he glanced at Imri for reassurance and saw that Imri had tensed as if ready to defend himself.

"Ah. Now I see it, Rieuk," said Linnaius with a disdainful little curl of the lip. "You're in thrall to an Emissary."

"I'm with Imri because I choose to be." It was taking all Rieuk's self-control to keep his voice steady. He could sense that familiar chill and intimidating aura emanating from his old magister. And as if to confirm his fears, a sudden sinister breath of wind shivered through the desolate valley.

"You're his lover." The cold eyes mocked him. "You fool."

"The Arkhan's aethyr crystals," said Imri. "Give them back and we'll let you go free."

"I hardly think that you're in a position to talk of making a trade." Again that flicker of dry laughter in the Magus's voice. "You failed to stop me last time." Linnaius turned and began to walk away.

"Tabris!" cried Imri. The smoke hawk issued from Imri's breast and darted after the Magus. Rieuk noticed that Linnaius's index finger had begun to move, almost imperceptibly, tracing a tiny spiral in the air. At the same time he sensed a change in the atmosphere, a sudden drop in pressure. "Imri, look out!" he shouted. A gust of wind ripped through the air and caught Tabris, flinging the hawk far up into the sky, out of control.

Imri staggered as if he had been hit.

"Go, Ormas." Rieuk felt his Emissary emerge from his body and soar into flight. "Attack!" If only he could gain Imri valuable seconds to recover. Ormas's consciousness became one with his own and he saw, through the hawk's eyes, Kaspar Linnaius slowly turning as Ormas bore down upon him, saw for a brief moment of triumph the look of astonishment on the old man's face.

This time it was Linnaius who staggered and dropped to one knee as the smoke hawk's shadow wings beat furiously in his face.

How dare Linnaius attack Imri! Suddenly all Rieuk's long-pent-up anger was flowing untrammeled into Ormas and the hawk began to claw wildly at Linnaius.

"*No, Rieuk.*" He faintly caught Imri's warning. "Call Ormas back."

Too late he saw the malicious glitter of ice-grey eyes. Then the full force of the wind hit Ormas and sent the hawk tumbling into the air. Rieuk was unprepared for the force of the gust. Dizzy, flailing, he lost his balance and sank to his knees as his mind went helplessly spiraling through the sky with Ormas.

"Rieuk!" As if from far away he heard Imri's horrified shout.

"They didn't tell you, did they, Rieuk Mordiern?" Linnaius was on his feet again. "When your Emissary is parted from you, you become vulnerable." Another twist of his fingers, and Rieuk cried out as Ormas began to fall, one wing torn. "When your Emissary is hurt, you hurt too." Shards of glass-sharp hail began to pelt down and as each icy pellet hit Ormas, so Rieuk felt his own skin scored and pierced until he collapsed, helpless.

"Leave him be, Linnaius." Imri's voice was dark as thunder. Tabris attacked Linnaius again, darting through the hailstorm, making for the Magus's moving hand.

Dizzy and bleeding, Rieuk sensed the sudden change in the air. Something was snaking toward them, something powerful and invisible. "A wouivre!" he yelled. "He's summoned a wouivre!"

He flung himself at Linnaius, toppling the old Magus to the

ground. But he was too late. A translucent air-dragon streaked through the sky as fast as lightning and attacked the smoke hawk.

Imri gave a choking cry and fell. In the sky above him, smoky feathers scattered and tumbled down like flakes of black snow. The wouivre was tearing its prey to shreds—and with every attack, Imri's body arched convulsively in agony.

"Stop, Magister!" Rieuk begged, crawling toward Imri. "Call it off!"

Splatters of crimson blotted the air. A hot rain of torn feather and black blood showered down as Rieuk stumbled toward Imri to shield him. Too late. All he could hear was Imri's agonized cry, mingled with Tabris's dying screams. All he could see was Imri flung spread-eagled on the ground, his chest and neck a mangled ruin of torn flesh and bone, his long black hair fanning out around him, his life fast-ebbing away as the sand beneath him turned dark . . .

"Imri, no. *No!*" A sob of denial tore from Rieuk's throat.

"You're . . . unharmed." Imri's eyes focused briefly on his, but the golden mage fire was dimming fast. Imri's hand rose shakily as if trying to touch his face, to make a last connection.

Rieuk gripped the bloodstained hand in his own. "Don't leave me, Imri. Stay with me. Don't leave me behind."

A swirling cloud of dust arose; Kaspar Linnaius's sky craft was lifting off, flying away across the desert.

Ormas was slowly, raggedly winging toward Rieuk through the swirling sand.

"Wait!" Rieuk sent his mind into the darkness of oblivion, hurtling after Imri's fast-receding figure into the Ways Beyond.

"*You must come back, Master. You must not follow him. It is not your time.*" Ormas confronted him, his hawk eyes burning, bright and cruel in the chaotic darkness. "*If you stay here, you'll become a Lost Soul and then you can never be reunited.*"

Imri's body lay, encased in a casket of aethyr crystal, illuminated by the light emanating from the Rift. The magi had washed the clotted blood from his torn body, had clothed him in clean robes, combed the black silk of his hair, and crossed his arms across his damaged breast.

His face was no longer distorted with pain, but calm, yet distant, as if carved from the same white, translucent marble as the statue of Azilis.

Lord Estael stood gazing down at the crystal casket. He did not even turn around as Rieuk approached.

"Imri," Rieuk whispered. "Oh, Imri . . ." His hands instinctively reached out and touched the crystal, as hard and chill as ice. "What have you done to his body, my lord?" He slid slowly to his knees. To be so close to Imri, yet never able to touch him again, was a torment beyond endurance. His fingertips, pressed against the ice-cold crystal, were fast becoming numb.

"Why are you grieving?" asked Lord Estael distantly. "Imri was an Emissary; there's still hope."

"What do you mean *there's still hope*?" Rieuk's throat ached with weeping. "Not necromancy?"

"Foolish boy, why would I suggest such an abomination?" Cruel eyes bored into his. "Have you forgotten how much he meant to me? I will keep his body here in the Rift, entombed in aethyr crystal, until you have completed the Arkhan's mission. In the Rift, the flesh will not decay."

Rieuk shuddered at the bluntness of Lord Estael's words. "But Imri taught me that the longer the soul is out of the body, the harder it is to reunite the two."

"In the case of ordinary mortals, that is so. But his soul is linked with his Emissary's; Tabris will shelter Imri's soul." Lord Estael took out a soul-glass, quite unlike the others Rieuk had seen. Within lay two distinct glimmering strands, intertwined in a spiral: one warm as amber, the other smokily black.

"W—wouldn't it be kinder to let him go?" As Rieuk knelt there, he heard himself speaking as if from a great way off. *What am I saying? Why am I arguing against bringing him back, when I'm not even sure I can make it through the night without him at my side?*

"When did kindness come into this?" Lord Estael's voice dinned in his ears, harsh as the beating of a brass gong. "You made a vow to the Arkhan. So you—Rieuk Mordiern—you *must* continue with the mission. If not, I have orders from the Arkham to destroy this glass."

Linnaius tottered from the sky craft and leaned against the mottled trunk of a silver birch, trying to get his breath. He was all but spent. Summoning the wouivre had used up too much of his spiritual energy. Even the clean, cold air of Tielen had not cleared his head.

"Magus?" called a voice. "Are you all right?"

Through the haze of exhaustion, Linnaius saw a figure hurrying toward him through the trees. "H—highness?" he managed, recognizing the fair hair and incisive gaze of Prince Eugene. "What are you doing all the way out here at Swanholm?"

"I'm on leave from the academy. I rode over here to see you. And I saw rather more than I bargained for. I wasn't imagining it, was I, Magus?" Eugene's voice was husky with excitement. "You flew. In that little craft you've hidden back there."

So the prince had learned his secret. "I beg you, highness, please don't tell a soul."

Eugene broke into delighted laughter. "And even if I did, would anyone believe me?" Then he added earnestly, "Don't worry; your secret is safe with me. But have you flown far?"

"I went to collect more aethyr crystals," said Linnaius. "Your father plans to establish a linked information chain, with devices in every embassy." He stumbled and the prince steadied him.

"You look exhausted. You must take better care of yourself."

"I think I shall find plenty to occupy my time here, highness. I don't plan on using my craft for a very long while."

"Teach me, my lord." Rieuk went down on his knees before Lord Estael. "Teach me how to become strong enough to destroy Kaspar Linnaius."

Lord Estael put out one hand to Rieuk's face; Rieuk flinched as the Magus stared probingly into his eyes.

"You are no match for Linnaius," said Lord Estael bluntly. "He would crush you. And your desire for vengeance is not nearly as strong as your desire to find death." He let go of Rieuk, who slumped to his knees, drained. "You are the Arkhan's Emissary now, so I must forbid you to go anywhere near your old master."

Rieuk could not hold back the sob of frustration that burst from his throat.

"You lost Imri before your training was complete," Lord Estael said, a little less harshly. "I will take you on as my apprentice and prepare you for the Arkhan's mission. After that, we will see if you are ready to confront the most powerful of our order."

"Y—your apprentice, my lord?" Rieuk had not anticipated that Lord Estael would suggest such an arrangement. Before he could stammer out another word, Lord Estael raised him to his feet and briefly pressed his dry lips to his forehead.

"There is so much you need to learn, Rieuk. Follow me."

Ormas followed Lord Estael's Emissary, Almiras, deep into the Shrine at Ondhessar until both shadow hawks hovered above the white statue of Azilis, the Eternal Singer. Rieuk gazed down on her through Ormas's eyes while Lord Estael began to tell him the secret the order had protected over the centuries. "Your countrymen know her as Azilia, the mortal woman who achieved sainthood through her good deeds and self-sacrifice. But they are ignorant of her true story. And Enhirre has paid dearly for their ignorance. If the Commanderie knew her real identity, they would pull down her shrines, for she is one of those they regard as the Enemy."

"The Enemy?" Rieuk repeated, not understanding.

"One of the Transgressors. The Rebels. She is the child of a forbidden love: a love between angel and mortal. An act of rebellion that brought about the downfall of her father and his followers, and led to their eternal imprisonment."

"So she was half mortal, half angel?"

"And she, in turn, fell in love with a mortal and bore his child. But years passed and her body, which was mortal, began to fail. Yet her spirit endured."

"But who sealed her spirit within the Lodestar? Who committed such a cruel act?"

A sad smile passed across Lord Estael's face. "Can't you guess, Rieuk? The Angel Lord, Prince Galizur. She was sealed here, in this world, so that she could not be reunited with her rebel father, Nagazdiel."

"And *I* set her free?"

"It seems, Rieuk," Lord Estael was regarding him with a quizzical expression, "that you are quite unique. There has never been a crystal magus with such potential in our order before. In fact—"

A Guerrier came into the Shrine and began to light votive candles.

"Return, Almiras," commanded Lord Estael. The Guerrier glanced upward as the flames flickered wildly in the breath of the hawks' wings. Ormas retreated, flying swiftly after Almiras.

Lord Estael greeted his hawk as Almiras alighted on his shoulder. To Rieuk's relief, Ormas came fluttering down out of the darkness a few moments later.

"Our order, Rieuk, was created to guard her crystal prison, in the hope that one day we could reunite her with her father. All true magi—all elementals like you, Imri, and Linnaius—we are all descended from that first, forbidden union that created her."

"We are?" Rieuk heard the words but could not begin to grasp the immensity of their meaning.

"We have angel blood in our veins."

Angel blood. The words sent a thrill through Rieuk's body; they resonated with the promise of unspoken, unimaginable mysteries. "But if our magi powers are angelic powers, why does the Commanderie persecute us? I thought they revered angels."

Lord Estael gave a short, bitter laugh. "The Commanderie seeks to destroy us because their founders allied themselves with the Warriors of Heaven to defeat Prince Nagazdiel and his followers. As we are Nagazdiel's children, they are bound to destroy us, too. I believe that there is a whole chapter of the Sacred Texts devoted to that subject. Yet the chapter you were taught at school is not the original. The original was suppressed."

"B—but how can that be?"

"The truth about our origins is the secret knowledge that we have guarded here over the centuries. Secret, because the followers of Sergius and Argantel have burned every copy of the original Texts they've laid hands on. The Guerriers of the Commanderie are dedicated to the destruction of magic and all who use it."

Rieuk's mind was spinning. He knew himself now to be the descendant of an angel. But his angelic ancestor was one of the Fallen—a rebel whose tremendous powers had not saved him from a terrible punishment.

CHAPTER 11

Père Albin's voice droned on, dull as the buzz of the fly trapped against the narrow classroom window. Jagu tried not to sigh too loudly as he dipped his pen in his inkwell and dutifully scratched down the dictation. The pen nib was slightly bent and, try as he might, he could not write with an even hand. He stopped, trying to pry the crossed prongs apart with a fingernail, dirtying his fingertips in the process.

An ink pellet suddenly flipped over his head, spattering his work with drops of black, and landed with a small splotch on Père Albin's desk. The elderly teacher paused and gazed down at the pellet. There came a smothered laugh from behind Jagu. *Kilian!* Never able to resist a prank, even in Père Albin's catechism lessons.

The boys waited, breath bated, to see how Père Albin would react. Glaring over the top of his spectacles, he reached for the cane with one gnarled hand. He brought the cane down on the desk with an ear-bruising whack. Jagu winced. Père Albin's fingers might be knotted with protruding veins and distorted with rheumatism, but he could still deliver a painful dose of the cane that his pupils did not forget in a hurry.

You idiot, Kilian.

"Which boy was responsible?"

Silence. Jagu stared at his blotted work, not daring to raise his head.

Père Albin walked between the desks, slowly tapping the end of the cane on his palm. Jagu had no love for the master who some-

how contrived to make the most inspiring and beautiful verses of
the Holy Texts dull, but he was in awe of his considerable scholar-
ship.

"Own up now, and your punishment will be brief. Remain
silent, and the whole class will suffer for your impudence."

Jagu could hear the old man's testy breathing as he approached
from behind. He crouched lower over his work.

"What's this, Rustéphan? Splashes of ink?" Jagu could hear the
barely restrained choler in the master's voice. "Show me your
hands." He glared round at the cowering boys. "Whoever made
that pellet will have ink on his fingers."

Jagu slowly raised his hands and turned them over for the master to inspect. Père Albin let out a cry of triumph. "Aha! Just as I
thought!" He grabbed hold of Jagu's right hand. "Inky fingers!"

"It wasn't me—" Jagu began, but down came the cane on his
outstretched palm. The pain made his eyes fill with tears.

"Sir," piped up Paol, "he's got organ practice at four."

Jagu bit his lip, praying the tears would not spill out and disgrace him in front of the other boys. He tasted blood as the cane
came down again and again,

*Quicksilver ripple of air . . . strange stillness . . . everything
ceases . . .*

Père Albin's arm froze in midstroke, and Jagu felt his heart stop.

The cane dropped to the floor with a clatter. Jagu blinked. The
burning pain in his hand brought him back to himself. He saw
Père Albin make a sudden move and instinctively ducked out of
the way. But Père Albin's attention was diverted. Where his jowled
face had been red with anger, it was now a pasty white. The master
staggered toward the window. The sky outside was black with a
sudden swirl of crows, as if all the birds in the seminary garden had
erupted into crazed flight.

"May the Heavenly Ones protect us," Père Albin muttered under his breath. The other boys were gazing at one another, mystified. Paol nudged Jagu. "You all right?" he whispered. Jagu
nodded, nursing his swollen hand. He was still aware of the
strange, stilling sensation that had seemed to stop his heart. Even
now, there was an odd, unsettling taint to the air.

Kilian, who was nearest the window, let out a piercing whistle.
"Will you look at *that*!"

Suddenly all the boys forgot Père Albin and scrambled toward the window, pushing and shoving to get a better view. And what was most extraordinary was that Père Albin made no move to stop them. He seemed for the moment as fascinated as they. Jagu, taller than his peers, gazed out over their heads, while agile Paol wriggled his way through to the front of the throng.

The dark flock of birds swirled over the ochre-and-grey-tiled roofs of the town of Kemper like thunderclouds, scattering a hail of jet feathers. The classroom door banged open and other boys came rushing in, jostling Père Albin's class to get a better view.

Jagu stood his ground, fascinated in spite of himself. The unpleasant feeling emanating from the darkly swirling birds was growing stronger. He felt a disorienting sense of nausea, as though the natural order itself had been disrupted.

"Thaumaturgy," Jagu heard Père Albin say in a strangled voice. "And here, in our very own town." The chapel bell began to clang—a fast, frantic clamor.

"Père Albin!" Jagu turned to see the imposing figure of Abbé Houardon, the seminary headmaster, in the doorway. He was glowering at their form master. "Bring your class down to the chapel at once. And Jagu, run to the library and fetch Père Magloire. If I know our librarian, he won't even have heard the warning bell."

Unlike most of his rowdier friends, Jagu was usually pleased to be sent to the seminary library. He liked the calming silence, and the dusty smell of old books entranced him with the promise of amazing tales and arcane secrets to be discovered within their faded bindings. Even though Jagu was one of the younger students in the seminary, the elderly librarian, Père Magloire, had begun to recognize him and nod kindly—if a little absently—at him whenever he was sent on an errand. The library overlooked the seminary gardens, and the many old and rare trees that had been brought from across the seas by a keen botanist priest over a century ago. Bookcases of varnished oak lined the walls and tall ladders could be wheeled along the sides on a rail so that Père Magloire could reach the highest volumes. Although of late, Jagu had always offered to scale the ladders in his place, fearing that the frail, wisp-bearded old man might fall.

When Jagu entered the library, Père Magloire was not at his desk. Blinds had been pulled down to protect the books from the sun, yet daylight still penetrated the faded linen, coloring the air with a yellowish tinge. The bell had stopped. But the disconcerting sense of wrongness still permeated the air; if anything, it felt stronger in here.

Jagu hurried along each row of bookcases, searching for the librarian. A fresh breeze and a splash of daylight made him notice that, unusually, one of the blinds was rolled up and the window gaped open. He reached the far end of the lofty room and gazed around, perplexed.

"Père Magloire?" he called, disturbing the silence.

There was no reply.

And then he felt it again: that horrible, unsettling sensation of nausea. The air in the library rippled before his eyes, as if an invisible layer of gauze were being peeled away. Every instinct told Jagu, "*Run!*" Yet when he tried to turn and flee, he found that he could not move.

A shadow skimmed the top of his head, drawing his gaze upward.

Père Magloire was tottering on the highest rung of one of the library ladders. As Jagu watched, helpless, the shadow took shape, revealing itself as a swift-flying smoky hawk, making straight for the elderly librarian.

"Mon père!" Jagu felt his mouth frame words of warning, but only a strangled sound issued from his throat.

Père Magloire turned to stare at him. But instead of the old man's customary rheumy, benevolent gaze, Jagu felt himself transfixed by eyes that were blank and empty. The librarian pulled an ancient volume from the top shelf, releasing a little cloud of brownish dust. The hawk seized the book in its outstretched claws and darted away, making for the open window.

Jagu gave chase. "Thief! Come back!" But the hawk had already swooped out the window and was winging swiftly away.

Frustrated, Jagu leaned out, trying to trace where it was going.

There, in the seminary gardens, stood a stranger beneath the spreading branches of one of the ancient trees. Jagu froze, hands clutching the sill, as the smoke-winged hawk flew straight toward the man, the book still grasped securely in its claws.

He saw the stranger raise his hands to take the book. He saw the hawk alight on the man's wrist. The air rippled . . . and then a cloud passed across the sun, plunging the garden into shadow. Jagu blinked, rubbed his eyes. The hawk was gone. But the man was still there, his head raised, staring directly at Jagu.

And he was smiling.

Jagu slowly backed away from the window. The intruder had seen him. He could identify the thief, but the thief knew who he was.

"What am I doing up here?"

Père Magloire's voice jolted Jagu out of his stupor. The old priest was wobbling dangerously, trying to regain his balance.

"Mon père, hold on!" Jagu hurried over and grabbed hold of ladder. "Can you climb down by yourself? Shall I help you?"

"I feel a little dizzy," quavered the old man.

"What on earth is going on, Rustéphan?" One of the final-year students appeared around a stack of books. On seeing Père Magloire, he launched himself forward to take his weight just as the old man loosened his hold and slid downward. All three ended up in a heap on the floor. As Jagu extricated himself, he recognized the student from his hazel-brown curls as Emilion, the senior prefect—a studious, conscientious young man destined to rise high in the priesthood.

"Go and get help," ordered Emilion, untangling himself from the unconscious librarian. Keen to escape, Jagu sped off.

"You saw the thief, Jagu? You actually saw him?" The boys whispered together excitedly in the chapel pews as they waited for Abbé Houardon to address them.

Jagu nodded numbly. He had been grilled by the priests in the headmaster's study for over an hour and was exhausted.

"What was he like? What did he do?" Paol kept pestering him with questions. "D'you think he really was a magus?"

"He put a spell on Père Magloire." Jagu felt a chill as he remembered the old librarian's expression. "His eyes were . . . *weird.*"

Kilian was not convinced. "Père Magloire's always weird. Is it so surprising, after working here all these years? He must be getting on for a hundred."

"And he stole a book."

"From our library? Huh! Good luck to him, then," said Kilian with a shrug. "Every book in there is as dusty and dry as Père Albin's sermons." He leaned back and propped his feet over the pew in front, causing the younger boys sitting there to squeak with annoyance.

"But which book?" persisted Paol as Kilian continued to torment the little boys.

"It was from the shelf where Magloire keeps the books about the missionary fathers. Remember? He showed us after he gave us that talk about his work in Enhirre."

Paol mimicked the librarian's quavering voice. " 'Bringing the heathen unbelievers to the light is the noblest cause a young man can devote his life to.' "

"Why would anyone want a book about missionaries?" Kilian yawned widely.

"Maybe it was a book one of the missionaries brought back." If only he had managed a closer look before the dark bird flew straight at him, clutching the book in its talons.

And there, in the green garden below, stands the waiting figure of the Magus, the breeze stirring his long locks of hair, unmoving, yet terrifying in his stillness.

Would I recognize him if I saw him again? This thought had been troubling Jagu since he had seen the intruder. *And, worse still, would he recognize me?*

"Stand *up*, Kilian!" Abbé Houardon strode down the aisle in a swirl of grey robes, stopping to glare at Kilian, who sullenly removed his feet from the pew and stood up with the rest of the boys. "See me after chapel," muttered Père Albin to Kilian as he followed in the headmaster's wake.

Abbé Houardon positioned himself below the tall statue of Argantel, the seminary's patron saint; the other masters took their places on the steps below. The headmaster cleared his throat and glared intimidatingly at all his students. "After today's incident, we must all be vigilant. I never thought that any servant of darkness would be so rash as to attempt to infiltrate a seminary, but it appears that our enemies are becoming bolder. The Commanderie has warned all devout believers to be on the alert."

Kilian raised one eyebrow in an expression of bored cynicism. This lecture was not a new one; the fathers were always warning the boys that they were entering an age of uncertainty in which their faith would be tested to the limit.

"Although the Inquisition destroyed that nest of vipers in Karantec—those malefactors who dared to call their study of the Dark Arts a science—it now seems that not every member of the College of Thaumaturgy was tried and executed, as we thought. This cowardly attack on Père Magloire bears all the hallmarks of the Forbidden Arts, although I'm delighted to be able to tell you that our librarian is making a good recovery from his ordeal."

Jagu leaned forward, listening with full attention now.

"I have sent to Lutèce to request an investigation from the Inquisition. And I and my fellow priests will perform a cleansing rite tonight."

Is no one going to explain why we were targeted? Jagu, disappointed, gazed expectantly at the other masters but they all stood listening in silence.

"I advise you boys to be on your guard at all times. Report anything suspicious instantly to one of the masters. Don't try to deal with it yourself." Abbé Houardon's stern gaze swept over the congregation, thick brows drawn together. "We may be attacked again." And with this abrupt warning, he made the sign of blessing over the pupils and left the lectern.

"Be on your guard?" Jagu mouthed to Paol. "Against what? Who *was* that man?"

"Jagu de Rustéphan, I want another word with you. Come with me."

Jagu looked up to see Abbé Houardon towering over him. "M—me, sir?" he stammered, wondering what misdemeanor he was to be punished for this time.

"You're such a troublemaker, Jagu," whispered Kilian with a malicious grin, as Jagu squeezed past him to follow the headmaster out of the chapel.

The headmaster's study looked out over the seminary gardens, and as Jagu stood before Abbé Houardon's desk, he realized that he could see the very spot where the intruder had been standing. The spring sunlight created shifting shadows on the grass beneath the spreading boughs of the old tree. A froth of tender green had appeared on the bare branches, as the first leaves began to unfurl.

"I can see the tree," Jagu said as the Abbé searched through a pile of papers. "The tree where *he* was waiting."

"What?" The headmaster looked up. "Oh, this has nothing to do with our intruder. I received a letter from Lutèce today. An eminent musician who once studied here in Kemper is visiting the city. You'll be pleased to learn that he is going to honor his old school with a recital."

Jagu forgot the intruder. "A musician?" His heart began to beat faster with excitement. Questions tumbled out of his mouth. "Will he give lessons? What's his name? When will he be here?"

A slight curl of the lips that might have passed for a smile altered Abbé Houardon's habitually severe expression. "He's called Henri de Joyeuse. And according to this letter, he'll be arriving on the diligence from Lutèce tomorrow evening. The bishop has invited him to play in the cathedral, so you're very fortunate that he's agreed to spend a day with us. He's just been appointed chapel master at the Church of Saint Meriadec."

"And he studied at this seminary? Just like me?"

"I still regret that Henri was never ordained as a priest, but the lure of the music was too strong." Abbé Houardon seemed to be lost in reminiscence. "He left us to study fortepiano and composition at the conservatoire in Lutèce. And now, it seems, he has found favor with the royal household . . ."

A real pianist! Jagu had always dreamed of being taught by a proper musician rather than his elderly and rheumatic music master, Père Isidore. He often took Père Isidore's place in chapel on cold days when the old man was too stiff to climb the steep spiral stair to the organ loft.

"So we thought that you should meet Maistre de Joyeuse. How do you feel about that?"

Jagu nodded enthusiastically. His fingers were itching to play.

"Report to me here tomorrow after vespers. Oh, and Jagu," said Abbé Houardon quietly as Jagu turned to leave, "it was . . . ah . . . unfortunate that you were the only one—apart from Père Magloire—to see the intruder."

Jagu stopped. Was the headmaster warning him that he was in danger? The good news had put all ominous thoughts out of his head.

"What was the book?" he blurted out. "The book *he* stole?"

"It was Père Laorans's *Life of Saint Argantel*." An expression almost resembling a grin had appeared on the headmaster's face. "I can't help wondering if that magus wasn't as clever as he thought. I'd like to see what sense he makes of the life of our patron saint! But be on your guard, Jagu, in case he returns. Because you're the only one among us who could identify him."

The grin had vanished; Jagu saw that Abbé Houardon was in deadly earnest.

" '*But how can we protect the faithful against the wiles of those cursed with daemon blood?' asked Archimandrite Sergius of the angel.*

"*Then Galizur struck the living rock with his sword of flame and breathed on the fragments that broke off. The rock became as clear as glass. 'Take these seven stones,' said the angel, 'and if they turn as dark as night, then you will know that evil is at hand.'*

"*With one of these angel-given stones, the Blessed Sergius tracked the Drakhaoul-daemons that were terrorizing the empire and destroyed them . . .*"

Rieuk shut the *Life of Saint Argantel* and passed a hand over his eyes. Where did the historical facts end and the legends begin?

His investigations had eventually brought him to Kemper and the seminary dedicated centuries ago to Argantel. The faithful companion of Saint Sergius—and founder of the Commanderie—had died in Kemper and was interred in the chapel. Every year on the date of his death, Saint Argantel's Day was celebrated and the saint's relics were displayed to the faithful. That day was but a fortnight away.

Saint Argantel's Day was approaching. And he had to inveigle himself into the seminary fast, or risk losing his chance of discovering the hiding place of the Commanderie's precious Angelstones.

"Whom shall I become? Old Père Magloire? As librarian and archivist, he must have access to all manner of ancient seminary secrets. Or better still, one of the students, one closely involved in the preparations for their saint's day?

"Wake up, Ormas. Go and reconnoiter. I want to see what's happening in every dormitory, every classroom, even the gardens."

Ormas silently flew away into the gathering dusk.

"Show us where you saw this evil magus, then, Jagu." Kilian pushed open the rusted ironwork gate with Paol and Jagu trailing behind.

The three boys had sneaked into the seminary gardens after vespers. And now, as dusk painted the boughs of the ancient cedars inky black against the slowly darkening sky, Jagu began to wish that they had come in daylight. The long grass beneath the trees was already damp with evening dew, and from the branches of the walled garden a blackbird let out a shrill warning cry.

"Keep up, Jagu," ordered Kilian. "We're supposed to be following *you*."

Jagu, increasingly uneasy, glanced up at the mullioned windows of the old library behind them. He reckoned that the intruder must have been about twenty paces from where he was standing.

"What's the matter?" jeered Kilian. "Scared?"

Was Kilian deliberately trying to provoke him? "You weren't there." Jagu could not shake off the nagging feeling that there was still some trace of that malignant presence lingering in the twilit shadows.

"So where was he?"

"There." Jagu pointed.

Kilian went up close to the gnarled trunk of the tree. He walked all around it. "There's some kind of metal label on it. But the writing's worn away."

"Isn't this one of the rare trees Père Ninian brought back from his mission to the Spice Islands?" said Paol, examining the label. "I think it might be a Serindhan malus. A paste made from the rotting fruit is said to cure scabies and—"

"Ooh, listen to our clever little scholar here. How come you've turned into such a swot, Paol?"

Paol neatly ducked Kilian's backhanded swipe. "Abbé Houardon says that the king was so impressed that he offered Père Ninian the post of Royal Botanist."

"It's getting too dark to see." Jagu could not get rid of the feeling that they were being watched. "Let's go."

"But Père Ninian never got to take up the post. He fell sick with some mysterious illness and died here in Kemper." Paol's voice grew quiet.

"And now his ghost haunts the gardens . . ." Kilian's words came floating through the twilight. Normally, Jagu would have laughed at his fooling. But tonight his nerves were on edge.

"Well, I've got keyboard practice." He forced a careless laugh as he started back toward the gate. "See you later . . ."

A shadow slipped from behind a tree. "Now you are mine, boy," a hoarse voice whispered in his ear. Hands covered his eyes and mouth. Jagu wriggled around and lashed out wildly, his fist connecting with flesh and bone.

"Ow!" Kilian went sprawling on the grass. "That hurt." He clutched his chin.

Jagu, breathing hard, had been about to say, "Serves you damn right." But a sudden flap of wings above their heads made him whip round. A bird lifted off from the upper branches of Père Ninian's tree and was flying away with slow, deliberate strokes. Dimly silhouetted against the star-prickled sky, its shadowy serrated wings were just like those of the bird he had seen in the library.

"Did you see that?" said Paol.

"Probably a crow." Kilian was still massaging his jaw.

"It was almost as if it was watching us. Jagu, d'you think it was—"

"I don't know," Jagu said curtly. He didn't want to think about it.

Paol suddenly shivered, hugging his arms to himself. "I'm cold. Let's go back."

Waiting for them in the doorway to the dormitory wing stood Père Albin, slowly, menacingly tapping his cane against his palm. "The headmaster told you quite clearly that the garden is out of bounds. What have you got to say for yourselves?"

Jagu lay on his stomach, unable to sleep. It wasn't just that his backside stung from raw weals inflicted by Père Albin's cane. It was that the bizarre incident in the library seemed to have left some residual scarring in his memory. Every time he closed his eyes, he saw the magus smiling at him, with a look of such chilling malignance that he awoke, shuddering.

What did he really want?

Staring down the dark dormitory filled with the soft breathing of the other boys asleep, punctuated from time to time by the odd staccato snort or grunt, he determined that he was going to find out.

The library was usually occupied by the older students at this time of day. Slumped over their essays, or thumbing frantically through old dictionaries, they struggled with their translations of the Sacred Texts from Ancient Enhirran. But the final year were being examined on their knowledge in the main hall and the intermediate boys had been sent away to a remote island monastery on a retreat. So when Jagu, Paol, and Kilian cautiously opened the door, they saw that the library was empty.

Shafts of sunlight shimmering with dust motes slanted between each tall bookcase onto the floorboards.

"This place could do with a good cleaning," said Kilian, pulling a face. "It stinks of old books."

"I love that smell," said Paol, smiling as he drew in a deep breath of dusty air. "Old books are filled with fascinating secrets. You should try reading one sometime, Kilian."

"Huh." Kilian scowled, kicking at the base of one of the cases. "So where was Musty Magloire when you found him, Jagu?"

"Over here." Jagu pushed a library ladder along the rail until it reached the central stack, where he had seen Père Magloire.

"Paol, you keep watch." Kilian had taken charge of the operation. "Cough if you hear anyone coming."

"Why do I have to be the lookout?" complained Paol.

"Because you're the youngest. Off you go."

Paol stuck out his tongue at Kilian but did as he was told.

"I'll hold the ladder steady. You shin up," said Kilian.

Jagu gripped the sides of the slender ladder and climbed up until he could see the titles on the top shelf. "Ugh. Layers of dust covering everything. Titles . . . faded. Difficult to read." He squinted sideways at the indistinct lettering, wobbling as he tried to keep his balance. "Nobody's taken these out in years."

"There must be a gap," said Kilian, "where the stolen book was shelved."

"*A Mission to the Spice Islands,*" read Jagu. "*Botanical Specimens from Serindher.*"

Kilian yawned loudly. "Bo—ring."

Jagu pulled out *Botanical Specimens,* a large, leather-bound volume. A small cloud of dust rose from its spine, tickling his nose and provoking a violent sneeze. Something dislodged itself from inside the covers and fell, bouncing off Kilian's head.

"I said bring them down, not throw them at me."

"Sorry," said Jagu cheerfully.

"What have we here . . . ?" Kilian relinquished his hold on the ladder. Jagu felt the ladder sliding away sideways and made a grab for the shelves to stop himself from falling off.

"For heaven's sake, Kilian, hold on—" The sound of frantic coughing interrupted him.

"Damn. Someone's coming," said Kilian, stuffing the object that had fallen from the top shelf into his jacket. Jagu slid down the ladder, burning the palms of his hands in his haste.

"What are you boys doing in here?" To Jagu's relief, he saw not Père Albin but doddery old Père Servan, who taught classes on the Sacred Texts.

"Er, Père Albin sent us to do some research on the prophets," said Paol swiftly.

"The prophets? You're looking in the wrong section." Père Servan pointed with his walking stick to another stack at the opposite end of the library. "You'll find no prophets here; these shelves are devoted to the history of the Commanderie and the missions overseas." He turned to Paol and prodded him in the chest with the end of his stick. "Unless you're planning to follow in the footsteps of Laorans and join our brothers at the new mission in Serindher?"

"Well, I've always dreamed of traveling abroad." Paol pushed his spectacles back up onto the bridge of his nose.

"It's not the traveling, it's the desire to spread the holy word that should inspire you," said Père Servan severely. "Have you young men today no sense of vocation?" He shook his head and continued on past Jagu and Kilian, muttering under his breath, "No spiritual rigor!"

Paol caught Jagu's eye and gave a quick nod. The boys moved toward the library doors, slowly at first, then quickening their pace before Père Servan asked any more questions.

Outside in the empty corridor, the boys huddled together to examine their discovery.

"It's just another book," said Kilian, disappointed.

"What did you expect to find in a library?"

"I thought that magus might have made his bird conceal something in there. Something magic—an 'eye,' maybe, so that he could spy on us from afar."

"An eye?" echoed Paol incredulously.

"Not a real flesh-and-jelly eyeball, stupid, some kind of necromantic device. A magic stone."

"You have a weird imagination," said Paol. "Why would anyone want to spy on schoolboys?"

Jagu had been wiping sticky cobwebs from the cover of the little book with his handkerchief as the other two bickered. He opened it carefully, prising the first two puckered pages apart. "It's handwritten," he said. All his earlier feelings of excitement faded, faced with an almost unintelligible blur.

"How can we read this scrawl?" said Kilian impatiently. "It's useless."

Paol peered at it through his awry spectacles. "It's all blotched. The book must've got wet."

"So why were they keeping it in the library?" Jagu took it back from him and opened another two pages. "Wait . . . this looks like a date at the top. Monday. Then Wednesday. D'you think it's a diary?"

The bell for the midday meal began to ring.

"You two scholars can decipher it if you want. I'm starving." And Kilian, with a careless wave of the hand, hurried off in the direction of the refectory.

Jagu wavered, torn between the need to eat and the desire to find out more about the book. "It's in our own tongue, at least."

He stared again at the looping script and began to make out words. "Hey, Paol, I can read this bit. 'Reached the Enhirran border . . . sunset . . . the local tribesmen made us welcome . . .' "

"Enhirre?" said Paol, his eyes wide with surprise behind his round lenses.

The midday bell stopped ringing. Jagu's empty stomach had begun to rumble.

"Whatever it is, we'll miss our meal if we don't hurry."

During his daily journeys to practice in the organ loft, Jagu had discovered many secret places in the old chapel. Behind the organ loft was a poky little room where piles of dusty choir music were stacked from floor to sloping ceiling in overspilling ledgers. And the steep, claustrophobic spiral stair leading to that room continued on upward until it opened out onto a hidden, sunny lead-lined platform between the sides of the chapel roof that allowed access to the bell tower beyond.

After Jagu had finished his practice, he, Kilian, and Paol hurried up onto the roof. As both the others had been working the bellows for him, no one would question their whereabouts for a little while, affording them some rare free time to examine their discovery without interruption.

"What are you eating?" demanded Paol.

Kilian smiled secretively but didn't reply.

"Aniseed drops. Don't deny it, I can smell them on your breath! But how—?"

"One of the Intermediates owed me a favor. He happened to be going into Kemper on an errand, so I made sure he called at the sweetshop on his way back." Kilian lay back on the sun-warmed lead, hands clasped behind his head, smiling in self-satisfaction.

"An Intermediate student owed *you*?"

"Don't waste your breath asking, he's never going to tell," said Jagu. Kilian had several "business arrangements" with the older boys; Jagu suspected that Kilian had acted as go-between, arranging the occasional forbidden tryst with the girls at the nearby convent school. "The least you could do is share them round, Kilian."

"Not till you've told us about my diary."

"Yours? *I* found it."

"Ah, but it fell on *my* head."

The feathered whisper of wings made Jagu glance round, dreading what he might see. But it was only a pair of collared doves, alighting on the ridge above their heads. "I think," he said slowly, removing the diary from his pocket, "that it's Père Laorans's journal. The master who was sent to Serindher to the new mission. Informal notes, jottings, place names, observations about the local flora and fauna . . ."

"And that's interesting because . . . ?" Kilian's eyes were closed; he appeared to be half dozing in the sunshine.

"There's some really gruesome stuff about the magi of Ondhessar. It says they practice soul-stealing."

Kilian rolled over onto his stomach and grabbed the journal from Jagu, eyes moving avidly over the intricately looping handwriting. "I'll bet this never made it into the official record of the mission."

"Read it out aloud!" insisted Paol.

"Then don't blame me if you can't sleep tonight." Kilian rolled his eyes dramatically. Then in a hushed voice he began to intone, " 'In the moonlight, a strange yet chilling sight was revealed. Many ruined towers lay below, the last vestiges of a lost, ancient civilization. At this point our guides refused to go any farther. They told us that the hidden valley was haunted by soul-stealing *ghaouls* who preyed upon the unwary traveler. One, Jhifar, related how he had once been unwise enough to enter the valley with his brothers. At nightfall, the eerie sound of a woman's singing began to issue from one of the ruined towers below. It was so strange yet so beautiful that the eldest brother went in search of the singer. Later he returned to their campfire. "You must come with me and hear her sing," he told them. They followed him but as they drew near to the first of the towers, a host of shadow birds swooped down upon them, feeding upon their life essence, sucking out their souls, while the shell that had been Jhifar's brother looked on and laughed. The evil magi had made him their puppet to lure the unwary travelers into their trap to feed their accursed shadow birds.' "

"Um . . . what was it you said about the magus in the garden?" said Paol with a slight quiver in his voice. "Didn't he have a bird with him?"

"Surely you don't believe any of this, do you?" Kilian looked up over the top of the book. "Ooh, Jagu, poor little Paol's scared. I don't think we should read any more, in case he has nightmares."

"Cut it out." Paol made a swipe at Kilian and snatched the journal from him. " 'Even more obscene is the rite Jhifar described to us,' " he continued in a loud voice, " 'to initiate a new member into the secret cult of soul stealers.' " He squinted at the book, turning it upside down. "It's illegible. Pity. Something about a fresh corpse . . . and its tongue—"

"Give it here." Jagu took the journal back and turned to the passage that had been puzzling him.

"Are you planning on boring us to death, Jagu?" Kilian got to his feet and stretched. "Since when were you so keen on ancient history?" He went to the edge of parapet and leaned over to scan the courtyard below.

"I haven't got to the curse yet."

"There was a curse?"

Paol crept up behind Kilian, hand reaching toward his jacket pocket.

"The guides told Père Laorans that anyone who entered the hidden valley would be cursed by the magi, fade away, and die."

Paol made a sudden move and snatched the bag of aniseed drops from Kilian's pocket.

"Give those back!" Kilian made a lunge but Paol was too swift. Crowing with delight, he darted away and disappeared down the stairwell, with Kilian hurrying after. Jagu sighed and followed.

"So you're Jagu de Rustéphan." Henri de Joyeuse was standing in the music room, one hand resting on the worn ivory keys of the fortepiano. "I've heard much about your gift."

Jagu opened his mouth and stammered a few words of greeting. "And I—I've heard so much about you." The fortepiano stood half in shadow and he could not quite distinguish Maistre de Joyeuse's features. His hair was fair, pale as ripening summer barley, and far longer than any priest's in the seminary, tied back at the nape of the neck with a black ribbon.

But what was I expecting? He trained in Lutèce. He must have adopted the fashions of the royal court.

"Perhaps you'd like to play something for me." The Maistre's voice was softly modulated, yet unusually kindly in tone for a teacher.

"What, now?" Jagu had not expected this. "But I'm supposed to show you round the seminary."

"The tour can wait. I'm eager to hear you play first." Joyeuse moved away from the keyboard, gesturing to Jagu to take his place.

Jagu felt suddenly unsure of himself. "What shall I play?"

"Whatever you like."

Jagu's mind blanked for a moment. And then he remembered the prelude he'd been practicing that morning, the fifth of six by Marais, where the familiar melody of an old plainchant hymn to Saint Argantel was woven through an intricate pattern of running notes. It required both dexterity and control to let the melody sing through the decorative figuration and Jagu had been working on it for months, refusing to be defeated by its difficulty.

Maybe it was a rash choice. Maybe he wasn't ready to perform it yet. But it was a piece that he cared about, that he had labored over for a long time. He raised his hands over the keys and saw to his shame that they trembled. Yet as soon as fingers touched the familiar yellowed keys, his nerves melted away. Absorbed in the demands of the prelude, he forgot that Maistre de Joyeuse was watching him until he played the final chord.

"Marais's Fifth Prelude?" Joyeuse was smiling. "You've mastered the technical difficulties extremely well for a student of your age."

Jagu heard the words as he surfaced from a trance of deep concentration. He felt himself blush with pleasure at the compliment and swiftly lowered his head.

"But there's so much more to this piece than just playing the notes. Listen . . ." Jagu slid off the stool to make way for him. "Close your eyes."

Jagu obeyed. The prelude began to reveal itself beneath Joyeuse's swift, sure fingers. The plainchant melody sang through the gentle patter of notes, like birdsong heard through falling rain. Joyeuse made it sound so effortless. When he had finished, Jagu did not know what to say. Now he wanted to blush with shame at the clumsiness of his own playing.

"How about that tour of the school?" Joyeuse closed the lid and stood up. "I hear the new chapel organ is a fine instrument."

"Oh. Of course. Please follow me, Maistre." Jagu didn't know whether he felt grateful or disappointed that there was to be no further analysis of his playing tonight. As Jagu held open the door, Maistre de Joyeuse stopped and put his hand on Jagu's shoulder. "You're young, Jagu. To play that prelude as Marais intended, one must have lived a little."

Jagu stared up at him, not understanding. Maistre de Joyeuse was smiling at him again, an enigmatic smile, reserved, yet kindly. None of the priests had ever treated him with kindness; they controlled the boys with strictness and frequent applications of the cane. As Jagu led Maistre Joyeuse from the music room, he was not sure whether he knew how to handle the situation. He was used to resenting and fearing his teachers.

Paol climbed slowly up a library ladder, carrying a pile of books. In Père Magloire's absence, Abbé Houardon had arranged a library roster and the senior prefects had been deputed to ensure that the boys did not shirk their duties. And the seniors preferred to send the youngest ones to tidy the highest shelves, while they lounged about at the front desk, "keeping an eye on things." Anyone—like Kilian—who dared to argue was dismissed with a cuff and extra duties. But this afternoon, the library was deserted, as the senior students were being examined on their knowledge of the Holy Texts.

"Take care, Jagu." Paol was just leaning out to replace the last well-thumbed volume when a quavering voice called out. He grabbed at the ladder, almost losing his balance. He looked down and saw the Père Magloire peering up at him through cloudy spectacle lenses.

"I'm Paol, mon père. Jagu is showing a visitor around the seminary, so I've taken his duty instead."

"Ah well, I suppose you will have to do for now . . ."

"Are you feeling better?"

"Yes, thank you, Paol." The elderly librarian was smiling at him and nodding.

Paol reached the bottom rung of the ladder. "It's good to see you back in the library."

"And it's good to be back. Although there are misplaced books everywhere I look," said Père Magloire, pointing to a nearby shelf. "Someone has mixed the saints up with the prophets." He pulled out a thick volume. "And since when have the learned commentaries of Erquy been classified as mathematical theorems?"

"I'll sort them out for you." As Paol knelt down, he thought he saw a flicker of shadow out of the corner of his eye. He blinked. A bird must have fluttered across the window blinds . . .

CHAPTER 12

Jagu's eyes kept straying from the mathematical problem he was supposed to be solving to the classroom window. It had rained all morning but since midday the clouds had dispersed and now the sun shone in a sky of fresh-washed blue. But what drew Jagu's attention was the dark bird that had soared past the window for the third time. As he watched, it disappeared amid the snowy dusting of blossom that had appeared overnight on the trees in the walled garden. *Surely it couldn't be the Magus's familiar . . . ?*

"Rustéphan!" Jagu started and saw Père Albin towering over his desk. "Would you kindly stand up and repeat to the class what I just said?"

Jagu had not heard a word. Paol whispered, "Measure the angle—"

Père Albin's cane thwacked down on Paol's desk, making him let out a startled yelp. "Is *your* name Rustéphan?"

"N—no, mon père."

"If I want to hear your voice, Paol de Lannion, I'll be sure to ask you. *Rustéphan?*" Père Albin rolled the "r," like a mastiff growling. He patted the end of the cane on his palm. "I'm waiting."

Jagu looked the hated Père Albin in the eyes. He would not be intimidated by the choleric old man. "I'm afraid I didn't hear, mon père."

"As I suspected! Daydreaming again. You know what happens to boys who daydream in my lessons?"

"Show me." It was an order, even though Henri de Joyeuse's voice was quiet. Jagu reluctantly obeyed. Joyeuse gently took his hands in his own to examine them more closely and Jagu heard him softly draw in his breath between his teeth.

"And what crime did you commit to earn this barbarous punishment?"

Jagu could not meet Joyeuse's eyes. "I wasn't paying attention in class."

There was a silence. "I see," Joyeuse said eventually. "And the master who did this to you?"

"Père Albin." Jagu raised his head, realizing what Joyeuse intended. "But please . . . please don't take it any further."

"Because he'll only make your life more miserable if I do?" Joyeuse's pleasant expression had hardened into a look of stern determination. "I can't allow a master to subject you to such abuse and ruin your prospects as a musician in the name of classroom discipline."

Over the past months, Jagu had forced himself to endure Père Albin's punishments in silence, hiding his misery, even from his friends. Now he realized that he had an ally, a protector who was prepared to stand up to the sour-tempered old master, and he was not at all sure how he felt about it. He had never understood why Père Albin had taken such a dislike to him. He had needed a great deal of willpower to arm himself against Père Albin and he feared that Joyeuse's kindly words might erode his defenses. He stared at the worn floorboards, studying each knothole, not knowing what to say.

"You have a God-given gift for music, Jagu," Joyeuse said, almost as if reading his thoughts, "and in the years to come you will encounter more people, like Père Albin, who are jealous of that gift, who resent you for it. Such people are to be pitied rather than despised."

"B—but you're leaving," Jagu blurted out.

"And when I've gone, it will all be just the same as before?" A mysterious smile had appeared on the musician's face. "I've already spoken with Abbé Houardon and he has agreed to allow you an extra hour a day to practice. It will mean extra duties substituting for old Père Isidore at matins and vespers in chapel, of course. But I don't believe you will find that so disagreeable, will you?"

Jagu felt as if a sudden shaft of brilliant sunlight had illuminated the music room, brightening every dusty corner. He gazed up at Maistre de Joyeuse. "You did that for me? Thank you, Maistre." His voice came out huskily and to his embarrassment he found that his eyes had filled with tears. He had never wept once when Père Albin was caning him, not even when the pain was so intense that he had bitten his lip till it bled to stop himself from crying out. But now he felt that if he began to weep, he would never stop.

And then he felt the lightest touch on his cheek, wiping away the single stray tear that had begun to trickle down. "If ever you need a recommendation, Jagu, I have many friends at the conservatoire of music in Lutèce. I'm not asking you to rush this decision. Practice diligently. And if you still want to make music, whether it be in a few months or a few years, contact me." The musician's gentle fingers tipped Jagu's chin upward until the soft grey eyes gazed intently into his. "Promise me that you will."

Jagu nodded, still fighting back the tears. This unexpected kindness had undone him utterly.

"And now I must bid farewell to *my* old form master."Henri de Joyeuse was already at the door; he glanced back over his shoulder and Jagu saw the ghost of a mischievous grin. "Of course, back then, he wasn't headmaster, and his hair hadn't turned grey. But we were all in awe of him, even the senior students."

"Abbé Houardon was *your* form teacher?" Jagu tried to imagine Henri at the same age as himself; had he been small and studious, like Paol, or a rebel like Kilian?

"Till we meet again." With a salute of the hand and a smile, Henri de Joyeuse was gone. Jagu, his emotions in disarray, stood in the center of the room, not knowing what to do. Then he noticed the little pile of music on the lid of the fortepiano. Maistre de Joyeuse had forgotten it; he would have to run after him.

A note addressed to "Jagu de Rustéphan" lay on top of the pile. With swollen, clumsy fingers, he opened it and read:

"Dear Jagu,
    "These pieces are for you. The first is a book of chorale preludes that I composed for the organ at Saint Meriadec. The sec-

ond is Marais's *Variations on a Ground Bass*. Both are challenging works. I have marked the fingering, expression and phrasing for you. Take your time in learning them. And when you have mastered them, come and play them to me in Lutèce.

"Your friend, Henri de Joyeuse."

"His own compositions?" Jagu took up the chorale preludes and leafed through them eagerly. At a first glance he could see that they were far more difficult than anything he had ever played before. Learning them would take weeks of practice; reaching performance standard might take years. But he relished a challenge. He clutched the precious book tightly to him.

"Thank you, Maistre," he whispered to the empty room.

"Lannion? Where's Rustéphan?" demanded Emilion as a slender, fair-haired boy appeared in the vestry. "He's missed his chapel duty again."

"He, um, asked me to deputize for him." Paol de Lannion had a distinctly distracted air. "He's having a music lesson with Maistre de Joyeuse."

"There's quite enough to be done for Saint Argantel's Day, without you little squirts skipping duties. You'll have to do, I suppose. Tell him to see me later. He's not getting off so lightly." And Emilion turned to the altar, bowing respectfully, before removing the candlesticks and the jeweled Golden Crook. "Come here, Lannion. All these will have to be polished. What are you waiting for?"

He turned round and saw that Paol was tottering on the first step of the altar. One hand was clutched to his shirt collar as if he was finding it difficult to breathe.

"What *now*?" Emilion said impatiently. The boy began to back away. His eyes had a haunted look. "Look, Lannion," he said, a little less fiercely, "just do the candlesticks, will you? There's polish and dusters in the vestry."

The boy nodded dumbly, slowly retreating, one unsteady step at a time.

"*Angelstones, master . . .*" Rieuk clutched at the ancient Serindhan malus tree to support himself as Ormas caught a tremor of the stones' latent power. "*They're here, hidden in the altar.*"

Rieuk concentrated again and looked around the chapel through Paol's shortsighted eyes. He could sense the strong, clear wave of energy emanating from the Angelstones, slowly draining Ormas of his strength.

"*This one is too weak to support me.*"

The bright flame of the boy's life essence was fading; separated from his soul, his heart would not be able to sustain the Emissary's presence much longer.

Rieuk knew that his plan was going awry. He had detected the location of the Angelstones but Ormas was not able to approach them without being affected. And with the union between Emissary and Paol failing so fast, he would have to find some other means to extract the stones and destroy them.

"Ormas. Bring the boy Paol to me in the garden. We need to find someone older to get the stones. Someone stronger."

Jagu could not sleep.

A trickle of moonlight leaked in through the high dormitory window, illuminating Paol's empty bed. Paol should have been back by now. It was only chapel duty, after all. And it was odd that neither Père Albin nor the senior monitor patrolling on dormitory duty had noticed his absence. Had they caught Paol trying to sneak back in and hauled him down to the headmaster's study to be punished? Jagu felt guilty now, for letting Paol cover for him while he spent time with Maistre de Joyeuse. He crept over to Kilian's bed and shook him by the shoulder.

"What's the matter?" Kilian mumbled.

"Paol's not back."

"What?" Kilian, still half-asleep, sat up, blinking at Jagu. "Where's he got to?"

"I'm going to go look for him."

"Wait. I'll come with you." Kilian grabbed his breeches from the end of the bed and started to pull them on; Jagu did the same. Holding their shoes, they tiptoed to the door and quietly let themselves out.

"I'll scout round outside," said Jagu.

"I'll check the library," said Kilian. "The little swot may have forgotten what time it is. You know how he loves to read."

"Meet me back here in a quarter of an hour," Jagu called over his shoulder as Kilian sped away. Jagu took the back stair, which led out into the quad. Lights were burning in the masters' study windows; he inched along the wall before risking a quick look inside through the lozenge-paned glass. Père Albin was marking the essays they had handed in earlier, frowning as he scribbled critical comments in the margins. He could hear two of the senior masters discussing the bishop's recent sermon.

Howls of laughter erupted from the opposite side of the quad, where the older students were housed. Jagu and his friends often wondered how the seniors amused themselves in their rare free time. Had they sent Paol out on an errand?

Jagu slipped silently across to the seniors' dormitory and stood on tiptoe to look in.

"And if any one of you wastrels has failed to gain full marks in the translation paper," one of the seniors was imitating Père Albin's choleric manner and the others were doubled up with laughter, "I shall take pleasure in applying the cane with more than my usual enthusiasm. You, boy! Yes, you, bend over . . ." Jagu could smell liquor fumes and spotted a couple of empty wine bottles on a desk. But there was no sign of Paol.

And then he heard a cry, distant and high-pitched, from the direction of the garden. It could have been a hunting owl, or its terrified prey . . .

Jagu sped from the quad, tearing along the path, scuffing up gravel as he ran.

A full moon was rising, turning the dark seminary garden into a lake brimming with silvered light. The cedars stood starkly black against the brightness and the white blossoms on the trees glimmered like stars. An unfamiliar perfume drifted on the air, sweet yet bitter-spiced, as if a thurifer had been burning incense beneath the trees.

The cry came again.

Jagu ran faster now. He trod on something that crunched like glass beneath his foot. Bending down to see what it was, he picked up the twisted metal frame of a pair of spectacles. Fragments of one shattered glass lens fell onto the path through his fingers.

"Paol!" he called. "*Paol!*" He reached the tall ironwork gate and rattled the catch, but it was locked. There was no choice but to clamber up the crumbling stones of the high wall, clinging to the ivy to pull himself to the top. The feeling of dread was growing stronger all the time, like chill fingers slowly closing around his heart.

The creamy scent grew stronger as Jagu hurtled through the dark garden. The tree was a mass of lacy blossom, luminously white against the shadowy foliage. And the light radiating from the tree seemed to be intensifying, growing brighter, as if it were leeching brightness from the moon. He skidded to a halt.

A boy lay at the foot of the tree, his fair head lolling against the trunk and a man was kneeling over him. For a moment, Jagu dared to hope that one of the masters had come to the rescue. Then he knew that no one had heard the cries but him.

As Jagu watched, a shadow issued from the boy's mouth and darted upward, outspread wings black against the moon's white disc.

Jagu tried to move. He could not even blink. He was paralyzed. He could do nothing to help.

The boy's body went into sudden spasm, his head jerked upward, and a faint cry issued from his mouth. Only then did Jagu recognize him.

"Paol?"

The man turned around. In the moonlight, Jagu recognized the magus, his green eyes glittering. At the same moment, he heard voices calling his name.

"Here!" he shouted, standing his ground, silently daring the magus to attack him when help was on its way. "In the garden!"

The magus raised his arm and his hawk familiar swooped down onto his shoulder. A cloud covered the moon and when Jagu looked again, he was gone.

"Paol!" Jagu stumbled forward and cradled his friend in his arms. "Stay with me!" But there was something about the unnatural way that Paol's head drooped against his shoulder that told him he had come too late.

Jagu could not control the trembling in his legs. He was afraid he was going to fall over.

"Drink this." Abbé Houardon placed a steaming cup in his hands. "It'll make you feel better." Jagu automatically raised it to his lips and obeyed. The hot sweet tea contained something strong that stung the back of his throat and made him cough and splutter. Through watering eyes, he saw the headmaster pour a measure of spirits into his own teacup and swallow a mouthful.

"I'm going to have to ask you to answer some questions, Jagu."

Jagu nodded. He supposed that he was still in shock. Everything that he had witnessed in the garden seemed like a confused dream.

"I want you to be completely honest with me, Jagu. You have nothing to gain by lying. Did you cause Paol's death?"

Jagu's head whipped up. "No! Paol was my friend."

"This wasn't just a boyish prank that went wrong? Or a dare? I want the truth, Jagu." The headmaster leaned out across his desk, staring searchingly into Jagu's eyes.

"I swear to you, on—on Saint Sergius's crook, I had nothing to do with it."

"I've had to inform the constables of the watch. They'll want to investigate the area where the crime took place. They'll also ask to interview you. Do you feel ready for that? I'll stay with you."

Jagu did not want to have to relive the past hour so soon. Yet he knew he must do it if only to ensure that no one else died as horribly as Paol had. Though how the constables of the Kemper Watch could track down a magus as cunning and devious as this one, he had no idea. He stared at the floor, studying the sanded whorls and knots in the polished boards. "Thank you, sir."

"And I have the sad duty to send for Paol's family, of course." Abbé Houardon seemed almost to be talking to himself. "But I've written again by express post to the Commanderie, Jagu. We need an experienced exorcist. This is beyond my skills. We're all in danger until this evil man is brought to justice."

Jagu is walking through the seminary garden beneath a slow snow-fall of white blossom.

There, beneath the tree, stands the magus, soft green eyes

*glinting through the pale cloud of falling petals, his hawk familiar
perched on his shoulder.*

*"Did you really think I would let you escape me, Jagu?" he asks
softly. "You have seen my true face. And for that you must die."*

Jagu turns and breaks into a run.

*The hawk comes flying after him, swooping down, knocking
him to the ground. He flings up his hand to shield his eyes, but the
hawk's sharp beak pecks and pecks at his wrist, until it burns like
fire.*

*"It's no use; you won't get away." The magus leans over him,
taking hold of him by the wrist. "See? I have put my mark on you.
Now you will do as I bid you."*

*A sigil glows in raw, red fire on the inside of Jagu's wrist, over
the pulse point.*

Jagu opens his mouth and screams.

"Jagu. Jagu!"

Jagu woke with a start to see someone leaning over him in the
half-light. He gave a shout of fear and struck out wildly.

"Idiot, it's me, Kilian." Kilian grabbed him by the wrist before
he could hit him again. "You were dreaming."

Jagu sat up, staring about him, certain that the magus's hawk
was still hovering in the shadows above his bed.

"D'you want to wake the whole dorm?" hissed Kilian.

Only a dream. Yet it had been so vivid. Jagu could still feel the
stab of the hawk's beak as it burned the magus's mark onto his
wrist. He left his bed and went to the window, pulling back the
loose sleeve of his nightshirt to examine his skin.

"What now?" grumbled Kilian, joining him.

Jagu stared. Even in the dull light before dawn, he could see the
faint shimmer on his wrist, above the pulse point—a mark that
looked just like the sigil in his dream.

"Look." He thrust his wrist in front of Kilian's face. "Now tell
me I'm only dreaming."

CHAPTER 13

Does it ever stop raining in Armel? Ruaud wondered as the sky darkened and the cold drops began to spatter down again. After serving in the searingly dry desert heat of Enhirre, he still found the moist air of Francia's western province seeped into his bones.

Maistre Donatien had established an efficient post-horse service for this kind of emergency, but even with this advantage, Ruaud had already been four days on the road to Kemper. And as he rode on through the mist and rain over the bleak moors that surrounded the distant cathedral city of Kemper, he began to wonder if it might not take five.

It was high summer, and yet the moors were swathed in low cloud that filtered out the sun. "Unless this is some mage-mischief designed to slow me down," he muttered to his horse as he pulled up his damp collar against the persistent drizzle. He passed bedraggled sheep sheltering in the lee of a ruined barn. He had not seen another traveler in the past three hours, and was beginning to wonder if he had lost his way in the mist. He had been so absorbed in his own thoughts, going over and over the facts of the case as set out in Abbé Houardon's letter, that it was possible he might have missed a vital milestone.

"I suspect that this may be the work of Kaspar Linnaius," Donatien had told him when assigning him the mission.

"But why would he risk coming back to Francia, where there's a price on his head?"

"Be careful, dear Ruaud. Linnaius is a cunning and dangerous adversary . . ."

Had Donatien's farewell smile, as he offered him his ring to kiss, been wholly sincere? Ever since Ruaud had been on the road, he had been wondering about the Grand Maistre's decision. It was, of course, his duty as a Guerrier to go wherever his commanding officer sent him. But relations between the two of them had been more than a little strained of late. Ruaud had twice been forced by his conscience to openly disagree with Donatien's decisions in council meetings. From odd little comments and digs, he could not help wondering if Donatien suspected him of plotting to take his place.

Yet the brutal facts of the Kemper case were enough to make Ruaud put aside these concerns: a boy had been murdered. And worst of all, Ruaud feared from the evidence that the victim's immortal soul had been stolen. Other children were in danger if this magus was still at large.

The mists were lifting at last and traces of whey-thin sunlight began to penetrate the cloud. A signpost appeared ahead through the shreds of mist; a bird of prey was sitting hunched on one of the arms. As Ruaud rode closer, he saw that it was a hawk, regarding him coolly with its bright, cruel amber eyes. Suddenly the bird lifted on powerful wings in a shower of glittering wet drops and skimmed silently away.

"Only a hawk." And yet why had he shivered so violently as if another drenching shower were about to fall? Stronger shafts of sunlight pierced the clouds; the rain had stopped.

Ruaud reined his horse to a stop and gazed up to see which way he should take. Rain dripped from the peeling sign. KEMPER read the arm that pointed in the direction taken by the hawk. Below him the moor mists were slowly parting to reveal the hazy outline of a good-sized city and, beyond, the sea.

"Ormas. Return." Through the shadow hawk's keen eyes, Rieuk had seen enough. A Commanderie officer was approaching. And he was not just one of the regular military; he wore the golden insignia of the Order of Saint Sergius. Like his patron saint, he would be trained in exorcism and the casting out of daemons.

Rieuk stood at the open casement, watching the rooftops for sight of his Emissary. From time to time, he closed his eyes, merging his consciousness with Ormas's to scan the terrain beneath for any other signs of approaching danger. This officer might be just the first of a whole troop of Guerriers.

"So I merit a visit from a top-grade Commanderie exorcist? I'm flattered." But even though the thought brought a wry smile to his lips, he knew that the danger was real. A skilled exorcist would seek to use the very Angelstones Rieuk had come to destroy against him.

A flecked shadow swept toward him across the sky.

"Ormas." The shadow hawk alighted silently on Rieuk's outstretched arm. Amber eyes stared challengingly into his. "Help me find the boy. There isn't much time left."

Jagu sat in the dormitory staring at Paol's empty bed. The shouts of the other boys kicking a ball around the seminary courtyard drifted up through the open window. He had slept badly again, convinced that he had heard Paol calling his name in the darkest hour of night.

"Sitting here moping won't bring him back."

Jagu's head jerked up. Kilian was standing behind him, the light blue of his eyes bright with a harsh, angry light.

"I know. But I can't stop thinking it was my fault. Why didn't I get there in time to save him?" This feeling of guilt had been eating away at him, and it was unlike anything else he had ever experienced, shadowing everything he did, leaching the taste from his food, the colors from the daylight, even the pleasure of playing music.

Kilian gave a shrug. "We're one player down. You're needed on the team."

"And I could do nothing. Nothing to help Paol!" Jagu kicked his heel against the bed leg. "I just stood there. While he—he—"

"Are you coming or not?"

Jagu heard Kilian at last. But he was not in the mood for playing games.

"Suit yourself, then." The dormitory door slammed behind Kilian and Jagu was left alone again with his thoughts.

Why couldn't Kilian understand? They had been friends, the three of them, united since their first day at the seminary. Was this Kilian's way of dealing with Paol's death, throwing himself into physical activity?

"*Jagu* . . ."

That voice. So faint, yet so familiar. Jagu went stiff, sensing that he was no longer alone. Slowly, unwillingly, he turned his head.

There, standing beside his bed, he could just make out Paol's diminutive figure, but indistinctly, as though peering through thick glass.

"Paol?" he whispered. "B—but you're—"

"*Help me, Jagu.*" Paol's elfin features were twisted into a heartrending expression of terror and pain.

Jagu rubbed his eyes, certain he was hallucinating. Was this Paol's ghost? The insubstantial image looked like Paol, but there was a taint of corruption about it; his wispy hair looked like dusty spiderthreads and his dulled eyes were sunken too deep in their sockets.

"Wh—what do you want?" Jagu stammered.

"*Set me free, Jagu.*" Paol's hollow eyes implored him. "*The magus has stolen my soul. Even though my body has begun to rot, I'm still bound to this place. I don't want to be trapped here forever. Or worse still . . . to be forced to do his will.*"

"But how can I set you free? I'm no match for that magus. I don't know what spells he's used to bind you."

"*All you have to do is to find the soul-glass, and shatter it.*"

"This soul-glass, where is it? And what is it?"

"*Follow me. I'll show you.*"

Jagu hesitated. "How do I know you're not leading me into a trap?"

"*You'll have to trust me. And you'll have to be quick too. The magus is distracted at the moment.*" A quizzical little frown appeared on the ghost's cloudy features. Jagu saw it with a quickening of the heart, recognizing one of Paol's most familiar expressions. "*But he won't stay distracted for long.*"

That little frown, if nothing else, had convinced Jagu that the apparition was not an illusion. He followed Paol's shadowy figure as it flitted downstairs and along the vaulted passageway.

A triumphant cry came from the outer courtyard as one of the teams scored. "One to us! One-nil!" Jagu felt a pang of regret, wishing now that he had gone with Kilian. Kilian would be in a foul mood for the rest of the day if his team lost.

"Where are you taking me, Paol?" In daylight, Paol's ghostly image was so pale that anyone glancing out of a classroom window would not even have noticed it. But when they reached the chapel, Jagu saw the apparition slide right through the weathered wood of the door, disappearing from view. "The chapel?" This seemed so unlikely a place for a magus to conceal a soul-glass that Jagu hesitated.

But he had to do this for Paol. And Paol had assured him that the magus's mind was occupied with other matters. Jagu's fingers closed around the iron door handle and the chapel door slowly opened.

As Ruaud rode into Kemper beneath the Armel Gate, he gazed up at the slender spires of the cathedral piercing the drifting clouds. The glistening sheen of rain on the slates was drying fast as the sun broke through. Why was the saint's benign influence not strong enough to stop this magus infiltrating the city and wielding his dark arts within the holy precincts?

He passed through the market-day bustle of tradesmen and farmers who had set up their stalls in the cathedral square, past cages of squawking chickens and plump ducks, fishermen with slopping buckets of dark seawater, filled with fresh mussels, crabs, and oysters from the bay.

Just another ordinary day in a provincial cathedral city . . .

Jagu gazed warily around the empty chapel. Since Paol's funeral, he had been unable to make himself come here, not even to play the organ. A shaft of rain-washed sunlight pierced the somber stained glass, highlighting the fine carvings on the altar that Père Albin had taught the boys to identify: Sergius's crook; Mhir's rose; seven stars for the seven Heavenly Guardians.

"Protect me," he whispered to Saint Argantel.

"*Over here!*" He caught sight of the apparition slipping through the arch to the little spiral stair that led up to the organ loft, and the disused room that had become the boys' secret hide-out. No one else would have thought to look there; the priests' embroidered ceremonial robes were kept locked in the vestry below. Jagu followed up the narrow winding stair in time to see Paol beckoning him on.

As he opened the door, a voice said, "So there you are, Jagu."

Jagu stopped abruptly on the threshold.

A bespectacled stranger rose from the table piled with dog-eared psalm books and broken-backed missals. "I've been waiting for you."

Jagu turned on his heel and darted for the stair, but the stranger, taller and stronger, made a lunge for him, catching hold of him by the wrist. Jagu struggled, trying to kick him in the shins. The stranger caught hold of his other wrist and pinned him against the wall, hands above his head. Piles of prayer books cascaded to the floor, sending up clouds of dust.

A slow smile spread across the stranger's features. Jagu recognized that knowing, chilling smile; he had seen it before in the seminary gardens. And in that moment, he knew that behind that smile lurked the grinning face of death—his own.

The headmaster's study brought back memories of Ruaud's own schooldays: the faint taste of chalk dust in the air, the brackish smell of ink, the pile of half-marked essays on the desk.

Ruaud sneezed violently and searched in his pocket for a handkerchief.

"Captain, I've kept you waiting and you're still in wet clothes." Abbé Houardon hurried in. "Whatever must you think?"

"It's nothing." Ruaud blew his nose vigorously. His head felt heavy and his nose still tickled; he suspected he might have caught a summer cold.

"The weather can be treacherous up on the moors. I take it you came that way?"

"Next time, I'm traveling by ship," Ruaud said ruefully.

"You must have a hot drink to warm you. You're in Armel now and we're famous for our cider. The kitchen will heat you up some punch; nothing better for driving out the damp."

A shadow briefly fell across the single source of daylight, an arched window set high in the far wall. The great hawk with smoke-flecked wings flew through the dirt-filmed glass to alight on the magus's shoulder.

"So he's arrived," murmured the magus. One hand gripped Jagu by the throat. "Downstairs, Jagu."

"D—downstairs?" Jagu managed, half-choked.

"A clever ruse of the Commanderie's, concealing their Angelstones under the protective eye of their founder." The magus forced Jagu down the narrow stairs, keeping such a tight grip on his shoulder that escape seemed impossible.

"W—what are you going to do with me?"

The magus's fingers stroked Jagu's cheek. "If only there were some other way . . ." To Jagu's surprise there seemed to be a note of regret in his voice. The magus took off his thick-lensed spectacles and gazed at Jagu. "You see, I can't touch the Angelstones. They drain me of my powers. So you will act as my shield and bring them to me."

Such astonishingly green eyes . . . Jagu forgot to struggle as he gazed back, entranced. It was as if he were slowly drowning in deep, jade waters. The magus's face began to blur, as if glimpsed from far beneath a rippled surface.

"So the boy who witnessed the murder is still here?" Ruaud took a mouthful of the hot cider punch and felt its warmth soothe his sore throat. "Why not send him home to his family to recover from the shock?"

"We felt he might be more vulnerable away from the seminary. Here, at least, he has the protection of his friends and teachers. Besides, he insisted he wanted to help you with your inquiry as much as he could."

The clock on the mantelpiece struck four.

"Jagu's late." Abbé Houardon checked the time on his fob watch. "I told Emilion, our head prefect, to find him and send him up here so that you could interview him. Where's he got to, I wonder?"

Ruaud set down his mug. "Jagu's the witness?"

"And our organ scholar. He's probably practicing in the chapel and lost track of the time."

"Let's go and find him, then." Ruaud took up his leather travel bag containing Judicael's exorcism equipment.

"You don't think—"

"I don't want to take the risk."

"Wait, Captain." The headmaster stopped him. "Did your superiors ever tell you of Saint Argantel's Angelstones?"

"I've heard the legend." Ruaud was impatient to make sure the boy was safe.

"It's no legend. Since the magus attacked Paol, I took the precaution of removing one from the altar." He pulled a chain from around his neck and handed it to Ruaud; on the end was a crystal in the shape of a tear. "Do you see that black streak at the heart? It means that the magus is still nearby."

"Thanks." Ruaud swiftly hung the chain around his neck and hurried out of the door. There had been something else in the legend of the Angelstones . . .

One thought and one thought alone dominated Jagu's mind as he walked toward the altar. He had no doubt that once the magus had used him as his "shield," he would kill him.

I must get away from him.

The school chapel, which had once been his quiet, safe haven, was filled with distorted shadows and strange, sinister rustlings.

"Seven stars," said the magus.

Jagu was eyeing the side door. The magus might not be aware that there was another exit from the chapel. A quick dash past the altar and he could be free.

The magus extended one hand toward the altar. Jagu became aware of a faint vibration that slowly began to increase in intensity. The tiled floor beneath his feet trembled.

"Look at the altar, Jagu," ordered the magus. "Memorize the sequence."

The carvings had begun to glow; first Sergius's crook, then Mhir's rose, lastly each of the Seven Stars in turn.

"Go. You must touch each carving, following the sequence."

Jagu hesitated.

The mark on Jagu's wrist throbbed with a sudden searing pain. Jagu cried out.

"Do it!"

Jagu knelt down and, his wrist still throbbing, pressed the carvings, murmuring the holy names under his breath in the desperate hope that one of the Heavenly Guardians might hear and protect him. "Galizur; Sehibiel; Taliahad; Ardarel . . ."

The vibrations were growing stronger still. A little door opened in the altar.

The magus clicked his fingers and a second door opened.

"There is a box inside. Take it out." The magus's eyes were shut, one hand pressed to his eyelids, as if he were in a deep trance.

How can he know? Can he see through stone? Jagu's fingers closed around the smooth wood of a little casket. He drew it out and held it up to show what he had found.

The magus gave a gasp and went down on one knee. "Stand aside. Stand back."

Whatever's in this box is powerful enough to make him weak. Jagu felt the wood of the casket trembling violently in his fingers; the hinges burst and the lid fell off, revealing three dazzling crystals within. *Angelstones.* Each one was humming at a different pitch. Jagu, with his accurate ear, could have named the pitches if the vibrations were not so powerful.

"Put the box—on the altar."

Jagu hesitated.

"On the altar!"

Jagu felt the mark on his wrist burning with such agonizing intensity that he almost dropped the box onto the altar stone. The humming grew louder still. He stepped back and felt the magus's arm clasp him, holding him pressed against his body like a shield.

"Hold still," the magus murmured in his ear. The resonance from the stones was setting off other vibrations; the organ pipes began to tremble in sympathy and the stained glass rattled until Jagu felt his ears would burst with the sound.

Then the box exploded in a burst of light and crystal shards.

"What in Sergius's name was that?" Abbé Houardon stopped, gazing at the heavens. "A lightning strike?"

Ruaud set off swiftly across the courtyard, making for the chapel, the headmaster following close behind. The sky had darkened. Ruaud felt a sick, strange feeling overwhelm him. Looking up, he saw a great flock of ragged-winged crows, black as storm, swirling around the chapel spire. Even as he raised his head, the cloud of crows came swooping down toward him, scattering jet feathers like blackened leaves.

"Take cover!" yelled Houardon, running for a doorway.

"It's a diversion. Stand your ground." Ruaud clenched his fists and strode on toward the chapel door as the crows came diving down to mob him, their raucous cawing and screeching making his ears ache. Maddened eyes, red with rage, glinted in the whirling featherstorm. He was taking a considerable risk, calling the magus's bluff in this way—but if his guess was right, the birds were nothing but a delaying tactic, designed to distract and confuse.

Sharp beaks stabbed at his head and neck. These birds were no illusion! Ruaud broke into a run. A trickle of blood dripped from a graze on his head, into his left eye. The malignant will driving this storm cloud of birds was more powerful than anything he had encountered before.

Overhead, the crows wheeled and turned, gathering for another onslaught.

Ruaud dashed the last few yards, one arm raised to protect his head, the other hand clutching his leather bag. He tugged hard at the chapel door handle—but it was shut fast and would not open. The magus had made sure that all the doors were locked.

"Side door!" shouted Houardon, gesticulating and pointing. Ruaud hurried along the wall of the chapel to the little porch that probably led into the vestry. Blood was still dripping across his eyes; he dashed the back of his hand across his forehead, the fingers coming away wet and smeared with crimson. The ragged phalanx of crows swept down again as he wrestled with the vestry door. When that also refused to open, he drew out his pistol, hastily primed it, and, aiming at the lock, fired just as the first of the attacking crows flew into his face.

His aim was good; the wood sizzled as the ball passed through the mechanism. And the crows, startled by the loud report, scattered in confusion. Ruaud took advantage of this and tugged the door open. He had intended that ball for the magus. Now he would have to reload. He leaned back against the door, breathing hard, scanning the dim chapel for signs of movement.

"Let me be in time," he muttered. "Let the boy still be alive."

The silence inside the chapel was more disconcerting than the frenzied onslaught of the crows outside. Ruaud delved into his bag for Judicael's standard tool: the pistol shot impregnated with holy water. As he hastily loaded shot and powder, he scanned the shadowed aisles of the chapel, aware that the next attack could come from anywhere.

It was an act of reckless audacity that this magus had dared to wield the Forbidden Arts on sanctified ground. But to use innocent and vulnerable children to accomplish his dark designs was unforgivable.

Saint Argantel's reminded Ruaud of the chapel at the school he had attended: plain lime-washed walls, simple columns, wooden pews scuffed by the booted feet of countless little boys, and a lingering stale smell of snuffed candlewicks that even the most pungent incense could not quite dispel.

"Come out, Magus!" he called, hearing the echo of his voice return to him. "Let the boy go and I'll spare your life."

There was no reply.

Am I too late? Has he already escaped, using the crows to cover his flight?

Ruaud moved out into the main aisle of the chapel, checking out every angle of the building for any hint of movement. And he knew that he was being watched.

Then he saw the altar. The ancient stone had cracked in two. And powdering the altar steps was a fine covering of glittering shards, as if someone had scattered crushed ice everywhere. At the same time, he heard someone cry out a warning. Wheeling about, he caught a glimmer of green eyes in the gloom, and a creature of smoke and flame came darting toward him.

Instinctively, his hands closed around the Angelstone to protect it. But a shaft of light issued from between his fingers, piercing the gloom with its brightness.

Jagu saw the Guerrier standing there, alone and vulnerable to the magus's attack. "Look out!" he shouted. The magus tightened his grip around Jagu's throat before the second word was out. And he loosed his familiar, sending it hurtling toward the Guerrier.

But as Jagu watched, helpless, he saw a white light unfurl around the Guerrier, as if great wings had sprouted from his shoulders. For a moment Jagu saw another figure superimposed—a tall, winged warrior whose silver hair crackled like lightning. With one powerful thrust, he loosed a dazzling spear toward the magus's familiar. The shadow creature swerved, but not before the brilliant spear shaft had grazed one black wing tip.

The magus cried out and loosed his hold on Jagu. Jagu sagged, going down on one knee, clutching his bruised throat. When he got unsteadily to his feet again, the brilliant light had dimmed, and the magus was gone.

As Ruaud's dazzled eyes adjusted to the dimness, the boy came uncertainly toward him. Ruaud saw at once that, in spite of all that he had undergone, he was making a brave effort to control his fear. He was tall for his age, with long hair as black as jet and thick-lashed eyes too dark against his pale skin. Some pale-skinned people flushed red with fright, but this boy's pallor only seemed to have increased, lending him a poignant look of fragility.

"Jagu." Ruaud spoke his name quietly as if gentling a startled colt. "You're safe now."

Jagu nodded. "The soul-glass," he said stiltedly. "I have to find it. And set Paol free."

Jagu was never sure afterward if he had really heard Paol's voice calling to him from the little music room, or if chance had led him to search there.

But with the captain following close behind, he hurried up the spiral stair. This was where Paol's ghost had led him; the magus must have concealed the glass somewhere among the piles of old hymn books. The magus had fled; surely the soul-glass was of no importance to him anymore.

"What are you looking for?" asked the captain, wiping a smear of blood from a gash in his cheek.

"I don't know what a soul-glass looks like," admitted Jagu. And then he felt a faint breath, as though a dusty shadow had slipped past him. "Paol?" he said, feeling the goose bumps rise on his chilled skin. Was that his ghost in the corner, pointing with one hand, faint as a skeletal leaf?

"There it is." On the top shelf, wedged between a stained vase and an old tin of brass polish, stood a delicate phial fashioned in the shape of a flower. As the captain reached up to take it, Jagu saw the cloudy swirl of an evanescent substance within the glass.

"Can so precious a thing as a mortal soul be contained in this little glass?" said the captain wonderingly. He passed it to Jagu, who held it carefully in his cupped hands a moment.

"Good-bye, Paol," he said. "Now you're free." Then he pulled the glass stopper out and the pale, hazy essence within melted away into the air. Paol's sad, insubstantial figure wavered, dwindled . . . and was gone.

"I saw the angel." Jagu was gazing at Ruaud with solemn adulation in his dark eyes.

"Angel?"

"The angel you summoned to defeat the magus. He was so . . . so beautiful. And so powerful."

Had the ordeal affected the boy's wits? Or had he, in that one transcendent moment, been a conduit for an angelic power? Now his whole body ached and the wounds on his face and neck were stinging. But he still felt an echo of that golden brilliance deep within his heart. He looked at the last remaining Angelstone and saw that the dark streak had almost disappeared in its clear crystal heart.

"Thank you," said Jagu faintly. He began to sag; Ruaud caught him before he hit the floor.

Ruaud went up to his guest room after sharing a measure or two of the local apple brandy with the headmaster. Time to start packing; he would have to leave at dawn the next day. He was not relishing breaking the news to Maistre Donatien that the last remaining Angelstones had been destroyed. Although one thought troubled him. *Why didn't Donatien tell me the stones were here? Doesn't he trust me? What other vital secrets is he keeping from us younger officers?*

The cathedral clock had just finished striking midnight when there came a polite tap at his door. Ruaud opened it and saw Jagu standing there.

"Why, Jagu—shouldn't you be resting?"

The boy gave a little shrug. "I couldn't sleep." Ruaud noticed that the strain was beginning to show; the fine skin beneath the boy's eyes was stained with bruises of fatigue. He had been through a terrible ordeal; Ruaud was only surprised that, as yet, he showed no other signs of damage.

"How can I help you?"

"Are you leaving so soon?"

"Duty calls me back to Lutèce." Ruaud turned back to his packing.

Jagu came farther into the room. "I want to train to be like you, Captain. If I come to Lutèce, can I join the Commanderie and learn to fight too? I'm not afraid of hard work. Please take me with you."

There was an air of sensitivity about him—but also, Ruaud realized, an underlying strength. He had suffered, but the ordeal had not broken him. A weaker personality would have been crushed by this encounter with the powers of the dark, but Jagu de Rustéphan was obviously made of stronger stuff.

"I want to ensure that no one else has to suffer as Paol suffered."

Ruaud looked searchingly at Jagu and saw the boy's eyes burning with the desire to serve. "How old are you?" he asked gently.

"I'm eleven. But I'll be twelve soon. And I'm tall for my age."

Ruaud could not hide a smile at this persuasive piece of reasoning. He reached out and tousled Jagu's black hair.

"You're too young. I was eighteen when I joined the Commanderie cadet force. But I like your attitude. And . . ." The smile faded when he remembered that the magus had escaped. The boy was still in danger. The magus could return at any time and destroy him. "What about your music? Abbé Houardon tells me that you were planning on studying at the conservatoire."

Jagu nodded with genuine enthusiasm. "Maistre de Joyeuse promised he would teach me if I came to Lutèce."

"Henri de Joyeuse, no less?" The boy must be very talented to have impressed the king's Maistre de Chapelle. "But what of your parents?"

A dismissive, defensive shrug. "I'm the youngest son. I was always destined for the church."

How could the boy's family show such lack of interest toward their gifted and sensitive child? "Then let's strike a bargain. You come to Lutèce with me and study music at the conservatoire until you're eighteen. Then if you still feel the call to join the Commanderie, I'll be your sponsor. Is it a deal?" Ruaud held out his hand. Jagu stared at him a moment, as though astonished by the offer. Then he reached out to grasp Ruaud's hand, his grip surprisingly firm for one so young.

"It's a deal, Captain."

"You used the last Angelstone?" Grand Maistre Donatien's face had turned red. "So now we have none?"

"I saved a boy's life! Isn't that the reason they were given to us, to save lives?" Ruaud could not understand Donatien's attitude. Had the responsibilities of leadership warped his mind? Disgusted, Ruaud pulled out the chain from beneath his shirt and handed the crystal to the Grand Maistre. "Abbé Houardon asked me to return it to you. And now, if you'll forgive me, I have duties to attend to."

"Wait." Donatien stared down at the last Angelstone. "Have you noticed this crystal is still clear? When the others were used, they lost their brilliance. Could it be . . . ?"

"This stone is different from the others?" Ruaud turned around, wondering what Donatien was suggesting.

"Take it to Père Judicael. And report to me on his findings as soon as you can." Donatien handed the Angelstone back to Ruaud. As Ruaud took the stone, Donatien's fingers closed tightly around his. "We thought we had destroyed the magi," he said, his voice low, intense. "All except Linnaius. So where did this magus come from?"

Ruaud had been wondering the same thing. "Ondhessar?"

"It's time we exerted some pressure on their patron and protector. I've suspected Arkhan Sardion's hand in this for a long while. He's resented our presence ever since we took Ondhessar. But there's trouble brewing between Enhirre and Djihan-Djihar." Donatien smiled, a slow, calculating smile. "And Shultan Fazil has always been Francia's ally. If Sardion attacks Ondhessar again, Fazil has promised to send his troops to help us." He let Ruaud go; his grip had been so tight, it had left marks on Ruaud's skin. Beneath that calm, controlled manner, Donatien must be seething at the damage inflicted by the magus on the Commanderie's holy relics. "This magus's little triumph will prove short-lived."

"So you think that this Angelstone is different from the others?" Père Judicael took the crystal from Ruaud and held it up to the candlelight.

"When I used it against the magus, I felt a burst of light flood through me. It was as if I became . . . a weapon." Ruaud found it hard to put into words, fearing that the old priest might pour scorn on his account. "And the boy I rescued told me that he saw a winged figure. Of course, the child was utterly terrified. Fear does strange things to the mind . . ."

"Have you noticed that the crystal is still remarkably clear and brilliant?" said Père Judicael. "Once the other Angelstones were used against the magi, they became dull and clouded. I wonder if this stone might be the Stone of Galizur? Ah well, there's only one way to be certain." He shuffled into the center of the arcane chamber, placing the stone at the heart of the Circle of Galizur. "Extinguish all the candles," he ordered.

Ruaud obeyed, and as he snuffed out the last candle, the silver traces marking the exorcist's circle began to gleam in the darkness.

"But what will this show us, mon père?"

The Angelstone had begun to radiate a clear, cold brilliance, glittering like ice in sunlight.

"Only the Blessed Sergius was pure enough in heart to summon the Winged Guardians. I don't see how I . . ."

"Sssh!" hissed Judicael. "There is still a trace of angelic power at the heart. It reacted to the Holy Sigils inscribed within the circle." He gazed at Ruaud, the Angelstone's penetrating light throwing the deep lines on his weathered face into sharp relief. "There's no doubt; this is the stone of Angel Lord Galizur." He removed the stone from the circle and the icy light faded as he handed it to Ruaud. "I doubt it would defeat a magus again, but it will still alert its wearer to the presence of evil."

Ruaud's fingers closed around the crystal and in the gloom he murmured a fervent prayer of thanks to the Commander of the Winged Guardians for saving Jagu's life.

CHAPTER 14

Rieuk never remembered how he found his way to Fenez-Tyr or the ship bound for Enhirre. In the aftermath of the Guerrier's attack, he moved like a sleepwalker, mind and body drained by the Angelstone's power.

Two days out of port, fever claimed him. He drifted in and out of consciousness, too weak to leave his bunk, lying in his own sweat and filth.

In his delirium, Rieuk wandered across a hot, dusty plain where the sands had been burned the color of blood by a pitiless sun. Where was Ormas? Had the hawk been fatally injured by the angelic power of the stone? He could only sense the faintest hint of the hawk's presence.

Lost, with no sense of which way to go, he trudged doggedly on, forcing his aching body to move until, exhausted, he dropped to his knees and crawled. His mouth was parched chokingly dry by the baking sun, and the coarse granules of red sand grazed his hands and knees till they were raw, yet still he went onward.

"Ormas . . . where are you?" he cried, even though his throat felt as if it were raked by thorns every time he tried to speak.

Suddenly a dazzling figure blocked his way. Blinded by the light, Rieuk flung his forearm to protect his face, glimpsing only the faintest outline of great snow-white wings, half-furled, and eyes that seared to the very core of his being.

Rieuk became aware that someone was wiping clean his burning skin with a cool, wet cloth. The cold shock of the water against the heat of his body made him shudder and cry out.

"Your fever is too high. This is the only way to bring it down," said a voice in his native Francian, a voice that though firm was also young and persuasive. Through the heat haze, Rieuk glimpsed his savior bending over him, pausing to push back a lock of hair. The image hovered in and out of focus: long hair, like silvered gold, and pale eyes so translucently blue they were the color of daybreak.

"Who . . . are you? Are you . . . an angel?" he said out of his delirium, still unsure what was real and what was conjured from the heat of his fevered brain.

The apparition laughed. "I've been called many things but never angel before. I guess I should be flattered."

Rieuk felt a wash of shame. "That was . . . a stupid thing to say . . ."

"It was the fever talking, nothing more. I've heard far worse, believe me. Now drink this draft. It will help bring your fever down." He raised Rieuk's head and held a little bowl to his dry lips. Rieuk swallowed, gagging at the bitter flavor.

"Vile . . ."

"I never said it would taste good." The kindly stranger's face swam in and out of Rieuk's vision, as if steam rising from his burning body were drifting across his sight, until he lapsed back into confused dreams.

"The fever's responding at last."

Rieuk opened his eyes at the touch of a cool hand on his forehead.

"I thought I'd lost you there a couple of times," said his savior cheerfully.

"You cleaned me up?" Rieuk felt deeply ashamed that this stranger had washed the encrusted filth from his body; he had only vague memories of the last days but he remembered the young man's voice and the feel of hands, firm yet careful.

"Well, you were stinking up the lower deck; I wasn't acting entirely selflessly!"

Rieuk could not remember a time since he had been with Imri

when anyone had taken care of him. He felt humbled by the young man's ministrations. "But . . . why? Are you a doctor?"

"No exactly. The name's Blaize. Père Blaize."

"A priest?"

Blaize laughed in that charming, self-deprecating way that Rieuk had first heard as he surfaced from the incoherence of his fever dreams. "I promised myself that I would come on pilgrimage to Azilia's Shrine to test the strength of my faith."

This young man could not be that much older than Emilion at Saint Argantel's Seminary.

"Why did you save me? You must know what I am. Why didn't you just walk away?"

"To me you were suffering and in desperate need. I wasn't prepared to abandon you just because you happen to be a magus." The amused look faded, replaced by a regard so keen and incisive that Rieuk knew Blaize was no naïve, inexperienced student.

"But you—your order—you're sworn to destroy us." Rieuk struggled to sit up.

"I'd never seen one of your kind before. Your eyes are quite . . . remarkable." Blaize caught hold of him and eased him back down. "Easy, there. You're in no state to go anywhere yet."

"My spectacles . . ."

"So that's how you go unnoticed among us?" Blaize was examining the thick lenses thoughtfully. He glanced up. "Don't worry," he said, grinning. "Your secret is safe with me."

Rieuk had used up what little strength he had; he felt his eyelids closing in spite of his will to stay awake. As he lapsed back into sleep, he found himself wondering how far he could trust the young priest. Or did Père Blaize plan to hand him over to the Commanderie when they reached the next port?

"This hawk tattoo on your breast. It's so realistic. Such artistry." Blaize wiped the wet cloth gently over the inked feathers. "What does it signify?"

Rieuk gazed up at Blaize. "If I were to tell you, you'd never believe me," he said without blinking.

Blaize looked a little hurt for a moment. Then he laughed and shrugged the rejection away. "As you wish."

Violent summer storms off Smarna blew the ship off course and the ship's master was obliged to put into harbor at Vermeille until the bad weather passed.

Too weak to leave his bunk to go ashore, Rieuk found himself looking forward to his visits from Blaize, who brought back fresh fruit for his patient: luscious black Smarnan grapes and white-fleshed peaches. And, little by little, he learned more about the young man who had saved his life.

"After Enhirre, I'm on my way to Serindher, to join the missionary fathers."

Rieuk closed his eyes. "To convert the ignorant natives?" he said, unable to keep the cynicism from his voice.

"To care for the poor and the sick."

Rieuk opened one eye. "Why would you want to do that, Father Blaize? Aren't you as like to get sick yourself in all that heat and humidity?"

Blaize paused a moment. Then he said, with a glimmer of a mischievous smile, "If I were to tell you, you'd never believe me."

Rieuk smiled back. "Touché."

"*Master . . .*"

Rieuk heard Ormas's voice calling to him through the confusion of his lightning-riven dreams. He woke, heart pounding, as thunder crashed overhead, setting the ship timbers trembling. A second later, the sound of torrential rain drummed on the deck above.

"Ormas?" Rieuk sat up too fast in his eagerness. The cabin spun and he pressed one hand to his forehead, as the blood rushed away from his temples. Lightning flashed again, silver-bright against the Smarnan night. And in the lightning's brilliance, Rieuk saw a hawk-winged shadow silhouetted against the cabin porthole. A fierce joy surged through him. Fighting the dizziness, he swung his legs off the bunk as the thunder rolled deafeningly again around the bay.

"Where have you been?" he cried out over the thunder. "I thought I'd lost you for good!"

"*I went to the Rift to be healed. I'm sorry, Master, that I abandoned you.*" Ormas sounded contrite. "*Can you forgive me?*"

"Welcome back," Rieuk said softly, opening his arms to his Emissary. Another silver flicker lit the humid night as Ormas lifted from the porthole. The cabin door opened. Blaize came in just as Ormas flew to Rieuk, melting into his tattooed breast.

Thunder rumbled as both men stared tensely at one another. And then Blaize began to laugh. "Amazing the tricks that lightning can play on the eyes! I could have sworn that I saw a hawk in here . . . but such a thing is impossible. Isn't it?"

When the storms died down and the ship set off again for Enhirre, Rieuk had regained enough strength to leave his cabin. Standing on the deck with Blaize beside him, he watched the sun setting, bleeding scarlet light into the deep blue of the waves, and relished the fresh tang of the wind on his face and hair. Once he and Imri had stood together like this and . . . For a moment, the fiery light blurred and dimmed as tears stung his eyes. He hastily blinked them away, not wanting Blaize to see.

"So what are you going to do when we reach Enhirre?" he said. "Hand me over to your superiors?"

"And why would I do that?"

"I'm your enemy. *The* Enemy." Rieuk had come to feel so much at ease in the young priest's company that he took pleasure in teasing him. He was still too weak to do anything else.

"Well, *you* thought I was an angel," Blaize said after a pause. "So, perhaps I was mistaken too."

As the ship sailed into the bustling harbor, making its way between the hundreds of little fishing boats bobbing about in its wake, Rieuk knew with a terrible certainty that he wanted the voyage to continue forever. He would rather have sailed over the rim of the world than return to his cruel and exacting master, the Arkhan. The very smell of Enhirre—dusty, hot spices mingled with excrement and rotting fruit—produced a feeling of profound loathing.

"So this is where our ways part," said Blaize. In the intense sunlight, Rieuk saw how young and vulnerable he looked in his white priest's robes. He feared for him.

"I don't know how to thank you—" he began lamely, when to his surprise Blaize flung his arms around him and gave him a swift, hard hug.

"Take care, Magus." Then, without another word, he strode swiftly down the gangplank and disappeared into the crowds of merchants and sailors thronging the quay.

Rieuk stood staring after him, feeling as if he had just lost something more valuable than he had realized.

"A Guerrier attacked you with the last Angelstone and you *survived*?" Arkhan Sardion's blue eyes widened with astonishment. At his side, Alarion, Sardion's eldest son, stared challengingly at Rieuk with eyes as startlingly blue as his father's.

"This streak of white in my hair is where the stone's power caught me." Rieuk pointed to the snowy lock that stood out amid the rich brown above the silvered angel-scar on his left temple.

"You're either lying, Emissary Mordiern," said Prince Alarion, "or you crystal mages are made of stronger stuff than your peers."

Rieuk held out the few fragments of shattered Angelstone that he had retrieved before the Guerrier had attacked him. "This is all that remains of the Angelstones in Kemper. But there was something different about the stone the Guerrier used." He was still weak from the aftereffects of the duel in the chapel but he didn't want to admit that to the Arkhan, or his fierce-eyed son.

Sardion took the shards of crystal and held them up to the daylight. "It's difficult to believe that these dull chips of stone were once touched by an angel. By my reckoning, all seven stones have been used up and the Commanderie have nothing left to use against us."

"Now we can win Ondhessar back," said Alarion, his eyes alight. "Without the Angelstones, the Francians are vulnerable. Let me lead a raid against them, Father!"

"Fifteen is too young to fight," said Sardion sternly.

"But Eugene of Tielen fought alongside his father when he was only fifteen," protested the boy.

"Prince Eugene was born a military tactician. At the age when you were happy enough to chase butterflies in the palace gardens, he was already planning campaigns with his lead soldiers. We must bide our time and strike when the moment is right."

Alarion scowled and stalked off without another word.

"Headstrong boy," said Sardion, although Rieuk thought he heard a note of pride rather than censure in his voice. "You must be tired after your long journey, Emissary Mordiern. And I believe Lord Estael has some news for you. Go to him."

News? Rieuk, who had been drooping in the soporific heat, was suddenly alert again. Had he earned his reward, and would the precious souls of Imri and Tabris be released at last from the soul-glass?

"You've done well," said Lord Estael. Rieuk stared at the tiled floor. "You've drawn the Commanderie's teeth. Let's see how valiant they are without their Angelstones to protect them."

"But I was careless. A boy died." Rieuk could not meet Lord Estael's penetrating gaze. "And one of the Guerriers bested me in a duel. I still have much to learn, my lord." Yet he had seen the mission through because it was for Imri, and he knew he would do it all again, if only in the vainest of hopes that it might bring Imri back. Yet the question was choked in his throat; he hardly dared to ask, for fear that the answer would not be what he so fervently wished for.

"And Imri, my lord? I've fulfilled my part of the agreement."

"Imri," Lord Estael repeated distantly. He seemed preoccupied, as though some other matter was absorbing his attention.

"Has anything happened? Is the soul-glass still intact?" He could not bear to think that his all efforts might have been in vain.

"Come with me."

Rieuk followed Lord Estael to the top of the Rift Tower. As he climbed the winding stair, he suddenly sensed Ormas's heart start to beat more rapidly. Rieuk pressed one hand to his tattooed skin, feeling the excited throb beneath his breastbone.

"*Will you let me go to greet them, Master? It's so long since I flew with my kin.*"

"How could I deny you?" Rieuk said, smiling in spite of the sadness he felt on returning to the place where Imri had first revealed the mysteries of the Rift to him.

He reached the top and as he came out into the misty verdant light, Ormas gave a triumphant cry and burst from his breast, darting off over the shadowed trees, Almiras following in his wake.

Rieuk leaned on the wall and gazed down on the vast forest that stretched into the distant horizon. The only sound was that of the breeze stirring the boughs of the fir trees. He wished that, like Ormas, he could fly free and unconstrained, leaving behind the burden of grief and duty that weighed so heavily on him.

"There's a revivifying quality in the air of the Rift," said Lord Estael, gazing out after his shadow hawk. "Yet, look closely, Rieuk. Do you notice anything different?"

"Different?" Rieuk had been away for so long that he could not be sure if his memories of the Rift were reliable. "The emerald moon looks a little hazy tonight. The light is not so intense, perhaps, as I remember." *But when I was with you, Imri, I experienced everything so much more intensely . . .* He raised his head to stare at the unfamiliar constellations glittering faintly above. "And the stars are not so bright."

The shrill, wild cries of shadow hawks broke the silence of the moonlit night and Rieuk recognized Ormas and Almiras. A flock had come swooping down to feed on the oozing sap of the Haoma tree.

"Night after night, the order has been monitoring the Rift. At first we thought it might be a temporary anomaly, but if you study our charts, Rieuk, you will see that we are observing a distinct change. The emerald moon is waning. The Rift is slowly closing."

"But what of Imri?" Rieuk stared at Lord Estael, aghast. "If the Rift closes before . . ." His voice trailed away as the unthinkable implications sank in.

The light in Lord Estael's eyes was bleak as a wintry sky. "I cannot say. This situation is new to us."

"And what of Tabris, Ormas, Almiras—"

"Our Emissaries draw their strength from the Rift. And if our Emissaries grow weaker, so will we. We have never found ourselves in such a perilous situation before."

This revelation had set Rieuk's thoughts spinning. He had risked so much to destroy the Angelstones, strengthened by the belief that the magi would be invulnerable once it was done. It had never occurred to him that their powers could be diminishing for quite another reason. "But why is this happening, Lord Estael?"

"Azilis."

"How could it be Azilis?"

"We first observed the changes after Kaspar Linnaius stole the Lodestar. We hoped that it was a temporary abnormality. Since then, matters have been deteriorating." Lord Estael slowly shook his head. "It seems that her presence alone was powerful enough to keep the Rift between our world and the Ways Beyond open. But now . . ."

"*Master* . . ." Ormas was calling to him. "*My kin are leaving. The Haoma tree is dying. They must fly farther in to search for another. What should I do?*"

"Come back to me now, Ormas." Rieuk tried to quell the panic in his voice. If Ormas abandoned him, he would be utterly alone. He turned to Lord Estael. "Did you hear? The Haoma tree is dying. The shadow hawks are leaving."

"This is worse than I feared." Lord Estael leaned far out and Almiras fluttered down to perch on his forearm. Rieuk anxiously scanned the sky for a sight of Ormas. At last he spotted three hawks skimming in a breathtaking aerial dance across the luminous disc of the moon. *What if Ormas doesn't want to return?*

"Is it possible, Rieuk, that the book in which your magister sealed Azilis was *not* destroyed when the college fell?"

Rieuk was still watching Ormas, and Lord Estael's question startled him. "You mean that all this while we've assumed she's free, and she's still trapped in Hervé's book?"

"Just suppose that your magister hid the book in a safe place? Or smuggled it out of Karantec before the Inquisition struck? Someone in his family might have it in their possession now and be keeping it safe from the Inquisition."

"His family?" Little Klervie playing with her fat grey tabby cat on the doorstep, soft-voiced Madame de Maunoir bringing him homemade lemonade when he was working late for her husband . . . it had never once occurred to Rieuk that the book might have survived the Inquisition's brutal purge.

"I want you to go back to Francia, Rieuk, and look for any clues you can unearth. If there's the slightest chance that you can track her—"

"Go back?" To return to Francia meant assuming another false identity, living on the edge, constantly in fear of the Inquisition. He had done terrible things in Kemper and all in the belief that it was for Imri. And now Lord Estael was telling him that it was not enough, and Imri's immortal soul was in peril.

"Wouldn't it be better to try to restore Imri now?" He heard the desperation in his own voice. "Before the Rift closes any farther?"

"We are proposing to undertake a very risky and delicate operation." Lord Estael's wintry expression grew icier still. "For there to be any hope of it succeeding at all, the Rift must be stable. The consequences of failure are too dreadful to be imagined."

Ormas silently alighted on Rieuk's shoulder. Rieuk closed his eyes, relieved beyond words that the smoke hawk had not flown too far into the Rift and abandoned him. *Don't leave me like that again, Ormas. You're all that I have now, my only companion.*

"If you don't bring Azilis back to us, Rieuk, there's a very real risk that next time you set Ormas loose in the Rift, he may not return at all."

Had Lord Estael read his thoughts? Rieuk drew in a slow, resigned breath. "Very well. I'll do it. I'll go back to Francia."

"Don't stay too long within the Rift," Lord Estael had warned. "Even with our Emissaries' protection, our bodies are not able to tolerate the rarefied atmosphere for long."

Imri's tomb shimmered dully in the hazy light in the clearing at the foot of the Emerald Tower. The clear crystal had become more opaque, as if layers of ice had encrusted the case, making it harder to see Imri's still form within. Yet just to glimpse the indistinct outlines of those familiar, beloved features, so perfectly preserved within the aethyr crystal, brought sudden tears to Rieuk's long-dry eyes.

"I couldn't leave again without seeing you once more." Rieuk slipped to his knees, one hand touching the chill aethyr crystal. "Where are you, Imri?" he whispered. "Can you still hear me?" He slowly let his head rest against the casket, close to Imri's. "Are you at peace?" He could not forget what he had done to Paol. The child's spirit had been so frail and vulnerable out of his body. "Or are you in torment, trapped in the soul-glass? If only you could tell me. I don't want to make you suffer." All he wanted was to hear Imri's voice, gently, affectionately chiding him as he often had when they were together. "I keep telling myself that this is all for you, to give you your life again, but am I deceiving myself? Am I being selfish, wanting to bring you back from the dead?"

The dreamlike atmosphere within the Rift must have begun to affect him . . . or was the growing numbness he felt seeping from the chill of the aethyr crystal? A slight breeze stirred the branches of the trees nearby and set the hairs at the nape of Rieuk's neck prickling. Was it his imagination? Or had he felt the touch of invisible hands drifting a brief caress?

He raised his head. There, on the edge of the clearing, half-clothed in shadow, stood Imri, his black hair loose about his shoulders.

"Imri?" Yet there was something indistinct about his lover, as though a gauzy veil was separating them, softly trembling in the breeze from the Rift. Yet Rieuk found himself stumbling headlong toward him, hands outstretched, even though sense told him that he could not embrace a shade. "Is it really you?"

"*Stay with me, Rieuk. Stay here.*"

"Rieuk." A harsh voice was calling his name. He felt the sting of a hand-slap across his face. "Rieuk, wake up!"

"No," Rieuk murmured angrily. "Go away. Leave us be."

"*Stay with me, Rieuk . . .*"

"Us?" Someone gripped him by the shoulders, pulling him to his feet. "You fool! I warned you not to stay in here too long."

Groggily, Rieuk opened his eyes to see Lord Estael glaring at him. "But Imri was here—"

"Look around you! There's no one here but ourselves."

CHAPTER 15

Sister Kinnie bustled down the chapel aisle, accompanied by a chestnut-haired girl.

The Skylarks' singing wavered. Celestine tried to keep her gaze fixed on Sister Noyale's moving hands as they shaped the contours of the musical line and marked the beat. Sensing that Rozenne and Koulmia had lost concentration too, she stared at the visitor . . . and thus failed to notice the ominous frown wrinkling the choir-mistress's face.

"New girl," muttered Katell and then, too late, clapped a hand over her mouth.

Sister Noyale's dark eyes narrowed. Her hands dropped. The singing raggedly petered out. She beckoned to Katell.

Katell hesitated.

"Out here. *Now.*"

Celestine had a sinking feeling. Sister Noyale had an implacable look that all the Skylarks knew well. At one time or another, each girl had transgressed in choir practice and learned to regret it. But impulsive Katell never seemed to remember.

"Did I hear you speak, Katell?" Sister Noyale was deliberately ignoring Sister Kinnie and the new girl.

Katell nodded, eyes lowered.

"Hold out your hands."

Celestine instinctively clenched her own fists, knowing what must come next.

Katell held out her hands, palms up. The sharp swish of Sister

Noyale's leather strap slapped down once, twice. Celestine winced, as did the other twenty-two Skylarks, feeling the stinging pain in sympathy with Katell.

"Return to your place." Sister Noyale placed the strap back on her music stand, her face impassive. Then she turned to Sister Kinnie and the new girl. "I will not tolerate any chatter in my rehearsals," she said crisply, staring at the girl as she spoke. "So you must be Gauzia."

"Demoiselle Gauzia de Saint-Désirat," said the newcomer in a clear, cool voice. "Youngest daughter of the Vicomte de Saint-Désirat." She stared back boldly at the choirmistress, with dark-lashed hazel eyes, more green than gold.

"So you are a vicomte's daughter?" Sister Noyale repeated in a disparaging tone the Skylarks knew well. Celestine sensed the other girls squirming, partly in embarrassment, partly in anticipation of the put-down to come. "Here we are all equal in the eyes of God, all servants of the Blessed Azilia. And I hope for your sake that you have some semblance of a singing voice, or you'll soon become very well acquainted with the convent kitchens."

Gauzia seemed not in the least cowed by Sister Noyale's chilly welcome. "What would you like me to sing for you?"

Koulmia gasped and several of the older Skylarks nudged each other. Celestine watched Gauzia, impressed in spite of herself by the new girl's self-confidence.

"I take it that you have prepared something?"

Gauzia cleared her throat, softly hummed a single pitch, and, clasping her hands together at her breast, began to sing. Celestine recognized the melancholy cadences of the old evening hymn "Guard Us Through This Night." Gauzia's voice was low but strong and sweet. She had been well trained, Celestine realized with a little pang of envy; she knew exactly when to take a breath as well as how to shape a phrase. And she used her soulful eyes to good effect; Celestine observed Sister Kinnie smiling and nodding her head in time as she listened.

"Your voice is strongest in the lower register," said Sister Noyale as Gauzia reached the end of the second verse. "Go and stand in the back row. To my right. Make room for her, Katell and Margaud."

Gauzia stared at her, mouth a little open, as if about to object.

She did not look too pleased to be placed on the back row. Then she closed her mouth, pressing her lips together. Celestine, unable to quell her curiosity, turned around to watch her. So did the rest of the front row.

Sister Noyale tapped her music stand briskly with her baton. "Any girl not looking in my direction will stay behind to polish the candlesticks instead of having her supper."

In the dormitory, the Skylarks clustered around the new girl, chirping questions. Celestine found herself on the outside of the circle, unaccountably reluctant to join in.

Am I just a little jealous of her?

"No, I'm not an orphan." Gauzia seemed so self-assured, answering as she unpacked her few belongings. "But my father made a vow that one of his children should be given to the church. I'm the youngest of six sisters. By the time he'd paid for my sisters' dowries, there was nothing left for me." She spoke in such a matter-of-fact tone as she shook out her woollen stockings that it sounded as if she had merely been forgotten when a tray of sweetmeats was being shared around, rather than being confined to a convent for life.

"But that's so unfair!" cried Katell.

Gauzia shrugged. "My oldest sister died in childbirth last month. My next sister was married off to a vile-tempered colonel who stinks of brandy. My—"

"We understand, we understand," chorused the girls.

Gauzia ignored them, staring at Celestine, the only one not joining in. "You're very quiet. What's your name?" The question was not framed in the friendliest of tones.

"Celestine."

"Just Celestine?" The bold hazel eyes challenged her. "Don't you even know your father's name? Or perhaps you never had a father." There was barely concealed scorn in Gauzia's voice now. Celestine opened her mouth to reply, and then remembered. When Maman lay dying Klervie had promised her never to reveal Papa's name. She closed her mouth again. None of the Skylarks had ever questioned her about her parentage. The Abbess had told them she was an orphan, rescued from the slums of Lutèce.

"Does it matter? We're all orphans here," said Rozenne, placing her arms around Celestine's shoulders protectively. "We leave family ties outside the convent walls."

Celestine leaned back against Rozenne, grateful beyond words that she had come to her rescue.

Gauzia shrugged and turned back to her unpacking, but not without giving Celestine a long, penetrating look. This matter was not over, Celestine sensed it, even as she nestled against Rozenne.

That night she dreamed of fire again.

The pyre burns so fiercely that she can feel the heat on her skin as she and Maman cower in a doorway. "Don't make a sound," warns Maman. But the stench of burning human flesh chokes her and she begins to cough and retch.

Garbed in black, the faceless soldiers seize her and start to drag her toward the flames. "Maman, save me!" she shrieks, but the shadowy crowd surges around her and her mother's anguished face disappears from sight.

At first it was just a malicious glance or a snide little comment. But one rainy morning, as the Skylarks were coming out of chapel after a rehearsal punctuated by coughs and sneezing, Gauzia hurried after Celestine and Rozenne, holding out a little cloth bag.

"You're on kitchen duty? Sister Noyale gave me these spices to put in the soup today. She says they're medicinal and will help to cure the sore throats. But only put in three spoonfuls."

If it was Sister Noyale's instructions, Celestine reasoned as she stirred the black spices into the soup, it must be all right.

"Are you certain it was three spoonfuls?" Rozenne asked, ladling out the soup at lunchtime.

But when the sisters and the girls started to drink the soup, there were cries of disgust and much coughing and spluttering.

"What is the meaning of this?" Sister Noyale marched up to the two girls. "Are you trying to poison us?" Her eyes were watering. "Have you even tasted this soup?"

Celestine glanced unhappily at Rozenne. She shook her head.

"Try it now," insisted Sister Noyale.

Reluctantly, Celestine lifted a spoonful to her mouth and swallowed. It burned like fire. "P—pepper," she wheezed.

"You can pour the soup down the drain; not even the pigs will touch it. Then you can spend the afternoon scrubbing out the washrooms and latrines. Perhaps that will teach you both to take more care with your cooking and not waste good ingredients!"

As Celestine straightened up to stretch her aching back, she saw Gauzia watching her and Rozenne from the washroom doorway, a little smile on her lips.

"You set us up!" said Rozenne. "You told us to put three spoonfuls in the soup."

"Oh, did I say three spoonfuls? How silly of me; I must have got mixed up. I think Sister Noyale said three pinches. You really shouldn't pay any attention to me, I know nothing about kitchen work. That was all done by the servants . . ." Gauzia's knowing expression belied the innocent tone of her voice as she walked off.

"That stuck-up demoiselle Gauzia. Her kind just makes me so—so *angry*."

Celestine looked in surprise at Rozenne. Her friend was sitting back on her haunches, scrubbing brush in hand, staring into the middle distance. Even-tempered, always ready to greet everyone she met with a smile or a kind word, Rozenne was never angry.

"Her kind?" ventured Celestine.

"She's a noble's child. She's had an easy life. She's never had to go without food or shoes . . . or a safe place to sleep at night. She has no cause to mock those less fortunate than herself."

Celestine nodded, pressing her hand over her stomach. "Hunger *hurts*." She would never forget how it felt to go without food from one day's end to the next, that desperate, gnawing, all-pervading emptiness. She looked up to see Rozenne still lost in memory.

"It hurts all the more when you know your father is living a fine life, while you go without."

"*Your* father?" Rozenne had not once spoken of her family. "Your father is still alive?"

Rozenne shrugged and dipped her brush in the water, scrubbing a new patch of floor with vigor. "My mother was maid to a great lady in Lutèce. She looked after her fine clothes, dressed her hair. But the lady's husband fell in love with my mother. When the lady discovered what had been happening, she turned my mother out without a sou. My mother had to go to the Salpêtrière, where I was born. They made her work very hard. When I was five, she died of consumption."

"Oh, Rozenne." So they had both lost their mothers to sickness. "But how did you come here?"

"She was always writing letters to my father. She told him that he should look after me, his daughter, if anything ever happened to her. She used to cry whenever she mentioned his name."

"You know who he is?"

"He's one of the convent benefactors. So he arranged for me to come here. But on one condition: that I never tell anyone that he's my father. I'm not supposed to know. Only the Abbess knows."

Celestine tried to imagine what it must feel like to be in Rozenne's place. She knew she would not be satisfied with just a name, she would yearn to discover everything about her negligent father. "But have you ever seen him? Has he been here?"

Rozenne nodded. "Once he came here on Saint Azilia's Day. With his wife and daughters."

"Your *sisters*?"

"Half sisters."

"How can you bear to know that?" cried Celestine. "How can you sing so sweetly, Rozenne, when you know that he wronged you and your mother?"

"I just can." Rozenne bent over her scrubbing. "Sister Kinnie says we must learn to endure. She says such wise things. I want to be like her, one day."

"Endure?" Celestine sat back on her heels. The pyre flames from her dream suddenly flared across her mind. "I don't think I could ever learn to do that. There are things that I'll never be able to forget—or forgive."

"Dear sisters, I have exciting news." The Abbess's voice trembled as she addressed the nuns and novices in the chapel. "We are to entertain a visitor. A very special visitor. Captain de Lanvaux is to celebrate Saint Azilia's Day with us."

Katell nudged Celestine sharply in the ribs. "Look, she's blushing!" Celestine looked and saw that Katell was right. A rosy flush had suffused the Abbess's skin when she mentioned the captain's name. "The good captain has just returned from a pilgrimage to Saint Sergius's Shrine in Azhkendir and he has generously agreed to tell us about his journey. And so, even though it is our blessed Azilia's Day, Sister Noyale has decided to add an extra choral work to honor our guest. 'Hymn to Saint Sergius' by . . . by . . ." The Abbess glanced pleadingly at Sister Noyale, obviously having forgotten the significant details.

"By an Allegondan composer, Talfieri. It has a demanding solo part too, so I shall be testing all our strongest singers," and Sister Noyale's keen gaze swept across the girls, "to see who is the most suitable."

"It should be *you*," Katell mouthed at Celestine.

Celestine shook her head. She was not sure she was ready for a demanding solo.

The instant the girls came out into the convent courtyard, they all began to chatter at once.

"They say the captain's very handsome," said Rozenne, with a yearning sigh. "And courageous too . . ."

"*My* father thinks the king favors him over Maistre Donatien." Gauzia's voice, full of self-importance, carried over the others.

"Has your father been to court?" asked Koulmia, wide-eyed. "Has he met the king?"

"Well, of course he has, he's a nobleman," came back Gauzia's tart reply.

"And you? Have you been to the Palais de Plaisaunces?" Skylarks crowded eagerly around her. "Or Belle Garde?"

"Well, I've seen King Gobain and Queen Aliénor." Gauzia gave a toss of her chestnut curls. "And Crown Prince Aubrey. He's so good-looking. Dark-haired, like his father, broad-shouldered . . ." Several Skylarks let out squeals of excitement.

"You should be the one to sing solo, Gauzia," said Koulmia fervently.

"Koulmia!" Katell tugged her plait hard.

"What was that for?" Koulmia said.

"What about our Celestine? Huh! Call yourself a friend?"

Celestine turned hastily away, but not before she had seen Gauzia fix her with a penetrating stare.

———

Ruaud de Lanvaux surveyed the congregation and wondered what he was doing addressing this avid audience of nuns and little girls. For it could not just be an illusion created by the golden shimmer of candleflames; he was certain that all the eyes staring at him shone with an air of almost . . . adoration. Certainly the atmosphere in the flower-garlanded chapel was uncannily hushed; not even one of the little girls had coughed as they gazed up at him. He recovered himself and murmured a prayer to Saint Azilia before he began his talk.

"Sisters," he began, and saw them all eagerly lean forward. "I have recently returned from a long journey. A hazardous pilgrimage that took me through a wild and barbaric land to find the last resting place of the bones of the patron saint of my order: the Blessed Sergius." As he spoke, he soon forgot the adoring eyes, losing himself in vivid memories of his travels: the icy White Sea, the sinister pine forests, the grey desolation of the Arkhel Waste . . .

"Who is your new little songbird, Abbess?" Ruaud asked after the service. "When she sings, that girl has a radiant, luminous quality . . . almost as if she were not of this world."

"It is you we have to thank for bringing her to us," said the Abbess, smiling fondly at him.

Ruaud blinked. "She's not that poor, half-starved little scrap I found wandering in the slums!" The snow-chilled memories of Azhkendir melted away as he saw again the ragged child wander blindly out in front of Tinidor, clutching her *Lives of the Holy Saints*. Those matted locks, framing a thin, dirt-streaked face, those blue eyes, dulled with despair and fever . . .

"The very same."

"You and the sisters have wrought a miracle." There was no suggestion of flattery in his words; he was genuinely amazed that in a few years his little foundling had blossomed into this angel-voiced girl. "May I see her?"

"Don't be shy." The Abbess beamed indulgently at Celestine as she hovered at the entrance to the parlor, uncertain as to why she had been summoned. "Captain de Lanvaux asked to see you."

Celestine ventured in, keeping her gaze fixed on the painted floor tiles, not daring to raise her head. She saw the captain's travel-worn leather boots and the long scabbard that hung from his belt. She saw the black jacket of his Guerrier's uniform—the same uniform worn by the men who had arrested her father. Searing hatred burned through her at the sight as the memories she had tried to suppress flared up, fierce as the flames of her father's pyre.

"Don't be afraid," said the captain gently.

How could anyone wearing that hated uniform speak with such warmth and sincerity?

"You owe Captain de Lanvaux your life," said the Abbess. "It was he who found you, ill and abandoned, and brought you to us."

Celestine slowly raised her head. "*You* rescued me?" She dared to look into his face and saw that he had tempered his steely gaze and was regarding her kindly.

"You don't remember me, do you, Celestine? Tinidor and I carried you here." His weather-tanned face crinkled into a smile.

"Tinidor?" She repeated the unfamiliar name mechanically.

"My charger. He's stabled here today. Would you like to meet him again? You could give him an apple; he loves apples."

"You saved my life?" Celestine was still trying to come to terms with the fact that one of the men who had destroyed her father had also been her savior.

"And having heard you sing today, I am doubly glad that I did so. You have a real gift, a God-given gift, Celestine. If you continue to work hard at your singing, I'm sure you will be chosen to sing in the royal chapel one day."

Celestine hardly heard the compliments. She was staring at the golden insignia on the collar, lapels, and cuffs of the uniform jacket.

"What do those mean?" she asked, pointing.

"Celestine!" Abbess Ermengarde said in shocked tones. "You mustn't speak so rudely to the captain."

"These?" Captain de Lanvaux beckoned Celestine closer. "This is the badge of the Order of Saint Sergius. Can you see the emblem of his crook? The crook with which he fought the Dragon of Azhkendir?"

Celestine had not been so close to a man since she entered the convent. Now, standing at the captain's side, examining the gilt buttons on his cuff, she felt overwhelmed. His skin exuded a different scent from the clean, soap-scrubbed smell of the Sisters, strong and rich as leather, salty like a breeze off the bay. She was aware of the slight hint of fair stubble on his tanned face, and remembered the roughness of her father's cheek when he kissed her good night . . .

The Guerriers who had arrested her father had worn different insignia on their black jackets.

"Then what do the emerald badges mean?"

"Emerald?" A puzzled look came over his face. "Ah. You must have seen the Guerriers of the Inquisition. But when—"

"The Inquisition," Celestine repeated slowly so that she should not forget. "What is the Inquisition?"

The Abbess clapped her hands sharply. "That's quite enough questions, child! Isn't there something you have to say to Captain de Lanvaux?"

Celestine wrenched her thoughts away from the black-clad shadows that still stalked her nightmares. Now they had a name: the Guerriers of the Inquisition. She was glad that Captain de Lanvaux was not one of their number. She raised her face to his again and, dazzled by the affectionate look he gave her, whispered, "Thank you, Captain de Lanvaux, for saving my life."

Tinidor let out an uneasy whinny and stamped one of his great hooves as Ruaud came into the stables.

"What's up, old fellow?" Ruaud stroked the charger's shaggy mane to calm him.

"Good evening, Captain." A dark-haired man appeared, his features half-illumined by the gilded aura of lamplight. How had he got in past the sentry? "Don't worry; I'm not an assassin." He smiled, revealing dazzlingly white teeth.

"If you were an assassin, I'd be dead by now." Ruaud spoke self-deprecatingly but inwardly he cursed himself for being so careless about his personal security.

"I make it my business to come and go unannounced, unseen. Let me introduce myself; my name is Abrissard. Fabien d'Abrissard."

Ruaud looked coldly at the stranger. "Should I know you?"

"The reason you've never seen me before, Captain, is that my job is to remain invisible. I and my kind deal with matters others would rather not dirty their hands with."

"You're a spy?"

" 'Spy' is such a crude term," said Abrissard fastidiously. "We prefer to refer to ourselves as agents of the crown. And our royal master asked me to have a little word with you before you take on your new role as Prince Enguerrand's tutor."

"So his majesty doesn't have complete confidence in me?"

"On the contrary. He chose you himself, purposely going against her majesty's advice."

"Let me guess; the queen favored Maistre Donatien?"

"It's no secret that she relies on Maistre Donatien rather too much since her brother's death."

"Is Prince Enguerrand in any danger?"

"No. But, as his tutor, you may be. There are dangerous undercurrents, Captain, beneath the smooth-flowing waters of court life. Old allies may come to see you as an unexpected obstacle to their ambitions."

"I see." Ruaud heard the warning concealed in Abrissard's metaphorical language.

"Just take this as a friendly piece of advice." And with an enigmatic smile, the agent of the crown was gone, slipping into the night as swiftly as he had arrived, leaving Ruaud with more questions than answers.

CHAPTER 16

Dark, charred ruins crowned the hill where once the college had towered above Karantec.

Rieuk stood staring at the devastation that had been his home for seven years. His throat had gone dry. His palms were cold and sweaty. He wished he had not been forced to come back. He laid his hand on his breast, gaining reassurance as he felt the slumbering Ormas quiver at his touch.

The cottage where Rieuk had last seen Hervé's daughter happily playing with her tabby cat had a sad, neglected air. The windows were boarded up, slates had fallen from the roof, and weeds were sprouting up vigorously all over the little garden.

A neighbor was sitting out by her front door, shelling peas.

"Can I help you?" she called in a loud tone that suggested help was the last thing she wanted to offer.

"I'm looking for Madame de Maunoir." He hoped she would not recognize him; the thick-lensed spectacles and white-silvered streak in his hair gave him the air of someone older than his twenty-two years.

"She's long gone."

"So I see. Would you happen to know where?"

"What's your business?" The woman put down the bowl of peas and scraped the empty pods from her apron into a bucket beside her chair.

"I'm a lawyer," said Rieuk. "I have news for her."

"Well, she's gone, and good riddance. Her husband was involved in some bad business. Last I heard, he was tried and burned with his treasonable books. No more than he deserved."

The barely disguised loathing in the woman's voice shocked Rieuk. The people of Karantec used to accept the magisters, taking a certain pride in their unconventional residents living on the hill. The Inquisition's campaign had changed all that.

"So you have no idea where we might find Madame de Maunoir and her daughter?"

"They followed him to the city. That's the last we heard of them."

"I see that the house is empty."

"No one will live there. They say it's cursed." The woman stood up, wiping her hands on her apron. "Is it a legacy, then? Has she come into some money?" There was an unpleasantly avaricious gleam in her eyes.

"I can divulge nothing, except to my Madame de Maunoir," said Rieuk, looking at her coldly over the rims of his spectacles.

"She had a sister in the capital. That's all I know." She took up the bowl and shuffled inside, slamming the door behind her.

Around the back of the deserted cottage, a shutter had been prised open and hung at an awkward angle, one hinge detached. Rieuk leaned over the windowsill and peered inside. He hardly recognized the interior of Madame de Maunoir's neat and pretty cottage. Someone had scrawled obscene graffiti all over the whitewashed walls. A few fragments of smashed china lay on the dirt-smeared tiled floor.

Rieuk turned away, wishing he had not troubled to look.

There were armed Guerriers out on patrol in the streets of Lutèce, and the very sight of their black uniforms set Rieuk's nerves on edge. It had taken him several days' intensive research in the records at the Hotel de Ville to discover Madame de Maunoir's family name, and several more days to trace details of any surviving relatives.

"And why should I talk to you?" Lavéna Malestroit stared at him with unconcealed hostility. "Isn't it customary with lawyers to put their business in writing first?"

"Very well, madame." Rieuk turned away. "We'll find some other way of contacting your sister."

"M—my sister?" Rieuk heard a catch in Madame Malestroit's voice.

"Didn't I say so? It's to do with the title deeds of her cottage in Karantec . . ."

"You've had a wasted journey. My sister is dead."

"Dead? Then you must be caring for her daughter, Klervie?"

Rieuk saw Madame Malestroit swallow hard. She seemed to be finding it hard to speak. "Klervie—is gone, too."

Klervie was dead?

"I should have taken the child in." Madame Malestroit began to sob. "After my sister died, that money-grubbing landlady couldn't even look after a little girl for a day or two. She turned her out. Oh, *her* story was that she'd sent Klervie to find me, but the child never arrived. I was told that a fair-haired child was seen nearby with a—a man. All they recovered was a shoe, her little shoe, muddy and bloodstained."

"She was murdered?"

She nodded, one hand pressed to her mouth, as though even speaking the words aloud made her want to retch. "Sick, evil pervert, preying on children. They never caught him."

So Klervie was dead. The image of the bright-haired child smiling up at him faded, tainted by the news of her sorry end. He retreated, stammering an apology. "I—I'm sorry to have disturbed you."

Rieuk sat down at a café in the nearby square and ordered coffee and a brandy. He rarely drank spirits but he was so shaken by the news that his hand trembled as he raised the glass to his lips. He drank the brandy down in one gulp, grimacing as it burned his throat. He had left without asking the weeping Madame Malestroit whether her sister had left any effects behind, let alone what had become of them.

Yet if Azilis had been in that house, surely I would have sensed her. I felt nothing. So where do I look for her now?

Hervé de Maunoir's book could have been sold off to an antiquarian bookseller, a private library, a university . . . A long and difficult search lay ahead of him. He ordered a second brandy and drank it in slow, ruminative sips, savoring the taste of burned sugar, wondering as he watched the passersby what new identity he would be forced to take. Scholar, collector, even Inquisition spy . . . ?

Was it just chance, or were all the lives Azilis had touched fated to end in tragedy?

CHAPTER 17

Winter at the convent was cold and dreary that year, drenched by frequent storms and persistent rain. The skies above the promontory on which Saint Azilia's Convent stood were perpetually daubed with a wash of cloudy grey, and even though the girls labored hard to keep the fires burning, a chill dampness pervaded every room of the convent.

"Snow would be better than this constant rain," complained Katell as she and Celestine carried firewood up the winding stairs to stoke the brazier in the Skylarks' dormitory. "At least we could play snowballs." The sound of persistent coughing echoed in the stairwell. "Listen to that!" Katell puffed. "Sister Noyale won't be pleased if the entire choir falls sick."

It was Katell's last month as a Skylark; in the spring, she and Rozenne would be old enough to move to the Novices' dormitory. The Novices followed a much more rigorous routine than the Skylarks, often singing for services late into the night. Celestine could not begin to imagine how she would endure life without Katell and Rozenne at her side. She had come to rely so much on the older girls that the thought of losing their companionship was hard to bear. There would still be Koulmia, of course, and a couple of others who grudgingly accepted her into their conversations, but Gauzia had divided the dormitory into factions, and Koulmia, fascinated by the charismatic Demoiselle de Saint-Désirat, was drifting away. Now there was whispering and nudging in the ranks whenever Sister Noyale singled Celestine out to sing a solo. Resentful glances, even snide comments could regularly be detected from Gauzia's followers.

The two girls trudged across the dormitory floor toward the brazier, where Katell let her bucket of firewood drop with a clang. Koulmia wandered over to greet them, wrapped in her blanket. "It's freezing up here," she complained.

"We'll get a good blaze going soon." Katell knelt to rake the faintly glowing embers. "Pass me those little sticks first, Celestine." A fierce gust of wind suddenly made the shutters rattle. Koulmia began to cough, a raw, ragged sound, and Celestine saw from the way she hunched her shoulders that it hurt.

"You don't look so well," said Katell, glancing up from the cinders she was raking. "Shall I take you to see Sister Kinnie in the Infirmary?"

"I'm just cold," said Koulmia. Her teeth were chattering. "Besides, I heard all the beds are full. Rozenne's gone to help."

"I thought only the Novices were allowed to help Sister Kinnie."

"All the Novices are ill. It's the lung sickness."

Celestine said nothing but a tight little knot of fear had begun to form in her stomach. Maman had fallen sick and she had never recovered. She glanced at her friends—Katell, a smear of ashes darkening her forehead as she stoked the fire; Koulmia, pale-lipped and shivering—and knew that she could not bear to lose anyone else she loved.

In the middle of the afternoon rehearsal, the youngest Skylark suddenly gave a sigh and crumpled to the floor. Sister Noyale shooed the others away as they hovered anxiously around her.

"Have you no sense, girls? Move back and give Karine some air!"

She knelt by the unconscious little girl and felt her brow and pulse. "Katell, run on ahead to the Infirmary. Gauzia, take charge while I'm gone."

The instant Sister Noyale left the chapel carrying Karine in her arms, there was an alarmed burst of chatter.

"I'm not staying in this plague-ridden place a day longer than I have to," declared Gauzia. "I've written to my father. He's sure to come for me. Or at the very least send his carriage."

"That's all very well for you, Gauzia," said one of her friends, red-haired Deneza, "but what about the rest of us? Will there be room for us in that carriage too?"

"Well, I couldn't rightly say. It would depend on my father. If the decision were down to me, you would all come," said Gauzia, pointedly addressing her adoring little circle, her back turned on Celestine.

Katell arrived back, out of breath, in time to hear this last remark. "I thought you were in charge here, Gauzia. Yet all I can hear is idle gossip. Don't you know how to conduct the choir?"

Celestine woke in the darkest hour of night. Someone was coughing incessantly. Peeping out from under her blanket, she saw by the wavering light of a lantern that Sister Kinnie and her assistant, young Sister Eurielle, were bending over Koulmia's bed.

"She's too sick to move," Sister Kinnie said in a low voice. "Besides, where would we put her? All the Infirmary beds are taken."

"But the risk to the other Skylarks?"

Sister Kinnie gave a weary little shrug. "What can we do? Like as not, they'll catch the sickness too."

"We just have to pray that they're healthy enough to pull through."

"Please get better, Koulmia," whispered Celestine.

The astringent medicinal odor of fumigating herbs made Celestine's eyes sting when she returned to the dormitory after completing her day's work in the kitchen.

"You must drink some of this chicken broth," insisted Rozenne, holding a cup to Koulmia's lips. "It'll give you the strength to get better."

Celestine saw Koulmia pull a face and turn her head away.

"Koulmia must be really sick," remarked Katell. "She usually eats anything."

"Do not . . ."

"You do so!"

"I helped Rozenne make the broth," Celestine said coaxingly. "We put in thyme and bay leaves, the herbs we picked and dried in the summer sun. Remember?" A draft shivered through the dormitory, making the door and shutters creak. Koulmia began to cough again, a harsh rattling sound. "Summer seems so far away now."

Rozenne rose from Koulmia's bedside. "I'll bring you some of Sister Kinnie's coltsfoot linctus. And another poultice to ease your throat." As she moved toward the door, she staggered, slopping broth onto the floor. Katell and Celestine hurried to her and caught her by the arms, supporting her.

"What's wrong?" demanded Katell.

Rozenne managed a weak smile. "Just tired. I haven't had much sleep recently."

Celestine felt a little stab of apprehension. Had Rozenne caught the fever too? She looked very pale, just as Koulmia had done before the heat of the fever began to sear her.

"Go and lie down. We'll fetch the linctus, won't we, Celestine?"

Celestine nodded vigorously.

"But there's so much to do . . ." Rozenne began to protest as Katell steered her toward her bed.

"Sleep. That's an order from Doctor Katell!"

Celestine took the cup from her and Rozenne slumped down onto the bed without any further protest. Katell tucked the blanket around her and beckoned Celestine away.

All night long, the raw, repetitive sound of Koulmia's coughing infiltrated Celestine's dreams. Toward dawn, she woke suddenly, sitting upright in bed, certain that someone had called her name.

Someone was coughing, but it wasn't Koulmia. It was Rozenne.

Celestine wrapped her blanket around her against the penetrating draft and shuffled across the cold floorboards to Rozenne's bedside. Her friend lay huddled up in the bedclothes, her body shaking with suppressed coughing.

"Rozenne," Celestine whispered. "What's wrong?"

Rozenne half opened her eyes. She seemed to have trouble focusing on Celestine's face.

"Shall I get you a drink?"

Rozenne nodded. Her face was pale, with hectic blotches darkening her cheeks. Celestine poured boiled barley water into a beaker and brought it to her. Rozenne seemed barely to have the strength to raise the beaker to her lips, and as soon as she had drunk a mouthful began to cough again.

"Oh, Rozenne, you're sick."

Rozenne nodded. "I thought I was strong, Celestine." She managed a weak, self-deprecating smile. "You should stay away from me. I don't want you to get sick too." She sank back onto the mattress. "You must protect your voice . . ."

Celestine felt another little twinge of fear. Rozenne had been like a big sister to her. She stretched out her hand to stroke Rozenne's head and felt how hot and damp her temples were beneath the unplaited strands of hair. She remembered how helpless she had felt standing at Maman's bedside as she lay murmuring incoherently in fever. If she acted now, there was still time to save Rozenne.

A bell tolled softly in the dawn. Sister Kinnie's face looked drawn and grey as she leaned over Rozenne's bed to take her pulse.

"She's too ill to be moved to the Infirmary. Although now there's two spare beds . . ." She spoke in a low, distracted voice as if she were talking to herself.

"What?" Gauzia said sharply, sitting up in bed. "Two?"

"We lost Aoda and little Karine in the night." Sister Kinnie wiped away a tear with her handkerchief.

"They *died*?" Gauzia's exclamation echoed around the dormitory; now all the other Skylarks were awake and staring in shock at one another.

"Hush, Gauzia. You'll upset the younger ones."

"Upset them?" Gauzia echoed contemptuously. "Don't you think they'll want to know where Karine has gone? What do we tell them? Lies?"

"You will tell them that it was God's will that the children were taken away from us." Celestine had never heard Sister Kinnie speak so sternly before. "Now get started on your day's chores, all of you. We will pray for our little sisters' souls in chapel later today."

"If the Abbess had called in a proper doctor, instead of relying on country remedies, this would never have happened." Gauzia's voice rose in pitch, unusually shrill and harsh. She gazed round at the other girls as they knuckled the sleep dust from their eyes. "And now we're all like to die of the lung sickness because Rozenne is 'too ill to be moved.' We're all breathing the same contagion in the air."

Celestine, her own emotions dulled by lack of sleep, realized that even the indomitable Gauzia was afraid.

"So where's your father and his famous carriage, then?" demanded a wry voice. Katell was glaring at Gauzia, her hands on her hips. "I thought he was coming to take you away from this plague pit?"

"He'll be here. It's a long way from our estate. But I know the carriage will come soon." But Celestine noticed a distinct hint of desperation in Gauzia's voice.

Celestine had never gone to pray in the chapel alone before. She pushed open the side door and stood a moment, gazing in wonder. A glow of saffron candlelight warmed the darkness, soft flames blooming like luminous saffron crocuses.

She took three slender candles from the box and lit them, placing them with the others before Saint Azilia's statue. "Onc for Aoda, one for Karine, one for Rozenne . . ." The shimmer was reflected in the statue's eyes of blue glass, glinting in the gold leaf gilding her long carved tresses. If she glanced up, it looked almost as if Azilia were alive and silently watching her.

But no . . . it must just be her imagination. She knelt and, clasping her hands together, raised her eyes to the saint's painted features and whispered, "Please, Blessed Azilia, please don't let Rozenne die."

The statue smiled calmly, distantly down at her. "I'll give you whatever you ask. I'll cut my hair." Celestine tried to think of some other, greater sacrifice that she could make. "I'll stay here and become a nun. I'll devote the rest of my life to the convent. Only please intercede for her. She's . . ." and Celestine felt tears welling up, ". . . she's always looked after me. Now I have to look after her."

Still the statue graced her with its benevolent, distant smile. Celestine wiped her eyes on her sleeve and stood up. Would her prayers be answered? A flicker of doubt entered her mind. How did prayer work? She was addressing an inanimate piece of carved stone. Did the chapel act as a conduit? Were her words carried to Azilia's spirit in the Ways Beyond mingled with the scented candlesmoke? And how could a spirit bring healing to an ailing mortal? Her own Faie had failed to help Maman when she lay dying . . .

Too many questions, too many doubts.

Celestine clapped her hands over her ears as if in doing so she could block out all these uncomfortable, troubling ideas that had begun to assail her. "Forgive me, Blessed Azilia. I shouldn't be thinking such terrible thoughts."

But if Rozenne doesn't recover, what will it mean? That my prayers weren't answered because I'm not worthy? Still the questions kept coming and each one punctured another hole in her faltering belief. *Or will she die because I didn't pray hard enough? Or because I dared to question your powers?*

After Maman's death, she had vowed never to let herself feel so vulnerable ever again. If only she had not let herself grow to care for Rozenne, if only she had kept herself armored against such strong feelings, she would not feel so weak and helpless now. As Celestine crossed the dark courtyard, shivering in the icy wind, she knew in her heart that no friend could ever replace Rozenne.

After all the lights were extinguished except the night-lights, Celestine slid out her father's book from its hiding place beneath her bolster. The Faie, in its guise as Saint Azilia, gazed at her, its eyes luminous in the darkness.

How different from the bland painted smile of the statue in the chapel. Even touching the book sent a little tingle through her fingertips; she could feel the Faie's power emanating from the pages.

"I need your help," she whispered. "My friend is very sick. I think she may be dying. Please, dear Faie, is there anything you can do for her?"

"*Mortal child, is your memory so short?*" The Faie's eyes gleamed, like moonlight silvering clear water. "*Don't you remember? I protect you, and you alone.*"

"But you're a Faie. You're supposed to grant wishes." Celestine's throat ached with the effort of holding back her tears.

"*I can no more heal your friend than I could your mother.*"

"If"—and Celestine clutched the book tightly—"if I were to bind you to Rozenne instead of me, could you heal her then?"

"*I am bound to you and you alone.*"

"So there's nothing I can do to save her?" This feeling of utter helplessness brought back the black, bleak terrors of those lonely days in Lutèce. She slid to the floor, crushing the book to her, her only comfort and shield against a rising tide of fear.

Fever candles burned in the hushed dormitory, emitting the scent of cleansing herbs to fumigate the air and to ease the labored breathing of the sick girls. But even the medicinal vapors could not mask the sickly stale sickroom odor that now seemed to permeate the whole building.

Katell sat at Rozenne's bedside, her head drooping. Celestine touched her shoulder and she started awake, rubbing her eyes.

"How is she?"

"Still very feverish. Sister Kinnie says to sponge her with a damp cloth. But every time I do, she shivers and pulls away, as if it's hurting." Katell gripped Celestine's hand, staring up into her face, her eyes clouded with worry. "Celestine, I don't want to hurt her. It's bad enough that she's sick. But to make her cry out like that . . . it can't be doing her any good."

Celestine held on to Katell's hand. Another shiver of apprehension went through her body as she looked at Rozenne. A strange rattling, wheezing sound was coming from her throat. She seemed to be struggling to breathe.

"Katell," she said, remembering hearing that sound once before in a drab attic room in Lutèce. "Go fetch Sister Kinnie. Go now!"

For once Katell didn't stop to argue. Celestine leaned over the bed. She stroked Rozenne's face and her hand came away damp and chill with sweat. At her touch, Rozenne murmured something inaudible and her fingers twitched fitfully.

"Rozenne," Celestine said urgently.

Rozenne's lids fluttered. Beneath the half-open lids, Celestine saw the whites of Rozenne's eyes. "Can you hear me?"

"Ce . . . les . . . tine . . . ?"

Rozenne knew her. Celestine clutched her friend's hand tightly. "Stay with me." It was a command.

"So tired . . ."

"Hold on, Rozenne. Don't go to sleep yet. Sister Kinnie's coming."

Rozenne's breathing was becoming more choked and irregular. The sound terrified Celestine.

Help me, Faie. She's drifting away, and I don't know if I can bear to lose her.

A faint luminescence began to glow in the gloom. Rozenne's eyes opened, but they were dulled and wandering, as though she could no longer focus on Celestine's face. Misty light illuminated the bed and silvered her livid features.

"Ohh," whispered Rozenne, "Blessed Azilia . . . ?"

Celestine glanced around to see that the Faie was floating behind her in the guise of Saint Azilia. It hovered in the darkness, long locks of gilded silver falling over its shoulders, blue eyes radiating an expression warmly suffused with love and concern. Slowly, the Faie raised slender fingers in a gesture of welcome, arms open wide as if to embrace the girls and draw them to itself.

Rozenne lifted her hands, reaching out to try to touch the shimmering vision. In the soft light emanating from the Faie, Celestine saw the sudden beatific smile that lit her drawn features.

And then Rozenne's outstretched hands dropped limply back onto the sheet.

"Rozenne. *Rozenne!*" Celestine, heart frantically drumming, shook her friend by the shoulder. "Oh no, please no . . ." But although Rozenne's eyes were still open, they stared blankly through Celestine, into the Faie's fading glimmer and beyond . . .

Celestine sat, clutching the book to her, as a sobbing Katell helped the sisters wrap Rozenne's limp, lifeless body in a sheet and carry it down to the Infirmary, where it would be washed and prepared for burial. Around her she could hear the other Skylarks talking in hushed whispers.

"Did you see . . . there was a light around her as she died . . ."

"You must have been dreaming."

"It was so pretty. All silver and gold, like summer starlight . . ."

"Was it an angel, come to take Rozenne to heaven?"

But Celestine was so angry with the Faie for failing to save Rozenne that her whole body shook.

"Which one of us will be next?" The shrill voice startled her. She looked up to see Gauzia standing in the center of the dormitory, her eyes burning with indignation. "Listen to you silly sheep, bleating about angels and silver light! Rozenne is dead. Don't you understand? Her life is over. And yours will be too if you stay here."

"You said your father was coming. With a carriage." Deneza glared at Gauzia. "It's been days since you wrote to him. So where is he?"

"Yes," said another of Gauzia's friends. "You promised us."

"Perhaps he just doesn't care about you."

Celestine heard Gauzia gasp.

"Of course he cares about me. But he's a very busy man—"

"So busy that he can't even spare a carriage to take you away from here?"

Gauzia was floundering. And in spite of all Gauzia's past unkindness, Celestine felt a little pang of pity. Maybe Gauzia had been lying to herself all this time, convincing herself that she was so much more to her father than yet another inconvenient daughter to be fed, clothed, and educated.

"Then the Abbess didn't send my letter." Gauzia, white-faced, had recovered enough to invent another excuse. "I demand to speak to the Abbess!"

"We've heard enough of your little fantasies, Gauzia de Saint-Désirat," said Deneza cuttingly. "If that *is* your real name, of course."

The moonlit dormitory was hushed in sleep when Celestine returned. She had been sitting, keeping vigil in the chapel by Rozenne's open coffin. She was not afraid to keep company with the dead. Rozenne's skin was so pale in death, like the smooth ivory wax of the best shrine candles. Her face was peaceful but expressionless, like a doll's.

All Celestine wanted now was to sleep, to lose herself in a place where no dreams would torment her. As she pulled the blanket up around herself, she heard the faint sound of stifled sobbing coming from the bed beside hers. Gauzia's bed.

She lay a while, staring into the darkness, uncertain of what to do. She felt too bruised, too vulnerable to risk provoking Gauzia's caustic tongue. Perhaps the sobs would subside soon . . .

But then she remembered Gauzia's face, white with shock.

"Gauzia." Celestine placed her hand on the heaving shoulders.

"Why?" Gauzia raised a face glinting wet with tears in the moonlight. "Why didn't Papa come for me? Doesn't he care if I live or die? Even if he was too busy, he could have sent a servant. He could have sent some medicine."

"Perhaps he never got your letter."

"Oh, I'm sure he got it. He just didn't want the inconvenience!"

"I'm sure there was a good reason—"

"How could you understand? You never knew your father."

Celestine withdrew her hand. Hervé's beloved face flashed into her memory, smiling affectionately at her over the rim of his spectacles as he drew a little sapphire flame from a crystal and shaped it into a flower for her. *Never tell anyone your true name or parentage.* "No," she said as she slipped back into her own bed. "I never knew my father."

There was a little silence, then Gauzia hissed, "And if you ever tell another soul about this, I'll make your life so miserable you'll wish you'd died from the lung sickness too."

Celestine, Katell, and Koulmia huddled together as the cold wind blew in across the convent cemetery from the sea. Celestine had found some hellebores in the bare wintry garden and placed the white and green blooms on the freshly dug grave. She had cried so much that she had no tears left anymore; her eyes, stung by the harsh wind, felt raw and dry.

Rozenne was dead. Soon Katell would move down to the Novices' dormitory. One by one, all those Celestine cared for were being taken away from her.

That evening at candlelit vespers, when the moment came for Celestine to sing the solo line in the Blessing, her throat tightened and only a whisper came out. She could see Sister Noyale frowning perplexedly at her as her beating hand moved on, sustaining the pulse of the music. She could sense the other Skylarks around her shooting little glances of surprise at her over the tops of their choir books. And then another voice, rich and strong, took over her part.

Gauzia.

When the service was over and the girls were filing out of the chapel, a firm hand descended on Celestine's shoulder. She looked up to see Sister Noyale staring piercingly at her.

"I—I'm sorry, Sister." Celestine could not meet Sister Noyale's forbidding gaze.

"Fortunately Gauzia had the presence of mind to cover for you." Sister Noyale's hand pressed against her forehead. "You don't seem to have a fever. Good. Nevertheless, we'd better not take any risks."

Celestine did not miss the look of triumph that flashed across Gauzia's face as she passed her. Sister Noyale beckoned Celestine to follow her into the side aisle and Celestine followed, dreading the inevitable scolding that was to come.

"Sing me a scale."

Celestine took a breath and opened her mouth. Two of the Novices were extinguishing the candles and the wreathing smoke irritated the back of her throat. A husky, dry sound issued from her mouth.

"Sing on," ordered Sister Noyale as the chapel grew darker. Celestine saw the two Novices slipping quietly away, leaving only the Eternal Flame watch lights burning at Saint Azilia's Shrine. But still she could not find her singing voice. She shook her head. "I—I can't, Sister Noyale." It was as if all the tears she had shed had washed away the music.

"It may be just a simple head cold. But the voice is a delicate, fragile instrument. It must be treated with care or permanent damage may be done."

"Damage?" Celestine heard a note of warning in the choirmistress's voice.

"You are not to sing a single note, Celestine, for the next fortnight. I want you to whisper when you speak to your friends—difficult for a young girl, I know. You must rest your voice. Every day you will drink a tisane of comfrey to soothe your throat. And you will wear a warm woollen scarf around your neck."

"I don't have a scarf—"

"I'm going to teach you how to knit one. That will keep you occupied while the others are at choir practice."

Sister Noyale was going to teach her how to knit? Celestine was so astonished that her mouth dropped open. She had never expected the forbidding choirmistress to be capable of such a gesture; it almost felt like kindness.

"Losing a friend is hard to bear at any age." Sister Noyale's voice drifted back to Celestine as she trailed after her through the darkened chapel. "But time will heal your sadness . . . and your voice will return."

In the dormitory that night, Celestine lay awake into the small hours, unable to sleep. The frame of Rozenne's bed still stood next to hers, stripped of its mattress and linen, which had been taken away for fumigation.

Will I ever be able to sing again? Or will I spend the rest of my days here as a lay sister, knitting and making healing linctuses?

"*Is that really what you want, Celestine?*" The Faie's voice was faint but clear as falling rain. "*To stay here forever?*"

Forever? No, what am I thinking? Restlessness seared through Celestine like a fever as she stared up into the darkness.

CHAPTER 18

The sun was setting over the sea and a lacy film of mist was slowly unrolling across the bay. Celestine, well wrapped against the chill in her Novice's robes of dove grey, knelt to place a bunch of winter hellebores and snowdrops, freshly picked, on Rozenne's grave.

"The winter hasn't been so harsh this year, Rozenne." She had taken to coming here at dusk to share her thoughts with her dead friend when she needed time to reflect on what was happening in her life. "Five years. I can't believe it's been five years since you left us." She straightened up. "And Sister Noyale says that soon I'll have to make some difficult choices about my future. I can't imagine living anywhere but here now. But suppose I'm offered the chance to go to Lutèce?"

After the last ravages of the sickness took little Sister Eurielle, life at the convent had slowly resumed its normal pattern. Under Sister Noyale's patient tuition, Celestine and Gauzia learned to write musical notation and were set to work to copy choir parts from the great missals of sacred music in the convent library. This year, Sister Noyale had even let them teach the youngest Skylarks their scales and exercises.

Yet, busy as her days were, Celestine often found herself looking out beyond the convent walls, gazing at the sky or the distant sea. Twice today, Sister Noyale had scolded her for making mistakes in her copying and she had been obliged to start the part again.

A sense of yearning washed through her again, as strong as a spring tide. But yearning for . . . what? This restlessness, when it came, swept all other thoughts from her mind. Never before had the convent walls seemed so confining.

An ordinary vespers on an ordinary day . . . The Novices were in the choir stalls, Sister Noyale was conducting, and the other sisters were sitting in their customary places in chapel. Elderly Sister Gwendoline had nodded off as usual, and her gentle snores could only be heard in the softest passages of the singing.

Celestine was the leader of the sopranos; opposite her stood Gauzia, leader of the altos. Nurtured by Sister Noyale's strict training, Gauzia's voice had gained strength and richness in the lower notes, whereas Celestine's upper register had developed clarity and brilliance. No longer rivals but equals, Celestine had come to realize that when they sang together, it was a thrilling, exhilarating experience.

Celestine rose for her first solo. Glancing out into the chapel, she noticed a stranger seated beside the Abbess. A man. It was very unusual for visitors to attend vespers. And there was something about the way that he sat, unmoving, listening with rapt attention as she sang, that distinguished him from so many other visitors who yawned or shifted restlessly through the services.

This man, she told herself, has come to hear the music.

As soon as the service was over, the Abbess rose and ushered her guest out. Twenty-four pairs of eyes fixed on the fair-haired young man as he walked beside the Abbess toward the doors. As soon as the Novices reached the side aisles, they burst into excited whispers.

"Did you *see* him?" squealed Deneza, grabbing Gauzia by the arms.

"Isn't he beautiful?" Koulmia sighed. "He must be of noble birth."

"But who is he? Why is he here?" Gauzia ran to the doorway to gaze after him.

Celestine alone said nothing. *If I speak, it will break the spell.*

"He's probably another of the Abbess's nephews," said Katell dismissively. "They're always coming to visit Auntie Ermengarde."

"I'd have remembered one as handsome as that," retorted Koulmia. "His hair . . . so long and so silky . . ."

"Stop drooling, Koulmia, and go and extinguish the candles." Sister Noyale appeared, holding her folder of music.

Celestine remembered that it was her turn to help Koulmia and went to follow her. But Sister Noyale stopped her.

"No, Celestine. I want you and Gauzia to come with me."

Gauzia looked at Celestine, one auburn brow flaring quizzically. They hurried after Sister Noyale, hearing Koulmia's disappointed wail echoing around the empty chapel.

"It's not *fair* . . ."

"Come in quickly, girls, and shut the door," ordered the Abbess. "We don't want to let our visitor catch cold. This old building is very drafty, Monsieur de Joyeuse."

A fire of driftwood was blazing in the Abbess's parlor and by its light Celestine saw the visitor rise to his feet to greet them.

"Monsieur de Joyeuse, may I present our two most promising singers? This is Celestine, and Gauzia." The girls curtsied dutifully.

"Demoiselles." The visitor bowed. "May I say how much I appreciated your performance? You, Demoiselle Celestine, shaped your phrases with genuine understanding and artistry." His voice was so pleasant to listen to, almost like a caress. "And you, Demoiselle Gauzia, you showed great flare in your interpretation."

He was paying them a compliment! Celestine stared resolutely at the floor, aware that her cheeks had flamed hot red. She could not remember the last time she had been so close to a man—and such an attractive young man at that. Beside her, Gauzia was far less shy, smiling at him boldly.

"Monsieur de Joyeuse has an exciting proposal to put to you girls," said the Abbess, settling herself in a cushioned fauteuil beside the fire.

"Excellent reports of your choirs have reached the court, Sister Noyale. Prince Enguerrand's tutor has spoken very favorably of the music-making here."

Sister Noyale gave a curt nod, as if she were unused to receiving compliments too.

"And so the young prince is planning to come here with his mother, Queen Aliénor, to the service on Saint Azilia's Day."

The Abbess was nodding vigorously. "Such an honor," she burst out excitedly. "The royal family coming to visit us here!"

"The prince has requested me to write a new setting of the service for your choir to sing, Sister Noyale."

"You honor us, Maistre," said Sister Noyale in level tones.

So he's a composer. Slowly, Celestine dared to raise her head. The firelight flickered across Monsieur de Joyeuse's face, catching burnished glints of gold in his long, fair hair. He was smiling at her as he spoke, and it was a smile of such pleasant warmth that she felt as if her heart were melting.

Before Celestine and Gauzia reached the dormitory, all the other Novices came running up to pester them with questions.

"Who is he? Why is he here? Tell us!"

Celestine blinked. She heard Gauzia explaining as if from a long way off. The squeals of excitement soon brought her back to reality.

"Prince Enguerrand here? With Queen Aliénor?" shrieked Koulmia, clutching Celestine's hands. "What an honor!"

"But just think, all the courtiers will accompany them in their fine clothes, and we'll be in our drab, grey habits," complained Gauzia.

"They're coming to hear you sing, not to look at you," said a dry voice. Katell had appeared in the doorway. As Senior Novice, soon to be faced with the decision whether to take her vows, she had not been judged to have enough talent to be sent to the choir of Saint Meriadec like Angelique. "And, royal visit or no, there are dormitory duties to be done before anyone gets into bed. If you must gossip, do it as you sweep and tidy up. I've seen cleaner pigsties. Koulmia, have you been eating in bed again?"

"Why would I do that?" Koulmia said in aggrieved tones.

Katell shook out her blanket and a little hail of crumbs and three brown apple cores fell onto the floor. "Just clean it up."

"You're such a slave driver, Katell," grumbled Koulmia, taking the broom from Celestine, who was standing, staring into the middle distance. "Well, look who's smitten with Monsieur de Joyeuse!"

"I was just wondering," said Celestine hastily.

"I wouldn't wonder too much," put in Gauzia with a malicious little laugh. "He's Maistre de Chapelle, isn't he? With a choir of pretty boys?"

"What do you mean?" Celestine did not understand.

"Are you really that naïve, Celestine?" Gauzia said pityingly.

For the second time that evening, Celestine felt herself blush as she realized what Gauzia was implying. "I'm sure Monsieur de Joyeuse is not like that!" she cried. He had smiled so warmly at her; surely she had detected something more than good manners in that greeting? It was as if they had an unspoken understanding, even though they had never met before.

Four months passed and still there was no music from Henri de Joyeuse. Spring softened the bare branches in the convent orchard with a white snow of apple and pear blossom. The harsh winds ceased to buffet the promontory, and were replaced by gentler southerly breezes. The days grew warmer and the girls shed their thick winter robes and wore lighter linen dresses. Celestine began to wonder if she had dreamed the whole episode.

"Perhaps he's been too busy to compose," she said wistfully to Katell.

Celestine was chopping vegetables from the kitchen garden when she received the summons to go to Abbess Ermengarde. Wiping her hands on her apron, she arrived to find Sister Noyale unwrapping a large package in the Abbess's parlor. The Abbess was fussing around behind her while Gauzia stood watching with folded arms.

"This arrived by special courier this morning," Sister Noyale explained, lifting out a plain leather-bound folder and opening it. On the first page, written in a bold, black hand, was the simple inscription:

Canticles for Saint Azilia's Day. Dedicated to my honored patron, His Royal Highness Enguerrand, prince of Francia.

So it was finished! Celestine glanced at Gauzia, wondering if she felt as dizzily excited as Celestine did.

"Well, Noyale?" said the Abbess impatiently. "What kind of piece has Maistre de Joyeuse written for us? Let's pray he hasn't composed anything too difficult for my girls to sing. We don't want to look foolish before the prince."

Sister Noyale looked up from the score. "It's challenging. He's made few concessions to the girls' youth and inexperience. But if we work hard, I'm certain that it will sound wonderful." Her brown eyes glowed with an enthusiasm that Celestine had only rarely glimpsed before.

"I know you love a challenge, Noyale," said the Abbess, "but if you think it's too difficult, you must tell Maistre de Joyeuse now and get him to change it."

"Here's your part, Celestine, and yours, Gauzia." Sister Noyale took no notice of the Abbess.

Celestine had been chopping onions for the evening soup and although she had carefully rinsed her hands before coming to the parlor, she sniffed her fingers, wiping them on her apron before touching the precious manuscript. Gauzia was already leafing through the pages.

"Do you think this is his own hand?" Celestine asked, looking at the strong black strokes on the staff.

Gauzia gave a careless little shrug. "Busy composers use a copyist."

"Oh." Celestine was disappointed. She had imagined that the pages she was holding had been hand-scribed by Henri de Joyeuse, that he had sat up late into the night, feverishly scribbling down these very notes especially for her to sing.

The Canticles were difficult. More difficult than anything Celestine had ever had to learn before. It was not so much that the notes were hard to pitch accurately, but more the way that the individual lines were woven together. It was little consolation to know that Gauzia was equally challenged by Maistre de Joyeuse's composition. She became obsessed with the drive to get to know this music as intimately as possible. As she sang alone in the empty chapel, she held in her mind the image of Henri de Joyeuse feverishly writing down the riot of notes flowing through his brain, lamplight like a golden halo burnishing his fair hair.

As Saint Azilia's Day approached, the Abbess began to fuss about the flowers for the chapel. Everything must be "perfect—no, better than perfect—for our royal guests," she insisted. The Skylarks were set to work binding floral wreaths and garlands to decorate the chapel; the Novices brought out ladders and, tucking up their long robes into their belts, climbed up to hang the garlands around the chapel pillars.

Celestine, her robes hitched up to her knees, was up at the top of a ladder held by Koulmia when she heard a sudden commotion below. All the girls had begun to chatter at once as noisily as a flock of starlings.

"Koulmia!" she called down. "What's all the fuss about?"

"He's here!"

"Who? Not the prince?" Celestine leaned out to try to see, just at the moment that Koulmia, distracted, let go of the ladder. "*Koulmia!*" She wobbled precariously at the top of the ladder, making a grab at a pillar to steady herself. "He-elp—"

"Good-day, Demoiselle Celestine," said a cheerful voice from below as firm hands caught hold of the ladder and steadied it. "I see I came just in time."

Celestine looked down to see Henri de Joyeuse gazing up at her. He must be able to see her bare legs! She climbed down, hastily shaking the tucked-in folds loose.

"Thank you," she mumbled, unable to meet his gaze.

"It's all right," he said confidentially. "I averted my eyes."

She looked up at him then, astonished that he knew what she had been thinking. His face had crinkled into a mischievously playful smile. She didn't know whether she wanted to slap him or hug him for rescuing her.

"Is that *really* Prince Enguerrand?" said Koulmia in a shrill whisper. "Isn't he rather . . . young? And he's dressed in black, like a schoolboy."

Even though the girls' heads were respectfully lowered, every Novice had angled herself so that she could look down the aisle and see the prince and his mother, Queen Aliénor, as they left the chapel after the service.

"He's Aubrey's younger brother, stupid," said Gauzia in scalding tones. "He *is* a schoolboy. What did you expect?"

"I expected someone a little more princely," said Katell. "So princes wear spectacles?" She made a disparaging click of the tongue. "What d'you think, Celestine?"

Celestine was still staring after the departing royal party. She was certain now: It was Captain de Lanvaux at the prince's side, ushering him out of the chapel, beneath the garlands of lilies and white roses, to the open doorway where his bodyguard awaited. The prince's tutor had spoken highly of the music-making at Saint Azilia's. Had Ruaud de Lanvaux arranged this prestigious occasion? She felt her heart warm with gratitude as she watched his tall figure, walking with the stiff bearing of a seasoned military man beside the young prince.

"I think that Prince Enguerrand has kind eyes," she said. "And a sweet, shy smile."

"Remember, girls, whatever you do, keep your eyes modestly lowered at all times," insisted the Abbess. "Don't look at the prince or his mother directly. That would be immodest and improper."

Celestine expected Gauzia to remind the Abbess that she had been presented to the queen before and did not need to be lectured on court etiquette. But Gauzia was silent, and when Celestine sneaked a look at her, she saw that her face was flushed pink. So even the worldly Gauzia was overcome at the prospect of a royal audience.

Two tall men of the royal household, resplendent in their uniforms of blue and gold, stood guard outside the Abbess's parlor. Celestine felt her knees go weak at the sight. But the guards merely opened the parlor door and the girls were ushered inside.

"May I present our two young soloists, your majesty, your highness . . ."

Celestine and Gauzia curtsied obediently. Queen Aliénor was talking with her ladies-in-waiting and she merely gave a brief approving nod. Celestine had never seen such richly dressed women before; the queen's costume of mulberry velvet was stitched with tiny jewels that glittered in the candlelight whenever she gestured. At her side, her son Enguerrand looked like a young cleric in his sober dark suit. But it was he who leaned forward and spoke to them, his low voice earnest and kind.

"Thank you for your beautiful singing. The service was truly uplifting. And Maistre de Joyeuse's Azilian Canticles were ravishing. I'd love to come here and listen to the choir again."

Even though she had been forbidden to do so, Celestine could not resist snatching a glance at his face as he spoke and she saw that behind the lenses of his spectacles, his dark eyes were gravely smiling at them. *He does look like a young priest; serious yet rather charming.*

"Thank you, your highness," said Gauzia boldly.

"Saint Azilia is my favorite of all the saints—after Saint Sergius, of course, Captain," Prince Enguerrand added with a hasty glance in his tutor's direction. "Her short life was so tragic, yet so inspiring."

Captain de Lanvaux turned around at this and gave an approving nod.

"You can go now, girls," said the Abbess hastily, shooing them out of the royal presence.

Celestine looked back over her shoulder for a glimpse of Maistre de Joyeuse. She had hoped that he would tell them if he had enjoyed their performance. She could just see the glint of candlelight on his fair hair as he listened attentively to one of the queen's companions, a dark-haired young woman, who was gazing at him with undisguised admiration.

Disappointed, Celestine turned away and followed Gauzia, who had already left the parlor, her head held high.

Gauzia stormed off through the cloisters; Celestine ran after her, the sound of their fast-pattering feet echoing around the moonlit courtyard.

"What's wrong, Gauzia? Everything went well. Aren't you pleased?"

"It makes me so angry." She spoke at last and her voice was choked with emotion. "To see those daughters of privileged families simpering around Queen Aliénor in their fancy clothes." She clenched her fists at her sides. "Why did we have to be born helpless women?"

"Helpless?"

Gauzia spun around on her heel. "What life is there for us, Celestine? We have no dowries, so we can never hope to marry. We have no money, no status, *nothing*."

"But we have our voices. We could make our careers from singing."

"Oh, wake up, Celestine." Gauzia took hold of her by the shoulders and gave her a little shake. "Try leaving Saint Azilia's and making your way on your own. Just try! How long would you last in the real world? A woman alone is easy prey. We've been sheltered here. Protected from the realities of life on the streets." She let go of Celestine. "It's different for men. Why can my brothers go into the army, the navy, the priesthood—and all that's left to me is to be shut away in this dreary convent?"

Celestine hung her head. She had no answer.

"Don't you have a dream? Do you really want to stay here forever?"

A little spark caught fire in Celestine as if she understood what Gauzia was saying for the first time.

Forever.

"N—no," she said dazedly. "There are things . . . things I have to do . . ."

The sharp clatter of hooves on the cobbles startled them both. Two horsemen rode into the convent courtyard; the first dismounted as the girls stared, carelessly flinging his reins into the hands of the second. A couple of shaggy hounds loped in behind them, pink tongues lolling out of their mouths as they panted.

"Good-day, little sisters," he called cheerfully, "can you take me to my brother? I thought I'd pay him a surprise visit."

"Your b—brother?" Gauzia was staring unashamedly. Celestine was tongue-tied. With his piercing eyes of dark blue, curling dark hair, and entrancing smile, she had never seen such a good-looking young man before.

"We've been hunting, haven't we, Locronan?" The newcomer turned to his companion, who grinned and nodded. "Bagged a fine brace of partridge out on the moors."

"Prince *Aubrey*?" Recovering, Gauzia dipped a swift curtsy and smiled boldly up at him. "Please follow me."

"Wait, your highness," cried his companion. "Your mother—"

"Will be delighted to see us!" called the prince, laughing as he strode after Gauzia.

As the royal party departed, all the sisters and students lined the courtyard to bid them farewell. Koulmia and Deneza clutched each other, barely able to restrain their squeals of delight as Prince Aubrey rode out of the courtyard, the hounds obediently trotting behind their master.

"And he spoke to you, Gauzia? He actually *spoke* to you?"

"He asked me to take him to his mother. It seems he was expected to attend the service but went hunting instead."

"Did you meet him too, Celestine?" demanded Katell.

Celestine nodded.

"But little Miss Mouse here was too shy to say anything," said Gauzia scornfully.

"Or you pushed her out the way so that you could take precedence."

"You take that back, Catty Katell!"

Katell, hands on her hips, faced her defiantly.

"Katell, please—" Celestine begged, catching hold of her arm.

"Celestine!" Sister Noyale said sharply. "Come with me."

"You haven't heard the last of this," Gauzia said under her breath as Celestine followed Sister Noyale toward the Abbess's parlor.

"So you want to steal away my best singer, Maistre?" Sister Noyale said, staring challengingly at him.

"I don't think I'm setting a precedent here, am I, Abbess?" Henri de Joyeuse looked to the Abbess for confirmation. "The convent regularly sends girls to sing at Saint Meriadec's in Lutèce. And excellent choirmistress that you are, Sister Noyale, you know that Celestine deserves the chance to develop her gift to the full."

There was a silence. Celestine saw Sister Noyale bite her lower lip. "You're saying that I've taught her all I know. And . . . you're right. She needs to be trained by a professional singing teacher like you."

Celestine stood watching the nuns and de Joyeuse discuss her future as the topic passed from speaker to speaker like the ball in a tense game of *jeu de paume*.

"But where is she going to live while she studies? She's an orphan, she has no relatives."

"She can stay with my family. They're used to hosting my students."

"Are you married, Maistre?" asked Sister Noyale pointedly. Celestine held her breath; for some reason she did not quite yet understand, his answer to Sister Noyale's question was of more importance to her than she could have imagined.

"No, I live with my aunt. My aunt was a renowned singer in her youth; she teaches technique to my students."

So he's not married. Celestine felt herself begin to breathe again.

"I think it would be more appropriate for Celestine to stay at the Sisters of Charity, in the care of Sister Angelique," put in the Abbess. "If she is to sing daily at Saint Meriadec's, she will have a companion to accompany her."

"Aren't we forgetting our other promising singer, Gauzia de Saint-Désirat? If you were willing to give them lessons together, there could be no talk of impropriety." Sister Noyale gazed sternly at the Maistre, as if challenging him to reject her suggestion at his peril.

"Her tone is distinctive but if she could learn to blend with the other choristers..." The Maistre smiled at Sister Noyale. "Why not? I'm sure that Gauzia will prove an asset to Saint Meriadec's."

"Gauzia's family would surely make no objection?" mused the Abbess. "Then I will write to the Mother Superior at the Sisters of Charity and ask her to take in our girls as lay sisters."

The mere hint that Gauzia might be her companion made Celestine squirm.

Leave the convent? The prospect was at once terrifying and thrilling. Celestine's heart had begun to flutter at the thought. She pressed a hand to her breast, trying to steady its wild beating. All her security lay here, confined within the convent walls: her dearest "big sister" Katell, her friends, the reassuring daily rhythm of the convent routine . . .

"So you're following Angelique?" Celestine whirled around to see Katell standing in the doorway, arms crossed, regarding her with a wry, sad smile.

"I don't want to leave you, Katell!" Celestine burst out.

"But you have to go?"

Celestine could not meet her friend's eyes. She nodded.

"Well then, that's as it should be. Go to Lutèce and make us all proud of you."

Was this really Katell speaking? Celestine slowly raised her head.

"Ever since you first showed us that amazing voice of yours, I knew you wouldn't stay. Heavens, we've been lucky to have you here all these years. You deserve this break, Celestine. You have to follow your dream." Katell's voice was steady, but Celestine could see a glimmer of tears in her eyes. "But you have to promise to come back every Saint Azilia's Day to sing to us."

Celestine flew to Katell and hugged her, hard. "Oh, Katell, you're all bones!" she said through her tears. "Thank you."

"What for?" Katell wiped her eyes on a corner of her apron.

"For standing up for me. I'd never have made it to today without you beside me."

"Enough of this nonsense!" Katell turned away so Celestine could no longer see her face. "I've got chores to finish."

"I wish you were coming to Lutèce with me, not Gauzia."

"So do I," said the departing back, stiff and straight as a broom handle. "Come back and visit. Visit soon. And don't forget to write!"

The following spring, the girls traveled by river to the capital city, where Maistre de Joyeuse met them in his carriage at the busy quay. As his driver skillfully negotiated his way between the other carriages jostling for room, the Maistre sat back on the seat, holding on to the strap to keep from being thrown by the violent lurches, and began to explain what lay ahead of them in their new lives.

"You'll be tutored in vocal technique by my aunt. She prefers to be called Dame Elmire by her students, but her stage name was Elmire Sorel, and she was once the toast of the opera houses in the city."

"Your aunt was an opera singer?" Gauzia clasped her hands together. "That's my dream—to act, to sing on the stage . . ."

"And don't be deceived by her friendly manner. In the music room, she's a ferocious tyrant! You'll have to work hard to keep up to her exacting standards."

During this conversation, Celestine had begun to feel an unpleasant and disorienting sensation. It was as if a thin, dark smoke were seeping in from the street outside, choking her with a nauseating smell of burning. She clapped both hands to her mouth, afraid she might retch.

"Are you feeling all right, Demoiselle?" Maistre de Joyeuse was looking at her with concern.

"You look quite green. You're not going to be sick are you?" asked Gauzia loudly.

"It must be the bumpy motion of the carriage over the cobblestones. Would you like the driver to stop?"

"No!" This inexplicable feeling of terror told her to get away as fast as possible. She felt so panicked that she wanted to wrench open the carriage door, jump down, and run until the feeling evaporated. "Where . . . are we?"

Maistre de Joyeuse checked outside. Then he rapped on the carriage roof and leaned forward to speak to the driver. "Turn off at once."

"Where are we, Maistre?" Gauzia tried to peep out but the Maistre leaned across and hastily pulled down the blind.

"I apologize. Why the driver chose to bring us by the Place du Trahoir, I have no idea. He may enjoy the sight of criminals swinging from the gibbet, but it's no sight for civilized citizens."

The Place du Trahoir. The name brought back terrible memories like a foul black sediment churned up from the depths of a still, clear lake. This was where they had executed her dearest papa, in the cruelest way imaginable, by searing flames on an oil-drenched pyre. Celestine leaned back against the seat and closed her eyes.

"So you saw?" She heard the Maistre's voice as if from far away. "I'm sorry, Demoiselle. We will soon be at my aunt's house."

"I'm feeling much better now." Celestine forced herself to regain her self-control. What must he think of her? It was not an auspicious start to her new life in Lutèce.

The frontage of Maistre de Joyeuse's town house could not be seen from the street, as like many others in Lutèce, it was protected by a high wall. But to Celestine's delight, behind the wall lay an intimate courtyard garden. When she gazed upward, she saw that the little garden was surrounded by other tall houses, and a single square of blue sky could be glimpsed high above. But she could hear sparrows twittering in the flowerpots among the scarlet tulips.

Maistre de Joyeuse went on ahead while the girls collected their bundles from the coachman. Celestine could not help feeling as insignificant and dowdy as the brown sparrows fluttering in and out of the rambling wisteria that framed the porch with its luscious-scented blooms.

"So where are our new students?" demanded an imperious voice from inside. "Don't tell me you've left them to make their own way in?"

The Maistre appeared in the open doorway with a grey-haired woman beside him. "Aunt Elmire, may I present Demoiselles Celestine and Gauzia."

The girls curtsied. Elmire Sorel regarded them with a keen and critical eye.

"You will be studying vocal technique with me. I'm a hard taskmaster and I expect you both to be diligent students."

"She's worse than Sister Noyale," whispered Gauzia to Celestine as they left the house to walk to the Sisters of Charity, their new home.

A tall, willowy nun was waiting to greet them in the austere entrance hall of the convent. Celestine stared.

"Angelique?" She ran to her and flung her arms around her, relieved to see a familiar face.

"Welcome to the Sisters of Charity," said Angelique, kissing her cheek. "Is this Gauzia? Let me show you to your room."

As Celestine followed the older girl through the hushed convent, she felt as if her new life was going to turn out all right if Angelique was there to guide and reassure her.

Every weekday the girls went to the Maistre's house for a singing lesson with Dame Elmire, then left after lunch to sing the afternoon service with the convent choir at the ancient Church of Saint Meriadec. Three times a week, the girls attended the Conservatoire for lessons in music theory and the fortepiano. To Celestine's disappointment, it soon became evident that the Maistre's busy schedule would only permit him to coach them from time to time. But when the day came for her first lesson, Celestine found herself filled with nerves at the prospect of a whole hour alone with him.

The lesson began well enough and she soon began to forget her apprehension, lulled by his sensitive accompaniment.

Suddenly he stopped playing. Celestine, surprised, stopped singing. He was leaning forward, arms draped over the music stand, regarding her intently.

"Did I sing a wrong note? I'm sorry . . ."

"No; the notes were perfect." Still he stared at her.

"My breathing, then. The phrasing?"

He slowly shook his head and she saw the hint of a smile on his lips. Was he teasing her? "Shall I sing the phrase again?" Used to Sister Noyale's strict regime, she felt baffled by his silence. She wanted so much to please him and win his approval.

He rose from the keyboard. "You've been well trained. Like all Sister Noyale's star singers, you have a good technique and produce a pleasing sound." He began to pace the music room as he spoke. *Pleasing.* From anyone else it would have been a compliment. Celestine watched him, alarmed. Every time he passed her, she found herself thinking not of her technique or her phrasing, but how there was a trace of golden stubble on the curve of his chin. She kept trying not to think of it . . . but the more she tried, the more her fingers longed to reach out and touch it, to feel the roughness against his smooth skin—

He stopped suddenly in front of her. "Do you understand what I'm saying, Demoiselle?"

She stared at him blankly. She had not heard a word, only the sound of his voice. And then she felt her cheeks flushing bright red. What must he think of her?

"Where is your real voice, Demoiselle Celestine? I want you to stop trying to sing the way other people have told you to." He was gazing into her eyes now with such intensity that she could not look away. "I want you to show me what this music means to you. I know you can do it. Who *are* you, Celestine?"

Who am I? The question came like a ram battering at a long-locked door. Celestine felt herself trembling. She had been Celestine for so long now, quiet, obedient, well-behaved Celestine, that the prospect of letting her true self loose was terrifying.

"I—I don't know!" She turned in panic and fled the room.

Little golden bees were busy about the blue buds of lavender, droning in the warmth of the sun. It was hard, in this little courtyard garden, to remember that the bustling city lay outside the walls with all its hateful memories. The roses had almost all finished except for one pale cream climber around the arbor seat that was still flowering prolifically. The roses had not even started to bloom when they left the convent; had they been in Lutèce so long already?

She could hear Gauzia's voice drifting through the open music room window, swelling as she sang, more rich and glorious in tone than it had ever sounded at the convent.

She's everything I'm not. Celestine paced the looping gravel path, unable to escape the sound of Gauzia's voice. *And how delighted he must be with her progress.* She stopped to pick a spike of lavender, sniffing the sharp scent on her fingertips. It took her back to the convent stillroom, tying bunches for Sister Kinnie to hang up to dry from the overhead herb rack. *Maybe I should never have left Saint Azilia's. Maybe I'm not ready to cope with life in the big city. But Gauzia is so confident, nothing seems to upset her. She's improving every day.*

Yet the thought of the two of them, Henri de Joyeuse and Gauzia, performing together pricked her imagination, sharp as a rose thorn.

I can't bear for him to pay her so much attention. I want him to play for me, to smile at me, I want . . . She imagined them smiling at each other over the music, a secret look of understanding that suggested a far greater intimacy than the usual relationship between master and pupil.

No! I can't afford to like him. Liking, loving, only leads to hurt. Loss. Loneliness. I must stay strong.

Maistre de Joyeuse had a composition to complete. He locked himself away in his music room, insisting that no one disturb him.

Celestine would tiptoe past his locked door and notice that his food tray had been left untouched, the delicious dinner cooked by Dame Elmire cold and congealing beneath its cover.

How wonderful to be so wrapped up in the world of sound that everyday necessities like eating and sleeping could be forgotten.

She stood very still, holding her breath, hoping to catch a faint snatch of the new sounds that he was weaving together. But all she heard were a few disjointed fragments.

Next morning, as Celestine arrived for her lesson with Dame Elmire, she heard Maistre de Joyeuse's voice. "Coffee!" he called. "Strong coffee."

She stopped, seeing him emerge from his room in his robe de chambre. He was unshaven and his hair was loose about his shoulders and disheveled, as though he had been dragging his fingers through it.

"You should be ashamed, wandering around the house in such a state," chided Dame Elmire. "Will you join us, Celestine?"

In the morning room, the housekeeper poured black coffee into delicate porcelain cups. Celestine was still unaccustomed to the drink—a luxury that she had not even heard of in Saint Azilia's—and she found its dark, burned aroma irresistible. When the Maistre had finished the first cup, he pushed it forward for a refill. As he did so, he glanced up at Celestine, acknowledging her presence with a rueful smile. "It took all night," he said. "But it was worth it."

"Your new composition?" she said, trying not to notice that she could plainly see a triangle of lean bare chest where the dark silk of his robe gaped open as he leaned forward to lift the cup to his lips. *Is that all he has on? Is he naked underneath?* she wondered, then felt herself blushing that she should think such an impure thought. "What are you working on, Maistre?"

"A work for Demoiselle Gauzia to sing on the Feast of Saint Sergius."

She thought at first she had not heard aright. "For Gauzia?"

"The Grand Maistre commissioned a new anthem. It's for a service at the Commanderie chapel."

"I see." Celestine turned swiftly away, hoping that he had not noticed her bitter disappointment.

"The Feast Day is only a week away. I need extra time to work on her part with her . . . so would you mind very much if we canceled our lesson today?"

Another sharp thorn pierced Celestine's heart. It was all she could do not to blurt out, "What am I doing wrong? Why didn't you choose me?"

CHAPTER 19

"*Gazette!* Get your copy of the *Gazette!*" sang out a paper vendor, passing by the front of the café. "Fighting in Enhirre, latest news!"

Rieuk leaped up, beckoning the boy over to buy a paper, hastily scanning the columns to discover what had happened.

"Our brave Guerriers have successfully repelled a raid on the Fort of Ondhessar by hostile Enhirran tribes. Ownership of the fort has long been contested by Enhirre and Djihan-Djihar, as it lies on the border dividing both countries. The household troops of his Excellency Shultan Fazil of Djihan-Djihar fought alongside the Francians to repel the invaders. It is reported that Arkhan Sardion's eldest son and heir, Prince Alarion, is among the many Enhirran casualties . . ."

The paper slipped from Rieuk's fingers. Alarion dead? But the Arkhan had forbidden him to fight. It had to be a mistake. And why had Djihan-Djihar entered the fray?

A hawk-winged shadow darted overhead and he heard Ormas's voice, low and urgent.

"Almiras is here. He has a message for us."

Rieuk cast coins on the table and hastily set off after the hawk. It must be an urgent message for Lord Estael to send Almiras so far from Ondhessar. At the end of the street he saw an avenue of plane trees leading to ornate ironwork gates. A sandy path led him into a shady public garden, where the distant voices of children at play carried over the splash of water spouting from a green-stained marble fountain. Rieuk stopped in the heart of an alley of sweet-blossomed lime trees, checked to see if anyone was watching, and set Ormas loose. There was a rustle high in the branches overhead and he saw both smoke hawks alight.

"*We are to return straightaway,*" Ormas conveyed Almiras's message. "*The Arkhan is demanding to see you.*"

The Arkhan's palace was hung with black. Black gauzes covered every window and only a faint, muted light seeped through. The sound of women's weeping, muffled and desolate, echoed through the vastness of the empty halls. The hushed, gloomy atmosphere only increased the ominous feeling of foreboding that had been plaguing Rieuk on the long journey back to Enhirre. Many weeks had passed since Alarion's death, yet as Rieuk followed the silent guards to the Arkhan's private chambers, he realized that Sardion was still grieving.

"I will never forgive them," said Sardion softly. "They took my son from me, my firstborn, my beloved Alarion. They will pay dearly for this. Francia will pay."

"I—I am sorry for your loss, my lord."

The Arkhan raised him to his feet, fingers clutching his shoulders. "And you will be the instrument of my vengeance." His blue eyes burned with a feverish glint in grief-hollowed sockets.

"Your vengeance?" Rieuk repeated, wishing he could retreat, yet held tight by the Arkhan's strong grip.

"The House of Francia will suffer as I have suffered. Let Gobain know what it is to lose a child, a child more dear to him than life itself."

"What do you mean, my lord?" Had Sardion been driven mad by Alarion's death? Rieuk could not follow what he was saying.

"My Emissaries have many skills at their disposal. They have acted as assassins before. Now it is your turn."

Assassins. Rieuk felt a chill in the pit of his stomach at the mere thought. "Please don't ask me to do this, my lord. Please, I beg you."

Sardion let go of him at last and reached into the breast of his robe. He withdrew a little phial which he held up in front of Rieuk's face. A translucent swirl of dark gold lit the lotus glass, intertwined with a spiraling thread of black. Rieuk's hands reached out toward the glass before he knew what he was doing.

"No, my lord, please not Imri—"

"Imri was dear to you, wasn't he?" The Arkhan's sleep-starved eyes glimmered like corpse candles as he snatched the precious glass from Rieuk's grasp. "And you will carry out this mission for the sake of the soul of the one you hold dear. Fail me, Rieuk, and I crush this soul-glass. And Imri Boldiszar becomes one of the Lost."

"We are magi," said Lord Estael dispassionately. "We achieve our ends much more subtly than a common hired gun. But we *are* just as deadly as a trained marksman. And much harder to track down afterward."

"The Arkhan wants me to *kill*?" Rieuk still could not believe what he had been ordered to do.

"You will bring about a death. There's a subtle difference."

"Why? Why must it be me?"

"You're a native Francian. You'll be able to get close to your target. Close enough to carry out your mission."

"And who is my target?"

"The heir to the throne. Prince Aubrey."

Rieuk went to the top of the Tower and gazed out into the night. A gust of breeze ruffled his hair, bringing with it the hot, parched scent of the desert.

If I were to close my eyes and let myself fall forward into the darkness, I would be killed instantly. And that would be an end to it. Their hold over me would be broken and I'd be free. In truth, he was weary, soul-weary, and wondering what there was left to live for. Magister Gonery's prophetic words kept whispering through his mind. "*They will promise you the things you most desire. And then, before you know what you have done, you will find yourself in thrall. Sealed into a contract that binds you until death—and beyond.*"

The eerie ice-light of Imri's Rift tomb shimmered in the darkness. Rieuk stood, one hand on the casket of aethyr crystal that encased Imri's body.

"Where are you, Imri? Can you hear me? Or are you far beyond the bournes of this world already . . . and this is just some cruel ruse to get me to do the Arkhan's will?"

Beneath the rime-coated crystal facets, he could hardly make out the form of Imri's body anymore. So much time had passed since they were last together. And Rieuk knew now how frail and vulnerable a soul was, once it was separated from its mortal body.

He slipped to his knees, resting his forehead against the chill crystal. "I don't know what to do. If only you were here, you'd tell me. Can I trust Lord Estael? If I carry out this mission, will the Arkhan keep his promise and set you free?"

CHAPTER 20

"Maistre de Joyeuse's new anthem is ravishingly beautiful, Celestine." Gauzia twirled around the girls' narrow convent cell. "I can't believe that he wrote it especially for me to sing. It's such an honor." She stopped for a moment in front of the little mirror and tweaked an errant curl back into place.

Celestine listened in silence, slowly dragging a comb through her hair. She could not be sure whether Gauzia was so excited that she could not contain herself, or if she was rattling on expressly to provoke her.

"We're leaving for the final rehearsal at ten. We're taking a carriage to the Forteresse. I suppose that means you'll have to manage without me somehow at Saint Meriadec's today. Though I heard the Maistre say that one of his younger students was going to play the organ in his place. We won't be back till late, after vespers."

Another lesson canceled—and he had not even taken the trouble to tell her himself. And what was with this "we"? It sounded as if there was more than a master-student relationship between Gauzia and the Maistre.

"Of course, all the most important members of the Commanderie will be there: the Inquisitor, Captain de Lanvaux, the Grand Maistre himself. And it's even rumored that Prince Enguerrand will attend. Sergius is his patron saint . . ." Gauzia stopped. "Listen to me, chattering on." Gauzia gave Celestine a condescending smile. "I must save my voice for the rehearsal."

Heart troubled with conflicting emotions, Celestine entered the chapel of Saint Meriadec. As she went into the vestry and took off her grey lay sister's hooded cloak, she felt that the cloth was damp. It must have started to drizzle as she walked through the streets and she had been so preoccupied that she had not even noticed.

"No Gauzia today?"

Celestine recognized Angelique's voice and turned around, grateful to see a friendly face. "It's her big moment. She's singing at the Feast Day in the Forteresse."

"I see." Angelique nodded, handing Celestine her choir robe. "I imagine she's pretty insufferable right now."

"She mentioned that there was a new student playing for the service today." Celestine changed the subject for fear she would say aloud what she really thought of Gauzia.

"He's only seventeen but very talented." Angelique gave Celestine a mysterious smile. "I heard a rumor from the older sisters that Captain de Lanvaux discovered him in Armel and brought him to Lutèce to study. So you share the same patron."

Another of the captain's protégés? Celestine was intrigued, in spite of her dejected mood.

The candles were lit in the choir stall glasses, for even though it was only four in the afternoon, the greyness of the sky outside made the light too dim to see to read the music. And as the choir began to sing, they were accompanied by the insistent patter of the rain against the stained-glass windows.

Maistre de Joyeuse's deputy had been dispatched to conduct in his master's place. Placid in temperament, he favored careful, easy-going tempi, taking no risks with difficult phrases. Celestine kept glancing surreptitiously toward the organ loft. Frustratingly, it was impossible to see anything of the new organist from her position in the choir stalls. And after a while, she forgot that a novice was playing, so competent and unobtrusive was his accompaniment. But when the time came for him to play alone at the end of the service, a paean of notes came tumbling out into the dimly lit chapel, lighting it up with the brilliance of its fanfares. The exuberance of his performance wiped all other concerns from Celestine's mind; she moved slowly as they filed out, entranced.

"Jolivert's 'Chromatic Prelude,' " whispered one of the elder sisters. "That piece is fiendishly difficult to play!" Celestine strained for a clearer look at the virtuosic organist but saw only the back of his dark head as he bent over the console.

In the vestry, the sisters began to chatter excitedly as they put on their cloaks. "What a magnificent technique! The boy's a real discovery. Such talent, so young . . ."

"We're leaving, Celestine," called Angelique. But Celestine stayed at the open vestry door, listening until the last blaze of notes died away. She was curious to see the gifted young musician with whom she shared a patron. After a little while, the lamp in the organ loft was extinguished. The bellows boys emerged from beneath the console, play-punching each other in a mock fight, and scampered off, yet still there was no sign of the organist. Had he already slipped away out of one of the rear doors? Disappointed, Celestine pulled up her hood and left the vestry—and almost bumped into someone crossing in front of the altar.

"Excuse me," he said.

"No, the fault was mine." The sacristan was extinguishing the candles; in the dreary rainlight slanting into the shadowed chapel, she saw a tall, lean young man clutching a folder of music. She had a brief impression of dark, intense eyes in a pale scholar's face and a skein of untidy black hair tumbling about his shoulders.

"You were the organist, weren't you?" she said, surprised at her own boldness. "Your playing was truly inspired. Thank you."

She saw his dark eyes widen at the compliment.

"Jagu!" a man called from the open doorway.

"Coming." The young organist turned and hurried down the nave toward the entrance. Celestine followed, but by the time she reached the open door, the chapel steps, glistening slick with rain, were empty. Even the beggars who usually sheltered with their dogs between the columns had disappeared.

Celestine pulled her cloak closer about her and, head down, set off through the puddles back to the convent.

The rain had stopped by the time the Maistre's carriage set out for the Forteresse. Celestine sat beside Gauzia, hands meekly folded in her lap, staring out of the window, while Gauzia chattered excitedly. Maistre de Joyeuse sat opposite, next to his aunt, Dame Elmire, who kept shooting reproving looks at Gauzia. Eventually she leaned forward and said, "Shouldn't you be saving your voice for the performance?"

Celestine had been paying Gauzia scant attention, having learned long ago to ignore her. Her mind was filled with music; ever since the afternoon, she had been remembering the magnificent performance that had lit up the dim chapel.

"So what did you think of our young organist today?"

Celestine realized that Maistre de Joyeuse was addressing her. Had he read her thoughts? "He's very talented. He played with such passion."

"I'm glad that Jagu acquitted himself well. Though now I have a serious rival!" She saw again that warm and endearing smile. *He really cares for his students,* she thought. *Is that because he had an understanding Maistre when he was a student? Or did he have to struggle?* She wanted to know everything about Henri de Joyeuse—and yet she did not dare to ask him such personal questions.

"Is Jagu really only seventeen?"

"Yes. He used to be a pupil at the Seminary in Kemper, my old—"

"There's the Forteresse!" interrupted Gauzia. "We're nearly there."

Celestine peered out of the carriage window and saw that they were traveling along a broad quay beside the river. Ahead, on an island, loomed a vast stronghold, whose crenellated fortifications and towers dominated the skyline.

"I believe it was originally built as a monastery," said Dame Elmire. "But the Commanderie converted it during the Religious Wars into a formidable citadel to defend the city. It's been theirs ever since."

As they crossed the bridge, Celestine saw that there were Guerriers standing guard, all garbed in somber black. Every time she saw those uniforms, the sight brought back a sick, shaky feeling.

This is not going to be easy . . .

The carriage rattled over a wide drawbridge toward the portcullis, and the coachman slowed the horses to a stop as two Guerriers approached.

"Your papers, please." The Guerrier addressing the Maistre spoke formally, with no hint of a threat, and yet Celestine felt a sense of panic rising. A band tightened across her chest, constricting her breathing.

"Here." Maistre de Joyeuse handed over their passes.

It was the Inquisition who took Papa. These are just ordinary Guerriers, like Captain de Lanvaux.

"Are you all right, my dear?" inquired Dame Elmire. "You look rather pale."

"Fine, thank you," Celestine managed.

"The jolting of the carriage can make one feel very queasy. I've brought a restorative tincture." Dame Elmire leaned forward to pass her a little brown glass bottle. "Take three drops on the tongue. That will make you feel better."

Celestine, grateful for the distraction, did as she was told. The drops were so strong they made her eyes water, but she felt a little less nauseous afterward.

"You're too delicate, Celestine," complained Gauzia. "You'll never be strong enough to be a professional singer if you can't take a simple carriage drive without feeling sick."

And then, as the carriage drove on into the vast parade ground beyond, Celestine caught sight of the ancient Commanderie chapel, its delicate gilded spire rising high to pierce the cloudy sky. A great rose window was set above the triple-arched doorway, dominated by tall statues of winged Guardian Warriors, their stern features almost worn away by centuries of wind and rain.

Many dignitaries and distinguished guests of the Grand Maistre were climbing the wide steps between a black-garbed Commanderie guard of honor. Celestine swallowed back her fear and straightened her shoulders.

"Would you let me take your arm, my dear?" asked Dame Elmire. "I don't want to miss a step and make a fool of myself in front of all these important people."

"Of course." Celestine managed a little smile, grateful for the distraction, and she and Dame Elmire set off up the steps, behind Maistre de Joyeuse and Gauzia.

After the service, the guests gathered for refreshments in the lofty Commanderie hall beneath a magnificent timber roof like the hull of an upturned galleon. Banners and bright-embossed shields adorned the walls, and carved angels gazed down from every gilded ceiling boss.

As Celestine escorted Dame Elmire into the throng, the retired singer was soon recognized and warmly greeted by two elderly clerics. Celestine stood watching as they began to reminisce, hoping that no one would notice her. She started counting the conical helmets and crossed scimitars displayed on the wall; trophies of some ancient Commanderie battle against the Enhirrans, she reckoned.

"Is my aunt neglecting you?" Henri de Joyeuse appeared behind her, startling her out of her reverie.

"Not in the least."

A peal of delighted laughter came from the other side of the hall. Celestine winced. Gauzia was surrounded by a little crowd of admirers, all eager to compliment her on her performance.

"Demoiselle de Saint-Désirat is in her element."

"She sang very affectingly," admitted Celestine. "But then, the anthem was very affectingly composed."

"I'm so glad you liked it."

But Celestine's attention was distracted. A guest had caused a chill in the atmosphere, just by entering the hall. Was he one of the nobility? He was soberly attired, with no jewelry or obvious badge of office. Yet she noticed that as he passed among the other officers, their conversation ceased and they instinctively drew back, as though deferring to him. She watched him reach Grand Maistre Donatien and bow. The Grand Maistre instantly turned to acknowledge him, a sure sign of the newcomer's importance.

"Who *is* that man?" Celestine whispered, still unable to take her eyes off him.

"One you don't want to have to do business with. That's Haute Inquisitor Alois Visant."

"Inquisitor?" she repeated mechanically.

"The head of the Francian Inquisition." Was that man talking with Captain de Lanvaux, exchanging the customary pleasantries, the ruthless mind who had hunted down and destroyed her father?

She wondered why he looked so ordinary; his hair was chestnut with the slightest shading of grey about the temples, his expression thoughtful as he conversed, giving little hint of his—

"Celestine?"

"What?" She started to find that Maistre de Joyeuse was gazing at her with concern.

"You were far away then. Very far."

"Forgive me, Maistre. I didn't mean to be so rude." Had she revealed too much? Trying to change the subject, she said the first thing that entered her mind. "What herbs are in your aunt's remedy? I feel much better now."

"My aunt's restorative drops?" He was smiling again. "Mostly brandy."

Rough hands seize her and bind her to the stake. The ropes cut into her flesh as she tries to struggle free. A hooded figure stands before her pyre. "Burn her," he orders the soldiers and they set flaming brands to the logs on which her bare feet rest.

"No," she whispers. Fire—such a cruel, horrible death. As the flames lick at her skin and the smoke stings her throat, she sees her executioner's face, his cold eyes reflecting the light of the flames.

Haut Inquisitor Visant.

All morning, Celestine went about her daily tasks in a daze, haunted by her dream. Last night's glimpse of Inquisitor Visant had brought home to her that she knew so little of the events that had led to her father's downfall. When Gauzia left for vocal training with Dame Elmire, Celestine could wait no longer. She took out the book and said, "Help me, Faie."

"*How can I help you?*" Each word pierced her brain like a shard of crystal. Glimmering light was emanating from beneath the protective cloth in which she had concealed the book.

"I was only a little child when the Inquisition took my father. I didn't really understand what was happening. Do you know why he was executed?"

The Faie, still in its guise of Saint Azilia, emerged from the cover until it towered above her, eyes luminous with concern, hands raised as though to bless. "*Lock the door.*"

Celestine checked the corridor; there was no one about. And

when she turned around again she no longer saw the sweet face of Saint Azilia smiling at her. A slender form, translucent as running water, gazed at her with wild, haunted eyes, faceted like glittering crystal.

"*I have a message for you. A message I was charged not to give you until you asked me.*"

The Faie's form rippled and began to take on a new identity. Brownish fairly short hair, a little untidy, a firm jaw, an endearingly slightly snubbed nose, two warm and smiling eyes the blue-grey of slate . . . a face that she had not seen in over ten years.

"Papa." She sank to her knees before the beloved likeness.

"*Klervie.*" Even the voice was his, not as deep or sensitively nuanced as Maistre de Joyeuse's, but warm in affection and good humor.

"*Dearest Klervie. If you are receiving this message now, it will be because my worst suspicions will have been proved true. I pray this will not be the case. I have bound this aethyrial spirit to protect and guard you until you are old enough and skilled enough to set it free. You have my blood in your veins, which means that you are different from other children. You were not born an elemental magus, like Kaspar Linnaius or Rieuk Mordiern, for which I thank God, but you do have a gift.*"

"I have a gift?" she murmured.

"*Listen carefully, child. The book to which I have bound the spirit is a book of magic. My grimoire. But however tempted you feel to use the glamours and spells concealed in its pages, I beg you to consider the consequences. Every time you use one, it will deprive you of some of that essential life force that the magi call the Essence. If you must resort to such desperate measures, do it only when your life depends on it. There is always a price to be paid for the use of magic, and you have not been trained how to conserve your strength.*"

Spells? Glamours? Celestine's mind was dizzied with the possibilities of this information. She could not take her eyes from this semblance of her father's face, trying to seal every detail in her memory. And then she heard footsteps on the stair. "Someone's coming!" But the Faie was still relaying her father's message and Celestine was desperate not to miss a single word.

"*I'm sealing this message in the book because I fear I have been betrayed. Kaspar Linnaius and I have been developing a secret de-vice, the Vox Aethyria, which transmits the human voice through the aethyr."*

"Kaspar Linnaius," Celestine repeated. And her memory cru-elly catapulted her back again into the Place du Trahoir, that terri-ble day that she had never managed to blot from her mind.

"We created a great invention together." Papa's bruised, swollen mouth twisted and contorted as he tried to enunciate the words. *"An invention that would have made our fortunes. Yet here I am, condemned to die—and where is Linnaius?"*

"He betrayed you, Papa." She vaguely remembered the older magus; he had always seemed forbidding and cold, never bringing her little treats, like Magister de Rhuys, or even smiling at her. Tears began to stream down her face. "Linnaius betrayed you to the Inquisition and stole your invention."

Someone rattled the door handle. "Celestine?" It was Gauzia, her voice shrill and petulant. "Why is the door locked? What are you doing in there?"

"Never forget that you are Klervie de Maunoir. But never tell another living soul. That name alone is enough to have you ar-rested by the Inquisition." Hervé's image began to shimmer, to fragment and dissolve as the rattling at the door handle grew more frantic.

"Don't go, Papa. Please don't go," whispered Celestine, reach-ing forward to try to embrace the fast-vanishing illusion. But her arms closed on empty air as the Faie faded swiftly into the book and became Saint Azilia once more.

"Celestine!" shrilled Gauzia petulantly. "If you don't open this door at once, I'll—"

Celestine opened the door.

"What were you doing?" Gauzia pushed in past her, looking around suspiciously, raising the bedcovers, opening the armoire door and peering inside. She turned on Celestine accusingly. "Was someone else in here? I thought I could hear voices."

"Oh, for heaven's sake, Gauzia." Celestine glanced away, not wanting to let Gauzia see that she had been crying. "I was learning song words, saying them out loud." She was still stunned by the Faie's revelation about the book. *My father left me his grimoire. A book of magic. And I have inherited a gift, his gift to use the glamours and spells inside . . .*

Gauzia came closer. "There's something different about you."

"My hair." Celestine cast around for her handkerchief.

"Have you been crying?"

"So what is so urgent that you had to break the door down to tell me?"

"It seems," Gauzia's hazel eyes were bright with a self-satisfied gleam, "that my performance last night found favor with quite a few people. Influential people."

"And?" Celestine only half heard what Gauzia was telling her. She wanted only to see her father again, to hear his voice instead of Gauzia's boasting.

"I've been asked to perform at a reception at the Muscobar Embassy. Many foreign dignitaries will be there. If they like my singing . . ." Gauzia spun around, clasping her hands together. "This could be my chance, Celestine, my chance to escape the convent at last."

Celestine began to understand why Gauzia was so excited. Celestine had never considered until this moment that she would ever be asked to use her talents except in the service of the church.

"Who made the invitation?"

"Why, the Muscobite ambassador, no less. A very handsome man, a count. I was presented to him after the concert." Gauzia sank to her knees by Celestine's bed. "And it gets better. I told him, 'But I've nothing suitable to wear, I can't possibly perform in this nun's habit.' And he said, 'We'll have a dressmaker visit you. Choose whatever style and color you like. And shoes to match.' "

Dresses and shoes meant little to Celestine except as a means to an end. She understood only that Gauzia had sung in public and been offered this extraordinary opportunity.

"And it's all thanks to Maistre de Joyeuse. I couldn't be more grateful. Do you think I should ask for a green gown, to match my eyes? Some people say it's an unlucky color . . ."

As Celestine lay awake with her thoughts, watching the moonlight fade, the clock of Saint Meriadec's struck two in the morning. She could not help repeating one name again and again. *Kaspar Linnaius*: the one magus to escape death at the stake. Memories, hazed by years of healing forgetfulness, began to flicker through her mind. Papa at work in his study, so intent he did not notice she was standing in the doorway, until she called his name. "Not now, Klervie, Papa's busy . . ." Sometimes there had been others there. The green-eyed young man who liked to play with Mewen, teasing him with a feather tied to a piece of string. And then she shivered. The older magus with eyes so cold that they gleamed like a wintry sky.

Then there was Papa's book, filled with forbidden knowledge. The Inquisition had burned everything in the magisters' library. Only this book remained.

Do I really have a gift? The gift to wield magic? The Inquisition had called it a Forbidden Art. If anyone else were to discover the secrets hidden inside the book . . . And yet now that she knew she had the key to unlock its hidden contents, this thought was dangerously attractive. She would never achieve anything if she was obliged to spend the rest of her days singing psalms with the Sisters of Charity. The answers lay beyond these safe convent walls, maybe far beyond the shores of Francia. But how was she, a young woman alone and without income or influence, to travel abroad?

Had Gauzia given her the clue?

Autumn had come early to Lutèce, bringing winds and sharp spatters of cold rain. Celestine went to and from the Conservatoire alone all week. Gauzia and Maistre de Joyeuse were busy rehearsing together for the recital at the Muscobar Embassy. Every time Celestine heard them, her heart was twisted with jealous anguish. Gauzia's voice seemed to have bloomed; even Celestine had to admit that her richly burnished contralto was a pleasure to listen to. Her technique had improved too, and she could sing a long, arcing phrase without skimping or snatching a little breath.

And then, the night before the concert, Celestine woke in the night to hear Gauzia sneezing. By morning, Gauzia was running a slight fever.

"It's only a head cold," she insisted, but Celestine could see the desperation in her eyes and hear the thick, clogged rasp of catarrh in her throat.

At Celestine's request, Angelique brought some linctus from the infirmary and a hot camomile tisane laced with honey.

"I'll be fine," Gauzia said again and again as she sipped the tisane. But the hoarseness in her voice was all too apparent. "You'll see."

"Will you turn the pages for me, Demoiselle?" the Maistre asked Celestine.

"Me?" Celestine was a little uncertain about this task; she did not want to risk turning in the wrong place and upsetting him.

"Don't worry; I'll nod so you know exactly when." He was smiling at her. "Shall we begin with a few vocal exercises, Demoiselle Gauzia?" He played a broken chord for Gauzia to pitch her first note, but Gauzia did not start to sing; she was surreptitiously trying to clear her throat, one hand covering her mouth. Maistre de Joyeuse played the broken chord again and Celestine saw Gauzia swallow hard before opening her mouth to sing. The notes that issued from her throat did not display the usual strong, well-rounded tone, but were far from the husky sound Celestine had expected.

But Gauzia was only ten bars or so into her first chanson when she broke down, one hand to her throat.

"Henri, this girl is sick!" pronounced Dame Elmire, marching in. "I could hear her coughing from two floors up. I forbid you to allow her to perform."

Gauzia let out a hoarse wail of protest, then lapsed into another bout of coughing.

"You should be in bed, young lady," said Dame Elmire. "Come with me to the kitchen and I'll give you a hot drink to soothe your throat. Then you're going back to the convent in the carriage." And before Gauzia could protest again, Dame Elmire took her firmly by the arm and marched her out of the music room.

Celestine rose from her seat beside the Maistre. "I'd better go to her."

He caught hold of her by the hand. "Can you take her place, Celestine?"

"Me?" Her first reaction was one of panic. "I can't sing Gauzia's songs!"

"We'll change the program. We'll choose a repertoire better suited to your voice. Who will know?"

"B—but it's tonight." The panic increased. "All those important people will be listening."

"And I'll be there to accompany you. What is there to fear?" He grinned at her, a disarming, friendly grin.

"But you said that my voice isn't ready."

He leaned closer to her. "Here's your chance to prove me wrong."

Her eyes widened. What was he implying?

"And I've nothing to wear."

"What about Gauzia's dress?"

"That won't be at all suitable!" pronounced a disapproving voice from the doorway. Dame Elmire had reappeared, glowering sternly at her nephew. "Green is definitely *not* Celestine's color. Not too mention the fact that Gauzia is rather more well developed than Celestine, and there's no time to take in the gown."

Celestine felt herself blushing again, mortified that Dame Elmire should have pointed out such a fact in front of the Maistre.

"So, Aunt, what do you propose?" said the Maistre wearily. "I can tell from the glint in your eyes that you have a plan."

"Indeed, I have! I've kept costumes from my favorite roles on stage. And I was a lot slimmer in those days. I was thinking that Comtesse Melusine would work very well. Follow me, Celestine."

"Well, what do you think, my dear? It's not the latest fashion, I know, but it has a timeless charm."

Celestine gazed at herself in Dame Elmire's mirror. Melusine's gown was made of the palest blue silk, with a delicate tracery of little flowers embroidered with sequins of turquoise and silver around the low-cut neck and hem. She had never worn anything so pretty or frivolous in her life. She wondered whether Sister Noyale would have approved.

"I don't feel like . . . me," she murmured.

"That's the idea! Let's see what Henri says."

The soft folds of the gown whispered as Celestine followed

Dame Elmire down the steep stair to the Music Room. *Such luxurious material. Will he disapprove?* Suddenly she could think of nothing else.

"Well? Will she do?" demanded Dame Elmire.

The Maistre looked up from the score that was laid out open on top of the fortepiano. *He hates it.*

And then she caught a darkening in his eyes, an intense focusing of the gaze, as if he were seeing her as he had never seen her before.

"You look . . . lovely, Celestine," he said without a trace of the playful, teasing tone he had used earlier. He closed the score with a snap. "The carriage is waiting. It's time to go."

A glitter of crystal chandeliers lit the crowded salon of the Muscobar Embassy. *What am I doing?* Celestine wondered, one hand clutching hold of the fortepiano. *If I make a mess of this, the Maistre will wash his hands of me. But if I'm a success, Gauzia will never speak to me again.*

So many well-dressed, elegant women and so many distinguished-looking men, all seated, looking expectantly at her . . . She was breathing too fast; she closed her eyes, remembering Dame Elmire's training. "*Inhale through your nostrils to the count of five, then exhale slowly through the mouth . . .*"

Yet when the Maistre began to play, the familiar phrases of the first song flowed around her like a comforting embrace and her fear faded away. When she opened her mouth to sing, she felt transported. She and the Maistre instinctively understood each other, working together to convey the subtlest nuances of the words and music. Only when the last notes died away did she become aware of the hush in the salon. And then guests rose to their feet to applaud. Bemused, she took the Maistre's outstretched hand and sank into a deep curtsy to acknowledge the rapturous reception.

"Well done," he whispered. "You charmed them."

"*We* charmed them." She felt as light-headed as if she had drunk sparkling wine.

"So this is your new songbird, Maistre?" The speaker was a distinguished-looking man of middle years. "Your performance was exquisite, Demoiselle."

"May I present Celestine, your excellency?" The Maistre

bowed. "This is our host, Count Velemir, the Muscobar ambassador."

Celestine was about to curtsy again, when the count took her hand and kissed it.

"Celestine? How mysterious that you use only your first name . . . You must tell me all about yourself, Demoiselle." He held on to her hand, leading her away from the Maistre, who was instantly surrounded by admiring women, young and old.

Servants were offering the guests silver trays with bowls of black, oleaginous globules heaped on crushed ice, surrounded by lemon segments. The contents gave off a faint, disagreeably fishy odor.

"What *is* that?"

"One of our national delicacies, my dear: caviar from the sturgeon that spawn in the River Nieva. You really must try some. It's delicious, I assure you." And as if to reassure her, he helped himself, spooning the eggs onto a tiny pancake, adding a squeeze of lemon juice, before popping it into his mouth. "Excellent. Now it's your turn, Demoiselle." And before Celestine could refuse, he was holding out another little pancake, heaped with caviar, for her to try. As she reluctantly opened her mouth, she caught Maistre de Joyeuse's eye as he listened to one of the Muscobite ladies and saw, to her annoyance, that he was vastly amused at her discomfort.

I can't afford to offend my host. She chewed the fishy mouthful and swallowed swiftly, trying to smile. To her surprise, the Count began to laugh. "Well done, my dear! You needn't disguise your disgust. It's an acquired taste. What you need now is a glass of vodka to wash it down." He clicked his fingers and one of the servants appeared with another tray.

"No spirits for my pupil, your excellency." Henri de Joyeuse had suddenly appeared at her side. "They damage the delicate vocal cords."

"And Demoiselle Celestine's vocal cords must be protected at all costs," said the Count, laughing again good-naturedly. "You are in good hands, Demoiselle. May we entice you to perform one day at the Winter Palace at Mirom?"

"Not until I have finished with her, dear Count," interrupted Dame Elmire. "Her training is not yet over. She's only sixteen."

Mirom, capital city of the northern kingdom of Muscobar. Her first invitation beyond the shores of Francia. Her first steps on the hunt for Kaspar Linnaius.

"If you are to begin your professional career, you need a name."

A name. Celestine lowered her gaze, studying the dusty floor of the carriage as they jolted along over the cobbles. *I have a name but it's one I can never reveal to you, dearest Maistre.*

"Don't make the girl feel ashamed, Henri," scolded Dame Elmire. "Is it her fault if she never knew her parents?"

If only I could tell you everything, then you would understand. She glanced up but the Maistre was staring out at the night, resting his head against the padded back of the carriage, lost in his own thoughts.

"As my student, you should take my surname," said Dame Elmire. Her eyes glinted in the darkness. "How does Celestine Sorel sound?"

"She's my student too," said the Maistre distantly, without turning his head. "Celestine de Joyeuse has a more euphonious sound."

"Celestine de Joyeuse," echoed Celestine. Even saying the name aloud gave her a glowing feeling deep inside.

"Of course, I was a Joyeuse before I married. So I suppose that taking our family name is a compromise. Although it could lead to misunderstandings. She could be supposed your sister, your cousin, even your daughter . . ."

As Dame Elmire prattled on, Celestine tried to make out the Maistre's expression as the occasional gold gleam of a street lantern briefly lit up the interior of the carriage. But he had withdrawn into his thoughts again. Only his fingers moved in a rhythm of their own making, silently tapping against the armrest.

He's composing again.

The city was already shivering under grey, glacial skies when Celestine heard a slow sad dirge of city bells tolling through the falling snow. She and Gauzia were helping Dame Elmire to toast slices of brioche over the glowing sea coals in the range in the kitchen.

"A good excuse to keep close to the fire," declared the old lady.

The kitchen door opened and Maistre de Joyeuse came in, stamping the snow from his boots. The icy draft made the burning logs sizzle and spit in the grate.

"Close the door, quick!" scolded his aunt. "So, what's all that tolling for?"

Maistre de Joyeuse came close to the fire to rub his hands; Celestine made room for him, but as she did so she saw the sadness in his eyes.

"Terrible news," he said. "Prince Aubrey is dead."

Gauzia let out a shocked cry and dropped the toasting fork.

"Heavens preserve us!" Dame Elmire hastily made the sign to ward off evil. "That fine young man, dead? How can that be?"

"A hunting accident. His horse threw him."

"But he was such an accomplished rider—" said Gauzia.

"Apparently a bird of prey flew down and startled his mount."

Celestine stood unmoving, remembering a tall, broad-shouldered young man, with an easy smile and an infectiously good-humored laugh, so full of life and confidence.

"This is a sorry day for us all." Dame Elmire retired to her seat in the inglenook, shaking her head. "He was so well liked. His poor mother. What must she be feeling now? And his father, the king . . . all his hopes for a secure succession dashed."

Gauzia had been fighting back sobs. Now she dashed from the room, slamming the door.

Snow still fell over Lutèce, softening the morning city clatter, dampening the metallic din of horses' hooves on cobbles, as cart and coach wheels stuck in the icy slush.

Celestine and Gauzia trudged to Maistre de Joyeuse's house through the snow, clutching their grey Novice's cloaks and hoods tightly to them against the bitter chill. The city's mood was as muted and hushed as the snowy streets; the Sisters of Charity had already planned an all-night vigil to pray for Prince Aubrey's soul.

Maistre de Joyeuse was seated at his desk, poring over a half-written score, the pale snow light leaching the gold from his hair.

He raised his head as they entered and Celestine saw there were grey smudges beneath his eyes as if he had been up all night.

"I wouldn't have called you here through the snow if the matter were not so pressing. There is to be a state funeral in three days' time and I've been asked to provide suitable music. Not the whole service, for which I thank God, but an anthem. The queen has specifically asked me to set some verses by the Allegondan poet Mhir. Given the lack of time, it's going to have to be mostly solo, alternating with brief choral passages." He was almost speaking to himself, indicating the relevant bars as he flipped through the score. "First verse—you, Gauzia." He tossed her a page. "Second and third verses, Celestine."

Celestine caught the sheets as he flicked them to her. The writing was not easy to read, hastily scribbled in the heat of inspiration—or desperation, she thought, given the tight demands of the royal commission. She glanced up and saw that Gauzia's lip was trembling again.

"The choristers of the Chapelle Royale will be singing the rest of the service, so you need only learn this. Shall we make a start? I'll have to set out for the Chapelle in an hour; the snow's all but brought the city to a standstill."

The aisles of the gloomy cathedral were filled with the noble families of Francia and the ministers of state and their entourages, somber in their mourning clothes. Outside, the streets were lined with the people of Lutèce, waiting in the snow to pay their respects to the dead prince. Celestine and Gauzia had left the convent at six in the morning to make their way to the cathedral before the crowds gathered. Since then they had endured an interminable wait in the cathedral vestry with the other musicians. The youngest choristers' behavior soon began to deteriorate and, forgetful of the solemnity of the occasion, one initiated a farting game. The head chorister grabbed the offender by the ear and dragged him outside. From the ensuing yelps, Celestine guessed that punishment had been swiftly administered.

"Little boys," said Gauzia scathingly, and Celestine nodded, though she had been rather grateful for the distraction. She could not help but remember Rozenne's funeral in the little chapel at

Saint Azilia's. Even though the cathedral of Saint Eustache was so vast and austere, she was sure she could sense similar thoughts emanating from the mourners: a young life, so full of promise, cut short before its time.

I wasn't able to sing for you then, Rozenne. But I'll do it today. As well as for the young prince.

When at length the signal came from the priests that the royal family had arrived, Celestine and Gauzia stood up to process in behind the choristers. Celestine was almost numb with cold and the boredom of waiting. She just wanted the ordeal to be over. The sight of one of the lay clerks clipping an errant chorister around the ear for chattering as they entered the nave only increased her sense of dislocation. They moved slowly down the side aisle to the steady rhythm of a solemn organ prelude. Then as they turned, she saw the prince's catafalque before the altar, the coffin draped with the blue-and-gold flag of Francia, and her heart seemed to miss a beat. In front of her, Gauzia's tread faltered.

Henri de Joyeuse came out from the choir stalls, ready to conduct the choristers as they approached. The boys' voices soared up into the shadowy heights of the nave, sounding, in spite of their earlier behavior, like a chorus of angels. Celestine, watching the Maistre's face as he conducted, suddenly felt comforted by his presence. His calm expression mirrored the mood of the music; he mouthed the shapes of the words to his young charges, who now sang their hearts out, their eyes soulful and yearning. His hands, as they shaped the phrases, moved gracefully, sinuously.

The chilly cathedral was filled with little braziers, glowing with coals sprinkled with grains of pungent incense, filling the cold air with blue wisps of twisting smoke. As the priests intoned the words of the service, Celestine became aware of the responsibility she was carrying. If she made a mistake, she would ruin the Maistre's composition and possibly his reputation. Worst of all, she would besmirch this final, heartfelt tribute to Prince Aubrey. Her stomach began to churn with anxiety.

She had never sung in such a vast space before and as she took in a breath, listening for her cue, she wondered if her voice would be too weak to carry to the congregation. The notes of the introduction, high, like distant morning birdsong, issued from the organ pipes. Beside her, Gauzia raised her head to watch the Maistre. The words chosen by Queen Aliénor from the writings of the poet-prophet Mhir took on a new significance as Gauzia's voice filled the cold air.

Celestine watched, as if in a frozen dream, as the members of the prince's family came forward, one by one, to place evergreen boughs on the coffin. King Gobain, his head bowed, Queen Aliénor, her face glacial, then Princess Adèle, holding Enguerrand by the hand, the young prince wiping tears from beneath his spectacles. Celestine felt a sympathetic tightening in her throat and checked herself, turning the page to begin her solo.

"The flame burned too brightly," Celestine sang, "and the snows of early winter extinguished its radiance. But the memory still burns in our hearts."

"I wanted to thank you, Demoiselle de—de —" Princess Adèle hesitated.

"De Joyeuse, highness. In honor of my mentor and teacher." It gave Celestine, eyes respectfully lowered, a little shiver of pride to say her adopted name aloud.

"Demoiselle de Joyeuse. You sang so beautifully for my brother's funeral."

Celestine heard from the tremor in the young princess's voice that Adèle was controlling her emotions with difficulty. "It was an honor," she answered quietly, not knowing what else to say.

"The others sang beautifully, too. But you"—and the princess moved closer to her—"you sang from the heart. I felt that you understood how it feels to . . . to lose someone you hold very dear."

Celestine looked up.

"Am I right?" Adèle said softly. "I am, aren't I?"

"I'm an orphan, your highness."

"So you lost your parents. That must have been hard to bear. Did you have any brothers or sisters?"

Normally Celestine would have resented this probing into her past. But there was something so sympathetic in the princess's manner that made her want to answer, if only to offer a little comfort or distraction. "No," she said, "but I had a dear friend, Rozenne; she was like a big sister to me. She . . . she died of a fever when I was eleven."

"I guessed as much," said Adèle. She put out her hand and took

Celestine's. "Come and sit with me. Tell me your story. I'm much in need of distraction."

Celestine let herself be led to the window seat, where Adèle settled herself, patting the silk cushions beside her. Below, the formal gardens of the palace, the intricate knotted beds and gravel paths stretched down to the river, in curlicued patterns of snow-dusted box, lavender, and yew.

"How old are you, Demoiselle Celestine?"

"Just sixteen, your highness."

"A year younger than I. Where did you learn to sing so beautifully?"

"I was trained at Saint Azilia's convent. I had a gifted teacher there, Sister Noyale." Celestine could not help smiling at the memory.

"So you are going to take the veil?"

It was a question that Celestine was not yet ready to answer, although she knew that one day soon she must make that difficult decision. "Gauzia and I lodge with the Sisters of Charity and sing with them in Saint Meriadec's every day. Many of the sisters in the choir were trained at Saint Azilia's too. So I suppose . . ."

"But with a rare voice like yours, you could fill concert halls. You could sing opera." Adèle clasped her hands together, her wan face lighting up at the thought. "I adore the opera! Have you ever been, Demoiselle?"

Celestine slowly shook her head. Such possibilities had never occurred to her. "Maistre de Joyeuse would not approve."

"Your teacher?"

"He says that one should not push a young voice beyond its natural limits. I'm not ready to sing in opera yet." Celestine became aware how serious and intense she must sound. And yet she sensed nothing but a kind and friendly regard; it was just like sitting chatting with Angelique or Rozenne

"Those verses by Mhir that Joyeuse set for Aubrey . . . *I* chose them," said Adèle suddenly. "Aubrey never had time for poetry. He was always so active, playing tennis, fencing, wrestling, riding." Celestine saw her bite her underlip, as though trying to hold back her tears. "But he had a good heart. Everyone liked him. We were utterly different in our tastes and interests . . . but he always had time for me."

"The verses were very aptly chosen."

Adèle sighed. She turned to gaze out over the snow-rimmed gardens, but not before Celestine had seen the glint of tears in her dark eyes. "I'd love to hear you sing again. When the time of mourning is over, will you come and sing for me?"

Celestine heard herself saying, "Oh yes, your highness, of course; you have only to ask."

Adèle unpinned a little jet brooch from her austere black dress and pressed it into Celestine's hand. "I want you to have this. As a token of my gratitude and friendship."

"Oh, I c—couldn't," stammered Celestine.

"I insist." Adèle closed her fingers around it. "It pleases me to make you this little gift."

"Thank you," whispered Celestine, pressing her closed fist with the brooch inside to her heart.

"What's that?" Gauzia poked a finger at the little jet-and-silver mourning brooch that Celestine had pinned to her dress.

"A gift."

"From whom? A secret admirer?"

"From the princess."

"Wha-at?"

Celestine had not told Gauzia of her invitation to the palace. But now Gauzia thrust her face into Celestine's. "From Princess Adèle? How so? And how come I didn't get a gift, too?"

Celestine shrugged. It gave her a certain pleasure to see Gauzia so annoyed. But now she knew that Gauzia would not give her a minute's peace, needling her for every detail of her meeting with the princess.

"She gave you the brooch herself? In the palace? What was she wearing? Not that you'd have noticed, Celestine. But why didn't she invite me? Didn't she like my singing?"

Angelique appeared in the doorway of the girls' cell. Her expression was grave.

"The Abbess wants to see you both in her office. You're to come with me."

Unlike soft-hearted and indulgent Mère Ermengarde at Saint Azilia's, the Abbess of the Sisters of Charity was a strict and stern-faced woman who did not tolerate the slightest lapse of discipline.

"What have we done wrong?" whispered Gauzia. "We're only lay sisters here. It's not as if we've vowed to devote ourselves to God. Yet."

Celestine shook her head, not wanting to say a word in case the Abbess overheard.

"I've received a letter," announced the Abbess as soon as they crossed the threshold. She frowned at them both over the top of the paper. "It states that you, Gauzia, have been offered a role in an *opera.*" She pronounced the word as if it were a mortal sin.

Gauzia let out a little shriek of delight. "What opera is it, ma mère?"

"The title is irrelevant. I cannot have one of my charges participating in such a frivolous, worldly entertainment. It is utterly inappropriate."

"So you're saying that I can't—" began Gauzia in tones of anguish.

"I'm saying, Demoiselle, that you must choose." The Abbess stared severely at Gauzia—and then at Celestine, who had been dreading this moment, even though her name had not yet been mentioned. "You are both approaching seventeen. An age at which most of our novices decide to take their vows or leave the convent for good."

"You're saying we must make our choice already?" Celestine was so alarmed at the thought that she dared to speak out. "But we've only been here a year. It will take another two years to complete our training at the conservatoire."

"Do you wish to perform in this opera?" said the Abbess, ignoring her and concentrating on Gauzia. "Because if you do, then you cannot continue to lodge here. It would severely tarnish the reputation of my convent if it were known that one of our girls is appearing in a *theater.*"

"B—but where shall I go?" Gauzia wailed.

"That, Demoiselle, is up to you. Please inform me of your decision by noon tomorrow."

"Is it truly your wish to become an opera singer?" Dame Elmire fixed Gauzia with a piercing stare. "Your voice is still developing. You'll be taking a risk."

"I've never wanted anything so much before," said Gauzia quietly. Celestine looked at her in surprise; for once in her life, Gauzia was not making a scene. This, more than anything, convinced her that Gauzia was speaking the truth.

"I see." Dame Elmire nodded but her expression still gave nothing away.

"But what opera is it? And what part am I invited to play?" Gauzia could not keep her excitement contained for long. "And who recommended me? Was it you, Dame Elmire?"

Dame Elmire sighed. "Petitfils, the manager of the Opera House, is an old friend of mine. He heard you sing at the cathedral and contacted me. The opera is called *Balkaris,* and the role is that of a slave girl."

"No wonder the Abbess looked so disapproving," said Gauzia with a giggle.

"But she said you must choose," Celestine quietly reminded her.

"What should I do, Dame Elmire?" cried Gauzia. "If I accept the role, the convent will throw me out and I'll have nowhere to stay. But if I turn it down, I may never get this chance again."

"So you are determined to go on the stage? You're not afraid of hard work?"

"I was born to go on the stage!"

The door opened and Maistre de Joyeuse came in, still wrapped in his greatcoat, the collar turned up against the cold. "*Peste,* it's freezing today. Will spring never come?" He held his hands up to the blaze, rubbing them together. A stray lock of golden hair fell forward, half-obscuring his face, and with a movement at once graceful yet unself-conscious, he shook it aside.

He looks so beautiful in the firelight . . . Celestine felt her face bloom with warmth at the sight; she glanced away, sure he must have noticed.

"It's as we suspected, Henri," said Dame Elmire. "The good sisters won't allow their name to be associated with the opera house. If Gauzia is to appear in your opera, we'll have to make other arrangements for her."

Your opera? Celestine was jolted out of her dreamy state.

"Can't she stay here?" said the Maistre. "Your students have lodged with us before."

"I—I didn't know you had written an opera," Celestine blurted out.

"She'll need a chaperone," added Dame Elmire slyly. "Any pretty young actress is regarded as fair game by the gentlemen in the audience."

"Dear Aunt, I know you're longing to find an excuse to spend your days in the Opera House once more."

"Well, it's settled!" Dame Elmire's eyes glinted triumphantly. "I will write to the Abbess straightaway."

The girls returned to the convent through the falling snow; a fresh dusting was settling onto the frozen slush, making treacherous going underfoot.

"How generous of Maistre de Joyeuse to invite me to lodge at his house." Gauzia, oblivious of everything but her own concerns, was almost dancing over the ice. "And how good of Dame Elmire to offer to act as my chaperone. It's going to be so exciting, Celestine, starting rehearsals and meeting the other singers . . ."

Celestine, toes and fingertips numb with cold, hardly heard Gauzia's exultant chatter. She was lost in her own dulled thoughts. She must have been deluding herself not to notice. Now it was obvious.

He likes Gauzia. What man wouldn't? She's so lively, so self-assured. And she's pretty. No wonder he wanted her to play a role in his opera.

Compared to her, I'm a quiet little mouse. Every time I'm with him, I get tongue-tied. Or I say something stupid and blush. He must think I'm so naïve. Why can't I be more like Gauzia?

CHAPTER 21

As the last traces of snow melted from the roofs of Lutèce, Celestine realized that the few ties that had bound her and Gauzia together were fraying fast. Gauzia spent all her days at the Opera House, rehearsing with the Maistre. So when walking back from vespers one afternoon, Angelique happened to inquire, "How is Gauzia enjoying her new life?" Celestine answered touchily, "Oh, it suits her all too well; she's really in her element now."

"Ouch." Angelique blinked her wide blue-grey eyes. "I touched a nerve there, didn't I?"

Celestine stared at the cobblestones. "I'm sorry. I didn't mean to snap."

"Do you wish you had been the one chosen for the opera?"

"No! Well . . . that's not it exactly." Celestine had not realized until now how miserable she had been feeling.

"You must really miss her company. You were good friends together at Saint Azilia's for . . . how many years?"

"Not quite friends," Celestine said with a wry little smile. "Good rivals, more like. I was always closer to Katell and Rozenne."

Angelique stopped suddenly and, putting her hands on Celestine's shoulders, gazed searchingly into her eyes. "Your talent is very special. Use it. Because we're not young forever, and the bloom in our voices soon fades."

Celestine stared back at her, astonished. What had inspired Angelique to speak to her so bluntly? Was there some secret sadness, a disappointment that had blighted her life? But before she could summon the courage to ask, the church clocks began to strike.

"Six already! We're late and I'm on duty in the refectory." Angelique gave her a swift kiss on the cheek and hurried away after the line of nuns disappearing around the far corner of the street.

"You're much in demand, it seems." Maistre de Joyeuse passed Celestine a sheaf of letters, several bearing crests.

"Invitations for Celestine de Joyeuse . . . to sing at the Smarnan Embassy, at a soiree for the Marquise de Trécesson . . ." She looked up in astonishment, to see that his eyes were twinkling with amusement. "Are you certain that they want *me*?"

"It's wonderful what a little royal patronage can do."

"Princess Adèle?"

"Oh, there's a request from her royal highness as well."

"Then I must reply to her first of all." Celestine pressed the princess's letter to her heart, touched that Adèle had remembered her.

"There's one slight snag. I won't be able to accompany you for the Smarnan concert, or the princess's reception. The opera . . ."

"Oh." Celestine felt as if the sun had gone behind a cloud. "Then I can't accept."

"So I was going to propose Jagu de Rustéphan to take my place."

Celestine looked at him blankly. She was so disappointed that the Maistre would not be there to support and guide her that she had not even considered the possibility of another accompanist.

"Jagu substituted at Saint Meriadec's for me. Don't you remember?"

That pale, dark-haired young man who had played as if he were possessed, and impressed all the nuns? He was a capable performer, she couldn't deny it. Yet the idea of working with anyone other than Maistre de Joyeuse tied her tongue and she could only nod in reply.

"Perhaps Sister Angelique would agree to act as chaperone for you, while my aunt is escorting Gauzia?"

Celestine stared down at the invitations, the gold-rimmed cards, the ambassadorial crests. How had it ended up this way?

Gauzia and the Maistre together every day, and she partnered with an inexperienced student?

"Repertoire. What songs would be most suitable for the Smarnan ambassador, I wonder . . ." The Maistre seemed not to have noticed her dejection and was already leafing through a pile of music.

"B—but won't he—Monsieur de Rustéphan—need time to learn all the accompaniments? This Smarnan reception is only in four days' time!"

"Yes, it is rather short notice. Typical of the Smarnans: impetuous, hot-blooded southerners. But you need have no worries about Jagu; his sight-reading is far better than mine. Ah! How about this one?" He triumphantly held up a sheet. "My 'Spring Moon.' You sang it very affectingly at Count Velemir's. And the words are by a Smarnan poet."

Why was she hesitating? This was an embassy reception, so there would be dignitaries present from many countries. What better way to begin her search for her father's betrayer?

"I'll do it," she said.

A virtuosic flourish of notes from the fortepiano greeted Celestine as she arrived at the Maistre's house. She opened the music room door to see two heads bent close together over the music on the stand, one golden, one black as crow's feathers. The Maistre looked up and smiled welcomingly as she came in.

"Demoiselle, may I present your accompanist: Jagu de Rustéphan."

Jagu stood up rather too swiftly and knocked over the music, fumbling to pick it up. He bowed awkwardly, not quite meeting her eyes.

"We've already met," she said coolly. "At the chapel." Was he blushing? He sat down again, concentrating on shuffling the sheets of music into the right order. Not a promising start, she told herself. Clumsy—and gauche.

"We always begin with some exercises so that the demoiselle can warm her voice," the Maistre explained. "We use techniques that my aunt has devised to loosen the throat muscles and facilitate the breathing . . ."

As Celestine began the series of daily exercises, she felt ill at ease. Could Jagu de Rustéphan sense that she resented his presence? He had not looked at her once directly . . . and yet, as he followed the Maistre's instructions, deftly playing one broken chord, then another, to give her the correct note, she sensed that he was listening to her with a highly critical ear.

"And now let's move to the recital repertoire." Now Celestine was the one to blush, caught off guard by the warmth of the Maistre's smile. "Are you going to start with 'Spring Moon'?"

"Yes." *Though I've never sung this song with anyone but you, Maistre.* It was hard not to feel resentful, for the instant Jagu began to play the introduction, she realized that she had come to regard this as "their" song. She could sense Jagu's dark eyes watching her. Why was he looking at her with such intensity? Only then did she remember that these bars were her cue. Too late she snatched a short breath, and muffed her first entry.

"Again," said the Maistre lightly. Grateful that he had not berated her in front of Jagu, she clasped her hands in front of her. *Concentrate!*

This time she did not miss her entry and they reached the end of the song without further mishap. The Maistre made no comment and indicated that they should continue with the next song, then settled down to listen in his aunt's chair by the fireplace. His silence disturbed Celestine more profoundly than if he had chosen to criticize her performance.

After a half hour, they had reached the end of the recital.

"Show me how you acknowledge the applause." The Maistre began to clap. Celestine had not expected this either; flustered, she dropped into a low curtsy and, rising, turned to the fortepiano, where Jagu was sitting, glaring. Was he feeling as embarrassed as she? She gestured to him and he rose, still glaring, and managed a stiff bow.

"If the applause continues, you must beckon your accompanist to stand beside you."

Celestine cast him an anguished glance but he continued to applaud. *Are you tormenting me on purpose, Maistre?* Reluctantly, she beckoned Jagu to stand beside her.

"Offer Celestine your hand."

Celestine steeled herself to place the tips of her fingers on Jagu's outstretched palm. Deliberately not looking at him, she bowed and heard the Maistre break into delighted laughter. She snatched her hand away and, stealing a glance at Jagu, saw that an angry flush of dark red had brought color to his pale cheeks.

"If you two could only see yourselves." The Maistre wiped tears of laughter from his eyes. "Forgive me. If you can't even bring yourselves to hold hands, then we'd better devise a different conclusion to your program. Of course, a true professional . . ."

They were only words. When Celestine was learning the song by heart, they had seemed little more than pretty, inconsequential verses. Now they were imbued with a bitter, personal resonance.

"Spring moon sheds its silver light on lovers, hand in hand,
   Why am I still alone in darkness?
   Where is my spring-moon lover?"

A single teardrop fell onto the music . . . and then another. Celestine flung the sheets away from her, scattering them across the floor.

What am I doing, sitting crying over a few words strung together by some stranger? How could the man who wrote these verses know what it is to feel this sweet, secret pain? And how can the Maistre know what musical notes will express that feeling until it's almost too much to bear?

"Where is my spring-moon lover?"

Why, every time I sing this phrase, do I see his face, hear his voice? Why did he make me sing this song? Has he guessed how I feel about him? Is he using my feelings for him to extract a more poignant performance from me?

Is he more cruel, more manipulative, than I could ever have imagined?

"*Why am I still alone in darkness?*" sang Celestine, and broke off, glowering at her accompanist.

"What's wrong now?" Jagu asked, with a subtle emphasis on the final word. His voice held the slightest hint of weariness, as if implying that she was being picky just to annoy him.

"That's not how we practiced it with the Maistre. He holds back on that phrase, and then puts a special nuance into the echo of the melody in the right hand."

She saw a look of resignation cross his pale face. She heard the hint of a sigh. "From bar twenty-two?" he said, not meeting her eyes.

I love this song. But he plays it with such detachment. When the Maistre plays it, it's as if we have a secret understanding, as if he's putting feelings into the accompaniment that he can't communicate directly to me . . . She broke off again. *Is that why I'm angry with you, Jagu de Rustéphan?*

"Where *is* Angelique?" Celestine fretted as she waited in the Maistre's carriage. She was nervous enough about the evening's recital without this added anxiety.

Jagu came back from checking the street for a sign of their chaperone. "We'll be late if we wait any longer," he said brusquely. The patter of running footsteps broke the twilit silence of the peaceful little *ruelle*. Celestine leaned out of the carriage window and saw not Angelique but dumpy little Sister Monique puffing along, waving a folded paper.

"What's happened?" Celestine got out and went to meet her, but Sister Monique could only wheeze and clutch her sides. "Jagu, we must take her in to Francinette."

"The time," said Jagu between gritted teeth.

In the kitchen, Celestine and Francinette helped Sister Monique into a chair and poured barley water for her while Jagu opened the letter.

"Angelique sends her apologies; she has come down with a migraine and has sent Sister Monique to replace her as our chaperone." The clock in the hall upstairs struck eight. Celestine looked up from fanning the wilting nun and saw Jagu crush the paper in his fist. She had been counting on Angelique's calm demeanor to help steady her nerves.

"S—sorry," whispered Sister Monique.

"She's obviously in no fit state to go anywhere," he said. Celestine could sense his growing tension; his face was pale with apprehension about the coming performance. As if she didn't feel nervous enough already! "And if we don't leave now, we'll arrive too late. We'll just have to go unchaperoned."

The applause was appreciative. Someone shouted, "Bravo!" But as Celestine and Jagu took their bow, Celestine letting her fingertips rest as lightly as possible on Jagu's outstretched hand, she saw that many of the Smarnan ambassador's guests were still chatting, just as they had done throughout the recital. They had continued to drink and eat, as though the music were nothing but a pleasant background to their conversation.

A little girl came up to Celestine and presented her with a bouquet of white roses and bright yellow mimosa. Celestine kissed her and curtsied again, holding the bouquet across her breast as Dame Elmire had taught her, so that the thorns did not snag the delicate material. She noticed that the audience had already left their seats and returned to the buffet table.

"Time to leave," she said resignedly. Then she glanced at Jagu and saw that his customary frown had deepened and his fists were clenched at his sides.

"Do they have no manners?" he said through clenched teeth. "Talking while you were singing, as if you were just some cheap street singer begging for loose change."

"You're not leaving already!" The Smarnan ambassador approached, accompanied by a thickset man of middle years who walked with a confident, military swagger. "The Count was most eager to make your acquaintance."

"Alvborg at your service, Gunnar Alvborg." The Count bowed. "Demoiselle Celestine, your performance was ravishing." He clicked his fingers and a flunky came over and offered her a glass of wine from his silver tray. "But you must be thirsty."

"Thank you. Are you with the Smarnan Embassy?" Celestine moistened her lips with the red wine, then set the glass down, determined to keep a clear head.

"Lord, no! I'm from a colder clime. Can't you guess from my fair complexion, and my accent?"

Was he teasing her? "I'm sorry, Count, you have me at a disadvantage . . ."

"Our countries have not always been on the best of terms in recent years," he said, smiling. "I'm with the Tielen Embassy."

"You speak our language very well for a Tielen," she said, then winced inwardly as she realized how rude that must sound.

"And you blush very prettily." He moved a little closer. "Perhaps you and your accompanist would like to perform before Prince Karl and his court? Although from the sullen looks your accompanist is giving me at the moment, perhaps not. He looks the jealous type."

"So Prince Karl likes music?" Celestine asked.

"He's a great patron of all the arts and sciences. He's a very cultured man and likes to invite the most distinguished academics and musicians to Tielborg."

"Sciences?" she echoed.

"I'm sure we could come to an understanding." He moved closer still and as she took another step backward, her elbow grazed against the wall. Too late she realized that he had cleverly maneuvered her into a little alcove. "One that would be mutually beneficial."

"I don't quite follow—"

"Has anyone ever told you how bewitching your eyes are?" He placed one hand on the wall above her head, leaning over her, so close that she could smell the wine on his breath. "Such a celestial shade of blue. Whoever named you chose well . . ."

Celestine had never found herself in such an intimate situation before. She mustered all her courage and stared challengingly up at him. "If you'll excuse me, Count—"

"And how provocative when you're roused." His smile widened and she saw from the glint in his eyes that he was enjoying her discomfort. "I swear, Demoiselle, that I just can't resist such a blatant challenge."

Was he about to touch her? To kiss her here, among all these illustrious guests? All her plans to secure her first invitation to sing abroad vanished in a single, all-consuming urge to flee.

"And how prettily you blush," murmured her admirer, hand sliding down the wall to catch her by the shoulder. "Where are you going, Demoiselle? We had only just begun our conversation."

"Let go of me," she said in a fierce whisper. Her whole body was burning with embarrassment; she was sure that she must have turned bright crimson. The hand that rested on her shoulder strayed onto bare skin, fingers wandering along the line of her bodice to touch her breasts.

Before she knew what she was doing, she had slapped him. But he just caught her by the wrist and pulled her close. "You're a spirited little tease, aren't you?"

"Let her go!"

Celestine felt his grip relax. Turning around, she saw Jagu advancing on them, his fists clenched, his pale face a mask of fury.

"Keep out of this, boy. This doesn't concern you."

"Let her go," repeated Jagu. Celestine twisted her hand free and ran to Jagu's side. The raised voices had attracted attention and she could see the ambassador whispering to a servant.

"What gives you the right to interrupt our tête-à-tête?" The charming, attentive expression had vanished, to be replaced by a vicious sneer. The count took a step toward Jagu, who stood his ground. "Do you know who I am?" The conversation died as the salon fell silent. All the guests were staring. "I am Count Gunnar Alvborg."

"I represent the demoiselle's guardian, Maistre de Joyeuse," said Jagu with calm dignity. "He placed her in my care tonight. I cannot allow anyone to molest her."

"Why, you—" Count Alvborg lurched forward, taking a swing at Jagu. Several female guests shrieked. Celestine saw Jagu move with lightning swiftness. His hand caught the man's thrusting fist and, with a sudden twist, pulled the assailant's arm up behind his back. As the ambassador's servants came running through the guests, he slammed the count's face against the wall.

"Damn you," shouted Alvborg, through puckered lips. "You'll pay for this, you impudent little nobody. I demand satisfaction. You'll—" The servants caught hold of him and removed him, still shouting abuse, from the salon.

The ambassador came over to Celestine. "I must apologize for the count. His behavior was unpardonable."

Shaken, she nodded. She wanted only to retreat, to vanish from all the staring, curious eyes. She turned to Jagu and saw a thin gash of scarlet marring his pale face.

"Is that blood on your cheek? Did he hurt you?"

His hand flew to touch his cheek; he looked at the fingertips as they came away smeared with blood. "It's nothing. His signet ring must have grazed the skin."

She pulled out her handkerchief to dab at the cut but he shook his head, turning abruptly away. "It's time we left," he said curtly.

Celestine's head was spinning by the time they were ushered down to their waiting carriage. The ambassador had kissed her hand, with many flattering compliments, but she had hardly heard a word. As the carriage rattled away from the torchlit courtyard, she leaned back against the leather seat and closed her eyes. When she opened them again, the carriage was moving along the wide avenue and the light from the street lanterns they passed illuminated Jagu, sitting silently watching her.

"Thank you," she said. "You rescued me."

"I was only following the Maistre's instructions."

"But Alvborg is a big, well-built man. And you disabled him so swiftly. Where did you learn to fight like that?"

A shrug. "I train with the Commanderie cadets once a week."

Now that the initial shock was wearing off, she began to feel angry with herself that she had wasted such a valuable opportunity. She had genuinely believed that Count Alvborg had approached her to invite her to perform. She must not allow herself to be so easily gulled again. "If only I could train with the cadets too. I don't suppose they accept women?"

He was staring at her as if she were mad.

A woman alone must devise strategies to defend herself. If I'm to go out into the world, I must become stronger.

Rehearsals continued—this time for the princess's soiree—and the frustration that had been building all week suddenly exploded. Jagu brought both fists crashing down on the fortepiano keys, and Henri de Joyeuse flinched.

"Why did you pair us together, Maistre? She's impossible! Nothing I do is right. You told me that she was a convent girl, sweet-natured, a little shy and retiring, yet she does nothing but complain that I don't play the way you do."

The Maistre said nothing for a while. He appeared to be studying the music, his head bent, his long strands of fair hair obscuring his face.

"Is that so?" he said eventually. To Jagu's annoyance, there seemed to be a little smile playing about the Maistre's lips. "I wondered if sparks might fly . . ."

That throwaway comment made Jagu even more angry. What exactly was the Maistre implying?

"I can't do it. You'll have to find another pianist. I've made up my mind."

"This is a *royal* recital." The Maistre shut the score and came over to the keyboard. "Do you want me to be frank, Jagu?"

"Yes." Jagu's chin went up defensively, ready for whatever blow the Maistre was about to deliver.

"Celestine is right. These last weeks you've been playing as if your heart isn't in the music anymore." The Maistre leaned on the fortepiano case, looking at him keenly. "So, what's changed?"

Jagu turned away, not wanting to meet his eyes. He had been dreading this question for some time. "It—it'll be my eighteenth birthday next week."

"Surely a cause for celebration?"

"Have you forgotten, Maistre?" he blurted out. "It's the age at which a man can enter the Guerriers."

"Ah. Your promise to Captain de Lanvaux. No, I hadn't forgotten. I'd just hoped that, with reflection, you might have changed your mind." The Maistre's gaze, usually so mild and encouraging, had become uncomfortably penetrating.

"Changed my mind? I owe him my life!" Jagu was indignant that the Maistre might have thought him so shallow that he would go back on his word.

The Maistre turned away from the fortepiano. "It's your decision, Jagu."

Jagu scowled down at the wet cobbles beneath his feet as he walked away through the rain.

I don't want you to be understanding, Maistre. If only you'd shouted at me, told me I was making the worst mistake of my whole life, it would have made it so much easier for me to walk away.

"Jagu. *Jagu.*" Jagu heard someone calling his name.

"What is it?" he mumbled. His eyelids were sticky with sleep. "Who's there?"

A wan face appears, hovering above his in the darkness.

"Paol?" *Jagu whispers.*

"*I can't sleep, Jagu.*" *Paol's fair hair has faded to wisps of dusty spidersilk and the fine skin over his delicate features is discolored, like ancient parchment. "Stay with me. Don't leave me alone in the dark."*

"*It's all right, Paol. I'm here.*" *Jagu reaches out to catch hold of Paol's hand, but the frail fingers crumble to dust in his grasp.*

Jagu sat up suddenly. He was shivering. His heart was pounding and his nightshirt was soaked with cold sweat.

"Paol."

His attic room was dull with the half-light before the sun rose. Shadows clustered in the far corners. He had not dreamed of Paol for some months now. He looked down at his right hand, feeling again the skeletal fingers disintegrating in his grip.

The magus's mark gleamed faintly in the dawnlight.

He's still alive, the one who did this to you. I don't know his name, I don't know how to begin to track him down, but I have to make sure that no other child suffers such a horrible death.

Jagu pushed back the crumpled sheet and went over to the desk, where his precious books of music were stacked. He drew out the document that he had placed for safekeeping in the Maistre's book of chorale preludes.

Enrollment in the Commanderie Cadets.
I, Ruaud de Lanvaux, recommend Jagu de Rustéphan as a suitable candidate for cadetship.

As the applause rippled around the salon, Celestine saw her patron smiling warmly at her. She curtsied, smiling back at Adèle. The program had been planned to include several of the princess's favorite songs, concluding with Henri de Joyeuse's achingly beautiful "Spring Moon." To Celestine's surprise, Jagu had played with sensitivity and expression. But in the anteroom after the performance, he seemed even more distant than usual.

"I won't be accompanying you again after tonight, Demoiselle," he said stiffly. "I'm about to enroll in the Guerriers."

This revelation shocked Celestine. "You're abandoning your musical career? When you have so much talent? Why throw away all these years of hard work?"

"Because I made a promise. A promise to a friend."

"You vowed to join up together?"

"I vowed to avenge his death."

"How did he die?" Her voice dropped to a whisper. There was something about his eyes that told her he must have been through some terrible ordeal. He must still be nursing scars from that experience. She found herself wanting to know what had happened to damage him so deeply.

"Besides," he said, avoiding her question, "I also owe Captain de Lanvaux. He saved my life."

"The captain saved you?" She became aware that she was looking at Jagu differently, wondering what had happened to him, how deep the scars ran. "What happened? Was it overseas? He fought in Enhirre, didn't he?"

"It wasn't overseas." He began to pack away his music, sliding the scores into his music case. So he didn't want to talk about that either. She felt hurt that he didn't want to confide in her. "I promised him I'd join up when I was eighteen." There was that determined, resolute tone in his voice again. And it infuriated her that he could be so sure of himself, so certain that he was doing the right thing.

"But what about the Maistre? What did he say when you told him?"

She saw him swallow and knew that she'd touched a raw place.

"He tried to dissuade me," he said stiltedly.

"It must be difficult for him to see one of his best students throw everything away. It must feel like a—a rejection." The words came out before she could stop them. But when it came to the Maistre, her feelings were so strong, so unpredictable that she could not always guard her tongue.

"He said it was my decision!"

"But he's given you so much. Is this how you repay his generosity?"

"How can you know what's right for me? You, with your sheltered convent upbringing? How can you know *anything*?" He seized his case and stormed out, slamming the door behind him.

CHAPTER 22

The greenhouse was hot and humid, and the fronds of trailing plants brushed Rieuk's face as he made his way to Magus Aqil's laboratory. The moist air was heavy with strange scents, some peppery and vivid that tickled his nostrils, others musky, tinged with a fetid odor of decay.

Aqil's gift lay in the culture and uses of plants. Rieuk supposed that he should have guessed that such a talent would make the secretive magus a master of poisons as well.

"Ah, there you are, Rieuk." Aqil looked up from his work; earthy tubers lay sliced open on a marble board beside a pestle and mortar. "Oranir, bring me the elixir we prepared for Emissary Mordiern."

A dark-eyed youth appeared from the inner room, carrying a phial, which he presented to Rieuk, bowing his head. As he looked up, Rieuk felt a sudden jolt of recognition. The boy was regarding him gravely with a gaze that reminded him painfully of Imri, although the mage-glitter in his black eyes was not warm amber but the scarlet and gold of burning magma.

"Oranir?" Rieuk said dazedly. "An earth mage?" Oranir vanished swiftly into the inner room before Rieuk could thank him.

"My new apprentice. He somehow found his way to Ondhessar from Djihan-Djihar. He doesn't say much. I'd guess from the scars on his body that he was treated very harshly when his mage blood first asserted itself."

Aqil's words stirred bitter memories in Rieuk. The thought that anyone could have been cruel enough to damage the boy's flawless olive skin sent a stab of bright anger through him.

"So in spite of the Inquisition's purges, there are still children being born with the gift?"

"Oranir is the first since you came to us, Rieuk. We are a dying breed," said Aqil, lightly enough. "Now, this elixir works in two ways. It will give Gobain of Francia the illusion that the cancer eating away at his bowel has been cured."

"Isn't that more cruel than poison?" Rieuk held up the phial, examining the viscous liquid within. It had a purplish tinge, reminding him of the dusty bloom on the skin of fresh-picked grapes. "To give him false hope?"

"If you really want to be arrested and executed as a poisoner and regicide, then I can give you a far swifter poison to administer," Aqil said mildly, taking back the phial. "But to allow you time to 'disappear,' you need your remedy to be seen to work."

"And the second stage?"

"The elixir will accelerate the growth of the cancer, making it much more aggressive. By the time you've left Francia, the king will suffer a sudden relapse and die. So your challenge is to find a way to administer the elixir. Have you worked out a strategy?"

Rieuk did not answer. He was trying to master a growing feeling of disgust. This deadly elixir seemed an underhanded and cowardly way to carry out the Arkhan's vendetta.

Rieuk took lodgings close to the Jardin des Plantes, the physic gardens renowned throughout the quadrant for their collection of medicinal plants from many countries. The most notable Francian physicians came to exchange ideas in the library and it was here that Rieuk went to present the specimens he had brought from Aqil's greenhouse.

"I doubt any of the Francians will have seen a scarlet-speckled fritillary or a white balsam poppy before; they only bloom in the hidden valley," Aqil had told him. "The poppy will pique the physicians' interest, especially when you tell them of its cancer-healing properties . . ."

"I've been listening to you with great interest, Doctor Suriel. This elixir that you claim can stop the growth of cancer . . ."

Rieuk looked up and saw a smartly dressed man addressing him. "And you are?" he asked levelly.

"Vallot, personal physician to his majesty the king."

"Emeric Suriel," Rieuk said, bowing. Aqil had helped Rieuk construct a convincing identity for his role, even down to inventing a Djihari physician father and a Francian mother.

"What proof do you have that this elixir of yours works where other remedies have failed?" Doctor Vallot said, regarding him intensely through his monocle, as if he were scrutinizing one of his patients. "And why should we trust your methods more than our own?"

Rieuk shrugged. "Indeed, why should you? I've studied in Enhirre and Djihan-Djihar for several years; the Djihari physicians use many remedies unknown to us in Francia." He could sense from his silence that Doctor Vallot was interested in his proposal. "But since you don't trust my methods . . ." He picked up his bag, turned, and made for the door, hoping that the ruse had worked.

"Wait."

Rieuk stopped but did not turn around.

"I'm sure you'll understand my reticence in this matter." Doctor Vallot's tone was almost placating. "It's the king's health we're dealing with here, after all."

"Of course." Rieuk still did not turn around.

"We'll need to check your papers."

"I'm sure you'll find that everything is in order," Rieuk said quietly. The Arkhan's secretaries had supplied "Emeric Suriel" with Enhirran passports and testimonials, confirming his status as a qualified physician. "But please don't take too long in making your decision. My visa only lasts for a few more days."

"Where can we find you?"

Rieuk turned away to hide a smile of bitter triumph. "I have lodgings at the rue de l'Arbalète."

CHAPTER 23

The great astronomical clock in the Plaisaunces inner courtyard struck ten.

Ruaud closed the *Life of Saint Argantel.* "We'll continue with our studies tomorrow, highness. It's late."

Enguerrand's hand shot out and caught his wrist. "Captain."

Surprised, Ruaud saw that the boy was gazing imploringly at him.

"There's a passage I need to discuss with you. It's been keeping me awake at night."

"Very well." There was something about Enguerrand's expression that made Ruaud pass him the ancient volume. "Show me."

"It's this passage. Where Saint Sergius turns to Argantel and says, 'I'm not ready to take on the task the Emperor has given me. Why has he chosen me? I'm just a simple man, not a warrior. All I want to do is go home—' " Enguerrand's voice faltered, " '—go home to the mountains of Azhkendir.' " He knuckled away a single tear that had trickled behind his spectacles. "Every night I lie awake asking myself the same question: Why me? Aubrey was raised to be king. I never wanted to be the heir to the throne." Enguerrand's voice had dropped to a whisper.

"Yet that simple man found the courage within himself to face the Drakhaouls, highness—"

"My father has no confidence in me. My mother thinks I'm weak. It's not that I didn't love Aubrey—I did! And I miss him very much."

So this was what was really troubling Enguerrand. He must have been bottling up his grief for Aubrey all this time. Ruaud looked at his charge, wishing that royal protocol did not forbid him from simply giving the boy a reassuring hug.

"But I can't bear the way *they* keep comparing me to him. I'll never replace him, and I'll never be good enough for them!"

There came a polite tap at the door and Fragan, Enguerrand's valet, appeared. "Pardon me, Captain, but her majesty asked me to ensure that the prince was not too late to bed."

Enguerrand nodded. He looked utterly defeated.

As Ruaud walked back to his rooms through the hushed corridors of Plaisaunces, he realized that it would take much more than readings about the life of Saint Argantel to give Enguerrand the consolation he so desperately needed. He determined to go to the king in the morning and ask him to take Enguerrand with him to the remote Monastery of Saint Bernez, high in the mountains, so that the boy could mourn his brother undisturbed.

His hand had already closed around the door handle when he thought he heard a scuffling noise inside. He glanced up and down the empty corridor; there was no sign of a servant or guard.

Why would anyone be in my rooms at this late hour?

Ruaud flung the door open. At the same moment there was a flash, a loud bang, and a pistol ball whistled past his cheek, embedding itself in the opposite wall.

"Who's there? Identify yourself!" he cried. There was a scramble of movement in the far corner of the antechamber. The emberlight from the dying fire revealed a shadowy form, fleeing.

Ruaud had left his sword hanging in its sheath. He drew the blade, seeing the emberlight glint on its keen steel. But the intruder had vanished. Baffled, Ruaud cast around, looking for a hiding place. Then he noticed that the tapestry that covered the main wall, a fine piece of Allegondan weaving depicting the Allegory of the Vineyard, was moving slightly. He lifted one corner of the heavy fabric and felt along the plain plastered wall behind, searching for a concealed door.

"Captain!" Friard came running in and stopped, seeing Ruaud's drawn sword. "Are you all right? I heard a shot."

"Get a light. And your pistol." Ruaud continued his search until his fingertips traced a thin crack in the plaster. Friard returned with a lantern and by its flickering flame Ruaud showed him the faint outline of a secret door he had discovered.

"There must a be a hidden catch. Ah." With a metallic click, the door swung inward, letting out a gust of cold, musty air from a dark passageway beyond. "Did you know of this, Friard?"

"No, Captain." Friard sounded as mystified as he was.

"I'm intrigued to see where this leads." Ruaud took the lantern from his lieutenant.

"Why the drawn sword, sir?" Friard asked as they edged along the dank, narrow tunnel.

"I disturbed an intruder in my rooms." Ruaud felt a breath of night air and spotted a small grille set in the wall far ahead, half-choked with weeds.

"It would be a little embarrassing if we were to emerge in the queen's apartments," came Friard's voice from behind him.

"What are you implying, Friard? That her majesty has been visiting me in secret?"

"Of course not! I'd never dream of such a thing." Friard sounded mortified at the suggestion.

Ruaud smiled in spite of himself; Friard was so easy to tease. "Here we are. Another door. Let's see where it's brought us." He heard Friard swallow hard as he eased up the rusty catch; the door opened inward. "Well, here's another mystery." He emerged into the night, gazing around to get his bearings. "We've come out in the gardens." A thick yew hedge ran the length of the wall, hiding the little door. He gazed up at the high wall of the palace wing towering above them. "My rooms overlook the main courtyard. Yet we're on the river side."

"And our quarry has escaped into the night," said Friard, gazing out over the darkened gardens to the distant lights illuminating the quay and the palace landing stage.

"Unless this was a ploy to lure us out of the rooms . . . while his accomplice slipped in, the minute we'd entered the passageway!" Ruaud hurried back into the passageway, Friard running after.

Someone had been rifling through his desk. The lock had been forced and papers were strewn all over the parquet floor. Ruaud swore. "I walked right into their trap."

Alain Friard lit candles on the desk, then helped Ruaud retrieve the scattered documents.

"Who could it have been?" Ruaud shuffled through the letters and dispatches, wondering what the thief had been searching for. "The Inquisition are much more subtle in their methods. This was so . . . blatant."

"I'll organize a guard on your rooms, Captain."

"I'm sure there's no need for that." Ruaud was puzzling over an empty folder; it had contained his recent correspondence with Konan, now Commander of the Guerriers occupying Ondhessar. "Why would Konan's dispatches be of any interest to anyone? Unless . . ." He looked up to see Friard regarding him with concern.

"Details of troop movements, numbers garrisoned at the fort," he said.

"Enhirran agents?" It was the obvious assumption. Yet something didn't quite make sense; the Enhirrans could assess the situation at Ondhessar firsthand. No, the whole incident had an orchestrated feel to it, as if it had been devised to undermine his reputation . . . or send him a warning.

"This was a serious lapse in security, Captain. Leaving sensitive documents where they could be so easily stolen by our enemies has put our men in Enhirre at risk."

Ruaud stood stiffly before his Commanderie superiors, listening carefully to the charges. Grand Maistre Donatien presided over the tribunal, resting his head against his hand, his expression bland, almost absent.

"Permission to speak."

Donatien nodded.

"Whoever broke into my desk knew exactly what he was looking for. But I put it to you, Maistre, that an Enhirran agent would gain little knowledge that was not already available to him. It seems more likely," and Ruaud phrased the next assertion with care, "that this was the work of someone with a grudge. Someone who wanted to discredit me."

"And why would anyone wish to do that?" said Donatien in incredulous tones.

"Someone who resents my position at court. Someone who feels I may have too much influence over the prince." Ruaud was watching his superiors closely, testing to see if any of them reacted to his allegations.

"That's absurd!" Donatien turned to the others with a dismissive little laugh. "We all hold you in the highest regard, Captain."

"Then why am I called to justify myself before you?"

"An official reprimand is appropriate in the circumstances, don't you agree, gentlemen? But given Captain de Lanvaux's unblemished record of service, no further action need be taken . . . at this stage."

As Ruaud saluted his superior officers and left the chamber, he found Alain Friard waiting anxiously outside.

"Let off with a reprimand," said Ruaud, feigning a lightness of spirit that he did not feel.

"But it wasn't your fault, Captain—"

"I'll just have to be more careful in future." Ruaud was walking away at such a swift pace that Friard had to run to keep up with him. "It's a matter of Commanderie security, after all." He wanted to put as much distance between himself and Donatien as possible.

"There's more to this than you're telling me, isn't there?"

Ruaud stopped on the bridge that led from the Forteresse to the city. "Friard, you've been a good and loyal officer to me. I don't want to implicate you in this."

"You know that I'd defend you to the death, sir," said Friard staunchly.

Ruaud leaned out over the stone parapet, feeling the breeze from the river flowing below cool his hot face. The clattering of carts over the cobbles would prevent anyone from overhearing their conversation. "I was set up, Alain. There's a schism in the royal household and Donatien has me marked as a king's man. But he's very close—too close—to the queen. And she resents me. She feels that I have too much influence over Prince Enguerrand."

Friard's eyes widened but he made no comment.

"It sounds so . . . disloyal to the Commanderie." Ruaud had not realized till he began to confide in Friard how disillusioned he felt. "I'd always looked up to Maistre Donatien. I modeled myself on him. And now . . ." He stared down into the churning waters of the River Sénon.

A hand gripped his shoulder. He looked round to see Alain Friard looking earnestly at him.

"*I* believe in you, Captain."

Ruaud grinned wryly and clapped Friard on the back. "You're a good man, Friard. I don't know what I'd do without you to cover my back. How about a glass of wine before we go back on duty?"

"Sounds good to me, sir!" said Friard, his face brightening at the thought. Yet as they set off toward the Pomme de Pin tavern, Ruaud found himself glancing uneasily over his shoulder to check if they were being shadowed.

I didn't want to believe Abrissard's warning. But now, I fear, Maistre Donatien, your allegiance to the queen has put us in opposite camps, and divided the Commanderie.

Jagu shaded his eyes as he gazed at the high walls of the Forteresse, a dark blur towering upward into the scalding brightness of the early-morning sun. He was still smarting from the comments Celestine had flung at him.

"This is for you, Paol," he said softly. He drew himself up to his full height and set off across the drawbridge. Minutes later, he was being led by a Guerrier not much older than he across the main courtyard. In the distance he could hear the sound of marching feet; in an inner courtyard he glimpsed a troop of Guerriers practicing drill to the insistent beat of a snare drum. It seemed so far from the corridors of the conservatoire and the idle, self-indulgent existence he had been leading.

"Welcome, Jagu!" Captain de Lanvaux rose from his desk to greet him. "Welcome to the Commanderie."

As Jagu returned the captain's firm handshake, he felt as though a heavy cloak were being lifted from his shoulders. He had made the right choice. A military career would be so much more rewarding than eking out his days in the salons of the rich, playing insipid music as background accompaniment to their little amours and scandals.

"You won't regret your decision," said Captain de Lanvaux. He watched as Jagu signed the commission, then added his signature below.

Regret? Jagu had spent many sleepless nights before making his decision. He was committing himself to a soldier's life, a soldier monk of the Order of Saint Sergius. And if that meant leading a celibate existence, dedicating all his energies to fighting evil, then he was strong enough to resist temptation. Ruaud de Lanvaux must have made a similar decision at his age, and he seemed the most well balanced man Jagu had ever met.

"You'll undergo the basic training, like every new recruit, including a tour of duty in Enhirre," the captain said, placing his hand on Jagu's shoulder. "But first, you must meet your superior officer. Come in, Guerrier Guyomard."

Jagu heard the once-familiar name, but did not instantly make the connection. A tall young officer entered and gave Captain de Lanvaux a vigorous salute.

"It must be a few years since you last saw each other." The captain was smiling as he spoke. "Guerrier, take Rustéphan to his billet and get him a uniform."

"Captain!" Guyomard turned to Jagu, who was staring at him in amazement. The flyaway thatch of ginger-blond hair might have been tamed into a more military cut, but the mischievous glint in those pale green eyes was unmistakable.

"Kilian?" Jagu said, staring at his friend.

"The same!" That roguish, lopsided grin was unchanged too. "How long is it? Six years, seven since you left Saint Argantel's in such a hurry?"

Captain de Lanvaux gave a discreet cough. Kilian instantly straightened up. "Forgive me, Captain. Follow me, Rustéphan."

Outside the captain's room, Kilian stopped, turned, and gave Jagu a friendly punch on the shoulder that almost knocked him off-balance. "Jagu! Where've you been hiding all these years?"

Jagu could not stop looking at his friend's face, trying to match it to his memories of the eleven-year-old Kilian. "Didn't Abbé Houardon tell you? The captain arranged for me to study at the conservatoire, here in Lutèce."

"So why join up? Or weren't you cut out to be a musician after all?"

Jagu gave Kilian a frank look. "Because I owe it to Paol." He saw Kilian's confident smile fade a little at the mention of Paol's name. And then he gave a careless shrug of the shoulders. "You'll have time in plenty to repay your debt here, cadet."

"Cadet?"

"You'll have to salute and call me 'sir.' "

Jagu suddenly began to laugh. He had never expected to enroll and find that Kilian was his superior officer, but on seeing Kilian's expression, he stopped laughing and saluted. "It's good to see you," he said, feeling that for once something was right with his world, and added, "Guerrier Guyomard, sir!"

"You sang so beautifully for us the other night, Celestine." Princess Adèle greeted her with both hands held out. Celestine had been about to curtsy but Adèle folded her affectionately in her arms and kissed her cheek, leaving a breath of her perfume, fresh as apple blossom. "I quite forgot my troubles listening to you."

"Your highness is too kind," Celestine murmured, surprised by the familiarity of Adèle's greeting.

"And we're alone, so no more of that 'highness,' please!" Adèle took her by the hand and led her to sit at a little table already laid with a tray of tea. "When we're together, tête-à-tête, call me 'Adèle.' This tea is delicious, you must try some. It's a new blend from Khitari. I prefer it with lemon, but Maman takes hers with milk."

Celestine accepted the delicate porcelain cup and tasted the tea. "What a delicate flavor," she said, nodding her appreciation.

"I thought you would like it." Adèle took a little sip, then put down her cup. Celestine could tell that something was troubling her. "This has been such a strange week." She looked up suddenly and asked, "Have you ever felt that you've lost all control of your own destiny?"

Celestine was surprised by the directness of the question. She glanced around, wondering if they were truly alone in the little rose-papered salon, or if some hidden court spy was listening in on their conversation. Adèle was gazing earnestly at her, waiting for her reply. She wanted to say, "When my father was burned at the stake as a heretic," for that would have been the most truthful answer of all. But instead, she had to content herself with saying, "I've been very fortunate. Ever since Captain de Lanvaux rescued me from a life of poverty, I've been offered choices along the way. And I've been blessed with a kind and sweet royal patron, Adèle."

Adèle nodded, acknowledging the compliment. "How I envy you, Celestine. I wish we could change places, even for a week or two! But I sing like a crow, so no one would ever seriously accept me in your stead. Can I confide in you? My father wants me married."

"Married?" Celestine could tell from Adèle's dejected expression that the princess was not at all enamored of the idea. "Does he have anyone in mind?"

"So far, there are three prospective husbands." Adèle pulled a face. "And when I said it was too soon, I was treated to a long lecture by Papa on duty to my country and my family. But two of the three are far older than I! First there's Eugene of Tielen; his wife has just died in childbirth." She shivered. "How could I marry a Tielen, Celestine? After they killed so many of our countrymen?"

Celestine had never given serious thought to what it might mean to be married. She shook her head in sympathy.

"Then there's Ilsevir of Allegonde. Twenty-six. I last met him when we were little children and he played a horrible trick on me. He gave me a biscuit to eat with some red jam on it. But it wasn't jam, it was hot paprika paste!" She showed Celestine a miniature in an oval gold case.

"He looks . . . pleasant," said Celestine. Prince Ilsevir could in no way be described as handsome from this little portrait. She saw a rather ordinary-looking young man, with mouse-brown hair, his plain features redeemed by an endearing smile.

Adèle sighed. "How he looks, what manner of man he is, matters little to Papa. Above all, the match must be advantageous to Francia. Now, if he were only as handsome as your accompanist, I would have nothing to complain about."

"Jagu? Handsome?" Celestine had never thought of him in that way. "But he always looks so surly and bad-tempered. I've never even seen him smile."

"Ah, but the way he was looking at you with those brooding dark eyes when you were singing. You couldn't see it, but I could." A teasing glint lit Adèle's eyes.

"An accompanist has to keep looking at his soloist." Celestine could feel the color rising to her cheeks. The princess was certain to interpret this as a sign of her secret affection for Jagu, when nothing could be further from the truth!

"You make a very attractive pair."

"Not any longer," Celestine said huffily. "He's just enrolled in the Guerriers."

"No!" Adèle looked shocked. "But doesn't that mean he has to take a vow of celibacy? My poor Celestine."

"I don't care what he does with his future." What *was* the princess implying? "If he wants to stay celibate all his life, that's his affair."

"Or . . . have you rejected his love and sent him away in such despair that he'd rather go fight in the desert than stay near you, knowing you can never be his?"

Celestine's mouth dropped open in surprise. It had never occurred to her until then that Jagu might have been hiding his true feelings for her. They had done nothing but argue over everything for the past weeks. And yet there had been that incident at the Smarnan reception, when he had defended her, standing up to the odious Tielen count. Had there been other subtle hints that she had missed, obsessed as she was with Henri de Joyeuse?

"It's too late now," she heard herself saying.

"You heartbreaker."

"You mentioned three prospective husbands," Celestine said swiftly. "Who is the third?"

Adèle rose and went to a little escritoire. "Andrei Orlov." She showed Celestine a second miniature, painted in jewel-bright colors like a little icon. The face that stared boldly back at Celestine was striking: a beautiful, dark-browed, blue-eyed boy with a wild tousle of black curls. "Why did you keep him hidden away? He's so handsome," she said, studying the portrait. "Although there's something willful, almost arrogant, about his expression."

"Do you think so?" Adèle leaned over her shoulder for a closer look. "I hear he's got himself into trouble at the Naval Academy more than once. And he likes to gamble."

"So he's heir to the throne of Muscobar?"

Adèle gave a shiver of revulsion. "In wintertime, the hours of daylight in Muscobar are so brief. And it's so cold that the rivers freeze over for months on end. I could endure the cold . . . but not the lack of the sun." She took the miniature back from Celestine, addressing the prince's portrait. "But if you're the one Papa favors, then I may have to learn to love the snow."

———

When Jagu tried to recall his first weeks as a cadet Guerrier, all he could remember was bone-aching exhaustion and a never-ending bombardment of shouted commands. The cadets rose before dawn, attended prayers in the Commanderie chapel, then were put through a series of drills and physical exercises on the parade ground. In the afternoons, they left the Forteresse to practice maneuvers on horseback in the river meadows beyond the city walls. There they also learned how to assemble, load, and fire muskets and small pieces of ordnance, before returning to the Forteresse for blade work with sabers and foils, or wrestling in the Salle d'Armes.

Jagu was certain that he'd made the greatest mistake of his life. Night after night he would collapse onto his hard, narrow bed, feeling every muscle in his body protesting. It was especially galling to find that Kilian was his superior; maturity had not tempered the malicious streak in Kilian's nature. He seemed to relish his role as Jagu's commanding officer, finding all manner of subtle ways to embarrass him in front of the other cadets.

One evening, returning exhausted to the cadets' quarters, he pushed open the door, only to trip over a rope stretched across the opening and crash headlong to the floor. Gales of helpless laughter erupted from the other cadets. Jagu looked up to see Kilian standing behind the door.

"For God's sake, Kilian, what are you trying to do, get me killed?"

Kilian crouched down beside him. "Ah, but I can't be seen to be favoring my old schoolmate, can I, cadet?" Jagu glimpsed the glint in his pale eyes. "Tongues would wag soon enough. Besides, if you're going to serve in Enhirre, this is just the kind of surprise attack you need to be prepared for."

Jagu rolled over onto his back, eyes closed, and let out a sigh, knowing himself defeated.

Throughout the long ride to the Monastery of Saint Bernez, Ruaud had much time to wonder about the enigmatic summons he had received from the king.

"We need to talk. Make any excuse you can for leaving Lutèce—but don't reveal to anyone that you are coming to Saint Bernez."

Why was the king so insistent on secrecy? And why had he requested him, out of all the Commanderie Guerriers? Yet as he rode up the narrow mountain path toward the monastery, the stark beauty of the sunlit peaks overwhelmed him, making his concerns seem insignificant.

As Ruaud entered the cloisters, he caught sight of Gobain in the herb garden, bending down to pinch a leaf of lemon balm, sniffing the scent it left on his fingertips.

"I hope I haven't kept you waiting, sire."

Gobain straightened up. "Not at all; I was enjoying the silence. And the sunlight. Now I see why you brought Enguerrand here on retreat; there's a healing quality to the air in the mountains."

"And the brothers are skilled gardeners." Ruaud surveyed the wide kitchen gardens and orchards beyond. "They say that nothing heals the pain in a man's soul better than an hour or two of energetic digging."

"Walk with me, Captain." Gobain set off at an easy pace toward the orchards.

Ruaud matched his step to the king's, nodding to the monks they passed, busy at work among the neat rows of cabbages and lettuces in the kitchen gardens. As they passed through the doorway into the orchard, a flutter of bright-feathered bullfinches took off in zigzagging flight from the nearest branches. Still the king had said nothing, leaving Ruaud wondering what the true purpose of the summons might be.

"How sweet the air smells up here," said Gobain. "Even the rain has a fresh scent. It would be a pleasant place in which to end one's days."

"Surely your majesty is not contemplating leaving us so soon . . ." began Ruaud, and stopped as he saw the king's dark eyes regarding him keenly.

"Let's proceed a little farther."

It had not escaped Ruaud's notice that the apple orchard was deserted except for the bullfinches. Gobain must have brought him here to talk about a matter of some sensitivity.

Gobain walked on. "I'll be frank with you, de Lanvaux. The doctors have given me six months; a year if I'm lucky."

Ruaud stared at the king; he could see no hint of sickness in his ruddy complexion. "Surely they're mistaken, sire."

"I look well for a dying man, don't I?" said Gobain with a grim chuckle. "My only consolation is that I've outlived Karl of Tielen."

"Prince Karl is *dead*?" Ruaud tried to make sense of two such startling pieces of information. With Karl dead, the balance of power in the quadrant might shift back in Francia's favor.

"A stroke, from what our agents have gleaned so far."

"All the more reason now, sire, for proving your doctors wrong."

Gobain gave a sigh. He had stopped close to a stone bench set beneath the crooked apple trees and eased himself down onto it. "I'm confiding in you, Captain, because Enguerrand respects you. He listens to you. You've wrought a change in my son; I can see it already, a change for the better."

"He's a credit to you, sire, a good-hearted, studious boy."

"Studious?" Gobain echoed contemptuously. "What use is a love of books and libraries when you have a kingdom to govern? Listen, de Lanvaux, I want you to devote yourself to making a man of him. A man fit to reign in my stead."

Enguerrand's earnest, bespectacled face flashed before Ruaud's eyes. The prince was the complete opposite of his father; he loathed hunting and was equally clumsy with a fencing foil or a tennis racquet.

"Enguerrand is at an impressionable age. His mother doted on Aubrey. Enguerrand is a disappointment to her and he knows it. He'll need all the encouragement and support you can give him when I'm gone."

Ruaud nodded, moved by the king's stoical attitude to his own mortality.

"Besides, it won't have escaped your notice that the queen listens to Donatien, Captain. And I consider Donatien to be a dangerous influence on my wife. He's even been interfering with my plans for Adèle."

"Interfering, sire?"

"I don't know what Donatien's motivation is, but he has convinced Aliénor that the alliance with Muscobar I've been planning will be disastrous for Francia. They've dreamed up a devious little scheme of their own involving Ilsevir of Allegonde."

The conversation had taken an unexpected turn; Ruaud had not expected the king to share such personal concerns with him.

He thought carefully before framing his next question. "Do we know what her majesty's objections are to the Muscobar alliance, sire?"

"She loathes the Grand Duchess Sofiya. It all goes back to some incident at a ball when they were girls. She's felt slighted ever since."

Ruaud raised an eyebrow. Surely the fate of Francia could not be influenced by so trivial a matter?

"To be frank, Lanvaux, I'm extremely uneasy about Allegonde. Ilsevir has proved himself pretty ineffectual so far, too easily manipulated by his politicians. And then there's the Allegondan Commanderie."

Ruaud was listening with intense concentration now. "The cult of the Rosecoeur?"

"What's *your* opinion on the Rosecoeurs?" Gobain's eyes suddenly lit with a penetrating, inquisitive light.

"I'm a follower of Sergius of Azhkendir, sire." Ruaud spoke from the heart. "I distrust anything to do with cults."

"Good man." Gobain nodded his approval. "That's why I want you to know that I'm placing all my trust in you. I'm going to allow Donatien just enough rope to hang himself. And when he does, you'll be Grand Maistre in his place."

"Me, sire?" Ruaud had never imagined himself at the helm of the Commanderie; he had always assumed that he would be sent back to Enhirre when Enguerrand came of age.

"So you weren't aware of the communications that have been secretly traveling to and fro between Donatien and the Rosecoeurs?"

Dumbly, Ruaud shook his head.

"Watch your back, Lanvaux. Aliénor wields a great deal of influence. If she suspects that you're working against her plans for her daughter, she will do all she can to have you removed."

Ruaud was feeling increasingly uneasy. He foresaw an uncertain future, in which he would have to go everywhere accompanied by bodyguards.

"Enguerrand will come of age soon, but he's still impressionable and, dear me, so unworldly. He'll look to you for advice, and Aliénor will resent that. If she had her way, she'd be Queen Regent until he's twenty-one, and that would be a disaster for Francia."

"A disaster, sire?"

"Imagine Allegondan Rosecoeur fanatics infiltrating the court. The nobles would take sides, Raimon de Provença would try to seize the throne, and the whole country would disintegrate into civil war." Gobain gripped Ruaud's hand, pressing it between his own. "Promise me on your life that you won't let that happen," he said in a voice hoarse with desperation.

Ruaud felt the viselike grip of the king's fingers burning into his own. He saw the pearls of sweat on the king's forehead and read the bitter knowledge of his own imminent death in his eyes.

"Even if it means opposing the queen and my own commander-in-chief?"

"Swear, Lanvaux. Swear on whichever saint you hold most dear."

Ruaud went down on one knee and, bringing out the gold chain he wore about his neck, he clasped the little icon of the saint that rested close to his heart. "I swear on my duty to the Blessed Sergius," he said quietly.

Gobain closed his eyes and let out a long, halting sigh.

"We will all pray for you, sire."

"Hah! Don't waste your breath." The king was regarding him, his bloodshot eyes dark with cynicism. "Nothing short of a miracle would save me now. And I don't believe in miracles."

CHAPTER 24

Gauzia was taking tea with Dame Elmire in the salon when Celestine arrived for her lesson with the Maistre. To Celestine's surprise, Gauzia rose and embraced her, kissing her on both cheeks, as if they were the closest of friends.

"Is there no rehearsal this afternoon?" Celestine asked, a little overwhelmed by the warmth of Gauzia's greeting.

"We finished early so that the scene painters could finish the sets. Only two days till the first performance!" Gauzia let out a little squeal of excitement. "You'll be there, won't you, Celestine?"

"I will?" Celestine said warily.

"You'll be sitting with me, my dear," said Dame Elmire, pouring her some tea. "In a box!"

Celestine had never been to the theater, let alone an opera, and had no idea what a box might be. Rather than inquire and expose her ignorance in front of Gauzia, she asked, "Where's the Maistre?"

"Oh, he had to stay behind to rehearse with Aurélie."

So he had forgotten that he had arranged her lesson for four this afternoon. "Who is Aurélie?"

"If you weren't living in your own little dreamworld most of the time, you'd know!" Gauzia exclaimed. "She's the talk of the city: Aurélie Carnelian, the diva from Bel'Esstar. She's playing the lead role, Balkaris."

Celestine tried to make sense of this information.

"Why don't you tell Celestine the story of the opera?" suggested Dame Elmire gently.

Gauzia raised her eyes heavenward. "It's called *Balkaris, Queen of Khendye*. I play a slave girl who's really the daughter of the Arkhan Sulaimon, but she's pretending to be a slave so that she can stay close to her brother, who's the queen's secret lover . . ."

Celestine set down her teacup. "And this is all the Maistre's work?" Gauzia's talk of slaves and lovers seemed a world away from the ascetic purity of his sacred music.

"Of course not, silly! A playwright wrote the libretto."

"Libretto?"

Gauzia threw up her hands in a theatrical gesture of despair as Celestine stared at her uncomprehendingly. "Just wait till you see the performance. Then you'll understand."

"So," said Celestine, choosing her words with care, "Aurélie Carnelian. Tell me more about her."

"She's a fine dramatic soprano," said Dame Elmire. "And she turns all the men's heads; they're absolutely besotted with her! She trained at the Conservatoire in Bel'Esstar, but every time I see her fiery dark eyes, I suspect that she has Smarnan blood in her veins. Henri must have had her in mind when he began work on *Balkaris*; she was born to play the part."

"So the Maistre has worked with her before?" Celestine heard herself asking even though she was not sure she wanted to know the answer.

The clock in the hall whirred and struck four.

"My dear, I fear you've had a wasted journey. I apologize on behalf of my nephew. Would you like me to give you some vocal coaching instead?"

Celestine tried to hide her anguish. "Thank you, that's so kind . . . but I must hurry if I'm to be in time for vespers."

Wearing another of Dame Elmire's altered stage costumes, Celestine followed the retired diva into her box.

"Ah yes, such a beautiful shade of sea blue; that was Dahut's gown from *The Bells of Ys*." As Dame Elmire had lifted out the delicate silken folds of the dress from the trunk, she began to hum an unfamiliar melody, full of leaps and strange intervals. "But oh, what a difficult role to sing! The composer wrote the most complex and challenging music and it went right over the audience's heads.

The opera closed after only five performances! I hope Henri will fare better with *Balkaris*."

Celestine perched on the edge of her velvet seat, gazing down at the audience. The players in the orchestra took their seats and began to tune their instruments. Where was the Maistre?

A little ripple of applause broke out in the stalls below. "There he is," remarked Dame Elmire, pointing with her black ostrich-feather fan. Celestine craned so far forward to see him that Dame Elmire tapped her sharply on the shoulder with the fan, whispering, "Careful, my dear, you don't want to fall on the unsuspecting souls beneath."

Three loud knocks resonated throughout the house. The audience's chatter slowly subsided as the Maistre raised his hands to give the first beat.

"The overture," Celestine breathed. She had not heard so many instruments playing together before: The sweetness of the violins and flutes was so exquisite that it made her want to cry. Or was she so moved because they were playing the Maistre's music? For now the tantalizing fragments of melody she had heard issuing from behind his locked door over the past months began to make sense.

Yet she was unprepared for what followed. The velvet curtains were drawn back, revealing many singers, dressed in vibrant colors, bright as a flock of summer butterflies. When they drew breath and began to sing, Celestine felt as if she might faint from the intensity of the sound. She had never imagined that men's and women's voices blended together could provoke such a powerful reaction in her.

I want to be a part of this.

The chorus were kneeling now, hands raised in supplication, all facing in the same direction. She heard the yearning anticipation in the music, the implication that someone important was about to appear. And the rest of the audience sensed it too, beginning to clap and shout as a tall woman entered, a diadem glittering in her black hair.

"Aurélie Carnelian," Celestine whispered. The audience fell silent as the diva opened her crimson-painted lips and began to sing. Her voice combined a sensuous beauty of tone with extraordinary power. Celestine felt as if her hair had risen up on her scalp, windblown by the sheer force of the diva's singing. When the aria was over, there was a little silence as if everyone present had quietly exhaled, and Celestine found that she was gripping the front rail of the box.

Then the cheers began, filling the silence. It was only as the diva acknowledged her admirers that Celestine noticed Gauzia, standing behind, carrying a palm fan. Her costume was shockingly revealing; loose pantaloons and a low-cut bodice of amber and purple silks.

"It's disgraceful," exclaimed Dame Elmire beside her.

"No wonder the nuns were against the plan," agreed Celestine. And then she realized that the Maistre must have seen Gauzia like this during the rehearsals. Had Gauzia no shame?

"Stopping the flow of the drama to kiss her hands to her admirers—so unprofessional," continued Dame Elmire with a sniff of disdain. "These young divas today are quite shameless."

The curtain slowly fell as Balkaris plunged the dagger into her heart and fell back on the tomb of her lover. The last hushed, somber chords died away and the Maistre laid down his baton. Suddenly the house broke out into cheers and when the curtain rose again, there stood the whole cast, bowing to acknowledge the applause.

Celestine clapped until her palms were sore. Roses were flung onto the stage, and one of Balkaris's page boys darted around the stage, gathering them up to present to his mistress, who smiled and blew kisses to her admirers.

Celestine felt as if she were still floating on clouds of the Maistre's sublime music, every phrase infused with his feelings, such sadness and such desperate longing.

"But what are they really applauding?" Dame Elmire asked pointedly. "Henri's music, which was divine, or Aurélie Carnelian's performance?"

At last, Aurélie, her arms overflowing with crimson roses, held out her hand to the orchestra, beckoning the Maistre to join her on the stage.

Celestine leaned far forward, applauding fervently as he bowed, making the orchestral players stand to receive their share of the recognition. He turned in her direction and gave her a little secret smile, the luster flames glinting in the lenses of his spectacles. Then he turned back to Aurélie and, to the enthusiastic shouts of her supporters, raised her hand to his lips and kissed it.

Celestine stared, her hands frozen in midclap. She saw the look that passed between them. It was an intimate look. It was a look shared between two people who had known each other a long time.

The applause continued around her but now it was as the distant patter of falling rain. She could do nothing but stare at them, Aurélie and her beloved Maistre, still hand in hand, bowing and smiling.

All this time I've been jealous of Gauzia, and I never even suspected there might be someone else.

After the performance, Dame Elmire insisted on dragging Celestine backstage. Bemused, Celestine followed her through the shadowy press of people: perspiring singers wandering around still in their stage makeup, and stagehands shifting the large scenery flats so that at one moment they found themselves passing through a shifting forest of painted trees. She feared that Dame Elmire might be knocked over, but the old lady navigated all the hazards with the practiced skill of an old performer. Every singer they passed greeted her warmly; she seemed to know every member of the cast by name.

A clamor of excited voices came from a dressing room whose door was ajar; inside, Celestine glimpsed Aurélie sitting in front of a candlelit mirror, wiping the rouge from her cheeks. Others had crowded into the little room, and she heard the heady sound of laughter bubbling up, mingled with the clinking of glasses. The little room was filled with vases of lilies and their strong scent wafted out, perfuming the passageway.

"I think we have a success on our hands!"

"Don't rejoice too soon, Petitfils, we haven't read what the critics have to say yet!"

Dame Elmire plunged into the throng of flamboyantly dressed artists. Celestine hovered outside, feeling superfluous.

"Dame Elmire," she heard a man cry out welcomingly. "Drink a toast with us to the success of your nephew's opera!"

"To *Balkaris,*" Dame Elmire said, raising her glass.

"And to our divine Aurélie," added a man's voice—a voice Celestine knew so well that her heart began to pound. As the others repeated the toast, she saw his reflection in the mirror, saw him raising Aurélie's hand to his lips again . . . and saw her caress his cheek, her slender fingers catching a stray lock of his honey-gold hair to pull his face down to hers. The gesture was so intimate, so revealing, that Celestine felt a pain as sharp as if Balkaris's cold steel had pierced her breast.

"Well, shall we go, my dear?"

Celestine started. How long had she been standing there, oblivious to everyone else around her?

"The carriage is waiting for us." Dame Elmire's cheeks were flushed from sparkling wine and the press of singers and admirers.

"Can't I stay for the party?" complained a familiar voice.

"You're too young, Gauzia," scolded Dame Elmire. "There'll be tobacco smoke, wine, and celebrating into the small hours. Ruin for a singer's throat! If you want to keep your voice and your part in this opera, you'll drink nothing but water."

"But the others—" began Gauzia as Dame Elmire hurried them along the narrow passageway to the stage door.

"I have a duty as your chaperone to ensure that you're home before midnight and in bed! Don't forget that you have to perform the whole opera again tomorrow, and the next night, and the next . . ."

Celestine wandered after them, hearing their bickering as if from a great distance away. He had not even noticed that she was there. But why would he, when the divine Aurélie was gazing at him with such blatant adoration?

"What did you think of my performance?" Gauzia demanded, once they were in the carriage.

Celestine looked at her blankly.

"*My* performance," repeated Gauzia, as if she were deaf.

"Oh! You were very good," Celestine said, trying to blank the image of the Maistre and Aurélie from her mind.

Celestine lay awake on her narrow convent bed, unable to sleep. The glorious music she had heard that evening kept playing and replaying in her head, tormenting and delighting her in equal measure. And dominating every phrase, every note, was the vision of crimson-gowned Aurélie, her voice darkly thrilling as Queen Balkaris prepared to kill herself rather than go on living without her lover.

"How can I bear the cruel light of day, knowing that your eyes are closed for all eternity?"

The Maistre must have been betrayed in love to be able to portray feelings of such bitter intensity in the music he had written for Balkaris. And yet the way he had looked at Aurélie as he took her hand between his own, pressing it to his lips . . . and the way she had let her fingers drift so sensuously across his cheek, had revealed a deep intimacy between them.

There's much more to their relationship than composer and artist. Lovers, a voice whispered in her mind. *They're lovers.* The thought was so agonizing that she felt as if a cruel hand had closed around her heart.

I must seem like a mere child to him, an innocent, inexperienced schoolgirl.

The dawn bell woke Celestine to a grey morning that only enhanced the dull sense of despair that returned the instant she opened her eyes. She lay inert, staring at the image of Saint Azilia on the far wall. How long had she been duping herself? Henri de Joyeuse was a kind and generous-hearted man . . . but he was kind to everyone he met, and she had been naïve enough to believe that in her case it meant so much more.

I will not give up on him!

She was sure that she had not consciously reached for the book . . . but suddenly she was sitting up in bed, holding it in both hands, gazing at the image of the Blessed Azilia.

"Help me, Faie."

The image of the saint began to dissolve before her eyes and in a swirl of soft radiance, the Faie rose up from the book.

"Why have you waited so long?" Eyes as translucent as the morning's cloudy light gazed down into hers. *"Do you wish me to reveal the secrets of your father's grimoire to you?"*

"Is there a glamour that will make the Maistre fall in love with me?" There! She had said it aloud; she had admitted how desperate she was.

"*What do you mean by 'love'?*" The Faie's crystal-bright gaze was blank. It was an aethyr spirit; how could it understand the complexities of a mortal heart? Celestine struggled to think of a means to express her wish in a way the Faie could understand.

"Love means . . . to dream of another person all the time. To want to be with them. To want to be in their thoughts constantly—" She broke off. What was she saying? Was this really love? It sounded more like obsession.

"*To alter the heart and mind of another mortal is beyond my power. I can only gift you, Celestine.*"

"Only me?" Was there some way the Faie could make her irresistible to men? Or would that just attract hateful and boorish predators, like the Tielen count?

"*In the grimoire, there are recipes for alchymical compounds that you can concoct to subdue your enemies, but no love potions.*"

"Narcotics? *Poisons?*" Celestine was not sure that she was ready to be trusted with such dangerous knowledge.

"*There are recipes for spells that will draw the truth from an unwilling tongue.*" The Faie was no longer hovering in front of her, it had floated to her side, its long crystalline strands of hair falling like a shimmering veil over its pale, androgynous body. The book opened and the pages began to flip over, as if turned by an invisible hand. Celestine caught tantalizing glimpses of engravings and dark-inked pictures in the margins: herbs, strange fruit, and rare plants. "*But you must remember that not a single spell contained within these pages can be cast without cost to you. How much of your precious life essence can you afford to expend on so trivial a matter?*"

As if from very far away, Celestine heard the distant, insistent ringing of the chapel bell. "Oh no. I'm late!"

The Faie swirled about her and she felt its breath, like a soft breeze from another world, stirring her hair as it stared deep into her eyes. Iridescent shadows flitted across her vision, dazzling her.

The door opened and Angelique came in. "Still in bed, Celestine?" Celestine blinked. The Faie had vanished and she was clutching the *Lives of the Holy Saints.*

"Late night at the opera?" Angelique began to brush her hair for her, deftly winding and pinning it into a knot on the back of her head.

"Oh, Angelique, it was amazing—"

"You can tell me all about it later. We'll have to sneak onto the back row of the choir stalls and hope that Mère Apolline doesn't notice."

Celestine heard men's voices coming from the music room.

He must have visitors. Have I come at the wrong time? Or has he forgotten my lesson again and made other arrangements?

Before she could even begin to feel aggrieved, the music room door opened and a tall, black-uniformed young man appeared.

Celestine gulped back an involuntary cry of dismay. The sight of that uniform still stirred memories so disturbing that they drove all other thoughts from her mind. Instinctively, she flattened herself against the paneled wall as he came toward her.

"And Godspeed, Jagu," called a familiar voice as the Maistre followed the Guerrier into the hall.

"Jagu?" she whispered, gazing up.

"Demoiselle Celestine?" He stopped abruptly, staring at her. He looked so different in his somber uniform jacket, his wild hair tamed and neatly trimmed to collar length.

"Cadet de Rustéphan is off on his first tour of duty overseas," said the Maistre.

"Overseas? To Enhirre? But you only joined up a few weeks ago."

"It's part of our training, to guard the pilgrim route to Ondhessar." He spoke as if he were on the parade ground, with no expression in his voice.

Celestine had heard stories of the dangers of military life in Enhirre: attacks from marauding desert tribesmen, sand fever, and dysentery. "But how will you keep up your music practice?"

"My question, too," said Maistre de Joyeuse, and she saw from his eyes that he was not in jest.

"I've made my choice," said Jagu, even more stiffly.

"When do you sail?" Celestine asked, trying to imagine how it must feel to be setting out into the unknown.

"My regiment leaves at dawn tomorrow. We travel by river to Fenez-Tyr, where we join our ship." He clicked his heels together, military fashion, and saluted. "Excuse me. I mustn't be late."

"Jagu," said the Maistre quietly. Jagu turned and suddenly all his rigid formality dropped away. He flung his arms around the Maistre, hugging him tightly as if he could not let him go.

"Thank you," he said in a muffled voice. "Thank you for everything, Maistre." Then he tore himself away, flinging open the door and hurrying down the path. The street door banged shut and he was gone.

Celestine found herself blinking away tears. "Come back safely," she called after him. She was ashamed; Jagu had shown all the determination and resolution that she lacked. And then she felt the warm pressure of a hand on her shoulder. Surprised, she looked up and found herself gazing into the Maistre's grey eyes.

"Tears for Jagu? And yet the pair of you did nothing but argue," he said, and she could not be sure from his expression if he was gently teasing her. *His hand is on my shoulder. He is touching me, trying to comfort me.*

"You're not implying that *I* drove him away?" she said, dismayed; the thought had never occurred to her till then.

"No, no . . . Jagu has daemons of his own that he has to come to terms with. I just wish they weren't driving him quite so far away."

She had not realized until then how much the Maistre cared for his rebellious student. "How long have you known Jagu?"

"He's been my student for six, seven years. Since he . . ." He went to close the front door and the blissful moment was over.

"Since?" She wiped her eyes with her handkerchief.

"It's not really my story to tell." He began to walk toward the music room; automatically she followed him. "But his best friend was murdered by a magus. It was a bad business, one that their school tried to hush up."

"A magus?" Celestine felt a little shiver go through her. "What was he called, this magus?"

"Jagu never knew his true name. The magus took the student's identity to infiltrate the seminary."

Could it have been Kaspar Linnaius? The thought transfixed her. *Do Jagu and I share the same enemy?* All these months they had worked together . . . and neither had once spoken of their secret fears and ambitions. And now it was too late to ask him. He could be gone for many months; if fighting broke out, he might get wounded, even . . .

"He could be killed," she said aloud.

"I had no idea you felt so strongly about Jagu."

"I only meant that—he's such a gifted musician—I wouldn't want him to be hurt—" This was far worse than she had intended. Now the Maistre would think she was trying to hide her feelings for Jagu, and the more she protested to the contrary, the more he would believe it.

The Commanderie barque lay at anchor where the river was at its broadest, beyond the Forteresse. But as Celestine hurried along the quay, she saw a column of Guerriers marching out across the bridge, then taking the stone slipway down to the riverbank, where a couple of rowboats were waiting. River mist, light as thistledown, was rising off the water as the sun's first light shone through the high clouds.

A group of women and children had gathered at the head of the slipway to wave the Guerriers farewell. Clutching her cloak close against the damp mist, she joined them, standing on tiptoes to try to spot Jagu.

As the Guerriers clambered into the boat, one turned around to gaze at the bank, and she recognized Jagu.

"Jagu!" she called out, frantically waving her handkerchief. Her hood fell back as the sun rose, dazzling her. "Godspeed, Jagu!"

Against the sun's dazzle, she saw one of his fellow Guerriers nudge him and point to her. He saw her. He saluted, stiffly—and then the salute changed into a spontaneous, boyish wave.

As the boat was rowed away downriver, Celestine and the other women waved until it disappeared under the bridge. A sudden feeling of desolation overwhelmed her as she walked slowly back along the quay.

I suppose I've come to care for him as a friend. And it's always sad to say farewell to a good and faithful friend . . .

Ruaud looked up from his dispatches to see Fabien d'Abrissard standing before him, shaking his head disapprovingly. He pointed his fingers at him, as if he were wielding a pistol. "I despair of you, Captain. You could be lying over your desk in a pool of blood . . ."

"To what do I owe the honor?" Ruaud asked, annoyed by Abrissard's theatrical arrival. Abrissard sat on the edge of his desk.

"The king is concerned for your safety. He asked me to warn you if I, or my associates, become aware of any potential threats."

Ruaud suddenly understood why Abrissard had come. "Someone has put a price on my head?"

"Someone very close to you."

Ruaud knew that he had made enemies, but he had never, till this moment, imagined that anyone judged him enough of a nuisance to hire an assassin. He sat back in his chair, pressing the tips of his fingers together in an effort to calm his racing thoughts. "Why me?" he said at last.

"Why? Aren't you going to ask 'who'?" Abrissard said, smiling.

"Should I feel flattered? I'm new to these palace political power games. I'm a simple soldier who's dedicated his life to following the teachings of Saint Sergius."

"The instant his majesty took you into his confidence and singled you out from your fellow 'simple soldiers,' " said Abrissard, "you became a marked man."

"So it *is* Donatien." The instant Ruaud had said the Grand Maistre's name, he felt a sense of revulsion. "I was his adjutant in Enhirre. I looked up to him. I told myself that I wanted to be like him one day. What went wrong? When did he lose his faith in me?"

CHAPTER 25

The Guerriers' watch fires illumined the ramparts of the ancient citadel at Ondhessar. Jagu, his cloak wrapped tightly about him for warmth, stared out into the darkness, searching for any sign of movement. He had never seen the stars burn so brightly in Francia; the unexpected chill of the desert night added a frosty sparkle to their brilliance in an ink-black sky. When night came to the crimson sands of Enhirre, it came suddenly, brutally, as the red sun sank behind the dunes, sucking the dry heat out of the atmosphere.

For centuries, the Guerriers of the Commanderie had taken on the role of protectors of the shrines and pilgrim ways. But since the siege of Ondhessar, a band of warriors calling themselves the Scorpions had been attacking both pilgrims and Commanderie strongholds.

"All quiet, cadet?" said a soft voice.

Jagu jumped. Behind him stood Kilian Guyomard, a familiarly malicious glint in his pale eyes. "Did I startle you?"

"What do *you* think?"

"Just checking my men are all awake and alert. The Scorpions like to attack at night. And as it's been a while since they last paid us a visit . . ."

Jagu leaned on the worn stone of the ramparts and scanned the black sands below that stretched far into the dark horizon.

"Nothing to report so far."

"Only a sliver of moon again," Kilian said, scanning the sky.

"Ideal conditions for a raid. According to Commander Konan."
The thought of a raid made Jagu's stomach feel distinctly queasy.

"You and me, up here, kind of reminds me of our old hiding
place on the chapel roof."

"You, me . . . and Paol."

"Who'd have thought it?" Kilian rested his arms on the rampart alongside him. The watch fire in the nearest brazier sputtered,
spitting out sparks. "That we'd both serve in the Guerriers one
day . . ." The glow illuminated his face and Jagu saw that his habitual mocking expression had faded. "I still dream about it, Jagu.
Finding Paol's body in the gardens. And you . . . half out of your
mind. You were damned lucky that de Lanvaux took you away
from Saint Argantel's. God, how I envied you."

"So . . . what was it like?" Jagu asked carefully. "After I left?"

"The facts got out, even though the masters tried to hush up the
whole matter. Boys were removed by their parents."

"But not you?"

"Ha!" Kilian let out a scornful laugh. "What did my father
care? He was just thankful I wasn't around to irritate him."

Jagu could not remember Kilian ever speaking so frankly at
school about his family. "Why did you irritate him so?"

Kilian gazed outward, not looking at Jagu. "He said once that I
reminded him too much of my mother. She died when I was six. He
remarried soon after, of course. My stepmother and I did not . . .
get on. So a good seminary education seemed like a convenient
way to dispose of me."

Kilian, always joking and playing tricks, hiding his feelings of
rejection and loss by acting the clown? "You played some pretty
unpleasant pranks on me. I got beaten in your stead—more than
once."

Kilian shrugged, with a hint of his old insouciance. "You were
just too easy to set up."

"Too easy?" Jagu echoed, stung. Kilian laughed and hooked his
arm familiarly around Jagu's neck. "No hard feelings, then?"

Jagu shook his head. He could not stay angry at Kilian for long;
in spite of all the torments he had inflicted on him, Jagu still felt an
instinctive liking for him.

Kilian unhooked his arm and turned around, leaning back

against the parapet. "I always wanted to ask you, but the masters wouldn't let me see you, and then you were gone."

"Ask me about what?" said Jagu. Was there some magic in the desert air that had caused Kilian to open up, or was it the camaraderie shared by brothers in arms, thrown together in a dangerous situation?

"Captain de Lanvaux fought the magus in the chapel. And you saw the duel. What was it like?"

"It was terrifying," Jagu said bluntly. "I thought that I was going to die. That magus was so powerful. He conjured a hawk spirit, all shadow and flame—it looked as if it had burst from a pit of darkness—and he loosed it on the captain. But then the captain summoned one of the Heavenly Guardians."

"He actually called down one of the Seven?" Kilian's eyes shone in the starlight. "And you *saw* this?"

Jagu had not once spoken of this with anyone before, not even Henri de Joyeuse. "I saw him. Though he was so bright, I could hardly look at him. For one moment, the captain and the angel . . . they seemed to be one. His burning eyes . . . they seared the magus. He pierced him with a flaming spear. He was . . . magnificent."

"But which of the Seven came? And how did he summon him?"

Jagu bowed his head. "He made me promise never to tell anyone."

"So it's true," said Kilian, half to himself, triumphantly.

"What's true?" Jagu wondered if he had said too much. Old friend Kilian might be, but Jagu had no desire to betray the captain's confidence.

"Your mentor. Captain de Lanvaux." Kilian's voice dropped to a whisper. "He's rumored to be the head of a secret elite company, specially trained to fight the Forbidden Arts. If we ever get out of this godforsaken desert alive, that's what I'm aiming for—"

An ululating war cry rang out, so shrill and ferocious that it made Jagu flinch. Immediately, there followed a blast of ear-cracking explosions. The night flashed white as grenades burst in the courtyard below. Chips of stone sprayed everywhere.

"Attack! We're under attack!" yelled a lookout. By the flickering watch fire, Jagu caught a glint of steel. Shadowy figures were running up the stair toward him and Kilian. Fear pierced him, like a cold blade, turning his limbs to ice.

This isn't an exercise. This is real.

"Jagu, cover the tower." Kilian grabbed his pistols and fired. One attacker fell. "How in Sergius's name did they get in?"

Jagu had never seen action before. And now black-robed tribesmen were swarming along the battlements, scimitars drawn. His mind a blank, Jagu discharged both pistols at the foremost of the attackers. The man went down with a grunt, but the others swarmed on over him. *No time to reload.* As Jagu drew his saber, he felt a sudden debilitating tremor in his arms and legs. Damn it, he was shaking. Shaking with fear! Furious at his own weakness, he backed up until he felt the cold stone of the fort wall behind him and there was nowhere else to go.

The flash and crack of pistol shots lit the night again and another attacker went down, tumbling into the courtyard below. Hurtling toward Jagu came a young man wielding a scimitar. Instinct alone made Jagu parry the first blow, the clash of steel shooting firesparks into the dark. The force sent tingling shocks up through his wrist and arm, but there was no time to recover. Another fierce diagonal slice followed, then another, the steel whistling past his ear so close that he was sure the blade had shaved off slivers of flesh.

In the heat of the moment, all Jagu's training seemed to have deserted him. This wildly slashing opponent was not observing the rules of saber-fighting that the cadets had been taught in the Forteresse Salle d'Armes. And from the fervent, crazed light in the young man's eyes, Jagu saw the very real possibility of his own death.

You may be ready to sacrifice yourself, but I'm not. Jagu knocked the scimitar askew with one swift, strong parry and carried his thrust forward with all his strength.

The shock as the tip of his blade pierced his attacker's chest jarred his arm from wrist to shoulder. The momentum forced the blade through flesh and bone. Blood spurted. The scimitar dropped to the floor with a clang. The eyes lost their crazed expression, widening to a look of surprise. Jagu gripped his sword tightly, tugging it from the man's body with both hands. As the blade came free, his attacker swayed on the edge of the parapet, then toppled over to crash onto the courtyard, many feet below. Jagu raised his hand to wipe the sticky wetness from his face, knowing it was his enemy's blood.

Don't drop your guard. He crouched, back against the rampart wall, brandishing his sword, gazing wildly around, ready to skewer the next assailant.

"Clear! All clear!" came the cry from the lookout.

Was it over so soon? Automatically he obeyed orders to assemble in the courtyard while the roll was called.

The young Enhirran he had run through lay sprawled in a pool of inky blood, his sightless eyes reflecting the chill glitter of the stars overhead.

"First kill? Don't feel too guilty," said Kilian, coming up behind him. He was grimacing as he pressed the heel of his hand into his shoulder. "Just remind yourself that it might be you lying there instead."

Jagu nodded, breathing hard. While his blood was still on fire, he could block out the reality of what he had done. "You're hurt." Jagu had spotted a dark, moist stain spreading beneath Kilian's fingers.

"Just a scratch," said Kilian dismissively. Then he staggered and Jagu caught hold of him. "All I know is it damn well hurts."

"God's teeth, that stings!"

Jagu came back into the infirmary just as the company surgeon was cleaning the scimitar slash on Kilian's shoulder with clear spirit.

"Give me that," said Kilian between gritted teeth. He seized the bottle from the surgeon with his sound hand and took a good gulp.

"You were lucky," observed the surgeon as he began to stitch the wound. "Another inch or so farther down and—"

"Yes, yes," said Kilian, irritably. "Anything further to report, cadet?"

Jagu stared at the surgeon's needle and thread as it penetrated Kilian's skin. His aching stomach began to churn. Clapping a hand to his mouth, he rushed to the latrines and was violently sick. Kneeling over the pit, wiping the slime from his mouth, he felt wretched and ashamed.

Am I made of stern enough stuff to be a soldier? If I'm sick every time there's a skirmish, I'll soon become the company laughingstock.

"What do we do with the bodies? In this heat . . ." Jagu did not finish; the thought of the smell of decomposition alone made his queasy stomach start to churn again. The desert sun was already burning fiercely and he dreaded hearing the telltale buzz of flies.

"Good question, cadet." Kilian, his arm in a sling, walked up to the corpses, which lay, stiffening, under bloodstained blankets. "What do we know of our attackers?" He crouched down beside them and with his sound hand lifted a blanket, looking at the dead face beneath.

"Interesting," he said. "See these marks?"

Jagu hesitated, then forced himself to take a look. This body was that of an older man, bearded, teeth showing beneath lips curled back in a slight rictus. In the morning light he could make out the pattern of a tiny intricate tattoo on the forehead.

"Where have you seen this before, Kilian?" he asked. Even though he could still taste the bile at the back of his throat, he made himself look again to be sure. "Don't you recognize it?"

"The magus's mark."

Kilian proceeded to check the other two corpses. Jagu hung back, knowing that one was the young man he had killed. "Look at the face of your enemy," Kilian insisted. "Ask yourself honestly: Would you rather be lying there in his place?"

Jagu said nothing. He was impressed by Kilian's utter lack of squeamishness. But then, Kilian had seen action before.

"There's another tribe mark here, on the right hand, see? On the index finger, leading to the wrist. Delicate work, like lace." Kilian let go of the dead hand and replaced the blanket.

"Who *were* these men? And why did they attack us? What is their grudge?" Jagu burst out. "And why are they prepared to die?"

A raw scream rasped out across the courtyard; Jagu flinched.

"It sounds as if Commander Konan is interrogating a prisoner right now."

———

The garrison commander was a seasoned Guerrier with many desert campaigns under his belt. Broad-shouldered as a bear, with a growling voice to match, Konan had served under Ruaud de Lanvaux, although Jagu had seen little of the captain's inspiring qualities in his successor.

"Guerrier Guyomard and Cadet de Rustéphan reporting on the enemy dead, Commander," said Kilian, obliged to salute with his left hand. "These raiders were not Scorpions. They all bear the same tattoo or tribe mark on their foreheads and right hand."

"I thought they'd all been exterminated when we took the citadel."

"You know who they are, Commander?" Kilian said.

"The 'A' was the badge adopted by the warriors of Azilis who protected this Shrine. It was also the emblem of the magi of Ondhessar."

Jagu and Kilian exchanged a look.

"You acquitted yourself well last night, young Rustéphan," continued Konan. "You'll be favorably mentioned in dispatches. I trust you've cleaned your saber blade thoroughly and checked that your pistols are in good working order?"

"Yes, Commander."

"They'll be back; no doubt of it."

"Are we going to negotiate with them over the return of the bodies?" asked Jagu.

"Barter with the enemy?" Commander Konan let out a scornful grunt. "When you've been here a few months, you'll learn that there's no point bartering with these heathens. The sword and the musket is the only language they understand. And if you want further proof . . ." He beckoned them into the next room.

An Enhirran warrior was shackled to the wall, sagging in his chains.

"We've got nothing out of the prisoner so far." Commander Konan was perspiring profusely; he peeled off his jacket, revealing a sweat-soaked shirt beneath. "Who sent you?" he demanded. "Who is your master?"

The prisoner said nothing. The Commander picked up his horsewhip and thrust it beneath the man's chin, forcing his drooping head up.

"Answer me."

When the prisoner still said nothing, Konan pressed the whip stock against his windpipe until, from the horrible gargling that ensued, it sounded as if he was slowly choking to death.

Jagu stared at the dirt floor, sickened. Was there no other way to gain information? No wonder the Commanderie were hated and feared.

And then to his surprise, the prisoner began to speak, pouring out a stream of embittered, impassioned defiance.

"One day we shall take back what is rightfully ours. And that day will come soon. You have no right to be here. This place is holy. Sacred. Your presence is sacrilege—"

"Are you working for the magi?" Konan pressed harder. "Who are you?"

Jagu saw sweat glistening like water on the prisoner's agonized face. "Who are we? We are your worst nightmare, Francian. We are the death that strikes silently in the darkness."

Outside, Jagu drew a bucket of water from the citadel well.

"Is it Commanderie policy to treat prisoners so brutally?"

"You always did ask awkward questions, Jagu." Kilian took a gulp of well water, then passed the scoop to Jagu. "Damn it, this scratch burns like hell. God help me if the blade was poisoned."

"But how are we ever to establish better relations with the Enhirrans if we torture and mutilate our prisoners?" He lifted the scoop from the bucket and drank, letting the last of the cool water from deep below ground trickle over his face.

"You're too soft. D'you think they'd treat us any differently?"

It began as a distant whispering, borne on the dry wind off the desert sands. At first Jagu thought he must have fallen asleep at his post and that the whispering came from the confusion of his dreams. But gazing out across the desert, he saw a smoky blur drifting across the red sand dunes, like mist. He rubbed his eyes. The whispering went on, in a tongue he could not understand, menacing, setting off strange chills in his body in spite of the heat of midday.

"Is anyone there?" Jagu gazed all around, shading his eyes with his hand. The sun was high overhead, its merciless light beating down on the back of his neck. All his senses were warning him that something was wrong. He gazed along the ramparts to the next guard post and saw through the slow-creeping haze that the Guerrier on watch had slid down to his knees. In the courtyard below Jagu spotted another lying slumped on the ground.

"What's wrong with me? Is it sunstroke?" Confused, he turned toward the tower door, willing himself to walk forward, but his musket fell from his nerveless fingers. *This isn't sunstroke.*

The next moment, he dropped to his knees. He began to crawl. At the back of his mind was a single thought: *Warn the others.*

The whispering was growing more insistent, more sibilant. The tower archway loomed, dark as a pit of hell. The stones inside were cold and rough out of the sun's furnace glare, and Jagu clung to each one as he made his way slowly, painfully, down, step by step. The whisper-voices echoed in the tower's vault, tainted with hatred. Shadows clustered closer, twisting into ghoulish forms, hideously deformed.

At the bottom of the stairs, the blinding sunlight seared his eyes like a wash of bright fire. He collapsed onto the dusty cobbles. Disoriented, he gazed around through blurred eyes. Another Guerrier lay doubled-up a few feet away.

Must . . . warn the Commander . . . Yet the short distance across the courtyard to the Commander's office seemed impossibly far.

He began to crawl again, pulling himself forward on his elbows, dragging his legs, which felt as if they were weighted with lead. Dust clogged his mouth and dried his tongue as he gasped for breath.

"Cadet! Get up!"

Jagu stared at a pair of leather boots that had appeared in front him. Commander Konan. He tried to speak but all that came out of his mouth was an incoherent groan.

"What in Sergius's name is the matter with you all?" The deep, growling voice seemed to come from very far away. "Are you ill? Is it sand fever?"

"No, Commander," said an unfamiliar voice. "It's poison."

Poison? The very word filled Jagu with a paralyzing black dread. *Am I going to die?* It seemed doubly unjust to have escaped death in the raid the night before, only to die ignominiously from such an underhanded trick.

"And who the devil are you?" demanded Konan. "How did you get in?"

"My name is Aqil; I am the Arkhan's envoy." He spoke the common tongue smoothly, with just the slightest foreign inflection. "And if you want to save your men's lives, I'd advise you to lower your weapon and listen to what I have to say."

Jagu tried to raise his head from the dusty cobbles to see his enemy's face; he could just make out a tall figure dressed in indigo robes, standing in the shadowy archway. The folds of his burnous obscured his features, but Jagu could see the gleam of his eyes.

"While our warrior brothers were keeping you distracted last night, we introduced a slow-acting poison into your well. Your men have already begun to experience the first symptoms: blurring of the vision, a creeping coldness that moves slowly from the fingers and toes through the limbs, up toward the heart."

Poison.

"I feel fine!" said Konan in stubborn denial.

"But take a look at your Guerriers. First paralysis sets in. Then the poison will reach their hearts, and they will die."

"You're bluffing."

"Am I? Can you afford to take the risk? In a few hours you will be the only Francian still alive in Ondhessar, surrounded by a detachment of stiffening corpses. Accede to our terms, and I will give you the antidote. But don't hesitate for too long. Soon your men will be beyond my aid."

"I will not give in to blackmail."

"Are you, perhaps, the only one not to have drunk from the well, Commander? My spies tell me that you prefer ale or wine."

In spite of the blazing sun overhead, Jagu felt as if liquid ice had begun to flow through his veins. *Poison . . . such an ignominious death for a soldier.* Through the whispering of his chilling blood, he caught the faint strains of a familiar melody. He struggled to cling to each elusive note, as if it were a lifeline.

I'm not ready to die.

"Your terms, Envoy." Konan spoke gruffly, as though barely controlling his feelings.

"You will return to us the bodies of our dead warriors. And you will surrender the fort. This land is rightfully ours. It belongs to Enhirre."

"Surrender?" repeated Konan. "Surrender the Shrine?"

The melody took words to itself, and the clear remembered timbre of a familiar voice. "*Spring moon sheds its silver light . . .*"

"Celestine," Jagu whispered.

Blue eyes, pure as a spring morning sky . . . She had chided him for playing without feeling and he had angrily rejected her criticism. But in his heart he had known that she had been right. Until the Maistre brought them together, he had been playing solely from his intellect, ignoring the sensual, expressive qualities that such a song demanded. And she had awoken all those feelings within him, bringing new color and life to his playing.

And what had he done? He had run away, never daring to tell her how he felt. And now he lay here dying, with such regret and longing welling up within him that he had been such a coward. "Celestine . . ." Jagu was drowning in the icy waves of a shadow-black sea. A single pearl of light gleamed far above him. *Spring moon.* He tried to reach for it, his fingers straining against the current. Liquid flowed into his mouth, acrid and foul-tasting; he coughed, heaving and flailing as he tried to expel the seawater from his lungs. He blinked the darkness from his eyes and found himself gazing up into the face of a stranger.

"Who—are you?" he gasped.

The stranger, who had been supporting his head, slowly withdrew his hand and reached for Jagu's right hand to check his pulse.

Jagu felt a sudden searing sensation as the stranger's fingers encircled his wrist. At the same moment, the stranger looked down. He murmured something under his breath and drew his hand swiftly away, as if he had burned his fingers. Jagu examined his wrist. The magus's mark glowed, raw as a brand, against his pale skin. When he raised his head, the Enhirran was walking swiftly away. Was the envoy a magus too? Jagu strove to speak, to call out after him, but no words would come, only a protracted groan.

"By Mhir's blood, I have such a headache. My skull is going to split apart."

Jagu saw Kilian sitting on a straw pallet close by, clasping his forehead in his hands.

"K—Kilian?" Jagu managed to pronounce his name, although

his tongue felt swollen and slow. Kilian rose to his feet and staggered toward him, wobbling like a newborn foal.

"So what dreams did their accursed poison give you?" Kilian slumped down beside him. "And who is she?"

"She?" Jagu felt the first ominous pounding in his temples. "What do you mean?"

"Celestine. You called her name as the antidote was working on you. Thought you were gone for good . . . and then you muttered that name. God, this is like the worst hangover ever. And without the fun of getting blind drunk before."

If Jagu had not felt so weak, he would have cursed aloud. Kilian would hound him mercilessly until he told him all about Celestine.

"Now I come to think of it, wasn't there that pretty blonde waving to you from the quay when we left Lutèce? I know you haven't got a sister, Jagu. What in hell made you sign a vow of celibacy with such a beautiful girl waiting for you back in Francia?"

Jagu closed his eyes. He didn't want to answer. He didn't want to think about it. Thinking hurt too much. The headache raged at full blast through his skull, black and violent orange, like a desert thunderstorm.

He caught snatches of the negotiations between Commander Konan and the Arkhan's envoy.

"Your men will feel debilitated for several days, as if they are recovering from a fever. But they are out of danger."

"I have a garrison of invalids and you expect me to march them out into the desert?" blustered Konan.

"Are you in any position to object? We made a deal, Commander."

"I can't believe that we've surrendered." Kilian and Jagu were loading a cart with munitions. Beside them, other Guerriers were packing provisions. Every man moved slowly, with the dragging gait of the convalescent. Jagu wiped the sweat from his forehead with the back of his hand; in spite of the furnace heat of the dazzling sun, he was still shivering with fever chills. Glancing around, he saw that the others were suffering too; every man had a gaunt look, with grey-brown bruising under their eyes and flaking, dried lips. "This is shameful. Humiliating."

"Is there nothing we can do?" Jagu stopped for breath; even the simple task of lifting a crate of muskets had depleted his strength.

"Captain de Lanvaux fought so hard to take Ondhessar. So many Guerriers gave their lives for the cause here." Jagu had not seen Kilian so grim-faced since Paol's death.

"You're saying we should stay and fight?"

"Damn it all, Jagu, even I know when the odds are against us."

Commander Konan's detachment began to wend its slow way across the sand dunes up into the foothills of Djihan-Djihar: some on horseback, others driving the wagons. Kilian had been deputed to bring up the rear, while Konan and his lieutenants led the column; Jagu found himself riding alongside another recent recruit, Viaud, a city boy from Lutèce who kept glancing around nervously.

"The Commander said they might attack at any time."

Jagu looked back; the red-stone fort loomed starkly against the sands, black in the sun's shadow.

"They promised us safe passage."

"And you believe them?" Viaud gave him a wry look. "They poisoned our water! Now we're so weak, they could easily pick us off, one at a time."

"And they could have withheld the antidote. Maybe they didn't want the bother of disposing of so many corpses." Jagu could be wry, too.

"Out here, the vultures will make swift work of us—" Viaud stopped. "What's that? Is it thunder?"

Jagu shaded his eyes, surveying the clear air rippling over the far horizon. "Not a sandstorm, surely."

"Your ears are keener than mine, musician."

"Whatever it is, it's drawing nearer."

A contingent of mounted men came riding over the foothills, following a standard rider bearing a banner.

"What did I tell you?" muttered Viaud. "We're dead meat."

"Stand firm!" bellowed Commander Konan. Jagu's right hand crept to his holster, feeling for his pistol; with his left, he kept a tight hold of the reins. His horse, sensing his master's apprehension, pawed the rocky path with one hoof. All about him, the Guerriers drew weapons, tensely waiting for their commander's next order. Jagu bit his lip. Was this the final confrontation? Was this where they would make their last stand against the Enhirrans? If only he could make out the colors on the banner, he would know for sure . . .

The standard-bearer came nearer. The emblem on the banner, fluttering in the hot wind, became visible.

"The Rosecoeurs!" Konan yelled. "Reinforcements!"

Jagu looked blankly at Viaud. The sound of hooves had increased from a low rumble to a clatter on the rock-strewn track.

"If it's the sign of the Rosecoeur, it must be the Allegondans," said Viaud, in puzzled tones. "But what are they doing out here, so far south?"

"Did the Commander send a message through to them?" Jagu pulled up his scarf to protect nostrils and mouth from the rising dust cloud scuffed up by the newcomers' horses.

The standard-bearer slowed his pace and the officer at the front of the column raised his hand to bring the cavalrymen to a stop. The banner was stitched with the crimson emblem of a heart pierced with a twisted branch; a single drop of blood hung from the last thorn. Jagu knew of the Allegondan Commanderie but had never encountered any of their number before. The Allegondans did not venerate Saint Sergius; they revered Mhir, who had died a martyr's death in their capital city of Bel'Esstar.

"Who the hell are you?" demanded Konan, riding up to the officer.

"Captain nel Ghislain," announced the officer, saluting Commander Konan smartly. "With reinforcements."

"You're too damned late. The Enhirrans have taken Ondhessar. They poisoned the wells. My men are too weak to fight."

Jagu saw Captain nel Ghislain cast a swift, scornful look over the ailing Francian detachment. "No matter!" He gave Konan a confident smile. "My men are in fine form. We'll take the citadel back in the name of the Commanderie."

CHAPTER 26

The city of Lutèce was in mourning for the king. Autumn fog drifted across the squares and boulevards from the river meadows, leaving water drops glistening on every bare branch and roof tile. Shops drew down their shutters, and all theaters and concert halls canceled their performances.

There was to be a grand funeral procession, with troops of guards lining the streets. Foreign crowned heads and dignitaries would follow the king's coffin, accompanying the members of the royal family. Celestine wondered how Adèle was enduring the loss of her father, so soon after the death of her beloved brother.

"How long will this official mourning last?" Gauzia, deprived of her nightly dose of adulation on the stage of the Opera House, restlessly paced the music room. Celestine gave a little shrug. Her thoughts were centered on the Maistre; the girls had been waiting over an hour for him to return from the palace with the music for the funeral service.

"When the late king's father died, the theaters were shut for four weeks," said Dame Elmire.

"What?" Gauzia let out a little shriek of horror. "I shall go mad with boredom. We've been rehearsing *A Spring Elopement*. I have a duet with Yann Kernicol—and an aria all to myself."

"There'll be plenty to keep you occupied," soothed Dame Elmire. "After the funeral, there'll be the coronation service."

Gauzia sat down in a flounce of skirts next to Celestine. "Have you heard the rumors in the city?" she said in confiding tones.

Celestine, startled out of her thoughts about the Maistre, shook her head. "They're saying it must be a curse. A curse laid on the royal house of Francia."

Celestine blinked.

Gauzia counted the points off on her fingertips. "First Francia was defeated by Tielen. Then Prince Aubrey was killed in a hunting accident. Now the king is dead. It has to be a curse. Who will it be next? Princess Adèle?"

"You know what Sister Noyale would say about such superstitious notions," said Celestine sternly.

"Everyone's talking about it. Kernicol, the tenor, reckons that it all dates back to the time when the Inquisition had those alchymists burned at the stake. He says that as they were dying, they put a curse on the royal family."

Celestine stared at Gauzia, aghast. *Those alchymists.* Did she mean her father? But before she could stammer out a question, the door opened and the Maistre came in.

"I'm sorry to have kept you both waiting," he said, putting a pile of folders on the fortepiano. He looked careworn and pale. "These sad formalities take so long to arrange. But you'll both be singing solo again, at the princess's request."

"Well, thank goodness that's over," said Gauzia, her voice echoing around the lofty fluted columns of the side chapel.

The choirs had stood in respectful silence as, to the slow beat of muffled drums, the king's coffin, draped in the blue-and-gold Francian flag, was carried from the cathedral. Only when the august guests and dignitaries filed out had they begun the final anthem. They had sung on until only the altar boys and sacristans remained.

"Hush, Gauzia!" Angelique gave her a severe look but Gauzia continued, regardless.

"How long was that? Three and a half hours?"

The Maistre appeared in the doorway, the smallest choristers of the Chapelle Royale milling around him, tugging at the long sleeves of his gown.

"Maistre, you promised us a treat if we behaved."

"You promised us cinnamon doughnuts."

"And hot chocolate."

"All in good time," he said, smiling at them. *He's so patient with the children,* Celestine thought fondly. *And they adore him.*

"Thank you, sisters," continued the Maistre above the little boys' clamor. "As ever, your contribution was exquisitely beautiful. I've heard that his majesty will soon be making a visit to the convent to thank you in person." The nuns glanced at each other in surprise. Celestine heard Sister Marthe whisper delightedly to Angelique, "King Gobain would never have troubled himself to visit us. But young Enguerrand has different priorities, it seems."

"So here you are, surrounded by all your little ones!" A woman, dressed in a cape of midnight velvet, came up to the Maistre. "Come, boys, follow me! We've laid on a fine spread for you in the vestry."

The choristers let out a cheer and surged around her as she led them into the side aisle.

"They'll love you forever, Aurélie." The Maistre took her hand in his.

Aurélie? Celestine saw the woman shake the hood from her head, revealing glossy black curls.

"Cupboard love?" The diva began to laugh, a throatily seductive sound. "You boys are so fickle!"

"No doughnuts for us, then?" said Gauzia in disappointed tones.

Ruaud was setting out the books in his study in readiness for his weekly tutorial with the young king, when the door opened and the queen entered.

"Your majesty, this is an unexpected honor." Ruaud bowed. When he looked up, he saw Aliénor regarding him coldly.

"I'll be frank with you, Captain de Lanvaux. I do not approve of your influence on my son. It's not healthy for a sixteen-year-old to spend so much time secluded with monks and priests. A king should take an interest in the welfare of his people. He should set a good example!"

Since Gobain's death, Aliénor had made no secret of her dislike for Ruaud, taking every opportunity she could to challenge him.

"With respect, majesty, what better example could a young

king set? He's devout and God-fearing." Ruaud knew he was treading on thin ice but could not resist adding, "Would you rather he spent his days gambling and drinking like so many of his peers?"

"Please don't patronize me, Captain. Of course I don't approve of the lax behavior of our younger nobles. But it wouldn't hurt Enguerrand to take up tennis . . . or hunting, a healthy outdoor sport. A young man should take plenty of vigorous exercise. I don't have to remind you what unhealthy urges can dominate the thoughts of boys his age. And what is this nonsense about going on a pilgrimage to the Birthplace Shrine? I absolutely forbid it. Enhirre is a dangerous, unstable country—you should know so better than most. And if you persist in encouraging this ambition, I shall be forced to intervene." The queen stared at him as though daring him to defy her, and Ruaud realized that he had no choice this time but to capitulate.

"Maman, what are you doing here?" Enguerrand appeared in the doorway.

"You're not a child, Enguerrand. Will you please address me as 'madame'?" Aliénor swept past her son, pausing in the doorway to add, "And you're not going to Ondhessar. You're staying here to ensure that your sister makes a good marriage. I've made my decision. And that's an end to it."

Enguerrand stood motionless, head bowed. When Aliénor was out of earshot, he said quietly, "I may be only sixteen, but I am king. And when I attain the age of majority, I won't let *her* tell me what to do anymore."

"The theaters will be reopening next week!" Gauzia's triumphant shriek cut across Celestine's vocal exercises. The next instant, Gauzia flung open the music room door.

Dame Elmire looked at her reprovingly. "Have you forgotten your manners, Demoiselle? I am coaching Celestine. Your lesson is not until four o'clock."

"But it can't be," Gauzia said breathlessly, "because they've called a rehearsal at the Opera House. With only a week to go, there's so much to do! Oh, and by the way, I'm going to stay with

Louise and Marcelle. Their apartment's so much closer to the Opera House!" The door slammed shut and she was gone again.

"Well!" exclaimed Dame Elmire. "A 'thank you, Dame Elmire' would have been appreciated. But theatrical people nowadays . . ."

Celestine said nothing. Gauzia had not even acknowledged that she was there.

"Not quite the glorious homecoming we'd planned, is it?" Kilian shaded his eyes as the sea mists parted to reveal their first glimpse of the distant coast of Francia.

Konan's Guerriers stood in subdued silence on the deck, watching the pale sun rise over the waters. Jagu shivered and pulled up the collar of his army greatcoat.

"It'll take a while to get used to the damp and cold again," said Kilian with a wry smile.

"What will they do with us? Punish us?"

"Demote us, most like."

"There is no rank lower than cadet," said Jagu dejectedly.

"Then it's the salt mines for you. Oh, don't look at me like that, Jagu. Must you believe everything I say?"

"It was the same mark, Captain." Jagu rolled up his sleeve and thrust his wrist in front of the captain's face. "The one that the magus put on me at Saint Argantel's."

Captain de Lanvaux leaned closer to Jagu over the desk. "Are you sure?"

Jagu grimaced. "How could I forget? There has to be a link between that magus and everything that's been happening in Ondhessar."

The captain sat back in his chair, pensively turning his pen over between his fingers. Suddenly he said, "How would you like to work for me, cadet?"

Jagu felt as if the clouds that had been dampening his spirits had suddenly lifted. He glanced up eagerly. "You'd take me on, Captain? In spite of what happened at the Shrine?"

"I've read the reports, and you acted honorably in difficult circumstances. I want you to join my personal staff as adjutant. You've developed some unique observational skills, and I want to put them to good use. Welcome on board, Adjutant de Rustéphan." He put out his hand and Jagu gripped it enthusiastically.

"Thank you, Captain."

Outside the captain's office, Jagu saw Kilian sitting on a bench, grinning at him.

"You, too?"

"Call me lieutenant now, Adjutant Rustéphan!"

"Damn!" cried Jagu. "You're always one step ahead of me."

"Are you sure this is where Captain de Lanvaux wanted us to meet?" Jagu murmured to Lieutenant Friard as he followed him down into the cold, musty air of the crypt of Saint Meriadec's.

Candles had been lit in the dusty alcoves; by their uncertain light, Jagu recognized the captain, Kilian, and old Père Judicael, flanked by two older Guerriers he had not met before.

"I've summoned you here because it's one of the few places we can be sure of privacy," said the captain, glancing at each man in turn. "There's been rather a puzzling turn of events in Enhirre. Lieutenant Kilian, would you explain?"

"The Rosecoeurs have taken back Ondhessar," said Kilian. "But they have stripped the contents of the Shrine and shipped them to Bel'Esstar."

"That's vandalism." Jagu was disgusted.

"The Arkhan has already expressed his displeasure to Prince Ilsevir," said the captain. "However, I'm surprised that our own leader, Maistre Donatien, has not registered an official protest at this act of violation."

"Ghislain," said Jagu, remembering the smartly turned-out young officer they had met in the foothills. He looked up. "We failed you, Captain. We let the Commanderie down. If we'd stayed, we might have prevented this."

"What happened to your regiment, Jagu, was another in a series of escalating attacks against Francia," said the captain. "I have reason to believe that this is all the work of the magi of Ondhessar."

"As to who is using them . . ." added Père Judicael.

"I want you all to be doubly vigilant. Your first duty is to protect the royal family. But I fear that there may also be a schism developing within the Commanderie. It may be that the magi are playing on our suspicions, setting one against the other." Jagu caught Kilian's eye. "But without the Angelstones to protect us, we are vulnerable. We have to rely on officers like you, Jagu, who have a sixth sense when it comes to mage-mischief."

A carriage was waiting outside the Maistre's house when Celestine arrived for her weekly lesson.

"Do you mind waiting, my dear?" Dame Elmire hurried out to meet her, bustling her with almost indecent haste into the salon next to the music room. "The diva has decided to pay him an unexpected visit." The dame then disappeared, muttering about fetching tea for their guest; Celestine perched on the edge of a fauteuil and tried to order her thoughts, which had been plunged into utter disorder by this news. Why had Aurélie Carnelian come to visit the Maistre? Was it to rehearse . . . or for quite another reason? Celestine did not hear a single note of music through the thin wall.

"I want you to come with me on this tour of Tourmalise, Henri."

Tourmalise? Against her better judgment, Celestine moved closer to the wall, to try to catch more of what was being said. *What am I doing, spying on him?*

"No one understands my voice as you do." The diva's perfect enunciation made every word audible, even through lathe and plaster. "We have a unique rapport, don't we?"

"You always know how to make a man do exactly what you want, don't you, Aurélie?" Celestine had never heard the Maistre use that tone of voice before; there was an intimate, teasing quality that implied a relationship far more close than that of singer and accompanist.

He's in love with her. He'll do anything she asks. She waited in growing dismay for his reply.

"But I have commitments in Lutèce. I can't just go off for a month, two months, and leave my choirs without their director."

"You have assistants. Let them take over. And you've been working so hard, you deserve a break. You don't want to make yourself ill." Aurélie's voice was so soft, so coaxing; how could he refuse? "Composers can burn out if they push themselves too far; you remember what happened to poor Capelian? You can relax at the spa in Sulien; I have a little villa there, overlooking the city. A rest will do you good."

Celestine heard the Maistre give a gentle, indulgent laugh. "It's impossible to resist you, Aurélie."

"So you'll come!" Celestine did not miss the triumphant ring in the diva's voice, which was interrupted by the silvery tones of the little clock in the hall striking the half hour.

"Goodness, is that the time? I have a student waiting. Forgive me."

"You see how busy you are, Henri? You must be more kind to yourself."

Celestine guiltily darted away from the wall and busily began to shuffle through her sheets of music as the salon door opened and the Maistre appeared. Behind him, Celestine glimpsed Aurélie in a tight-fitting traveling costume of mulberry, her glossy black hair elaborately curled and arranged.

"Demoiselle Celestine, please go on through to the music room."

Why was he speaking so formally to her? Was it because of Aurélie? Eyes downcast, Celestine had almost reached the door when Aurélie suddenly let out a little cry of vexation. "What am I thinking of? I'm leaving without the very piece I came to collect. Henri, would you be so good as to bring me a copy of *Faded Petals?*"

"By all means." The Maistre went back into the music room; Celestine went to follow him, only to find Aurélie blocking her way.

"So *you're* Henri's latest protégé?" The diva gave her a hard, appraising stare. "Ah yes, I believe I heard you sing in the cathedral. A sweet voice, but lacking any real substance." She stopped suddenly, gazing challengingly into Celestine's eyes. "I saw the way you looked at him. You're utterly smitten with him. It's written all over your face. So let's get one thing straight: Henri is *mine*. I understand his needs. An inexperienced child like you could never hope to satisfy him."

Am I that transparent? Celestine took a step back, dismayed that her rival had read her so accurately. *Are my feelings for the Maistre so obvious?*

"Besides, you really don't want to make an enemy of me, my dear. I have influence in every opera house and concert hall in the quadrant. I can put an end to your career before it's even begun."

Celestine was unprepared for such a blatant challenge. Even if she had found her voice, she would not have known what to say.

"And now that we understand each other," said Aurélie with the sweetest smile curving her red-rouged lips, "I trust I will never have to raise this delicate issue again."

"Here it is." The Maistre reappeared, waving a folder which he handed to Aurélie; Celestine noticed how the diva closed her hands over his as she took it, caressing his fingers. "Let me escort you to your carriage."

Celestine still stood in the hall as Aurélie stalked past her, leaving a waft of exotic perfume in her wake. As the Maistre opened the door, Aurélie flashed her a triumphant glance from beneath her strong, black brows.

She sees me as her rival! And she's so famous, so influential, what chance do I have, competing with her for the Maistre's affections?

Gauzia came clattering down the stair into the hallway, clutching her score.

Aurélie glanced around and saw her. Her expression altered, her tone became sweet and indulgent. "Why, if it isn't little Gauzia!"

"Aurélie!" Gauzia replied, with a winsome smile.

"Are you on your way to the rehearsal, my dear? Let me give you a lift in my carriage."

All three swept out of the house, the two women chattering animatedly about the Opera House. Celestine stood in the hall, feeling as if life had just passed her by.

CHAPTER 27

Garlands of fresh spring flowers were draped over every lintel and window of the Palace of Plaisaunces. All the drab, funereal hangings had been taken down and the courtiers had put aside their black clothes the instant the Queen Regent announced that the official period of mourning for her husband was at an end. Evenings that had been filled with contemplative readings from the Holy Texts by Grand Maistre Donatien and the hushed strains of slow and solemn music were free again for cards, masquerades, dancing—and for entertaining foreign royalty. The palace was abuzz with rumors about the splendid banquet that Queen Aliénor had arranged: The guest list read like a gathering of all the crowned heads of the western quadrant. It was little surprise that Prince Eugene of Tielen had declined to attend, as he was still mourning the death of his young wife—and, besides, Francia had not forgiven the House of Helmar for inflicting such a crushing defeat in the Spice Wars. And it was generally held (though no one said it aloud) to be a relief that the warlord Volkh of Azhkendir would not be making the long journey from his remote kingdom in the far north.

"My mother is calling it a spring banquet," Adèle said to Celestine, showing her the list of guests, "but it's really a marriage market at which I am to be sold off to the highest bidder."

Celestine scanned the list and her eyes widened. "You want me to sing before all these eminent people? Wouldn't it be better to ask a well-known diva, like Aurélie Carnelian?"

"I want *you*, Celestine." Adèle put her hands on Celestine's shoulders, gazing candidly into her eyes, and Celestine blushed. "Besides, who else can I discuss my mother's choice of suitors with? None of my ladies-in-waiting dare tell me what they really think; they're all too scared of Maman. I'm sure that she lines them up in front of her and makes them learn by heart exactly what she wants them to say to me."

Celestine was much relieved to hear that Adèle preferred her to the Divine Aurélie.

"If only Papa could have lived a little longer. I'm almost certain he didn't favor an alliance with Allegonde." Adèle's hands dropped back to her sides. For a moment she looked vulnerable and bereft. "But now that he's gone . . ."

The realization that Adèle was still grieving for her father stirred bitter memories for Celestine. "Do you miss him very much?"

"Do I miss him?" Adèle went to a little ebony-framed portrait of the king and picked it up, staring at it. "I'm not sure if I ever truly loved my father. I respected him . . . but he was not an easy man to love. When Enguerrand and I were little, we hardly ever saw him. He was always so busy." She carefully replaced the portrait. "Aubrey was his favorite. But strangely enough, I never hated Aubrey for it. I was . . . grateful to him, I suppose, for keeping Papa from interfering in our daily lives. And now they're both gone."

"Congratulations, Celestine." The Maistre looked up from Princess Adèle's invitation and smiled at her.

She looked away, biting her lip. The warmth in his grey eyes almost melted her resolve. *How can you look at me like that when you're Aurélie Carnelian's lover?*

"This could be the making of you. This could lead to many invitations to sing abroad. Let's review your repertoire, shall we?"

Helplessly, she felt herself being seduced all over again by his charm. In spite of her determination to stay aloof, she found that she had drawn nearer to him, looking over his shoulder as he flicked through a sheaf of songs, picking some, discarding others. "I see that the princess has marked 'Spring Moon' as one of her favorites; I'm flattered that she likes it—and so should you be, as I wrote it for you."

He turned and gazed into her eyes.

"F—for me?" Why had he chosen this moment to tell her? She gazed mutely back at him, unable to find words to express how moved she felt.

"When it's published, it will bear a dedication to you."

"It's to be published?" She was utterly confused now; did this mean that he might have feelings for her? Or did he just dedicate each piece that he wrote to its first performer?

Celestine glared at the Maistre's new song, "October Seas." Why was it proving such a trial? The poem, by Muscobite poet Solovei, was deceptively simple; it recorded the impressions of a lone woman going to the seashore every day and gazing out into the autumn fogs for a glimpse of her lover's ship returning to harbor. "*In vain*" was the refrain of the last verse, "*I wait in vain.*"

"All the Muscobite poets seem to relish gloomy subjects," the Maistre had said to her with a glint of a mischievous smile in his eyes as he handed her the music. "It must be because they're too far north to see much of the sun."

Since then, Celestine had been struggling to find the right way to convey the song's subtle melancholy. When she concentrated on refining the purity of her tone, aiming to let the words speak for themselves, it sounded too detached. And when she tried to interpret what lay behind the words, she got in a muddle.

"Is her lover dead?" she asked, perplexed. "Or does she think he's dead?"

"There are many possible readings." The Maistre looked up at her from the keyboard. "But you must find the one that unlocks the music for you. It's all to do with . . . love."

Love. She felt an involuntary shiver go through her. "*On the far horizon—*" she began, and broke off. This phrase was especially challenging as it skipped over the break in her voice. She took a breath and tried again. It was like trying to crest a high wave; each time she struggled, she fell back, floundering.

The Maistre left the fortepiano and came to stand close behind her, placing his hands on her diaphragm.

"Breathing. Control," he said softly into her ear, one of his favorite phrases. "Push against my fingers as you release those notes. Slowly. Don't strain. Let it sound effortless."

She drew in a breath, then let the notes float out. All she was aware of was the firm pressure of his hands on her waist and rib cage. *He's holding me. I can feel his breath warm on my cheek . . .*

"Now try it again by yourself."

He moved away from her, smiling encouragingly. Flustered, she tried to collect her thoughts. She reminded herself that he was merely instructing her, as he instructed his other pupils, young men as well as girls . . .

"Perhaps we'd better substitute another song," the Maistre said at length. "Perhaps you're not ready to sing this one."

Not ready? What had he meant by that? Aurélie had put it more bluntly, calling her an inexperienced child.

And now she lay sleepless, restless with longing, unable to forget what it felt like to be pressed against his firm frame, to sense the steady beat of his heart so close to her own . . .

It was all to do with love.

Was he implying that she could not sing the song with true understanding until she had made love? She felt her cheeks burning. But what did love mean to him? Was it possible for two people to love one another deeply, chastely, and never surrender to the sins of the flesh? All she knew was that every time she was with him, life seemed so much more vivid and intense. She longed for him to touch her, kiss her . . . and yet she also feared where such intimate contact might lead. The girls had frequently been warned at the convent about men and their importunate needs and desires. If she were to surrender to the strength of her feelings, she feared that she would lose all control.

But he is Aurélie's, and can never be mine . . .

In the first dawnlight, she found herself opening her father's book. For a brief moment she glimpsed the names of holy saints, then the printed text blurred, re-forming to reveal the spells and glamours hidden within. Flicking desperately through the faded pages, she searched for a cure for the unassuageable ache in her heart.

"*What are you looking for?*" The Faie was gazing over her shoulder, translucent eyes wide and curious.

"A remedy," Celestine muttered angrily, "to cure a broken heart." *Or to remove a spiteful rival.* Even though she had not spoken aloud, the pages fell open at a potion that claimed to cause youthful bloom to fade and wither. Tempted, she lingered over the words, wondering if the spell would work . . .

"*Why would you want to do that?*"

"Because the Maistre matters to me more than anyone else." She clapped her hands to her mouth. She had said it aloud.

"*More than your father?*"

"That's different!" Even though the Faie had asked the question without any expression or insinuation, Celestine heard the unspoken reminder.

I have a duty to Papa . . .

"Are you feeling well, Celestine?" the Maistre asked. "You look pale."

Why did he have to speak so sympathetically? One kind look from his soft grey eyes and she was quite undone. "I—I didn't sleep well. The birds woke me early," she lied. *If you only knew why I couldn't sleep, Maistre . . .*

He played a few bars and she recognized the introduction to "October Seas," as gently repetitive as the wash of the tide on the seashore in the bay below Saint Azilia's. She closed her eyes, remembering standing on the headland, gazing out across the grey sea. Before she realized what she was doing, she had sung the first phrase, letting the notes float into the misty horizon conjured from her memories. The Maistre continued playing, so she continued to sing, caught up in the notes' desolate spell.

"*In vain,*" she sang. "*In vain . . .*" The last note faded away. She opened her eyes, awakening from the trance, to see the Maistre had risen from the fortepiano.

"When did you learn to sing it like that?"

She could not even stammer out a reply.

"Only yesterday I was thinking of removing it from the program." He was speaking so fast in his excitement that she couldn't quite catch all his words. "And now you've managed to capture exactly that elusive quality of melancholy I was striving for."

His approval meant more to her than any amount of applause.

And even though he could never be hers, at least she had the bitter-sweet pleasure of knowing that she had brought his song to vivid and poignant life.

"The time has come, Celestine, for you to choose." The Mother Superior fixed Celestine with a stare so penetratingly severe that she began to tremble. "The sisters and I have tolerated your frequent absences from the daily services long enough. I have a letter here from Abbess Ermengarde asking me to take in one of the novices, Margaud, from Saint Azilia's. She has a genuine vocation and is eager to take the veil."

Celestine nodded, remembering Margaud, a solemn girl, two year's her junior, with a sweet alto voice. She guessed where this discussion was leading.

"We have little enough room to accommodate our own sisters here. And we survive on the charity of our benefactors. But you are eighteen years of age. You must decide, Celestine. Do you intend to dedicate your life to God?"

Gauzia had not given the matter a second's thought—but then, she had never pretended to have any kind of spiritual vocation. She had been sent to Saint Azilia's against her will. But Celestine had begun to agonize over the decision.

The sisters took me in and cared for me when I was orphaned. But if I leave, I'll be out on the streets again. I have no money, no family, nowhere to go.

"The very fact that you're hesitating just confirms what I've suspected for quite a while; you don't belong here." There was a sour hint of triumph in the Mother Superior's stern voice.

"I'm very grateful to the convent for all that you've done for me," Celestine burst out. "But if you're saying that I must give up my performing career, then I'm just not prepared to do that."

"Celestine must stay here, mustn't she, Henri?" Dame Elmire declared as she poured tea for her nephew. "We can't have the poor girl wandering the streets."

"Oh, but I couldn't possibly . . ." Celestine heard herself say and was not entirely sure why she was arguing so forcibly against

Dame Elmire's suggestion. The thought of living so close to the Maistre was both seductively attractive and disturbing.

"Nonsense!" said Dame Elmire briskly. "There's Gauzia's room."

"Isn't Gauzia coming back?"

"Why would she want to?" A knowing smile appeared on Dame Elmire's face. "She has her freedom, living with her fellow ingénues near the Opera."

"I'll do housework. And I want you to have any money I make from performing." Celestine felt her eyes brimming with tears of gratitude. "I can't board here for free, Dame Elmire."

Dame Elmire thrust a broom into her hands. "If you're not afraid of a few spiders, then you can start straightaway."

The little trunk Celestine had brought with her from Saint Azilia's lay open on the bed as she carefully folded her few clothes and laid them inside. She was required to leave behind her novice's gowns and linen; they would be washed and handed on to her replacement, Margaud.

There came a discreet tap at the door and Angelique came in.

"I can't believe you're leaving us," she said.

"Mère Apolline said I must choose." Celestine continued to pack, not wanting to meet Angelique's eyes.

"And you chose Henri de Joyeuse."

Why did I choose to stay close to him, knowing he can never be mine? "There are things I have to do. Things I can't accomplish if I stay here, safe inside the convent walls." Still she could not look at Angelique. As she struggled to fasten the strap tight around the battered leather, she felt Angelique's arms go around her.

"There's a shadow haunting you, isn't there? Ever since that first day I saw you in the Skylarks' dormitory, I've known. Maybe it's what makes your singing so poignant."

"Oh, Angelique, if only I could tell you . . ." Celestine closed her eyes a moment, longing to share the burden of her past. Yet if Angelique knew that she was an alchymist's child, would she still treat her so fondly?

"Take care. And if ever you need to confide in anyone . . . well, you know where to find me." Angelique kissed the top of her head and, unlacing her arms, hurried away.

The note, emblazoned with the royal crest, read:

> Please wear this for the recital. It should fit, as my maid is certain that you and I are almost exactly the same size.
>
> Your affectionate friend, Adèle.

Celestine carefully lifted the silken dress from its wrappings and held it up against her.

"The princess has an excellent eye for color!" exclaimed Dame Elmire, clasping her hands together in delight. "That deep hyacinth blue complements your eyes perfectly."

Celestine had never received so costly a gift before; she stroked the softly shimmering material, holding it up to her cheek. "How can I ever thank her?"

"By giving the best performance of your life, my dear."

Celestine gulped. Suddenly she felt overwhelmed by nerves. "I have butterflies," she admitted, pressing a hand against her breast.

"I would be worried if you didn't feel a little apprehensive." Dame Elmire helped her fold the silk dress. "I mistrust any performer who boasts that they never feel nervous. Such musicians rarely give a memorable performance—or they are consummate liars."

"Well? How does she look, Henri?" asked Dame Elmire as Celestine came down the stair. The dress was so light that she felt as if she were floating down on a cloud.

The Maistre was sorting through his music on the hall table. Celestine was sure that he would glance up, nod abstractedly, and go back to his sorting. But instead he let the sheets of music slide. He was gazing at her, almost as if seeing her for the first time. When he spoke, he stammered. "Ce—Celestine. You look . . . lovely." And then as she hastily bent to retrieve the scattered sheets, he said swiftly, "Forgive me. That must sound so lame. I never meant . . ."

"Let me help." Celestine darted forward and dipped down to hand him the pages she had rescued. His fingers gently grazed hers as he took the music, and she felt herself shivering at his touch. She gazed into his eyes and saw a look so intimate, so intense, that it seemed to strip away all her defenses, laying bare her innermost feelings.

"The carriage is waiting," said Dame Elmire, "and it really wouldn't do to be late for this recital!"

The Salle des Chevaliers was one of the most impressive halls in the Palace of Plaisaunces. The wooden beams of the ornate plaster ceiling were intricately painted in the style of the previous century, with white and golden lilies and fire-breathing salamanders, the emblems of the royal household. Embroidered banners hung from every beam, displaying the arms of the duchies of Francia: Provença; Armel; Vasconie. The walls were hung with crossed swords and spears, battle trophies from ancient Francian victories.

"Not the most intimate of rooms for a recital," said the Maistre, testing the tuning of the fortepiano. He took out a little tuning key and started tightening the upper strings, the sound echoing high into the vaults of the ceiling.

"And there are so many extra guards on duty around the palace tonight," murmured Celestine, as the heavily armed soldiers standing in every doorway shuffled and coughed.

"With half the crowned heads of the quadrant here tonight, they're taking no chances."

The great doors at the rear of the hall were pushed open, and the courtiers thronged in, all talking loudly. Odors of herb-roasted meat and rich wine wafted in from the banqueting hall beyond.

"It sounds as if they've all dined well," said the Maistre with an ironic lift of one brow. "Let's hope half of them don't sleep it off during our recital."

"His majesty, the king," announced a herald.

The whole company fell silent as King Enguerrand entered the Salle des Chevaliers. Queen Aliénor, somberly dressed in black-and-silver brocade, swept through the bowing guests toward her seat, looking straight ahead until she saw the Allegondan guests. Only then did a chilly smile of welcome appear on her face as she greeted Prince Ilsevir and gestured to him to sit beside her. Celestine, head lowered in a respectful curtsy, caught sight of Adèle's resigned expression as she sat down on the gilded fauteuil beside her mother. Where, Celestine wondered, was the young Muscobar prince and his entourage? King Enguerrand kept glancing around anxiously, as though searching for someone.

The murmur of conversation in the room ceased. Celestine realized that all the guests were looking expectantly at her, and her mouth went dry. She sent a swift, desperate glance to the Maistre. He looked over the top of the open music on the fortepiano and smiled at her. And suddenly she knew, in her heart, that she had no reason to be afraid. She managed a shaky little smile in return and slowly inclined her head—the signal they had agreed for him to start to play.

The instant the first chords rippled out into the salle, Celestine relaxed. The audience became a blur as she drew in a breath and began to sing. The music possessed her. There seemed to be a perfect understanding between them; her voice had never soared so effortlessly before and he was always there, supporting her, matching her. This moment was theirs and theirs alone. They finished the final song. As they took their bows, she felt the warmth of his fingers touching hers. Regret flooded through her as she realized that it was over.

If only it could always be like this, just the two of us, making music together.

"My dear young lady!" A distinguished-looking diplomat came through the press of people toward Celestine, his arms open wide. She recognized Count Velemir, the Muscobite ambassador. A young nobleman wearing an immaculate white uniform was with him.

"You've made a conquest tonight!" exclaimed the count. He kissed her hand and, rather than relinquishing it, drew her toward him. "Highness, may I present Demoiselle Celestine, our entrancing singer tonight?"

"Andrei Orlov," said the young man, making her a formal military bow, striking one hand to his heart.

"Prince Andrei," she murmured, curtsying. She recognized

those dark curls from the portrait Adèle had shown her. The portraitist had not flattered him; he was every bit as handsome in the flesh.

"To be honest, I'm no connoisseur of the arts, Demoiselle, but I really enjoyed your performance." There was the slightest hint of a roguish glint in his dark eyes. "I think my sister, Tasia, would love to meet you; she's much more artistic than I."

"Have you ever visited Mirom?" inquired the count pleasantly.

"No," said Celestine, trying to make polite conversation, "although I hear it can be very cold in winter."

Prince Andrei burst into laughter, and his laugh was so warm, so charming, she could not feel offended at his response. "You should come visit us in the spring, Demoiselle, when the snows melt and the frozen rivers thaw."

"I shall speak with Maistre de Joyeuse," said the count, raising his glass to Celestine, "and see if we can arrange a little tour. Although I have every hope that you will be invited to perform at a royal wedding before too long—"

"For heaven's sake, Velemir, let's not jump the gun!" Celestine could not help but notice the angry color that darkened Prince Andrei's cheeks at this suggestion. "I haven't even been properly introduced to the girl yet." *He doesn't look so keen at the prospect of marriage . . .*

Another Muscobite, a soulful-eyed young man in naval uniform, approached and murmured in Andrei's ear. The prince nodded and bowed to Celestine before following his countryman toward the princess's chair.

"Hobnobbing with royalty again?" said a voice in her ear. She jumped and, turning, saw the Maistre standing behind her, smiling. "We must talk," he said. "There's something I've been meaning to tell you."

She took his arm and for a while they walked in silence, Celestine moving as if in a blissful dream, oblivious to the jeweled and powdered courtiers, content to be so close to the Maistre. It was not so crowded at the far end of the great Salle, as most of the guests were milling around the princess, eager to see which suitor had attracted her attention.

"We've both been so busy," began the Maistre. "And what with all the rehearsals, there just hasn't been time . . ." What was he struggling to say to her? "I'm leaving Lutèce tomorrow."

"Leaving?" The dream shattered. "Where are you going?" Although she feared she knew the answer to the question already.

"To Tourmalise. The diva has asked me to accompany her on a recital tour." He was not looking at her as he spoke; he obviously felt ashamed to be breaking the news to her so late.

"How—how long will you be away?"

"Five, six weeks, maybe longer. I can't be sure. It depends."

"Oh." To her shame, she felt tears filling her eyes. She turned away from him, willing herself not to cry.

"My aunt will continue to coach you, as usual."

She nodded, not trusting herself to speak. She had been so blissfully happy a few moments ago and now he had spoiled it. But then, she had no right to expect anything; he was Aurélie's lover.

"What's this? You're not crying, are you?" he said gently.

"There's a speck of dust in my eye," she said angrily, blinking, as if to dislodge the imaginary speck.

"Celestine—" he began. A Guerrier hurried up and saluted. "Captain de Lanvaux presents his compliments, Demoiselle. He wanted to congratulate you in person, but has been called away on urgent business." He presented her with a letter, saluted again, and sped away.

Celestine opened the letter.

"What does the captain say?" the Maistre asked.

"He wants me to meet him in the Plaisaunces Gardens tomorrow afternoon."

CHAPTER 28

"Why an alliance with Allegonde, Grand Maistre?" asked Ruaud. "Muscobar will not react kindly to this snub."

Donatien gave Ruaud a shrewd look. "I'm only complying with the queen's wishes. She feels that Ilsevir will make a much better match for Adèle than Andrei Orlov. He's older, more levelheaded—"

"The queen's wishes?" Ruaud was becoming increasingly irritated by Donatien's smug attitude. "What about the king?"

"Oh come now, Ruaud, would you trust an unworldly sixteen-year-old to make such an important decision? One that will affect the future of Francia?"

Ruaud remembered his last conversation with Gobain. The late king's predictions were proving disturbingly accurate. "And the princess's wishes?"

"Princess Adèle will do as her mother commands."

Ruaud felt a faint flicker of panic; Allegonde would prove a weak and ineffectual ally if the recent intelligence about Eugene of Tielen was true. A brilliant military strategist, the young ruler was pouring funds into training his armies and constructing a second impressive fleet of warships. "But if Adèle were to marry into the Orlovs, we would have a strong ally against Tielen."

"Ally? Watch what you say, Ruaud. Anyone overhearing this might think you were planning military action against Prince Eugene."

Was Donatien reprimanding him? What was his real motive in

following the queen's wishes? Well, Ruaud could play mind games as well. "So what advantages will a match with Allegonde bring us? I hear Ilsevir is more interested in music than his armies."

"It's not your place to question the queen's wishes." Donatien's eyes had hardened. "And may I remind you that if you had brought Kaspar Linnaius to justice, he would no longer be supplying the Tielen armies with alchymical weapons."

Rieuk gazed down on the tall, slender trunks of eternal trees in the Rift, ghostly foliage wreathed in drifting mists, lit by the light of the emerald moon. It seemed an eternity since Imri had brought him up here to seek out Ormas. In the distance, he glimpsed a flock of shadow hawks skimming gracefully above the trees. Their wild cries carried back to him over the velvet darkness of the forest and he felt Ormas's heart quicken with longing at the sound.

"*Not yet, Ormas, it's not yet time.*"

"Rieuk . . ."

That voice. Rieuk gripped the parapet rim. He had been thinking of Imri as he climbed the endless stair. Had he conjured a spectre from his memory? Here, in the Rift, anything might happen.

"Rieuk, I'm cold . . ."

Rieuk slowly turned around. There, in the gloom behind him, stood Imri . . . or a semblance of Imri, his black hair loose about his shoulders, his face half-veiled in shadow.

"Imri?" Rieuk stood, staring. "Is it you? Is it really you?" He had wanted to see him so much . . . yet now this felt terribly wrong. "What have they done to you?" Yet even as he reached out to the revenant, it began to fade, leaving him clutching empty air.

Rieuk found Lord Estael conferring with Aqil and Oranir over a detailed plan of the citadel of Ondhessar.

"Well, Rieuk?" he asked, looking up.

"Was it your doing?" Rieuk demanded. "Was this some illusion you conjured up? Or was it really him?"

"I have no idea what you are talking about," said Lord Estael coldly.

"Imri came to me. In the Rift. I saw him. He spoke to me."

Rieuk shivered, rubbing his arms. Since the encounter he had felt chilled to the bone and could not get warm again, in spite of the fierce sun outside. He sensed Oranir's dark eyes regarding him curiously, but the reserved young magus said nothing.

"A trick of the Rift." Lord Estael shrugged. "We had hoped you might have made some progress in your search for Azilis . . . But your arrival is timely; the Arkhan has fresh instructions."

"What new mission has the Arkhan devised for me?" asked Rieuk wearily. It seemed that the more he did in the name of the magi of Ondhessar, the more the Arkhan required of him.

"The situation has become rather more complicated than we anticipated. The Allegondan Commanderie has removed the last of the relics from the Shrine. They have taken the statue of Azilis and are transporting it to Bel'Esstar. The Arkhan has already made a formal protest to Prince Ilsevir, but the prince has refused to listen."

"You're not expecting me to bring back a *statue*?"

"The Arkhan has asked us to teach the prince a lesson he will not easily forget," said Magus Aqil. "And the Guerriers who desecrated the Shrine will pay dearly. We are traveling to Bel'Esstar, Rieuk. To attend a royal wedding."

"It's been too long since we talked together," said Captain de Lanvaux as he and Celestine entered a shady alley, dappled with shifting sunlight filtering through the acacia leaves. The sound of hoeing came from a distant flower bed; they passed a gardener wielding his topiary shears with dexterity, clipping fresh growth from the box and yew.

"I've followed your career with great interest. And I've noticed that the princess is fond of you."

She had not expected the conversation to take this turn. "She's been very kind to me."

"So the feeling is mutual?"

Celestine nodded. "We understand one another."

"What if I were to ask you to go to Allegonde with her?"

"Leave Lutèce? For good?" The thought of being separated from the Maistre was intolerable, even if she could never be his. "Oh no, I couldn't—"

"The princess is apprehensive about the coming wedding. I thought it might help ease her into her new life if a few friends accompanied her to Bel'Esstar. I'm sure that a recital or two could be arranged. Bel'Esstar is famous for its opera houses and concert halls—but I'm sure you know more about that than I do," he added, with a smile.

Celestine felt emboldened enough by that kindly smile to dare to ask, "But a singer needs a sympathetic accompanist. Could—could you arrange for Maistre de Joyeuse to come, too?"

He paused, glancing around them as if checking to see if they were alone. "Have you seen the striped roses in the knot garden? They're at their best."

She followed him down the gravel path, thinking how incongruous it was to hear the captain talking like a keen gardener.

"We used to grow moss roses like these at Saint Azilia's." She bent to inhale the rich perfume exuding from the crumpled petals of damson purple. "The scent is heavenly, but the thorns are vicious!"

He drew closer to her, as if to smell one of the moss roses, and his voice dropped to a more intimate pitch. "We've learned of a threat against the royal couple's lives."

Celestine stared at him in alarm. "But who—?"

"Enhirran extremists, maybe . . . The Rosecoeurs' act of vandalism in stripping the Shrine of its treasures has provoked much anger in Enhirre. What better way to draw attention to the Enhirran cause than to disrupt a royal wedding? Or it may be from quite another source. The point is that we can't take the risk. That's why I'm asking you if you would help protect her."

"Me? But I have no training."

"I want to pair you with one of my agents." The captain kept his voice low, speaking urgently. "He has the experience, you know the princess; together, you should make a formidable team. What do you say?"

To Celestine's surprise, she heard herself answering, "I'll do it. For the princess's sake."

He straightened up as the sound of clipping shears came closer. "Good. Let's move on, shall we?"

She looked quizzically at him. "We're being observed? Even here?"

He nodded. "You're learning fast."

———

"I'd like to introduce you to your partner for this mission, Demoiselle. Although, I believe you already know one another." Was there a hint of a smile in Captain de Lanvaux's voice, Celestine wondered, as he opened the door to his study. A black-haired Guerrier rose from his seat and turned to face them.

"Jagu!" Celestine stopped in the doorway, staring. Jagu took a step back, gripping at the top of his chair to stop himself from tripping.

"B—but I thought you were in Enhirre," she stammered. She did not know if she was pleased to see him again, only that she had felt her heart beat faster at the sight of him.

"My detachment returned some weeks ago. Since then Captain de Lanvaux has been kind enough to make me his adjutant."

"Jagu served with great distinction in Enhirre," said Captain de Lanvaux, crossing the room to put his arm about his new adjutant's shoulders.

Jagu stared at the floor, evidently embarrassed by the captain's praise.

"But on to more pressing matters." Ruaud de Lanvaux gestured to them to sit. "The princess's wedding." He pulled a sheaf of papers from a drawer and spread them out on top of the desk.

"Is the threat to the princess, or Prince Ilsevir?" asked Jagu.

"We believe Prince Ilsevir to be the main target, but our intelligence suggests that his bride, Princess Adèle, is equally in danger."

Celestine tried to repress a shiver. The thought that any insurgents, no matter how desperate their cause, should regard sweet-natured Adèle as a target made her feel sick.

"And this intelligence comes from the Allegondan Commanderie?" Jagu's habitual scowl seemed to have deepened since his time abroad. She wondered what had happened to him in Enhirre. "Served with distinction" implied that he had seen action. Had he fought and killed the enemy?

"From several sources," said the captain enigmatically. "But you won't be traveling as Guerriers of the Commanderie. You'll be billed as two of Francia's most celebrated musicians. You'll be singing at the wedding ceremony, then at the reception afterward. But you'll also be there to protect the princess. There'll be other

Francian agents to back you up, but you'll be in a unique position."

"Do you have any idea yet what kind of attack might be launched? Are we talking of a grenade? Or a sniper?"

The captain's eyes darkened. "The only information we have is that there may be magi involved."

"Magi?" Celestine echoed. *Did he mean Kaspar Linnaius?* Beside her she noticed that Jagu had tensed, as if steeling himself to take a blow.

"It's not common knowledge, but I head a small elite squad within the Commanderie, established to hunt down and destroy anyone rash enough to practice the Forbidden Arts. That's how I first met Jagu."

Celestine did not miss the look that passed between the two men. *"His best friend was murdered,"* the Maistre had told her. *"Murdered by a magus."* She wanted to learn more about the terrible event that had scarred Jagu's early life. But the captain was already filling in more of the details of their mission and she forced herself to concentrate. "There will, of course, be all the usual bodyguards in attendance to protect her royal highness. But you two will be trained to identify the unusual, the unexpected, that others might disregard."

"The unusual?" Celestine echoed.

"And if we identify the presence of a magus," said Jagu, "how do we protect the princess?"

"I'm going to introduce you to Père Judicael. He taught me the skills of exorcism.

"If me, why not send Kilian too?" Jagu demanded.

"Because you, Jagu, already have a sixth sense when it comes to mage-magic."

"And why me?" asked Celestine warily. She was not sure that she wanted to meet Père Judicael. If he was so clever an exorcist, wouldn't he be able to detect the Faie's silvered aura clinging to her? Suddenly the prestigious mission didn't seem such an attractive proposition, after all.

"Of course, if Lieutenant Guyomard had even half as pretty a singing voice as Demoiselle Celestine, I might have seriously considered him," Ruaud said, laughing. Celestine saw for a moment

Jagu's stern expression soften and the hint of a smile made his face look younger, more relaxed.

"Kilian sings like a bear," he said. "Even at Saint Argantel's, he could never hold a tune."

"Does that answer your question?" Ruaud was still smiling as he looked at her. There was something in the fond way he looked at her sometimes that reminded her of her father. How could it be that he, who should by all reasoning, have been her enemy, had not only saved her life but watched over her all these years? She returned the smile even though there was pain in her heart. *For if Père Judicael discovers my secret, then we will be enemies.*

The Inquisition archives were housed in an unremarkable building on the right bank of the river, overlooking the Forteresse.

"I want you to research the magi," the captain had instructed her. "Find out everything you can, so that you are well armed against them, in case they strike in Bel'Esstar."

Celestine stood on the steps, waiting for her knock to be answered. She was dressed in regulation black, her new uniform, especially adapted by the military tailors, with a long riding skirt instead of the usual breeches worn by the men. They had even sewn on little gold buttons with the emblem of Sergius's crook. The irony of the situation did not escape her; a quarter of a mile away lay the Place du Trahoir, where her father had been executed.

Eventually the door opened and the Archivist appeared.

"What do you want?" he asked, peering at her over his pince-nez. "I'm very busy."

"I've come to do some research," she said. "For the Commanderie."

"A woman? In the Commanderie?" He clicked his tongue in disgust.

"Here is my letter of introduction, signed by Captain de Lanvaux."

The Archivist scanned the letter. "Well, your papers seem to be in order. You'd better follow me." Shaking his head disapprovingly, he led her into the archives. As they passed stack after stack of meticulously ordered black-bound volumes, each one with the year and title tooled in silver, she felt a strange, sick feeling in the pit of her stomach. "The trial of the heretics from the College of Thaumaturgy . . ." He muttered to himself as he searched along the shelves, stopping at last to pull out a thick volume.

"You'll find what you need in here. These records are very expensive to produce. Please treat them with care."

The sick feeling grew more acute as she turned the pages. The records of the trials were meticulously hand-scribed and arranged in date order, so she soon came upon the one she was looking for. There was her father's name, Magister Hervé de Maunoir, written alongside the other alchymists accused of heresy and practicing the Forbidden Arts: Goustan de Rhuys; Deniel; Gonery. Some dispassionate secretary had sat in court noting down every question posed by the Inquisitors, every halting response given by men whose limbs had been twisted in the Inquisition's torture chambers until they could hardly stand upright.

The words blurred before her eyes; she hastily wiped away tears, glancing around to check that the Archivist was not spying on her.

What *was* their crime? To have studied the science of alchymy in a country where free thought was held to be dangerous? Again and again, the Inquisitors referred to the magisters' experiments as "heretical" and "going against the natural order." And one name recurred: Kaspar Linnaius.

"What are you doing here?" A soberly dressed man stood staring down at her.

She forced her most detached expression as she snapped the book shut. He must have moved as stealthily as a cat for her not to have noticed him.

"Research. For Captain de Lanvaux."

The Inquisitor gazed coldly at her. "A young woman? Since when have women been members of the Commanderie?"

"I am one of his special agents," she said coolly. "And you are?"

"Haute Inquisitor Visant," he said, equally coolly. Now she recognized him—and now she knew that he was the one who had engineered the fall of the College. "I see you've been researching the trial of the magi of Karantec. May I ask why?"

"The captain has asked me to find out all I can about Kaspar Linnaius."

"And what makes you think, Demoiselle, that you will succeed where so many experienced Inquisitors have failed?" The suggestion of a sneer passed across his otherwise expressionless face. "No one is more eager than I to bring Magus Linnaius to justice. But he's snug and safe under the protection of Prince Eugene. No one can touch him in Tielen!"

"Tielen?" Celestine repeated the name rather more forcefully than she should. *At last I have a lead to pursue.* Then she noticed the curious way Visant was looking at her and forced herself to master her feelings. This was the man who had tried and condemned her father to death; she must never let her guard slip in his presence again.

"Then we will just have to find a way to tempt him out," she said levelly.

A carriage was waiting outside the Maistre's house. Celestine hesitated as she turned the corner, recognizing it as Aurélie Carnelian's. So the lovers had returned from Tourmalise.

"Shall I see you at rehearsals tomorrow, Henri?" Celestine drew back, hearing Aurélie's rich voice floating across the garden. Hastily, she hid in a recessed archway in the garden wall.

"I'm not sure what my plans are yet." The Maistre appeared at the garden gate, ushering the diva through. Celestine shrank into the archway, wishing she could make herself invisible. But the two seemed too involved in their own conversation to notice that she was there.

"Don't leave your work in the hands of that new repetiteur; he doesn't understand the way you compose. He mangles the rhythms." Was there a forced brightness in the diva's tone?

"But I have commissions to complete. I can't attend every single rehearsal, Aurélie."

"Must you work so hard? We've only been back a couple of hours." Aurélie wound her arms around the Maistre and, pulling his face down to hers, kissed him. Celestine turned her head away. She could not bear to watch. When she dared to look round again, she saw that Aurélie was leaning out of the coach window, kissing her fingers to the Maistre, as the carriage rolled away. He stood watching until it turned the corner of the street. Then he turned and went back inside.

So that's the way it is between them. I made the right decision. At least once I'm on my way to Allegonde, I won't have to watch them sighing over each other all the time. It's time to break the news.

"The Commanderie?" The utter bewilderment in the Maistre's eyes almost undid her. "First I lose Jagu, now you? What hold does Ruaud de Lanvaux have over you both?" An unfamiliar note of anger sharpened his tone.

"Captain de Lanvaux rescued me from the streets when I was sick and starving," she said defiantly. What right had the Maistre to interfere in her life when he was having an affair with Aurélie?

"But you're a woman."

"There's a special unit within the Commanderie that the captain is in charge of. A secret unit, employing both men and women."

"Secret?" The Maistre made an exclamation of disgust. "There's too much secrecy with the Commanderie these days. It smacks of something underhanded. Already in Allegonde they're telling artists how to think, what to write . . ."

"I owe him. I owe him my life. I would have died if he hadn't—"

"And me? Do you owe me nothing?"

Celestine stared at him. "Of c—course I do," she began. "Without you, I'd never have become a singer, or made a career, I'd probably have taken my vows, so I'm very grateful, thank you—"

"I'm not asking for gratitude." He moved nearer to her, looking at her so intently that she began to back away.

"Then what?"

He stopped, shaking his head. "I have no right." He seemed to be talking to himself. "They will say that I took advantage of you. And yet, I can't help myself—"

"Maistre?" she said softly.

"Don't you understand, Celestine? It's a torment to be with you; it's a torment to be away from you."

"Torment?" she echoed. *Am I hearing you aright? Aren't you*

Aurélie's lover? And then, before she knew what was happening, he had caught her in his arms, crushing her close to him.

"You can't imagine how long I've wanted to do this," he murmured into her hair. Celestine, pressed tight against his body, felt his heart beating fast close to hers as his lips touched hers, kissing her gently at first, then more urgently. This was what she had dreamed of for so long, and now that it was happening, she felt dizzy and confused with the suddenness of it.

"No, no, this is all wrong," she cried, pushing him away. "What about Aurélie?"

"Aurélie?" His grey eyes had grown dark, unreadable.

"Don't think you can just win me over with sweet words. You've just come back from her villa in Tourmalise. She told me you were lovers."

"Aurélie told you that? I see." He looked utterly deflated. "I had no idea she was quite so manipulative."

"Well? Is it true?" Though she longed to let him hold her again, she had not known until now that she was so proud. She would not be second-best to Aurélie Carnelian.

"We were lovers," he said gravely, "but it didn't work out. Our dreams were too different. We wanted different things. And then I met you."

What about those intimate looks exchanged with Aurélie, those lingering caresses . . . had they all been merely habit?

"You were so young. I tried to throw myself into my work to forget you. But it didn't work. I just couldn't stop myself from wanting you."

Tears blurred her eyes. She willed herself not to cry. If she cried, he would put his arms around her again and this time she would have no willpower to resist him. "But I saw you tonight," she said haltingly. "You were kissing her. Please don't pretend it was just a friendly farewell."

He turned away, hands raised in a helpless little gesture. "I've been a fool. How can I prove to you that she means nothing to me anymore?"

"Nothing, Maistre?" Celestine's heart was racing too fast; she was out of her depth and drowning fast. She wanted to believe that he no longer loved Aurélie . . . but was he just telling her what she wanted to hear? How could he be so sure?

"What else did she tell you?"

"It doesn't matter." She was backing away from him, even though each step was harder than the last. Every instinct made her want to feel his arms around her again, to feel that potent beating of his heart so close to her own, and to know it was throbbing so fast because of her.

"*Celestine!* I love you. Don't leave me."

She could still hear him calling her name as she left the house, and the despair in his voice almost undid her. But she forced herself to keep on walking.

CHAPTER 29

"Demoiselle?" A Guerrier came running toward Celestine across the rain-swept courtyard of the Forteresse. "I'm Alain Friard. Captain de Lanvaux has asked me to be your instructor in weapons skills. I'm sorry to have kept you waiting." Lieutenant Friard flashed her a friendly, apologetic grin. His face was framed by a fringe of damp brown hair that he kept shaking out of his eyes, reminding her irresistibly of a wet dog. "Terrible weather for midsummer," he called back over his shoulder as he set off. Celestine gathered up her skirts and followed him out into the rain. She hoped that she would not disprove the captain's faith in her.

He led her through a tall archway into a side courtyard and stopped outside a plain door.

"Forget that I'm a woman, Lieutenant." She had been rehearsing this speech all the way to the Forteresse. "Don't treat me any differently than you would treat any other cadet."

"W—with respect, Demoiselle, that hardly seems appropriate." Lieutenant Friard's eyes betrayed how confounded he was. She sensed that if he could have invented any excuse to wriggle out of this task, he would have seized it. What made him stand his ground, stuttering and flustered? Loyalty to Ruaud de Lanvaux?

"I think there must be a reason the captain chose you to instruct me," she said, less harshly this time.

"I'd do anything for the captain," he said, and then blushed. "I'm sorry; I didn't mean that instructing you—" He gulped. "That just didn't come out the way I intended, Demoiselle . . ."

"Shall we make a start?" She was sure that once he was on familiar ground, he would forget his nervousness.

"Oh yes, yes, of course." He opened the door, revealing a long, bare hall. "This is one of our firing ranges, with targets set up for small arms. To handle a pistol successfully, you first need to understand how it works." Pistols were laid out on a table near the door. "Here we have powder, which must be kept dry at all times, and shot, which comes in different sizes . . ."

As Celestine had suspected, Lieutenant Friard lost his earlier self-consciousness when demonstrating his expertise in handling weapons. He made her pick up one pistol after another, testing the weight, showing her how to balance and aim with a steady hand. He assessed which model and type best suited her. He showed her how to load and prepare to fire. He warned her that firing even the lightest of pistols would involve some recoil.

"Don't worry; I'm stronger than I look," she said, seeing him eyeing her slender wrists uncertainly. "I grew up in a convent, so I have strong muscles from doing laundry, gardening, mopping floors."

The first targets that he set up for her were tin plates, hooked on the far wall. She obediently copied him, priming the pan, inserting the ball, but when it came to squeezing the trigger, the deafeningly loud crack of the report bruised her ears and her shot went wide.

Disappointed, she lowered the pistol, the acrid fumes of the burned powder making her nostrils twitch. "I missed."

"You flinched as you fired."

She felt ashamed. "It was so . . . loud." She waited for the inevitable reprimand.

"You're a singer. You have sensitive hearing." He passed her two little pads of wool. "Put these in your ears. It will help protect them by deadening the sound."

She looked at him, surprised. "That's so thoughtful. Thank you."

Yet still her shots went wide. Forgetting his earlier inhibitions, he stood close to her, adjusting her arm position, balancing her wrist, getting her to fix her line of fire more accurately, until she managed to graze the edge of one of the target plates.

"At last!" she cried, astonished that such a little achievement should mean so much to her. And then she heard men's voices outside.

"Here come the new cadets," said Friard.

"Must I stop now? I was just beginning to make progress."

"May I suggest you put a warm poultice on your wrist tonight? And you may need to bind it."

She glared at him, hating the fact that he was probably right; her right arm was throbbing and her hand had developed a tremor from supporting the weight of the pistol. *I will not give in to this weakness; I will become stronger!* "Same time tomorrow, Lieutenant?"

He nodded. The door burst open and half a dozen cadets came in; on seeing her, they stopped in astonishment, nudging each other to let her pass. She wondered what they would whisper about her when she had gone . . . and whether they would tease Lieutenant Friard mercilessly about his new pupil.

When Ruaud arrived for his evening tutorial with Enguerrand, the young king's study was empty. Turning round, bemused, Ruaud wondered if he had mistaken the time—and saw one of the great tapestries twitch. Instinctively, he reached for the hilt of his sword.

"Who's there?" he demanded. "Show yourself."

Enguerrand appeared. "Ssh," he whispered, beckoning.

Ruaud hesitated, and then joined Enguerrand, wondering what he was doing. A concealed door was ajar, like the one he had discovered in his own study, and he could just catch a distant murmur of voices.

Is this palace riddled with secret passages?

"So Prince Eugene is building a second war fleet? Do we know what he intends to do with it?"

"My mother," mouthed Enguerrand silently, but Ruaud had already recognized Aliénor's clipped tones.

"Our agents suspect that he plans to finish what his father, Karl, began. And invade Francia." It was Donatien speaking, without a doubt.

"Then we must act to protect Francia. And if that means uniting with Allegonde, then so be it. I can see no alternative in the circumstances. Adèle must marry Ilsevir."

"Ilsevir has been secretly initiated into the Order of the Rosecoeur. He will do whatever the Master of the Order tells him is best. And as the Master and I have been in close communication . . ."

Ruaud could hardly believe what he was overhearing.

"We must face the truth, and that is that Enguerrand is unsuited to rule. He's sickly. Weak." Ruaud heard Enguerrand's sharp intake of breath at his mother's blunt words. "Sooner or later, Tielen will take advantage of that weakness. I will do anything in my power to prevent that happening. If it means making Enguerrand abdicate in favor of Ilsevir, then so be it. You have my blessing to go ahead with the negotiations . . ."

The voices faded away as the speakers left the room.

"I know my mother has never believed in me." Enguerrand had clenched both fists; Ruaud could see that he was making a heroic effort not to cry. "But to plan to give my throne away—isn't that treason?"

"What do you think, Celestine?" Princess Adèle came out from behind the lacquered Khitari screen and turned slowly around, her ladies-in-waiting holding up the long train of ivory lace.

"You look . . . ravishing," said Celestine, awed. "If Prince Ilsevir doesn't fall in love with you when he sees you, then . . ."

"But will I fall in love with him?" Adèle's expression was pensive as she smoothed down the billowing folds of creamy lace. "We only met a few weeks ago. He's practically a stranger. Imagine marrying a man you know no better than . . ."

"Then may you have many happy years together, to get to know each other well," said one of her ladies, wiping away a tear. "Your dear mother, Aliénor . . ."

Adèle shot Celestine a little look that said *You see what I have to put up with?*

The midnight summons was terse:

"Captain de Lanvaux—come to the king's apartments at once."

Ruaud, half-asleep, tugged on his uniform and followed the officer of the king's bodyguard, who had been sent to fetch him, through the hushed and darkened palace toward the royal apartments. As they drew near, Ruaud became aware of a stir of movement: servants silently hurrying along the dimly lit corridors. Something was far from right in Plaisaunces.

As they reached the king's rooms, the soldiers on guard immediately opened the doors to admit him. To his surprise, he saw the queen in the antechamber, in a velvet robe de chambre, her greying hair loosely twisted in a single plait, as if she had just been woken from sleep. Aliénor was usually so careful about her appearance.

"Enguerrand has been taken ill. Very ill."

This news caught him completely off guard. "Ill? But his majesty seemed well enough earlier today. A little abstracted, maybe . . ." Although, as Ruaud thought back to Enguerrand's tutorial this morning, he remembered that the king had looked pale and dull-eyed, as if he had slept badly, and had stumbled in his translation more than a few times. "What do the physicians say?"

"He has a high fever. He's delirious." Aliénor was twisting the cord of her robe between her fingers; even though her tone of voice was flat and controlled, Ruaud saw that she was genuinely anxious about her youngest child.

"Is it that serious?" Adèle came running in, also in her robe de chambre. "Serious enough to postpone the wedding?"

"It's far too late to do that, I'm afraid. Besides"—and Ruaud saw the queen bite her lip before continuing—"if the worst were to happen, it's vital that Francia has a strong ally."

"What are you saying, Maman?" Adèle glanced at Ruaud, as though desperately seeking his support. "I can't leave Enguerrand if he's that sick! I won't go. You can't make me." She began to sob.

"Control yourself, Adèle." Aliénor looked coldly at her daughter. "This is no time for hysterical outbursts. You will go to Bel'Esstar, and that's an end to it. I won't hear any more of this nonsense."

Ruaud wished that there were some way he could alleviate the princess's worries. It wasn't surprising that she was so distraught; already facing the prospect of marriage to a virtual stranger with whom she had little in common, her brother's illness must seem catastrophic.

"But if my brother isn't there to give me away?"

"Your uncle Josselin is quite capable of performing that role. It's more important that the wedding goes ahead, under the circumstances."

"Well, I hope you're satisfied." Gauzia's eyes flashed with a cold, contemptuous light. "Coming between two lovers. Breaking up a long and happy relationship." She flung down a broadsheet on Celestine's bed. The headline read: "Diva Storms out of *Balkaris* at Opera House." "You've ruined the Maistre's opera."

"What *are* you talking about, Gauzia?" Celestine was taken aback at the vehemence of Gauzia's outburst. She picked up the *Gazette* and read: "'The Divine Aurélie has walked out of *Balkaris*, accusing her fiancé, Henri de Joyeuse, of carrying on a secret affair with his ward, convent-educated orphan Celestine.'" The paper dropped from Celestine's hands.

"It's the talk of the Opera House. By tonight it'll be the talk of Lutèce. You and the Maistre. Poor Aurélie is utterly distraught."

"Now wait a moment—" began Celestine indignantly, but Gauzia was in full flow and would not be silenced.

"It's always the quiet ones. I'd never have thought of you as a troublemaker." She advanced on Celestine, thrusting her face close to hers. "You sly, devious little minx. Stealing him away from Aurélie. Carrying on with him behind her back."

"What?" Someone must have been spreading malicious rumors, and Celestine had a good idea who it might be.

"Just how long have you and the Maistre been at it?"

Celestine gasped. The unfairness of the allegation took her breath away. Before she knew what she was doing, she had lifted her hand and slapped Gauzia, hard. "How dare you?" she cried. "How dare you slander the Maistre? When you know nothing. Nothing at all!"

Gauzia, one hand clasped to her reddening cheek, stared at Celestine. Suddenly tears began to spill from her eyes. "You hit me. You *hit* me!"

Celestine stared back, horrified at what she had done. "Oh, Gauzia, I'm so, so sorry. I never meant to—"

"Don't come near me." Gauzia backed away, still weeping.

"Don't ever come near me again. I'm going back to the Opera. At least I know now who my true friends are." She turned and fled; Celestine heard her sobbing as she ran down the stairs.

Celestine was shaking as she picked up the *Gazette* and scanned the column again. How long would it be before Aurélie spread the slanderous gossip around the whole city?

"*I can put an end to your career before it's even begun.*"

Celestine paused in her packing for the journey to Allegonde and picked up the precious book to place it in the little trunk. "At least I'm starting out on my journey to trace Kaspar Linnaius," she told the Faie, and found herself wiping away a tear that had strayed unbidden down her cheek. "But leaving the Maistre is hard, so hard, I don't think I can bear it . . ."

Someone tapped at the door; imagining it to be Dame Elmire, she said, "Come in," without looking up. When she raised her head from the open trunk, she saw Henri de Joyeuse standing there.

"Maistre," she said, wishing that the mere sight of him did not make her heart ache so.

"How can I apologize for what has happened?"

"The *Gazette*?" She gave a little shrug, feigning indifference. "What's done is done."

"I knew Aurélie wouldn't let me go without creating some scandal. But she had no business dragging your name into this, and I can never forgive her for that."

"I'll be on my way to Bel'Esstar tomorrow," Celestine said, trying to sound more philosophical about the matter than she felt. "By the time I return to Lutèce, the whole affair will probably have been forgotten."

"Not by me."

"Maistre?" There had been something in his voice that made her heart miss a beat. "Aren't you supposed to be at the Opera House?"

"I can't bear to think that we'll be apart again," he said. His hair was untied and there were shadows beneath his grey eyes, as if he hadn't slept. Suddenly he moved, catching hold of her by the hand. "Promise me one thing. Promise that you'll not be tempted by the Allegondans to stay in Bel'Esstar."

"I'm not sure that I can." She was trembling; she was not sure that she was strong-willed enough to extract her hand from his. And when he pulled her close to him, all she wanted was to rest her head against his shoulder and stay folded close in his arms.

"Once they hear you sing, they're going to try to make you stay. The great Talfieri, Illustre Lissier, they have much influence with the prince."

"You have to let me go, Maistre. You know that the princess has done so much to advance my career. She's been so kind to me." Couldn't he see how torn she felt? Why was he making it so hard for both of them? "I can't let her down."

She heard him swallow hard, as though gulping back tears.

"Of course. I have no right to tell you what to do. You must follow the dictates of your heart." He took both her hands in his and pressed them to his lips. "Farewell, my dearest girl."

"Captain . . ." A hoarse voice issued from the king's bed.

Ruaud had nodded off. He jolted awake.

"Sire?" he said, hardly daring to hope.

"I'm thirsty . . ."

Ruaud hastily poured water and, supporting the boy's head, held the glass to his fever-cracked lips, gently wiping away the drops that spilled down the side of his chin.

"What day is it, Captain . . . ?" The dark eyes looking at Ruaud from the pillows were lucid, no longer hazed and wandering.

"You know me. Thank God." Ruaud had stayed at the king's side for five days and nights while fever racked the young man's body, ready to administer the last rites of the Sergian Church. Now his prayers had been answered. Enguerrand's hand fumbled for his.

"You stayed with me."

"It was nothing, sire." Ruaud looked at the king's slender fingers curled so trustingly around his own. Tears of relief trickled down his cheeks.

Is this how I would feel if I had had a son of my own?

"Don't . . . be sad." The pressure around his hand tightened. "I'm going to recover. I had a dream, Captain . . . I dreamed that the Angel Lord Galizur came to my bedside. He told me I must get

well again. He told me there was much for me to do. He warned
me that the Agents of Darkness were abroad, and that I must do all
in my power to fight them." Enguerrand gazed into Ruaud's face
pleadingly. "And he said that my sister is in danger."

"Your sister is protected by two of my best agents," said
Ruaud, as soothingly as he could. "They will do all in their power
to keep her safe." But he silently offered up a prayer to Saint
Sergius to watch over Celestine and Jagu.

CHAPTER 30

The journey across the mountains to Allegonde had taken the royal party three days longer than planned, due to an unseasonable fall of snow in the high passes. But Celestine did not mind; she was so excited to be leaving Francia for the first time in her life that every new occurrence was a novelty to her. She did not mind sharing a cramped bedroom with the princess's ladies-in-waiting, high in the eaves of a mountain chalet inn; when she flung the shutters wide on the first morning, the view over the peaks as the sun rose took her breath away.

She leaned out, watching the rising sun tinge the white snow with rose and gold.

If only you were here to see this with me, dearest Maistre . . .

A wave of yearning washed through her, so strong it made her shiver.

"Close the shutters, Demoiselle!" cried one of the ladies. "Do you want us all to catch a chill?"

While the court ladies complained about lumpy mattresses and the coarse, gritty porridge served for breakfast, Celestine ran outside to gaze at the snow-covered crags, still tinged pink by the sunrise, breathing in the crisp, sweet air.

"Enjoy the mountain air while you can."

She looked around and saw Jagu de Rustéphan leading his horse out from the stables. "Why so?"

"I hear it can get very oppressive down by the Dniera at this time of year. Snow in the mountains means thunderstorms on the river plain."

"Well, I can't wait to see Bel'Esstar. Surely you must feel just a little excited to be visiting the birthplace of Talfieri? And the Opera House . . ."

He came close to her and said quietly, "We have a job to do. Never forget that. Even up here, someone might be waiting . . ."

She glared at him, resenting the reminder that she was new to this role. "Do you think I've forgotten? But that intercepted message specifically mentioned the two of them. Together." Why did he have to be such a killjoy? "And that won't happen until we reach Bel'Esstar."

A bird suddenly rose from the stable roof and flapped away on dark wings. Jagu flinched and Celestine saw in that brief unguarded moment a look of fear in his eyes.

He's served in Enhirre and fought in battle. How can he be afraid of a harmless bird?

The Basilica in which Adèle and Ilsevir were to be married was a magnificent domed edifice, completed only thirty years ago. The exterior was deceptively and elegantly plain, but the instant Celestine entered the building, she was overwhelmed by the wealth of ornate decoration. White marble and gold leaf dazzled the eye; every fluted column was adorned with carved, rosy-cheeked cherubim playing musical instruments. A celestial *trompe l'oeuil* filled the inside of the vast dome, depicting golden-haired angels, floating on impossibly fluffy, snowy clouds, or hovering on rainbow wings in a sky of bright cerulean blue.

"And look at the organ," she whispered to Jagu, trying not to giggle. "It's like a wedding cake." The vast case was garlanded with painted festoons of flowers and fruit; fulsome angels blew gilt trumpets from every corner.

"Forget the exterior," he said brusquely. "It's the action that counts." Each word reverberated around the dome. "And such a resonant acoustic. Every quiet footfall, every stifled cough will be greatly magnified. An assassin would be setting himself an impossible task in here."

"A normal assassin, maybe. But one practicing the Forbidden Arts . . ."

He nodded, and she glimpsed again that fleeting look of pain she had seen before when he had let slip those few tantalizing details about his best friend's death.

"There'll be guards posted in the upper gallery, as well as in all the aisles, and covering every exit. I'll be in the organ loft . . ." He left her and hurried to the little door concealing the stairs that led up to the console.

"So I'll need to position myself over here to see you." Celestine went to stand on the marble tiles in front of the choir stalls. As Jagu appeared high above her, she said, "We're a long way apart. We need a signal." She thought a moment. "If I notice anything suspicious, I'll take out my lace handkerchief. If I drop it, be ready to take action."

"The view from here is quite limited." Jagu was checking how much he could observe using the organist's mirror.

"I'll go and investigate the rear exits." Celestine passed the altar and skirted around the back, where the flicker of many votive candleflames glowed in the shadows. She passed chapels dedicated to Saint Sergius and Saint Argantel, stopping as she came to a set of double doors, freshly varnished, set between two massive columns entwined with carved vines and gilded grapes.

She tried the door and found that it was locked. A sudden tingle of pain, thin and silvery, like a wire, shot through her head. She pressed fingers to her throbbing temples.

Two priests appeared.

"Why can't I go in?" she demanded in the common tongue.

"You need a special permit from the Grand Maistre," replied one, smiling. "This chapel is closed to visitors."

"But we are Guerriers of the Francian Commanderie." Jagu had reappeared, striding swiftly over to her side. "We're responsible for Princess Adèle's personal security. We must check every corner of the cathedral."

"You need a special permit," repeated the priest, still smiling.

"Why? What's in here?" Celestine asked, affecting her most innocent expression.

"The sacred relics brought back from Ondhessar."

"The relics?" Jagu repeated.

"Captain nel Ghislain and his men recovered the Elesstar statue and brought it here for safekeeping."

"But in doing so, they despoiled the Shrine." Jagu seemed to be controlling his temper with difficulty.

"More sacrilege to have left them there to be despoiled by the Enhirrans," said a calm, smooth voice. "If we hadn't arrived just in time to relieve you, these sacred treasures would be lost to us." A grey-uniformed Rosecoeur officer came toward them from the shadows; Celestine's eyes were instantly drawn to a small insignia, an enameled rose, dark crimson, on the lapel of his jacket. "Captain nel Ghislain at your service," he said to Celestine, saluting.

"Yes, I remember you, Captain," said Jagu coldly, returning the salute. "This is Demoiselle de Joyeuse; she will be singing at the ceremony."

Celestine nodded in greeting and as she did so, another silvered barb of pain pierced her skull. She hoped neither man noticed her wince.

"Would you like to see what we have rescued from the ruins of Ondhessar, Demoiselle?" Captain nel Ghislain addressed Celestine directly, ignoring Jagu.

"Ruins?" repeated Jagu ominously.

"Thank you," said Celestine, giving him her most gracious smile. She sensed a distinct animosity between the two men.

Ghislain took a key from his pocket and unlocked the doors, ushering them both into the chapel beyond.

"Ohh," she said softly. In the center of the chapel stood a life-sized figure carved from white marble, so pale, so translucent that it seemed to exude a gentle radiance. As she approached, she saw that it was the effigy of a woman, so skillfully sculpted that, had it not been for its unearthly pallor, she would have taken it for a living being.

"It seems only fitting that this exquisite image should be exhibited here, in Bel'Esstar, the city where the Blessed Elesstar was miraculously restored to life," said Captain nel Ghislain.

A thin, silvery melody had begun to whisper through Celestine's brain. As she walked slowly around the figure, she noted the unearthly beauty of the carved face, the cupped hands on the statue's breast, holding the open petals of a lotus flower.

What was that elusive, persistent melody? Was it a song she had heard before, many years ago? It was so sad it made her want to cry.

"Has the Allegondan Commanderie stripped the Shrine of *all* its sacred treasures?" said Jagu, still bristling with barely disguised disapproval.

The melody was growing louder. Celestine stretched out her hands, compelled for a reason she could not explain to touch the statue's delicate white marble fingers. The men's voices receded, to be replaced by the rushing sound of a distant, turbulent wind.

"Father . . . where are you, Father?" She is standing, alone and confused, on the edge of a barren, empty plain. Overhead, clouds scud unnaturally fast across a sickly, faded sky the color of fog. She stretches her arms out into the wilderness, calling for him in vain . . .

"Are you all right, Demoiselle?"

She started, blinking as she looked up into Jagu's face.

"And soon, God willing, we will start work on the new cathedral," Captain nel Ghislain was saying. "It is his highness's dearest wish that he should leave a lasting memorial to his late father. What better way than to build a Fortress of Faith to house this exquisite figure?"

"So much for the spirit of brotherhood between members of the Commanderie," muttered Jagu as they left. She could tell from the set of his mouth that he was genuinely upset. "They've despoiled the Shrine and taken the treasures for themselves. I can't believe that Maistre Donatien gave his agreement to such an act of vandalism. I'm going to notify Captain de Lanvaux."

The official book containing the complete list of wedding guests was on display in an anteroom in the palace, flanked by jade vases overflowing with late-flowering roses of pink, old gold, and cream, already drooping in the heat.

As Celestine and Jagu studied the list, the heavy scent from the roses balmed the warm air. Each eminent name was elegantly hand-scribed in curling handwriting, each dot and accent picked out in gold. Yet as Celestine turned page after page, she realized that, should the name "Kaspar Linnaius" appear in the Tielen contingent, she had not even formulated the beginning of a plan. There were plenty of Rosecoeur Guerriers on hand that she could call on to arrest him, but a powerful magus must surely be well prepared to counter such eventualities. Besides, if he was attending as a member of Prince Eugene's household, arresting him could spark an unfortunate international incident.

Yet there it was. Some lines below his royal patron, Eugene of Tielen, "Magister Kaspar Linnaius" was clearly written, followed by the title of Royal Artificier.

So he was close by. After all the years he had spent in hiding in Tielen, he must feel very secure in his master's protection to accompany him abroad. *And now that I know he's here, what am I going to do? How do I entrap a magus as powerful as Magister Linnaius?*

"Jagu." She pointed out the name. "It's him. The alchymist. The Magus. Is he the one, do you think . . . ?"

She saw him grip the edge of the delicate ormolu table until his knuckles whitened.

"Surely the Tielens wouldn't stoop to such a low trick?" he muttered. "Prince Eugene wouldn't dare employ the Forbidden Arts against his royal host and his bride."

"That's not what I meant. Is *he* the one who killed your friend?"

He turned and she glimpsed again that vulnerable, younger Jagu, his dark eyes blank with the raw pain that had never healed. He grabbed hold of her by the wrist. "How did you know?" His voice was unsteady. "Who told you?"

"The Maistre." She felt sorry now that she had been the one to reopen the wound he kept so well hidden.

"And how, how do *you* know that this man is a magus?" His fingers pressed harder into her flesh.

"The captain sent me to the Inquisition archives to do research. It seems that Linnaius was the only magus in Francia to escape the Inquisition's purge fourteen years ago." She was surprised at the ingenuous tone with which she gave her answer. "Jagu . . . you're hurting me."

He looked down at his hand, which was still tightly gripping her wrist, as if it were not his own. The grip relaxed. "I'm sorry."

"And he's coming to Bel'Esstar." His eyes had a distant, unfocused look, as though he was staring into the nightmare that had scarred his past.

"Would you know him again, if you saw him?"

"His smile still haunts my dreams," he said, with a shudder.

"What manner of man was he?" Even though he had let go of her, she stood close to him, speaking softly, as though of some intimate, shared secret. If anyone were to come in now, they might well imagine they had disturbed a lovers' tryst.

"The one who murdered Paol? Young, well favored, not some old grey-bearded scholar. Unless that was just the face he chose to show me. But his eyes . . . such a glittering, mesmerizing stare."

"Why did he kill your friend?" Celestine pursued the matter relentlessly, unsparing of his feelings.

Jagu hesitated. "He stole his soul. He used his body and deceived us all, moving around the school like one of the pupils, to get what he wanted."

"A soul-stealer? So this magus could take control of anyone here and use their bodies to do his will?" She began to fear for Adèle. "So if he is behind the death threats, he could become anyone. Even you, Jagu, or me. And then he could get close to the princess . . ."

A sudden chatter of voices outside made her break off; the ladies-in-waiting were returning

"We need to talk somewhere less public."

The East Wing music room overlooked the formal gardens of Ilsevir's palace. Celestine stood at the window, gazing out at the imposing prospect, which stretched far into the horizon.

"A white garden; what a curious conceit." The gravel was white; the beds were filled with white lilies, roses, and marguerites, and the borders with silver-grey foliage. The statues were all of pale marble: gryphons with folded wings, swans, and wan water nymphs. White peacocks trailed their long tail feathers along the paths and doves clustered together to drink from birdbaths shaped like upturned shells. The afternoon was muggy and close; Jagu's information about the soporific summer atmosphere of the low-lying city was all too correct. She could see courtiers drifting listlessly along the paths, fanning themselves, soon disappearing into the shade of tree-lined avenues.

Jagu lifted the lid of the fortepiano and played a series of arpeggios in quick succession, shaking his dark head as he did so. "I'm sorely out of practice."

"I need to warm up too." Already Celestine missed the rigor of her daily exercise routine, strictly imposed by Dame Elmire. "It's too easy to slip into bad habits."

They worked for a half hour or so until Celestine burst out with the question that had been troubling her since their last meeting. "How could you tell if I was . . . not myself, Jagu? How would you know if I had fallen victim to a soul-stealer?"

He stared at the fortepiano keys, as if lost in reminiscence. "It was impossible to tell with Paol. We were all deceived. So as part of my training, the captain sent me to research soul-stealing. But there was little information, even in the secret library. The technique drains both stealer and victim of much life energy. If the victim's soul is out of his body for too long, the body dies."

Celestine shivered, goose bumps prickling her arms, in spite of the clammy warmth of the afternoon. "And the victim's soul? What happens if the body dies?" She came over to lean on the top of fortepiano. "Is there no way of telling? Are there no words of holy exorcism to drive the evil influence out of the victim? Why are we so ill armed against the magi?"

A sharp tap at the door interrupted them and a grey-wigged flunkey announced, "His excellence, Illustre Talfieri."

Hearing the name of the eminent composer, Jagu rose hastily and Celestine dropped into a curtsy.

"Forgive me for disturbing your rehearsal." An elderly gentleman with an untidy mop of silvered hair entered. "But I come at his highness's special request."

"W—we're honored, Illustre," stammered Jagu. Celestine was trying not to stare as Talfieri placed a folio on the fortepiano and drew out a sheaf of music.

"Are you skilled at quick study?" he asked, regarding them with a glint of malicious amusement. "The prince asked me to write a little piece to celebrate the opening of the new shrine to Elesstar. He didn't give me very much notice, but that's the way of princes." He handed them copies.

"But why us, Illustre?" Celestine found her tongue. "Surely there must be many Allegondan musicians more worthy of this commission than—"

"Indeed," he said, nodding, "but the prince felt it would honor his new bride if her household musicians were to perform instead. So here I am, to coach you."

This isn't a clever ruse to distract us from our duties guarding the princess, is it?

"Let me play you the opening bars to give an idea of the tempo." Talfieri flipped the tails of his brocade jacket as he took Jagu's place at the keyboard. "You may have a little difficulty reading my handwriting," he said, leaning forward until his nose almost touched the paper.

Celestine shot Jagu a questioning look. He gave a little shrug. The great Talfieri was renowned. What could they do but comply?

Celestine had been quartered with one of the princess's ladies-in-waiting, the matronly Marquise de Trécesson and her maid, Mélie, a skilled seamstress. In the palace hierarchy, a singer's status seemed to be on a par with that of a maid, so both were allocated little beds in the narrow antechamber, while the marquise enjoyed the luxury of a spacious room. Mélie allowed Celestine a glimpse of her mistress's chamber; the walls and vast bed were hung with Khitari silk printed in an exquisite pattern of bamboo and dancing cranes, in subtle tones of jade, pomegranate, and black on ivory.

Mélie was busy with the final alterations to the princess's wedding gown when Celestine returned, sitting close to the window to make the most of the hazy afternoon light, a little pair of pince-nez balanced on her upturned freckled nose as she squinted at the seam she was sewing. Celestine looked at the voluminous folds of satin and delicate lace that swamped Mélie's lap and let out a sigh of admiration.

"How do you make those tiny stitches so neat and even?"

Mélie looked up over the top of her pince-nez and said, "Practice. And good light." As she spoke, a shadow passed across the windowpanes. Celestine glanced up.

"And now a cloud goes across the sun," said Mélie, glowering.

"No, a bird. It's hovering outside the window. It looks like a bird of prey."

"Chase it away! Let it go and catch its dinner somewhere else."

Celestine rapped loudly on the pane. Almost instantly, the hovering bird swooped around, so close to the glass that she was afraid it was about to crash through. She took a step back but not before she had seen it fix her with its fierce amber eyes. And then it was gone, darting away with astonishing rapidity, like a streak of smoke smeared across the blue of the sky.

"That's better," said Mélie, applying herself to her sewing again. But Celestine was overwhelmed with an inexplicable feeling of apprehension. Her first instinct was to check that the book was still safely concealed, wrapped in a silken scarf in her trunk. Her second instinct, as she gently unwrapped it, was to ask the Faie's advice. But as she knelt before the open trunk, gazing down at the image on the cover, she knew that it would be impossible while Mélie was in the room. Yet the urge to ask the Faie the questions burning in her brain grew stronger as she looked at the placid, beatific expression the Faie had adopted.

"Mélie! Is the gown finished yet?" the marquise called. "We're late for the final fitting."

"Coming, madame," answered Mélie, raising her eyes to heaven as she snipped off the thread and laid her needle down.

"Shall I help you?" Celestine offered, eager to have a few precious moments of privacy alone with the Faie.

"I daresay I can manage," said Mélie resignedly, lifting the voluminous folds of the dress and carefully wrapping it in a thin muslin sheet to protect its delicate fabric.

Celestine waited, all impatience, for both women to leave the marquise's apartments. When she was certain that Mélie would not be sent back to retrieve some vital item, she bolted the antechamber door, closed the shutters, and, in semidarkness, took out the book.

The Faie immediately issued from the book, almost as if she had been eager to escape its confines. And as her translucent form took shape, Celestine was disturbed to see that the Faie had assumed the image of the Elesstar statue, hands cupped at her breast, holding a pale lotus flower.

"Why do you look this way?" she whispered. "Is it because I've been unable to forget the statue since I saw it? Or is there a connection between you and Elesstar?"

"*I saw this image in your thoughts. It pleased you, and so it pleased me too.*"

"Can you read me so well?"

"*I've watched over you as if you were my own daughter. I've known your mind since you were a child. Does that trouble you?*"

Celestine had not expected to hear such caring words from the Faie. "No, not at all. But, dear Faie, something else is troubling me. How did my father find you? Did he summon you? What happened that night, the night I first saw you?"

The Faie extended one hand and let her translucent fingers drift over and around Celestine's face, as if caressing her. "*You heard my voice. And so did another. He had the power to set me free.*"

"So it *wasn't* my father who released you?" Till now, Celestine had believed that Hervé had summoned the Faie for the express purpose of protecting his daughter. To learn that another magus had been involved put quite a different complexion on the matter.

"*I saw you, Celestine, and in that one moment I knew that I wanted to protect you as my own.*"

The Faie's words were like balm, calming Celestine's worries.

"*And never more than at this time, in this place.*"

The moment of calm was shattered. "What do you mean?" Celestine cried, alarmed. "Am I in danger?"

"*There are powerful forces near at hand. They are gathering. I can sense them.*"

"The princess. Do they mean to harm the princess?"

The Faie's expressive eyes suddenly darkened to a sad, twilit amethyst. "*I do not know what they intend. But I fear for you, Celestine. I fear for your life.*"

Celestine had begun to twist her fingers together in agitation. "What can I do? I can shoot a pistol reasonably well. I can—"

"*Let me shield you and your princess.*"

"You?"

"*Pistols will be little use against their kind of power. But I can shield you from the darkest of glamours.*"

"But how, dear Faie?"

"*For a little while, just a little while, I will come with you.*"

Celestine still did not understand what the Faie intended. "With me? In the form you're in now? But won't that draw too much attention to us?"

"*I am bound to the book. And to you, by blood. I can be part of you, just as I am a part of the book.*"

Celestine recoiled. "You mean . . . in my body?"

"*Shall we try it? If you find the experience distasteful, then I will return to the book. I will do exactly as you wish.*"

It was hard to resist the Faie's sweet and persuasive tones.

"*Do you remember the day I gifted you? Did that distress you?*"

"No, but . . ." Celestine wavered, still reluctant to risk so much.

The Faie had drawn closer to her, so close that when Celestine gazed into her limpid eyes, she felt as if she were losing herself. "*Trust me,*" whispered the Faie, coming closer still. A cloudy mist filled Celestine's vision as the Faie swirled about her in a dazzle of pale light. And then the glimmer vanished and Celestine shivered, as though a sudden draft had gusted through the stuffy antechamber.

She could hear voices outside; the marquise and Mélie must have returned.

Celestine looked down at the book on her lap and saw that the cover was plain leather. The image of Saint Azilia had vanished.

The door opened and Mélie's thin face peered in. "The princess is asking for you, Celestine."

"I'll go at once." Celestine hastily replaced the book in her trunk.

"What a gorgeous perfume," remarked the maid, sniffing the air as she came in. "What is it? Lilies? And look at you; how do you manage to keep so fresh and radiant in this stifling heat?"

All the windows in the princess's apartments were open and the gauzy voiles hung across them to mute the sun's glare and keep out insects stirred a little in a hot breeze.

Adèle was reclining on a chaise longue, but the instant she saw Celestine, she sat up, opening her arms to embrace her.

"Isn't this humidity fatiguing? Even in this light muslin, I feel too hot and sticky to do anything strenuous. I hope I can persuade Ilsevir to leave the capital and spend the summer months in the country. He has an estate in the mountains."

"And how is his highness?" Celestine inquired as Adèle patted the seat beside her.

"His highness is well, thank you," said Adèle as Celestine sat down. "In fact, he has proved himself rather sweet and attentive," she added with a bubbling little laugh. "I fear I may have judged him rather harshly."

"But you were so certain that he had no redeeming features other than his love of music." Adèle liked to be teased, and Celestine felt confident enough in the princess's friendship to indulge in a playful dig or two.

"And in looks, he certainly comes a poor second to dashing Andrei Orlov. Yet"—and Adèle gave Celestine a coy sideways glance—"he has such an adorably shy smile. For once I have to admit that Maman made a wise choice. When I think of the other contenders . . ." Celestine saw her give a delicate little shudder of disgust. "Eugene of Tielen."

"Prince Eugene?" Celestine's playful mood evaporated.

"How could I have married a Tielen? My uncle Aimery died defending Francia against Prince Karl's war fleet. I was only six, but I've never forgotten Maman crying all night when the news came through."

"Azilis." Rieuk had sensed her for a brief moment, a pale shimmer, like the faint notes of a once-loved melody heard again after many years.

The magi had traveled by boat up the River Dniera to Bel'Esstar and were filing off with the other passengers onto the quay. Rieuk looked up at the merchants' houses of pale grey stone lining the wide banks and wondered why he had heard her calling.

"This is, after all, the city where Azilis spent most of her mortal life," said Lord Estael as they walked along beside the river. "Perhaps you can feel traces of her presence lingering here? Or can you sense the sacred relics that they stole from the Shrine?"

A patrol of grey-uniformed Allegondan Guerriers appeared, marching down the street, carrying a Rosecoeur banner. The magi quietly drew back into an alley as the Rosecoeurs went by.

"We must split up," said Lord Estael. "You all have your allotted tasks. The city is swarming with the Commanderie and Ilsevir's troops. Be careful. And remember that Kaspar Linnaius may be here as well; his name was on the list of guests."

Rieuk shivered at the thought that he might come face-to-face with Imri's murderer after all these years. He felt Lord Estael's hand on his shoulder and turned to see the magus's hawk-bright eyes staring warningly at him.

"Don't approach him. Don't do anything that might endanger our mission, or yourself."

CHAPTER 31

The cloying scent of orange blossom filled the basilica; the white petals were wilting and dropping in the stifling heat as the royal couple took their vows.

Celestine was drooping too; she fanned herself vigorously, trying to stay alert. The Duc de Craon, Adèle's uncle, kept nodding off and had to be nudged awake several times. The princess's bridesmaids fidgeted, fiddling with their posies of pink and white rosebuds. Prince Ilsevir was perspiring; Celestine saw him mop his shiny face with a silk handkerchief just before he exchanged rings with his bride.

Small wonder, thought Celestine, *as he must be unbearably hot in that heavy embroidered brocade jacket. But as for you, dear princess, you look exquisite in your white gown. How could any man fail to fall in love with you?*

Thus far, to her relief, the ceremony had proceeded without incident, apart from the moment when one of the littlest bridesmaids tripped during the procession down the altar.

Prince Ilsevir folded Adèle in his arms and kissed her tenderly.

To Celestine's surprise, her eyes filled with tears. She had remained dry-eyed through Prince Aubrey's funeral. A wedding was supposed to be a happy occasion! Yet she was not alone; she saw many lace handkerchiefs raised among the eminent guests and heard the sound of sniffing coming from Adèle's ladies-in-waiting.

A wave of longing for what could never be swept through her.

Never before had she missed the Maistre so desperately; his absence was like a burning ache in her heart.

Is this my own sadness? Or am I sensing the Faie's loneliness too?

The moment when the couple retired to sign the register was approaching. As the princess's bridesmaids lifted the train, Celestine raised her moist eyes to the organ loft, where Jagu was stationed beside Illustre Lissier, the basilica's Maistre de Chapelle. This was their cue; she moved out from behind the choir stalls where she had been sitting.

I must not let myself be distracted. The temptation to scan the congregation for a glimpse of the elusive Magister Linnaius was distracting enough. *I must sing like one of the painted angels overhead.*

The lavish reception filled the gardens of the palace. Only royal guests and a few select foreign dignitaries had been invited to attend the wedding banquet in the ornately gilded dining room, so Jagu and Celestine had been relieved of their duties by the royal bodyguards for the duration of the banquet.

"At least you've been spared the tedium of the Duc de Craon's speech, my dears," said the marquise. "Josselin has been known to drone on for a good half hour and more. Go and enjoy yourselves!"

Enjoy ourselves? Jagu never felt at ease when mingling with strangers. The younger son of the lord of Rustéphan, he had often escaped to the seashore when guests arrived at the *manoir,* leaving his older brother Markiz to play the "good son." Jagu's idea of enjoyment was an uninterrupted hour or two practicing the fortepiano, or a long, bracing walk along the rugged coastline near his home. Solitary pursuits. But Celestine was soon surrounded by admirers, and as he watched her he could not help thinking there was a radiance about her that afternoon, and yet also a vulnerability that made him want to protect her.

The oppressive heat was evidently proving a problem for the palace kitchens; buckets and yet more buckets of ice were sent for as the delicate fruit jellies and elaborate charlottes began to melt.

Page boys were set to work to swat the swarms of sticky black flies that hovered beneath the trees. Jagu, still ill at ease, stood apart from the wedding guests, keeping watch, while Celestine gracefully accepted the many compliments.

At length she rejoined him, carrying two glass dishes of a rose-pink dessert.

"Iced sherbet?" He shook his head; it smelled too sickly for his taste.

The sun was setting and a violet twilight bathed the grounds.

"Did you spot your magus?" she asked in a low voice. "In the Tielen contingent?"

Jagu slowly shook his head. "Perhaps he chose not to attend the wedding after all."

"Jagu, it's some years now since you saw him. Perhaps you've—"

"Forgotten?" *What could she possibly know about it?* "Oh no, I haven't forgotten. If only I could forget."

"But you said he was a soul-stealer." Her spoon clicked against the dish as she scraped the last traces of sherbet. "Perhaps even the face you saw in the school garden was stolen . . ."

"It's possible," Jagu admitted. "But the little I've learned tells that soul-stealing can drain the stealer of life essence, too—"

He flinched as a crow lifted from the tree branches above their heads, its wings black against the darkening sky. High overhead he saw a cloud of birds slowly circling above the palace.

"Birds," she said, staring upward too. "Tell me, Jagu, why are you so afraid of birds?"

"Because," he said, finding the courage to confide in her at last, "that magus had a hawk as his familiar."

"A hawk?" she repeated. "I saw a hawk yesterday. It flew close to my window and—"

"What kind of hawk?"

"How should I know? Its feathers were mottled, dark, like charcoal."

This was not what he had wanted to hear. "The magus's familiar had smoky plumage, too. It was unlike any hawk I've ever seen before."

"Jagu, you don't think . . ."

He wanted to reassure her. But the possibility that the magus who had placed his mark upon him was close by had set his nerves on edge.

"We must be on our guard."

Celestine lay on her little bed, unable to sleep for the heat. Even the sheet was damp with her perspiration, so she flung it off, wishing for a hint of breeze to cool her. The stifling night air was sensuously perfumed by the white stars of night-flowering jasmine growing beneath her windows.

It was Adèle's wedding night. What must it feel like to lie so close to Ilsevir, naked, all the wedding finery stripped away? To let him invade the most intimate, secret places of her body?

The thought was both terrifying and disturbingly, deliciously arousing. She moved restlessly on the crumpled sheet, wishing that she were not alone on this scented, sultry night.

"Henri," she whispered, "are you thinking of me? Just a little?"

Jagu gazes out across the Bel'Esstar rooftops, all the neat slates gleaming as if slicked with oil beneath the yellow, thundery sky.

A storm is coming. Far out on the dusty Dniera plain, heavy clouds are gathering, threatening torrential rain.

Yet this feeling is different, charged with a darker significance. He has felt it before; it stirs up memories he has tried to scour from his mind.

Quicksilver ripple of air . . . strange stillness . . .

"Wake up, Rustéphan!"

Jagu sat up in bed, gasping as if he were drowning.

Viaud stood over him, glaring. "That was some nightmare! How can I sleep if you're shouting like a madman?"

Jagu's heart was still pounding and as he pressed one hand to his chest, to calm its frantic beating.

What did it mean? Was it a warning? Or just a memory?

The instant he entered the chapel, Jagu sensed it. Faint, masked to conceal its presence, but unmistakable: the dark aura of a true magus. At the same moment, he felt a burning in his wrist as if the magus's mark had reacted, just as it had in Ondhessar. He pushed up his cuff and saw the sigil faintly glowing, angry red. For a moment he stood still, disoriented, fighting the urge to turn and run as fast as he could.

"Jagu?" Celestine gently touched his arm. "Are you all right?" Her eyes were dark with concern. Suddenly he was disgusted with himself for being afraid. She was depending on him. He must be strong to protect her.

"Be on your guard," he muttered. "Something's not right here . . ."

He scanned the guests as they took their seats in the chapel. Illustre Talfieri came in, leaning on his cane; he paused before sitting down and nodded to them.

As if it wasn't hard enough keeping vigilant in case of an attack, he and Celestine had to perform Talfieri's new and taxing composition under the critical eye of the composer. Jagu glanced at Celestine and noticed that she was practicing controlling her breathing to calm herself. He had to remind himself that she was only nineteen years old; this premiere must be quite an ordeal for such a young singer.

And then the audience rose to their feet as Prince Ilsevir and his new bride came in.

"And now I will call upon you, your highness," said the archbishop, "to say a few words on this auspicious occasion and declare the new Elesstar Shrine open . . ."

Celestine glanced at Jagu. The chapel was an intimate space in which to sing. It was also an ideal opportunity for an assassin to strike and make good his escape. Yet Jagu seemed withdrawn, lost in his own thoughts; she detected that his fingers moved silently on the arm of his chair. Was he mentally rehearsing Talfieri's music? The keyboard part was fiendishly difficult.

The prince clasped his hands together, head bowed, as if overcome by the emotion of the moment. "I—I can hardly find words to express my joy to be standing before these holy and priceless relics of the Beloved Elesstar." He raised his head and Celestine saw that his eyes glistened with tears. "Such a sight inspires the utmost humility in the heart of a devout believer like me."

Oh, Adèle, my poor Adèle, I had no idea that Prince Ilsevir could be such a prig. Celestine tried not to look in the princess's direction. She could imagine all too easily that Adèle was squirming in her seat, trying to conceal her embarrassment. Yet Adèle sat utterly impassively, showing a poise her mother, Aliénor, would have approved of.

"I'm honored to welcome the brave Rosecoeurs who brought back these treasures from Ondhessar. I shall be awarding each man the Order of the Rose, an honor accorded only to the most valiant and devout soldiers of our order."

Celestine was scrutinizing the audience. The Allegondan Guerriers to be honored were standing guard at the rear of the chapel, by the double doors; their captain, nel Ghislain, was seated behind the princess.

"But first I would like to invite Celestine de Joyeuse to sing a sacred aria in honor of Elesstar, especially composed for the occasion by our most eminent composer, Illustre Talfieri."

Celestine gazed around the candlelit chapel as she took a slow, calming breath, one hand resting on her lower ribs to ensure that she expelled the air slowly and regularly. She smiled radiantly, just as Dame Elmire had taught her, although within she felt nothing but a growing agitation.

Something's wrong. Can you sense it too, Jagu? She turned to him and saw him acknowledge her with a little inclination of the head. There was something about his calm, watchful air that comforted her; they were close together, ready to act as one, should the need arise.

Celestine's last pure notes, sensitively phrased, died away into silence.

Jagu waited, tense. Then Prince Ilsevir began to applaud, followed by the rest of the audience. Illustre Talfieri seemed pleased enough as he took his bow. Celestine smiled at Jagu. But as she smoothed down the silken folds of her blue dress, he couldn't help noticing that her hands were trembling. So she had been nervous! She had concealed it with consummate skill.

If only he could dispel the feeling that their ordeal was far from over.

The first of the Allegondans to be awarded the Order of the Rose approached the prince. Ilsevir turned to Captain nel Ghislain, who held out the medals on a crimson velvet cushion. The mark on Jagu's wrist suddenly throbbed. He flung himself forward. "Protect the princess!"

Quicksilver ripple of air . . . all movement ceases . . .

Celestine blinked. Everyone around her seemed frozen: the prince, half-turning toward the Rosecoeur, the red medal ribbon in his hands.

A flash of dark wings scored her vision. Then another and another, all swooping down toward the princess.

"*Adèle!*" Heedless of her own safety, Celestine flung herself in front of the princess, throwing her arms wide as the shadow creatures flew toward her. Behind her, Jagu pulled Adèle down, shielding her with his body.

The four Rosecoeurs waiting to be honored collapsed like puppets whose strings had been severed.

"Keep away!" Celestine's voice rang out, clear and hard with fury as the shadowy hawks attacked. "You shan't hurt her. I won't let you!"

Jagu, weakened by the throbbing pain emanating from the magus's mark, stared at Celestine, astounded. Her eyes blazed white fire. She stood there, her arms outstretched, and it seemed that a cold, pure light radiated from her body, as if she had created an invisible shield the shadow hawks could not penetrate. Jagu saw them fall back, repulsed, scattering little shreds of smoky feathers. One after another, they spiraled through the air, speeding toward the great windows overhead, flying through the stained glass as though it were no more solid than mist.

The instant they were gone, Celestine's bright aura vanished and she swayed, as if about to faint. Jagu caught her as she crumpled to the floor. Ilsevir dropped the medal he was holding and helped Princess Adèle to her feet. Everyone in the chapel was staring around dazedly.

"Celestine!" Jagu cradled her in his arms. She was white and her lips had a pale, bluish tinge. *Please let her be all right.*

Her head moved a little against him and her lips framed indistinct words. "Is . . . the princess safe?"

Jagu was so glad to hear her speak that for a moment he could not reply. When he managed to choke out an answer, he was almost incoherent. "She's safe, yes. Thanks to you. H—how did you do it? You were—"

"She's safe," she whispered, and her golden lashes fluttered closed again. Alarmed, he fumbled for a pulse in her slender throat and felt a steady throb against his fingertips. So she had just fainted. All around him, Captain nel Ghislain's men rushed ineffectually to and fro, and the eminent guests were hastily ushered out, but he just stayed there, holding her, thankful beyond words that she was alive.

But what *was* she? Was he the only one to have seen that brilliant shield of light that she had projected to protect the princess and himself? All the members of the royal household were fussing over the prince and princess, utterly ignoring them. Jagu prayed that no one else had seen what she had done. In Francia, such a display would have condemned her to the stake. Of course, it was always possible that Père Judicael had taught her a new rite of exorcism . . . but he doubted that to be the case. This slender girl in his arms concealed a considerable power.

Captain nel Ghislain was checking each of his fallen Rosecoeurs in turn. Jagu saw him rise, shaking his head. *Soul-stealing.* The magi had infiltrated the chapel by taking the bodies of the four Rosecoeurs. Now that the initial shock was wearing off, Jagu felt the old anger resurging, the feeling of utter impotence against such dark and forbidden powers. There were no Angelstones to protect them anymore against the powers of the dark.

"Mmm . . ." Celestine's head moved a little, nestling against his shoulder. He held her close to him, breathing in the sweet scent of her hair, all too aware how soft her body was, how fragile. If the magi's hawks had broken her barrier, he shuddered to think what damage they might have done to her.

"Jagu . . . ?" Her eyes were open and as she looked up at him, he saw that they no longer blazed with unnatural light but had returned to their soft, tender blue.

He had been holding her far closer than was appropriate; they were Guerriers, fellow soldiers. Reluctantly, for he could have held her close in his arms all night, he helped her to sit up slowly. "You fainted."

"How foolish of me," she said, sounding annoyed with herself. "I never faint."

"I do not think the magi will trouble your princess again."

Celestine saw the Faie hovering above her, a luminous shadow in the shuttered dark of the antechamber. From Mélie's bed close by came the sound of gentle snoring.

"But now they know that I am protecting you, they may come after us. You must be careful, dearest Celestine."

Celestine lay on the little bed in the Marquise de Trécesson's antechamber, the pale gold of her hair loose about her shoulders. Jagu gazed down at her anxiously; she looked so vulnerable asleep. And yet in the chapel yesterday when she defended the princess . . .

"She hasn't stirred since you brought her back," said the marguise quietly.

Jagu turned to tiptoe away. His news could wait until she had recovered. But her hand moved and reached for his. He stopped. Such a gentle touch . . . and yet it sent a tingle of longing through his whole body.

"Jagu?" she whispered.

"I'm here." He knelt down beside her bed. "Listen. Viaud and I have been out asking questions. And guess what? Prince Eugene never arrived in Bel'Esstar. The ambassador and his wife represented Tielen at the wedding."

Her eyes, still dulled by sleep, stared at him uncomprehendingly. "What are you saying?"

"It seems that there was a skirmish on the border between Khitari and Tielen and Eugene just rode off with his elite regiment to repel the invaders."

She sat up. "So if Eugene didn't come, then Kaspar Linnaius . . . ?"

"It's highly unlikely that he would have attended without his royal master." Jagu had been thinking about the possibilities on his way back to the palace. "No; the attack yesterday bore all the signs that it was the work of the magi of Ondhessar."

She looked so crestfallen that he wished he hadn't spoken with such bluntness.

"There'll be other opportunities," he said encouragingly. "You're one of the captain's agents now. We won't stop hunting for Linnaius, I promise you."

"You saved me." Adèle took Celestine's hands in her own, pressing them tightly. "I don't know how to thank you." The princess was pale and the dark smudges beneath her eyes told of a sleepless night.

"I'm just glad that I could be of service to you, your highness." Celestine tried to summon a reassuring smile. In truth, she was still deeply shaken by the events in the Basilica.

"And you, Monsieur de Rustéphan." Adèle turned to Jagu, extending one graceful hand. Jagu hesitated, then shyly took the proffered hand and kissed it. "You were so brave. And so quick to sense the danger."

Prince Ilsevir was standing watching. "I would like you to accept a small token of our thanks," he said shyly, and presented first Celestine then Jagu each with a velvet purse filled with coins.

"Your highness, this is too generous, I couldn't possibly—" stammered Celestine.

Adèle suddenly flung her arms around Celestine and hugged her. "I'm going to miss our little tête-à-têtes so much. Promise me you'll come back soon."

"Your voice has won the heart of our foremost composer," said Ilsevir, taking Adèle's hand in his. "Talfieri wants you to sing in the new mass he is writing." The intimate little smile that Adèle gave her husband did not escape Celestine's notice; she bit back an envious sigh.

"Azilis was there." Rieuk turned to the other magi. "Didn't you sense her presence? We may have failed to kill Adèle of Francia, but we've made a far more significant discovery."

"But how can that be?" Lord Estael's gaze was stern as a

hawk's settling on its prey. "You told us that your magister's daughter was dead."

"Unless Klervie de Maunoir didn't die after all and that young singer . . ." Fair-haired, blue-eyed, with the voice of an angel . . . The instant Rieuk spotted her in the chapel, he had felt an inexplicable shiver of recognition. "Celestine de Joyeuse," he said, pronouncing each syllable slowly, pensively. Was the long search over at last?

"Names can be changed. Perhaps the family faked the child's death and hid her away, fearing that the Inquisition would come looking for her."

"But why did Azilis use that young woman to foil our attack?" asked Aqil.

Estael looked troubled. "Azilis has selected this young woman so that she can enter the mortal world again. Perhaps she has no need for us anymore."

"What do you mean, my lord?" Rieuk had not imagined such a possibility. That night in Karantec, had Azilis been crying out, not to him, but to Klervie? Had she formed an indissoluble bond with the little girl all those years ago?

"She was once flesh and blood. After this eternity of imprisonment, she may have yearned to take human form again. Except she is so powerful that Celestine de Joyeuse will slowly lose her own identity and become her puppet."

CHAPTER 32

It seemed to Celestine as if many months had passed since she last stood in front of the Maistre's house, gazing up at the music room window. Faint strains issued, a tempestuous passage on the fortepiano, filled with yearning, unresolved phrases that crested, one after another, like storm waves crashing on a deserted shore.

This was unlike any music she had heard him play before.

"Are you sure you'll be all right?" Jagu had asked more than once as they parted on the quay by the Forteresse. The old Jagu would never have shown such concern for her safety. Yet since the attack in the chapel, he had become much more protective—endearingly so, at times. Even the Marquise de Trécesson had noted his concern, commenting with an indulgent smile, "That young man has become very attentive of late, my dear. I believe you may have made a conquest . . ."

And Celestine had dismissed the marquise's suggestion with the most pleasant of laughs. "Oh, it's a purely professional concern, I assure you."

She walked slowly up the path and raised her hand to knock.

I want to see him so badly. But I'm so nervous . . .

The music stopped, halfway through a phrase. She turned, hearing his footsteps coming closer. The door opened.

"Celestine?"

She turned around to face him. He stood in the doorway, his hair escaping its loosely tied ribbon, as though he had been raking his fingers through it. *How endearingly untidy you look, dear Maistre.*

"Welcome back," he said.

"Maistre." She lowered her eyes.

"Are we going to stand here on the doorstep all afternoon? Come in. My aunt is out. She said she couldn't stand the racket a moment longer."

"Racket?" Celestine followed him into the house. "Are you working on a new piece?"

He gave a self-deprecating laugh. "How did you guess?"

"Your unconventional style of dress, for one. You only wear that old robe de chambre when you're composing."

"How well you know me." He stopped on the threshold of the salon. "But where's your luggage? You weren't robbed on the way, I trust?"

"The marquise's servants will deliver it this evening."

"The marquise!" he said, gently mocking.

Already she was falling under his spell, forgetting all the resolutions she had made in Allegonde. "I understand, Maistre, that it will be difficult for me to continue living in this house," she began. "But with Prince Ilsevir's very generous gift, I have enough money to set myself up in my own apartment now." She had rehearsed this moment many times in her mind during the tedious coach journey back to Lutèce. "I'm very grateful to you for all you've—"

"Gratitude?" He came closer to her. "I never asked for your gratitude, Celestine. If you think that's the case, then I'm mistaken; you don't know me well at all."

His words hurt her. All her carefully planned phrases flew out of her mind. "Then what do you want?" she cried.

He moved closer still. "You."

She found she had no will to resist, gladly raising her face to his as he began to kiss her, light butterfly kisses at first, falling on her lids, her forehead, her hair, then, as his mouth touched hers, harder, more forcefully . . .

"But your aunt—" she murmured.

"I told you. Aunt Elmire has gone to the Opera House," he murmured back, his lips brushing her ear. "We're alone." And he swung her up in his arms, carrying her into his bedchamber.

Alone. His hands were moving down from her shoulders, and she shivered as they set off delicious little tremors of fire in her body. "I've been in love with you since I first saw you at the convent," he said softly.

"And I you, Maistre." She laced her fingers in his long hair, as she had longed to so often, surprised at the softness of it.

"Call me by my name. Call me Henri." They sank down on the bed, arms still wound around each other.

"*Henri.*" She had been calling him by his first name in her dreams for so long. But the difference between the Henri de Joyeuse of her imaginings and the man whose arms were crushing her close to him suddenly terrified her. This was real: the heat of his breath as he kissed her throat, the smell of his skin, like leather and brine, the urgency of his hands delving beneath her tight bodice to caress her breasts.

He's so strong.

This fusion of fear and pleasure was overwhelming. She had not known till now how intoxicating it could be to be held so tightly that she felt she might break. Or how vulnerable his face would look as he whispered her name again and again.

She no longer cared if what they were doing was sinful, she only knew that it was what she had wanted for so very long.

"There's something different about you, since you came back from Allegonde, Jagu." Kilian stopped Jagu as he left Captain de Lanvaux's room. "You look so damned pleased with yourself. The cat who got the cream."

"We foiled an assassination attempt," Jagu retorted, knowing full well that this was not what Kilian was referring to.

"*We,*" mimicked Kilian. "That would be you and the delectable Demoiselle de Joyeuse? Paired together all those long weeks away must have forged quite a strong bond between you, hm?" A teasing light danced in his eyes.

"We work well as a team," said Jagu staunchly.

"Oh, I see. Is that what it's called these days, working well as a team? I'd have said you were well and truly smitten. I've seen you smile on more than one occasion. Today I even heard you laugh!"

For a moment the bantering tone disappeared and Kilian put his hand on his shoulder. "It's good to see you like this, Jagu."

"But do I stand any kind of chance with her, Kilian? Is she worth giving up my Commanderie career for?" The questions that had been tormenting Jagu suddenly came pouring out. "Should I break my vow?"

"Why are you asking me? How on earth should I know?" Kilian gave him a little punch on the shoulder. "Shouldn't you be asking Demoiselle Celestine?"

As Celestine lay in Henri's arms, he threw back the tumbled sheets and said, "Celestine. I can't bear to live without you any longer. Marry me."

"M—marry you?" The unexpectedness of the proposal took her breath away. "You're teasing me, Maistre," she said uncertainly.

He pushed himself up on one elbow and gazed down at her. "Why would I tease the woman I love over such an important issue?" He bent over and kissed her, his hair brushing softly across her breasts, and she felt a wave of desire flood through her again. "Well?" he asked, his face close to hers, a little interrogatory smile on his lips. "So, will you have me, Demoiselle? With all my faults? My late nights at the Opera House, my pacing, my black moods when the muse deserts me?"

"You know I love you, with all your faults," she said, kissing him tenderly in return.

Downstairs, a door slammed.

"My aunt's back." Henri sat up, hastily fumbling for his shirt and breeches.

"If she finds us together like this—" Celestine's blissfully languorous dream shattered as she panicked, trying to adjust her disordered clothes.

"Hen - ri?" called Dame Elmire in full operatic voice.

A few minutes later, Celestine followed the Maistre downstairs, to see Dame Elmire standing in the hall.

"I have good news, Aunt," he said. His hand caught hold of Celestine's. "I'd like you to welcome a new member to our family. Celestine has agreed to become my wife."

Dame Elmire looked at them both in turn. Celestine waited, gaze demurely lowered, for Dame Elmire's response, aware that she was blushing from head to toe.

"Well, it's about time!" said Dame Elmire. "Come here, both of you." And she folded first Henri then Celestine in her arms. "So I'm to have a niece at long last," she said, giving Celestine a kiss. "Though are you really sure you want to take him on? He can be very difficult to live with."

"I'm just so happy," Celestine said, squeezing the Maistre's hand. She couldn't stop smiling.

"I'll make sure that the formal announcement of your engagement is in all the city news sheets by next week," said Dame Elmire. "We have a wedding to plan!"

"Once a Guerrier makes a vow before God, Captain, is it impossible to break?"

"Why, Jagu, have you had a sudden crisis of faith?" The captain fixed him with his keen eye and Jagu looked away, discomfited. Was he going to have to confess the truth? "What, then? Is it your music? Now that you've had a taste of the performing life abroad, have you changed your mind?" How did the captain read him so accurately? "Think of me as your confessor, Jagu," the captain added more gently. "You can say what you like to me here in the utmost confidence."

"It's the vow of celibacy." The confession came out in a rush.

"So you've fallen in love." There was no hint of censure in the observation.

Love? Was that what it was? Jagu had not put it quite so bluntly to himself. *Am I in love with Celestine?*

"And is your love returned?"

"I—I don't know."

To Jagu's surprise, Ruaud de Lanvaux began to laugh. "And there I was, thinking that you were about to confess you'd already spent a night of passion together."

Passion? Jagu felt color flood his cheeks at the thought.

"If you love her, my boy, and she loves you too, you're going to find it hard to lead a life apart. But don't throw your vow away for an infatuation. For once you turn your back on the Commanderie, you can never be allowed back in. You're fortunate, Jagu, you have your musical talent. But I've seen other men forsake their vows, only to lose both their love and their faith. Such a double disappointment is hard to bear."

Jagu managed a wry smile. "You're saying that women are fickle."

"You've proved yourself a real asset to the Commanderie and I have great hopes for you. You have the potential to rise very high. But you must put earthly distractions aside if you're going to dedicate yourself to God."

"Joyeuse? Oh, you must mean the king's Maistre de Chapelle," said the sacristan of Saint Meriadec.

Little by little, Rieuk was drawing closer to Celestine de Joyeuse. He had learned that her name was the same as that of the eminent composer Henri de Joyeuse. The sacristan had confirmed that Maistre de Joyeuse was the demoiselle's guardian and teacher. And now he stood in this quiet, secluded *ruelle,* gazing up at an old town house hidden away behind high walls.

"Wake, Ormas," he murmured to his Emissary. "Investigate."

He felt Ormas stir, and a pulse of dark energy caught fire within his breast. Then the Emissary separated from his body, soaring up into the air like a streak of smoke. Rieuk stood, back against the wall, concentrating on searching through Ormas's keen eyes.

The hawk circled slowly around the house, winging past each window. On the ground floor, Rieuk glimpsed a fair-haired man seated at a keyboard instrument, playing a note or two, then leaning forward to scribble rapidly on a wide sheet covered in empty staves.

"Can that be Maistre de Joyeuse?" Ormas flew past once more, giving Rieuk a second view. *He looks much younger than I imagined. Is he more to Celestine than a guardian and teacher? Is he her husband?*

There was no sign of movement in the first-floor rooms. Ormas rose higher, passing the attic windows. And suddenly Rieuk caught a faint yet distinct vibration that pierced his mind like a silver dart. He staggered, clutching at the grimy stones of the wall to right himself.

Azilis. There was no denying it; he recognized that elusive glim-mer, delicate, yet redolent of such great power. He felt light-headed, dizzy in the knowledge that his long search was at an end. He had been pursuing her for so many years, with still no hope of being reunited with Imri, forced to commit sickening crimes in the name of Enhirre. He had no idea yet how he was to infiltrate the household, or lay his hands on the book, let alone extract Azilis's spirit from its pages without shedding Celestine's blood. But this moment of triumph had been hard-won.

"Ormas. Return."

But as Ormas flew past the music room, Rieuk saw that a sec-ond figure had appeared beside Maistre de Joyeuse. "Wait. Go closer, Ormas," he ordered, concentrating all his attention on the newcomer. A golden-haired girl stood beside the composer, one hand on his shoulder, leaning familiarly close to read the notes he had been scribing. *Klervie.* As Rieuk watched, Maistre de Joyeuse pulled her to him, kissing her tenderly.

That's not the chaste kiss of a guardian and his ward. They're lovers. A dark, bitter pain pierced his heart. Why should she know happiness when he had suffered so much? *Would you kiss her so passionately, Maistre de Joyeuse, if you knew her secret? Or her real name and parentage?*

"*Shall I return now, Master?*" The hawk's appearance had caused the sparrows in the garden to scatter noisily in panic; their frantic chirping might draw attention to his presence. As Ormas silently folded himself into Rieuk's body once more, Rieuk turned and began to walk away. Going back to Ondhessar without Azilis was not an option. But how could he get inside the mansion with-out being observed?

There was a sharp hint of autumnal crispness in the morning air as Jagu left the Forteresse; as he crossed the bridge to the quay, he saw wisps of mist rising from the river, mirrored by the trails of smoke rising from the forest of chimneys.

He had spent half the night praying for guidance in the Commanderie chapel, yet his thoughts had strayed constantly to Celestine.

He missed her.

They had spent much of the trip to Allegonde in each other's company. He had looked forward to seeing her each day. He kept remembering little things about her: the unconscious frown of concentration on her face as she tied back her cloud of golden hair in the oppressive heat; her radiant smile when a difficult phrase in a song went suddenly to her liking; Celestine scattering crumbs from her breakfast roll every morning for the little birds on her windowsill. Celestine, Celestine, Celestine . . .

Kilian's right. I can't think of anything else. I must be in love. And yet it was an intoxicating feeling, one that put a spring in his step and a smile on his lips.

Jagu hadn't expected Celestine to open the door to him. Her smile, so open, so welcoming, put all thoughts out of his head.

"Oh, Jagu, the Maistre is out. I'm so sorry if you've come all this way—"

"It wasn't the Maistre I came to see. It was you."

"Me? Is it to do with . . . the magus?" She beckoned him into the music room, closing the door behind them. He stood there, feeling awkward. She had assumed that he had come on Commanderie business.

"Not exactly—" he began, but she interrupted him in a sudden excited torrent of words.

"I haven't told Captain de Lanvaux yet, although I must. Do you think he'll mind? It's just that I don't think I can continue to work for him now that my circumstances have changed. I'm so grateful to him for all he's done and I don't want to offend him in any way—"

"Wait." Jagu held up one hand to try to interrupt the flow. What had she just said? *My circumstances have changed.*

"Oh, but how rude of me; I still haven't asked you why you've come."

But Jagu had to know what she was babbling about. "Why can't you continue to work for the captain?" *Or with me, for that matter?*

A shaft of sunlight sparkled on the little drops of condens on the windowpanes, falling between the two of them l translucent barrier.

"You should be one of the first to know." She clutched both hands together in her excitement. Her eyes sparkled, bright as the sun-riven water drops. "We're to be married!"

"You?" Jagu felt as if he had been shot in the chest. "And the Maistre?" For a moment it seemed as if the sun were extinguished.

"The Maistre is going to ask you to play the organ at the ceremony." He could hear her, still happily chattering on, unwittingly increasing his anguish, for how could she know what he felt? He had never dared to tell her. And now it was too late and he had lost her. And lost her to the one he had always admired most in the world of music. "It'll be at Saint Meriadec's, of course, with the choir of the Sisters of Charity. I hope Angelique will sing a solo . . ."

Why had he not seen this coming? He looked at her from the dark cloud of his despair and saw how happiness had transformed her; this must be the source of the radiance that made her performances so entrancing. Then he heard the silence; she had finished and was looking expectantly at him. There was something he was expected to say.

"I—I hope you'll both be very happy." He managed to stammer out the words. "And now I'd better be going." He turned, making hastily for the door, fumbling clumsily for the handle.

"Thank you. But, Jagu, didn't you have a message for me?"

He stopped, his numbed mind racing. What on earth could he invent now to explain the urgency of his visit? "A message?" His dazed mind tried to find a reason that would not sound too lame. "I'm . . . I'm asking the captain to send me back to Enhirre." He heard the words before he understood fully what he was saying.

Celestine's bright smile vanished. "Back to Enhirre? Oh, Jagu, must you go? After your last mission there . . . won't it be dangerous to return?" He read concern in her eyes, but with the bitter consolation that she cared for him as a friend.

"There's nothing to keep me here."

The look of concern changed to one of disappointment. "We so wanted you to play at our wedding. But you'll be gone . . ."

"Long before," he managed to say, turning his face away so that she could not see his expression as he opened the music room door.

"Jagu?" He heard her puzzled tone as, head down, he strode down the hall and tugged the front door open.

"Got to get back." He mumbled some nonsense about roll call and weapons training.

Somehow even Enhirre doesn't seem far enough.

Rieuk had already inspected five rooms before he found one to rent that afforded a good view over Maistre de Joyeuse's secluded mansion. It was a garret at the top of a dilapidated hostelry on the main avenue; the concierge was elderly, with poor sight, and asked no questions of "Père Emilion" in his threadbare soutane once he had paid her a month's rent in advance.

The time Rieuk had spent at Saint Argantel's Seminary provided him with a plausible alias. Emilion would have been in the junior class at the time Henri de Joyeuse was completing his final year.

He returned to Saint Meriadec's to glean more information. The garrulous sacristan told Père Emilion that the Maistre and his ward were to be married at the end of the year. "They make such a charming couple!"

From his garret Rieuk kept a close watch on the Maistre's house, noting the students and tradesmen who came and went. To his frustration, he could detect no regular pattern to the hours that visitors called. He would just have to make his move.

That afternoon, about three o'clock, a carriage drew up outside the house.

"Ormas. Go!"

Ormas sped through the grubby window glass and flew over the garden as Celestine and an elderly lady left the mansion. Through Ormas, he heard fragments of their conversation.

"Princess Adèle's wedding gown was lace and satin. Do you think that your dressmaker—"

"But that was a summer wedding, my dear, and you're getting married in winter. Lutèce can be so foggy at that time of year. You don't want to catch a chill on your wedding day . . ."

He caught a glimpse of Celestine's face as Ormas flew back to the garret; she looked so happy, chattering away animatedly as she helped the old lady up into the carriage.

Henri de Joyeuse was alone in the house.

———

Rieuk walked up the overgrown path, treading on the lavender stems that spilled their brittle heads beneath his feet, releasing a faint, bitter memory of their summer scent.

His first knock went unanswered. From upstairs he heard the sound of the fortepiano. He knocked again and waited. Still the sound of scales continued. At his third attempt, the scales suddenly stopped. A minute later, the door opened.

"I'm disturbing you. That's unpardonable of me. I'll come back another time."

"I'm sorry. Do I know you?" Henri de Joyeuse looked at him quizzically, as though trying to recall his face.

"Emilion. The name's Père Emilion. We were at Saint Argantel's Seminary together. You probably don't remember me—I was only ten when you left, Maistre." It was a hazardous ploy; the Maistre might have kept in touch with his old school, Emilion might be dead . . . "But I sang in the chapel choir. And I've never forgotten your playing. You were so inspiring."

"Saint Argantel's?" A bewildered smile appeared on the Maistre's face. "You'll have to forgive me; I can't quite place you. So what can I do for you, Père Emilion?"

Henri de Joyeuse seems a genuinely good-hearted man. Rieuk hesitated. *Why do I have to do this to him?* Yet he was so close to his prize now that he could not afford any sentimental feelings. He had to be ruthless. "I've been overseas. At the mission in Serindher. I understand you have a list of the organists and choirmasters in Lutèce. I'm looking for a musician to join our mission and teach hymns."

"You'd better come in. I'll see what I can find for you. Saint Argantel's, hm? I haven't been back in many years." Henri de Joyeuse talked amicably on as he led Rieuk to the music room.

"And was Père Houardon still there?" asked Rieuk.

"No longer plain Père Houardon, but abbé and headmaster!" Henri de Joyeuse closed the music room door and went over to a glass-fronted bookcase filled with bound volumes.

"I was terrified of him; he was so strict." It was too easy to play this part; Rieuk kept his voice even as he slid one hand inside the breast pocket of his stolen soutane and took out the tiny crystal soul-glass. "He'd make an excellent headmaster."

"So, Emilion, you chose the church. Unlike me; I'm afraid I'm a disappointment to the good fathers."

"The sacristan at Saint Meriadec's told me you are to be married. May I offer my congratulations?"

Henri de Joyeuse turned around from the cabinet; his grey eyes were alight with an expression of such warmth and delight that Rieuk faltered. *Is there no other way? If I stay here, as Père Emilion, until Celestine returns . . .*

"She's a singer. My ward. And such a talented musician . . ." He checked himself, laughing. "Forgive me; there's nothing more tedious than having to listen to the ramblings of a man in love. Here's that list. Why not try Le Brun first? He's a skilled and patient trainer . . ."

Ready, Ormas? Rieuk steeled himself.

"Ready, Master."

As Henri de Joyeuse closed the glass cabinet door and came toward him, the paper in hand, Rieuk loosed his Emissary. The hawk darted straight toward the composer. The Maistre's grey eyes widened in surprise. The paper fell from his hands. Then as his legs began to buckle, Rieuk caught him, easing him slowly to the floor.

This moment, when he was caught between two consciousnesses, was always fraught with risk. Supporting Henri de Joyeuse's lolling fair head against his arm, he held the soul-glass to his victim's lips. And as Ormas melted into the composer's breast, the lotus glass began to fill with the essence of his soul, gently but firmly forced out by the Emissary. Slowly, the composer's gold-fringed eyelids closed as he breathed the last of his soul into Rieuk's glass and Rieuk pressed home the crystal stopper, murmuring the words of sealing.

Rieuk felt faint and disconnected from his own body. He willed himself to secure the soul-glass in his inner pocket. He willed himself to lay the composer's body down on the floor gently.

"Ormas," he said quietly. "Ormas, can you hear me? Are you awake?"

This was the moment that Rieuk dreaded. There was always the risk that he would lose control and damage his own mind as well as his victim's. *For you, Imri. Only for you.* He let his mind merge with Ormas's.

For a moment he lost himself in a fragmented confusion of

sensations, memories . . . Then, through his link with Ormas, he was looking at himself. Rieuk Mordiern stood over him, blinking behind the thick-lensed spectacles he wore to conceal the brilliance of his eyes.

"What is your name?" Rieuk Mordiern asked. As always it was disconcerting to hear his own voice through another's ears.

"My—name—is—" He stumbled, not yet fully inhabiting his victim's brain. "It's—Henri de Joyeuse." It would take some practice to manipulate a mind as subtle and gifted as this. He might not have long before Celestine and the old lady returned.

"You are my eidolon. My puppet. You will do as I command." Rieuk spoke the words of the rite to bind the stolen body.

"I am your eidolon. Your puppet. I will do as you command," the composer repeated in a dull, lifeless voice. The glamour had worked; through Ormas, he had become Henri de Joyeuse.

"Good-day to you, Maistre de Joyeuse." Rieuk backed away; he needed to retreat to the seclusion of his rented room, where he could concentrate all his strength on manipulating his victim.

He went slowly down the garden path, one uncertain step at a time. If the soul-stealing had been difficult, then this was harder still. His body was weakened, with only half his will to control it. All his vital energy, his life essence was infused into Ormas so that he could manipulate his eidolon-victim. If any of his enemies were to waylay him at this moment, he would have no strength to defend himself. He just had to hope that none of the Commanderie were close at hand.

The dressmaker plied Celestine and Dame Elmire with tea and delicious little macaroons while she took measurements for Celestine's gown and laid out samples of fabrics. She suggested ivory and gold-threaded brocade or white velvet as soft as new-fallen snow, although Celestine had taken a liking to a bolt of fine satin, with a waxy sheen like snowdrop petals.

They left the shop much later than they had intended and made their way home through the twilit streets, still animatedly discussing the dressmaker's suggestions. Celestine favored the satin but Dame Elmire preferred the brocade.

"With your pale porcelain complexion, a subtle touch of color would—" Dame Elmire broke off as they entered the walled garden. "No lamps lit in the house? And the sun's setting."

"Henri's probably not even noticed. When he's working, he loses all concept of time," Celestine said with an affectionate smile.

"Henri, why are you working in this poor light?" called Dame Elmire as they entered the darkened house. "Hasn't Francinette been up to light the lamps? Francinette!" She disappeared down the back stair to the kitchen to look for the maid.

The house was silent. Celestine tiptoed to the music room door. Henri must be composing at his desk, and she had no wish to disturb him, she just wanted to sneak a little look . . .

CHAPTER 33

"Back to Enhirre?" Jagu sensed that Captain de Lanvaux was looking at him intently, but he could not meet his gaze. "Why this sudden desire to leave Francia, Guerrier?"

Jagu stared at the floor.

"Ah. So she turned you down?"

Jagu managed the slightest, curtest of nods. To have to admit aloud that he had been rejected would only increase his humiliation.

"I see." There was no hint of censure in the captain's voice. "But to go so far . . . is that really necessary? I'd hoped that you would continue to work for me, as part of the special division. You and Demoiselle de Joyeuse acquitted yourselves with distinction in Bel'Esstar. You make a good team. I'd hoped that I could pair you together again."

"Well, that won't happen now," Jagu said brusquely, "as the demoiselle is getting married."

"Married? What happy news. And who is the lucky man?"

"Maistre de Joyeuse."

"Excellent!" Captain de Lanvaux was smiling broadly. "They seem made for each other. I can't help feeling a little responsible for this, as I brought them together at Saint Azilia's. I must pay them a visit to offer my congratulations."

The captain, his mind obviously distracted by Commanderie matters, had still not guessed the reason for Jagu's black mood. This conversation was only rubbing salt in Jagu's wounds. "May I be excused, sir?"

Captain de Lanvaux rose and walked round his desk to place a hand on Jagu's shoulder. Jagu looked away. "Please reconsider your decision. Your quick thinking in the basilica saved the princess's life. Not many have your experience when it comes to detecting the Forbidden Arts. Oh, and by the way, I'm recommending you for promotion."

Jagu's head lifted. "Promotion?"

"No one deserves it more than you."

Rieuk lay on the narrow bed. The faint light of the waning moon shone through the cobwebbed window of his rented garret room. He was conserving his strength for the time when he must make his move. Beside him on the windowsill stood the soul-glass, faintly luminous in the darkness with the essence of Henri de Joyeuse's immortal soul.

"Henri?" Celestine tapped on the music room door. When there was no answer, she opened it and peered into the room. "Won't you join us for dinner, Henri? You must eat."

He was sitting with his back to her, leaning over the open score on his desk, pen in hand.

"Later," he said distantly.

She ventured a little farther into the room, longing to fling her arms around his neck and kiss the top of his head. Yet he seemed so deep in thought that she did not dare disturb him.

"Shall I bring you some food on a tray?"

"Thank you."

She retreated to the kitchen, where Dame Elmire greeted her with a knowing look. "What did I tell you? He's always like this when he's composing, especially in the early stages of a new work. You've seen it before yourself! It's best to let him alone until he's ready to mix with us ordinary mortals again."

Celestine let out a little sigh. She had been longing to discuss wedding plans. But if Henri was in the throes of composition, she was loathe to disturb him.

Rieuk watched Celestine through his Emissary's eyes as she withdrew on tiptoe. There was still too much activity in the house to risk making his move, yet he could hear from the clatter of plates below that the servant was clearing away the remains of supper.

When she returns with the supper tray . . .

"I'm off to bed now," called out the aunt. "Good night."

"Good night," he heard Celestine reply.

"And Francinette, make sure you've safely extinguished all the lamps. We don't want to be burned alive in our beds."

"Yes, madame," came the surly response from the kitchen.

"I've brought you some soup and bread." Celestine placed the tray on the music room table. "It's pea and ham, your favorite. Don't let it go cold."

"Thank you." Again that abstracted voice greeted her; Henri was leaning over the score, his head propped on one hand, his hair escaping its black ribbon, half-obscuring his face.

"Your aunt wished you good night." She came closer. "The dressmaker took my measurements for the wedding gown today." She just couldn't resist telling him her news. "But I'm not allowed to say anymore; it's bad luck."

"Celestine. You're an orphan; you never knew your parents. Is that right?"

Why was he asking her this question tonight? He had never seemed bothered before.

"I don't remember them very well," she said, choosing her words carefully. "I was only five when they died." She longed to tell him all about herself, to share the secrets of her past with one who loved and understood her. But what if he looked at her with horror?

Yet even now he was looking at her oddly. "So you knew their names?" Was he testing her? Or worse still, had the jealous Aurélie been spreading malicious rumors?

"Is it important, Henri?"

"I thought there might be relations of yours that you would want to invite to our wedding. An uncle . . . or an aunt, perhaps?" His eyes had lost their usual brilliance and were dull and glazed.

"No one," she said firmly.

"Forgive me. I didn't mean to upset you."

"Of course. I forgive you." She went to him and, standing on tiptoe, kissed him full on the lips. "Good night."

Rieuk had been wondering where the book might be hidden when Celestine suddenly flung her arms about him and kissed him passionately.

The kiss, so intimate, so invasive, shocked all other thoughts from his mind. He was inhabiting the Maistre's body more easily now, moving with greater fluency. But seeing, feeling, *tasting* through another's senses was deeply unsettling. Distracting, too; the feelings that had flooded through him awakened memories of a time when he had loved and been loved in return. For that brief moment, he knew what it was to adore Celestine with every fiber of his being. The image lingered on and it took a supreme effort of will to wrench his thoughts back to his mission. Even then, the soft radiance of her blue eyes still haunted him.

As he suspected, she had not told a soul her true name. But why was she working for the Commanderie, the very organization that had destroyed her father?

He had noted a trunk in the corner on which she had placed a jug of pale late roses, a gift, perhaps, from her fiancé? But he could not detect the slightest trace of an aethyrial presence. Azilis must have concealed herself from Ormas's keen senses.

He stood on the landing, uncertain where to go. He had no idea which room was the Maistre's bedchamber. It would not do to walk in by accident on the old lady as she was preparing for bed. He could only retreat to the music room and pretend to work late into the night.

He already felt drained by the tremendous effort he had expended. Returning to his own body, he checked the soul-glass. Was it his imagination or had the starry glimmer of the composer's trapped soul begun to fade? He felt the first stirrings of panic. He had lost Paol de Lannion this way; he must not make the same mistake again.

A drop of Maunoir blood, that was all he needed to undo the binding spell. But it must be taken by stealth.

There had been roses in a jug on the trunk and they were

drooping, starting to shed their petals. And roses had sharp thorns . . .

"I thought you were made of stronger stuff." Kilian stood over Jagu as he packed his kit. "I never took you for the kind of man to run away."

"I just asked to be posted overseas again." Jagu did not even look up, suspecting that Kilian was trying to provoke him. "I'm not running away."

Kilian hunkered down beside him. "So she turned you down? The captain's made you an offer you'd be a fool to reject. And yet here you are, playing the rejected lover."

Jagu said nothing.

"Haven't you heard? Grand Maistre Donatien has resigned. He's retired to the Monastery of Saint Bernez. Very suddenly. Very unexpectedly."

Jagu raised his head. He had been so wrapped up in his own misery that he had been oblivious to other events going on around him. "Resigned? Is he ill?"

"There's all kinds of rumors flying around." Kilian leaned closer to Jagu and added in an undertone, "Some are even saying he's betrayed the Commanderie."

"Maistre Donatien?" Jagu gazed at Kilian and saw that, for once, his friend was in earnest.

"A canker eating away at the heart of our brotherhood. It could easily destabilize the Commanderie."

"You don't think that what happened to the regiment in Ondhessar—"

"All I'm saying is: Be careful. We're entering uncharted waters. The captain will need our support."

"Fresh roses, Henri?" Celestine took the little bouquet of blush-cream blooms from him and sniffed them, inhaling a faint memory of summer from their petals. He must have noticed that the others had died. "Autumn roses have such a delicate scent. Thank you." She stood on tiptoe to kiss him. "I'll put them in water straight-away."

The stems were studded with vicious thorns and, in spite of handling them carefully, she still managed to prick her thumb as she placed them in a vase. "Ow!" She sucked the tiny puncture.

"You should let the blood flow to flush out any dirt that might infect the cut." He held out his handkerchief.

"It's only a little thorn prick." But she was touched that he should worry about her, and taking the fine white linen, she pressed it to her injured thumb. "See? The bleeding's stopped already."

The glimmer in the soul-glass flickered, like a candleflame wavering in the breeze. Aethyric crystal had remarkable properties, but it could not sustain a mortal soul for too long once that soul was separated from its body, as Rieuk already knew to his cost.

"Henri, we're going out to the drapers' to choose trimmings and lace," announced Dame Elmire. "Look at you; you're a disgrace. You've been wearing the same clothes since the day before yesterday and you haven't even bothered to shave."

"I'm sorry, Aunt." *At last the house would be empty and he could complete his mission.*

He waited until he heard the front door close, then made his way upstairs and into Celestine's chamber, lurching in his haste and almost losing control of the Maistre's body. He knelt and took the jug of roses off the wooden trunk. Undoing the catch was frustratingly difficult with the Maistre's long, slender fingers but at last he managed it and flung open the lid.

"*There* you are," he breathed. Celestine, trusting soul that she was, had merely wrapped her father's grimoire in an old petticoat. He had no doubt that his long search was over, for as his fingers closed around the book's leather binding and he lifted it from its hiding place, he felt the telltale tingle of aethyrial energy in his fingertips.

But the image on the front of the book confused him: the title proclaimed in gold letters that it was a *Lives of the Holy Saints*. The cover showed a pious young woman with hands tight-clasped in prayer, and a modest, downcast gaze. Was he mistaken? Yet even as he puzzled over it, the woman in the picture slowly raised her head and fixed him with large, soulful eyes.

"You. It *is* you. Why have you been evading me for so long?"

He gazed back at her in wonder. "Don't you remember me? I set you free."

"*But you were too weak to bind me.*" Each word resounded in his mind like a clear crystal bell.

"I'm much stronger now. And I know your true name."

"*I am already bound to Celestine. Bound by blood.*"

Rieuk had never once imagined that the spirit would defy him. "I'm going to break that bond. I'm going to take you back to Ondhessar."

A shudder went through the spirit's translucent form. "*And what if I don't want to return?*"

"But the Rift is closing. And as it closes, our mage powers are growing weaker." She seemed not to be listening. Panicking, he tried a more personal appeal. "We're your children, aren't we? We need you, Azilis. We need you to keep the Rift between the worlds open."

"*Children? What children would keep their mother imprisoned against her will?*"

Rieuk had not anticipated this. "But you're in thrall to Celestine de Joyeuse. You're still a prisoner." *I've searched for you for all these years. How can you reject me in favor of Celestine?*

Fighting the growing sense of desperation, he drew out the handkerchief spotted with Celestine's blood and dipped it in the rose water, squeezing the stained fabric over the book. The trace of blood would be so diluted that it might not work.

"*Why are you trying to sever the link between us?*" The spirit rose up out of the book, towering above him. "*Celestine. Celestine!*" And that terrible, high keening that he had first heard in Hervé de Maunoir's study began again.

Something's not right. Celestine had been troubled by a faint feeling of unease ever since she left the house. She could not identify the cause, although there was a fitful, cold wind blowing that rattled the shutters and set the shop signs creaking as they swung to and fro above her head. It had rained during the night and there were many puddles to be avoided.

She had been looking forward to choosing the lace and ribbons to adorn her wedding dress but it was difficult to put her mind to such charming fripperies when she felt so jumpy.

The Faie's cry pierced her mind like a sliver of ice.

The book. Someone is stealing the book!

"Excuse me, I think I've dropped one of my gloves. I'll just run back . . ."

"I'll wait for you at the draper's shop," called Dame Elmire after her.

"*Celestine, help me!*" As Celestine ran, she heard the Faie's desperate cry again. She gathered up handfuls of her skirts so that she could move more swiftly, not caring who saw.

She pushed open the gates and stumbled up the path, banging on the door with both fists.

"Henri! Let me in!"

There was no reply.

"*Celestine!*" A high-pitched, unearthly scream came from upstairs, the same sound that had once woken her from sleep, many years before. She rattled the door handle frantically, fumbling for her key. Where was Francinette? Out at the market, perhaps . . . or scrubbing pots and pans in the basement kitchen, deaf to her cries.

At last Celestine found her key and with shaking fingers unlocked the door. As she ran up the stairs, the eerie, mind-splitting wail grew louder and more desperate till it blotted out all thoughts but one: *Stop the thief.*

She flung open her door. Henri knelt on the floor, her book in his hands. The Faie writhed above him, a pale, twisted shadow.

"Henri! What are you doing?" How did he know about the book? Had he been set up by the Inquisition to uncover her secret? Was this the reason for his increasingly strange behavior toward her during the past two days?

Slowly, interminably slowly, Henri turned around to stare at her with the same dull, dead expression that she had seen the night before.

"*This is not Henri de Joyeuse,*" the Faie told her.

"Who—who are you?" Celestine took a step back, overwhelmed by a sudden feeling of dread.

"This aethyrial spirit is not yours, Klervie." Henri's mouth framed the words and the voice was Henri's, but the intelligence behind them must be another's. Who else could possibly know her true identity?

"Magus," whispered Celestine, taking another step back. *He is here.* She had waited so long to find him and now he—or his consciousness—was here in her bedchamber. "Soul-stealer. Restore Henri to me."

"First give me the book and the spirit. And a drop of your blood to break your father's blood-bond."

Henri's body was moving without his own volition, a grotesque, terrifying puppet. "First restore Henri," she insisted, trying to control the shaking in her voice.

"*I want to stay with you, Celestine.*" The Faie gazed at her beseechingly. "*Don't give me to this magus.*"

"How can you make me choose between you?" Celestine gazed back at the Faie. The Faie had protected her, saved her life, and gifted her. She couldn't bear the thought of losing her. Tears started to her eyes. "I love you both so much."

"Hervé's book and the spirit, in exchange for Henri de Joyeuse's soul," said the magus quietly.

"Faie; help me."

The Faie, just as she had in Bel'Esstar, gathered herself and in a dazzling swirl of pale light, melted into her. Celestine felt the Faie's power seeping through her, infusing her with strength until her veins pulsed with a clear energy.

The thing that was and was not Henri flung up one hand to shield his eyes from the brightness. "Attack me, and you attack Henri de Joyeuse. Damage this body, and you damage the one you love." The magus clutched the book to Henri's breast like a shield.

He had outmaneuvered her. Celestine let out a cry of frustration.

"*If we render him unconscious, then the spirit bird possessing his body will be forced out.*"

"But we mustn't harm him." Celestine wavered, caught in an agony of indecision.

"*His vital signs are failing. If you don't act now, it will be too late.*"

Too late?

"*If body and soul are kept apart for too long, they can never be reunited. He will die anyway.*"

That decided her. Celestine's hand shot out, pointing at Henri's fair head. She felt the Faie's clear, bright energy surge through her, passing down her arm and through her extended fingers.

Henri's head jerked back and he crumpled to the floor, the book slipping from his fingers.

And as she watched in horrified amazement, a shadow began to slide out of his slack mouth, slowly taking a recognizable shape: first the sharp beak, then bright amber eyes, smoke-speckled wings, the feathery tips serrated . . .

"A bird. A . . . *hawk?*"

Suddenly a terrible rage flared up in Celestine; the magus had betrayed her father and now he had struck at the one she loved. As the shadow bird darted toward the window, she flung out her hand again, loosing another dart of translucent energy.

A shudder went through the hawk's body and it let out a piercing cry. She had wounded it! For a moment it veered off course, flapping raggedly, as though it could no longer see where it was going. Tatters of shadow flew into the air, falling like flakes of sooty snow.

Celestine, eyes dazzled by the brightness of the Faie's attack, saw the hawk recover—and fly straight through the windowpane, out into the daylight.

She stumbled after it, flinging open the window, gripping the high sill, as she leaned out to see where it was going. It was heading toward the backs of the main street, a trail of smoke against the cloudy sky. So he had been in hiding nearby, that damned magus. Why had she not sensed his presence? In her rage, her first instinct was to pursue the familiar and destroy it, once and for all.

But then she remembered Henri.

A shaft of whitefire pierced Ormas's skull. Searing pain knocked Rieuk to the floor as the injured hawk hurtled through the pane and melded with him.

My eye. My eye's on fire. I'm blind.

A terrible madness gripped him. He writhed on the floor, moaning, unable to gain control of his own body, living Ormas's agony as well as his own. *When your Emissary is hurt, you hurt, too.*

"Maistre?" Celestine threw herself on her knees beside him, trying to lift his head and shoulders. "Speak to me." But unconscious, he was so heavy that she could do no more than lift his head onto her lap.

"Faie, what shall I do?" she cried, desperate. "Why doesn't he respond? That cursed shadow creature has left his body." She clutched his wrist tight, feeling in vain for a pulse. "Henri, dear Henri, please come back." She kissed his face, his lids, his chill lips. "Come back to me!"

Azilis. Rieuk pressed one hand to the agony of fire that burned where his right eye had been, rocking to and fro. Gouts of seared blood and tissue dripped onto the boards through his clenched fingers.

For a moment, she had been within his grasp, dazzlingly luminous in her pure, aethyrial beauty. Then she had melted into Celestine's body, merging with her, rejecting him.

Why had he hesitated? Why, when he was so close to possessing her, had he held back? For in that momentary hesitation when, hurt and confused, he had not known what to do, she had struck, attacking Ormas, forcing him from the eidolon's body.

He opened his mouth and howled aloud his pain and frustration.

Ruaud stopped at the flower stall on the corner of the avenue.

"A bouquet, please."

"What would you like, officer?" asked the flower girl. "I've autumn roses, lilies . . ."

Ruaud knew nothing about flowers. "I leave the selection to you," he said, handing over his money.

He had just turned into the narrow *ruelle* that led to Maistre de Joyeuse's mansion when a streak of darkness passed overhead. He stopped, gripped by a vivid, chilling memory. That birdlike shadow . . . It was so like the magus's familiar that had attacked him in Saint Argantel's that for a moment he could not move.

But why would it be here? The magus had destroyed Argantel's

Angelstones years ago in Kemper. What possible reason could he have for returning now? Unless he had come for Lord Galizur's stone, which Maistre Donatien wore?

He shook his head, dismissing the thought. *I must be hallucinating.*

The front door to the Joyeuse mansion was ajar.

"Anyone at home?" Ruaud called. When there was no reply, he went in. The sound of smothered sobbing was coming from the upper landing.

"Celestine?" He hurried up the stairs and saw Henri de Joyeuse lying on the floor, with Celestine supporting his head in her lap. The Maistre's face was deathly pale and his eyes were closed.

"What's happened?" The bouquet dropped from Ruaud's hand. He knelt beside her and felt for a pulse in the Maistre's throat. "Did he faint?"

"That magus." She looked up and he saw the tears streaking her face. "He was here. He—he said—"

"*Here?*" But there was no time for questions; Henri de Joyeuse's pulse was so faint that he would soon slip from unconsciousness into death. "This is the work of a soul-stealer," said Ruaud as he straightened up. "I feared as much when I saw his shadow creature just now. I just could not believe—"

"Is there any hope for Henri, Captain?" Celestine broke in, her blue eyes blazing through the tears. "If there's anything I can do to bring him back, I'll do it. Just tell me what it is." He realized that, in spite of her tears, she was ready to fight for her lover's life.

"The magus must have his soul imprisoned in a soul-glass." He was remembering Paol de Lannion. "That's how they do it; they charm out the living soul and replace it with their familiar. If we hurry, there may still be a chance. Did you see where it went?"

She pointed toward the window. "The familiar flew toward the avenue. Several of the houses back onto the *ruelle.*"

As he ran down the stairs he heard her calling after him, "Please hurry!"

A line of black crows had gathered on the rooftop of one of the houses. As Ruaud hurried up the steps, he half expected them to rise up and attack him, as they had in Kemper.

He was only too aware that with every minute that passed, Henri de Joyeuse was slipping further and further away from life, and soon it would be too late to bring him back. Now that there was no vital spirit to animate his body, death would soon claim him.

"Commanderie!" he shouted as he pounded on the door. "Open up immediately!"

After what seemed an age, an elderly concierge opened the door and peered at him.

He charged past her up the stairs.

Soul-stealing was a coward's magic, an underhanded, devious piece of trickery. The magus could skulk out of sight, undetected, while using his victim's body to achieve his goal.

Ruaud could smell magic close by, a dark-spiced, feral odor. Before Kemper, he had not been able to detect it. But ever since his duel with the magus, he had developed a stronger instinct for the Forbidden Arts.

On the sixth and uppermost floor of the narrow building, the stink of magic grew stronger. He was confronted by a single door. "Open up!" he cried. When there was no reply, he kicked the door open.

He halted on the threshold. It was a tawdry, poky little room, half-lit by a grubby-paned window set in the eaves that afforded a good view of the Maistre's house below.

Spots of blood stained the bare boards; freshly spilled, Ruaud reckoned, from the look of it. If the magus had been here, he was injured and could not have got far . . .

He tugged the thin mattress off the bed, flinging it on the floor, frantically searching beneath for the soul-glass. The magus would have little use for it now.

And then he stopped, hearing the crunch of glass beneath his foot.

"Oh no." He knelt down and felt with careful fingers on the dusty boards. Soon they closed on sharp shards: the fragments of a delicate lotus glass with its priceless contents all leaked away.

CHAPTER 34

Quicksilver ripple of air . . .

Jagu felt it. Even within his quarters, within the hallowed stone walls of the Forteresse, the disturbance reached him. Faint, this time, yet unmistakable, that strange moment of stillness.

And at the same moment, the magus's mark on his wrist began to burn, just as it had in Bel'Esstar.

He pushed back his cuff, staring at it in disbelief, seeing the faint marks of the sigil on his skin darkening to an angry red, as if freshly branded there by the magus's perverted art.

How could *he* be here in Lutèce? And why had he come?

A thin filament of glimmering brightness spiraled through the air . . .

The Maistre's fair-lashed lids fluttered a little, then opened, revealing a hint of soft grey.

"Ce . . . les . . . tine?"

He knew her. He was his own self again.

"I'm here, Henri, I'm here."

He tried to raise one hand to touch her face. But then she saw the light fade from his eyes, and as it dimmed, so his hand dropped back. A little sigh escaped his mouth and she knew that he was gone.

"What's wrong, Rustéphan?" demanded Lieutenant Friard, glancing up from the roll call.

"Where's the captain, Lieutenant? I need to see him. Urgently."

"How urgently?"

"The magus is here," said Jagu. "In the city."

Lieutenant Friard dropped his pen, spattering ink over the neatly scribed list of names. "I believe he went to pay a call on Demoiselle de Joyeuse . . ."

Celestine? Jagu's heart twisted in his chest. Suppose the magus had come seeking her out after the thwarted attack in the Basilica? "Permission to go find the captain?"

"Granted." Friard took up his pistol. "Do you need backup?"

But Jagu was already running toward the Forteresse stables.

Jagu dismounted at the entrance to the *ruelle* that led to the Maistre's house and tied his horse's reins to the railings. He checked the mark on his wrist and saw that it was already fading.

He's getting away.

He hesitated a moment, torn between his duty to pursue the magus and his fear for Celestine's safety. And then he saw that the front door was open.

"Celestine!" he shouted, hurrying into the hall. "Maistre!"

He stopped, hearing the sound of muffled sobbing coming from upstairs.

Something was wrong here, very wrong. He hurried up the stairs, two at a time.

Through an open doorway, he saw Celestine weeping over the body of a man who lay with his fair head in her lap.

"Maistre?" Jagu stared down at his beloved teacher. He knelt beside Celestine and lifted the Maistre's wrist, feeling in vain for a pulse. "Maistre!"

Celestine raised her tear-streaked face to his. "Jagu, you're too late. He's gone."

Jagu was still holding the Maistre's hand in his own. "No," he said in disbelief. "He can't be." How could a healthy young man like Henri de Joyeuse be lying here dead? He leaned forward and felt for a pulse at the throat. "A doctor. You've sent Francinette for a doctor?"

"It's no use," said Celestine in a hard, low voice. "It was the magus, Jagu. He stole his soul. And when it returned to his body, it was too late and he . . . he died."

"But why?" Jagu could feel tears, useless tears burning in his eyes. Why was he reliving this nightmare? Why was the magus still at large, ruthlessly attacking all those he held dear? "Why use the Maistre?"

"To get at me." Her voice was even quieter. "He did it to deceive me. It's all my fault."

"How can it be your fault?" Jagu burst out, not understanding what she was saying.

"Don't ask me. Not now." Her blue eyes burned in her white face; he had never seen her look so fierce . . . or so desolate. And then the mask crumpled and the tears began to flow again. "Henri," she wept. "Why couldn't I save you? Why didn't I see what he had done to you? Why was I taken in by his deception?"

Immobilized by his own shock and grief, Jagu knelt, clutching the Maistre's cold hand, not knowing what to do. There was nothing he could say to alleviate her pain, yet he could not bear to see her so distraught. Would she have wept for him like this if he had died in Enhirre? And then he dismissed the idea; how ignoble of him to even think such a thing! He laid the Maistre's hand down and looked into his still, empty face, seeking in vain for a trace of the gentle, endearing humor that had so often animated it.

I came to save her, dear Maistre. I never once thought that I would lose you.

Blindly through his tears, he reached out to put his arms around Celestine. To his surprise, she turned to him, burying her face in his shoulder. They knelt there awhile, clinging to each other, until Jagu heard voices and the sound of booted feet on the stairs.

Captain de Lanvaux appeared in the doorway, his face grim. Jagu recognized several familiar faces from the captain's elite squad, foremost among them Alain Friard and Kilian.

"He got away," said the captain briefly. "He was wounded. We followed a trail of bloodstains. But we lost all trace of him at the quay."

"What's the meaning of this?" demanded a woman's voice querulously from downstairs. "Why is my front door open to the four elements?"

"Dame Elmire." Celestine started up. "I must go to her. We have to break it to her gently. She's elderly. The shock could kill her."

Ruaud de Lanvaux stopped her. "Let me tell her, Celestine." Celestine nodded.

Jagu dashed his hand across his eyes, hastily wiping away the wetness. He didn't care if the other Guerriers saw his tears for his teacher, but she would need him to be strong.

"Shall we move him?" Lieutenant Friard said quietly.

The Guerriers moved forward and respectfully, efficiently, lifted the Maistre's body and laid it on the bed. The lieutenant began, in a quiet voice, to say a Sergian prayer for the dead. They stood, heads bowed, until he had finished.

"It's all my fault, Jagu." Celestine's eyes were swollen with crying. "Henri died because of me."

"No," Jagu insisted. "You mustn't blame yourself. He died because the magus killed him. Just as he killed Paol." He wanted so much to put his arms around her again and hold her close. But the captain reappeared and Celestine hurried to him. "Dame Elmire is in shock," he said briefly. "The servant woman is with her. I've sent for the physician."

Much later that interminable day, the members of Captain de Lanvaux's squad returned to the house. Celestine, clutching the book, had been keeping watch over Henri's body. But as evening fell, she let the Guerriers take her place and went downstairs, still holding on to the book.

"Soul-stealing is damaging for the stealer as well as the victim," said the captain. "The magus must have used up much of his own life energy. He can't have gone far." He carefully drew his handkerchief out of his pocket. Wrapped inside were fragments of crystal glass.

"What is that?" Her throat ached and her voice was hoarse when she tried to speak.

"I found these on the floor of his room. He must have smashed the soul-glass when you thwarted his attack."

"Henri's soul was contained in here?" She extended her hand to touch the glittering shards, as if there were some tangible, lingering trace of his presence.

"Careful; they're sharp," the captain said brusquely.

"What kind of glass can preserve a mortal soul?"

"We believe the magi who practice soul-stealing use a special glass that they imbue with Aethyric properties."

"We're going to track him down and bring him to justice," said Jagu grimly. "No one else is going to die by the Forbidden Arts."

"How did it all go so wrong?" Rieuk lay, ill and in intense pain, in the darkened cabin of a barque sailing upriver. He could see nothing through the seared ruin of his right eye. His left eye watered constantly, half-closed and swollen in sympathy with its damaged twin. Even the slightest movement of the barque on the water sent agonizing barbs of pain shooting through his head.

Ormas had retreated into himself, nursing his own wound in silence.

Rieuk had not felt so alone—or so desperate—since Imri's death.

"Why did Celestine attack? Didn't she understand what would happen to de Joyeuse? I thought she loved him. I don't understand . . ."

"*Azilis made her do it, Master,*" came back Ormas's halting reply. "*Azilis took control of her. Azilis has chosen Celestine for her own.*"

"When am I going to wake up, Faie?" Celestine whispered. "When am I going to wake up and find this is all a vile dream?"

"*You protected me,*" said the Faie. "*And in protecting me, you lost the one you loved. I can never repay such a debt.*"

"Why can't you bring him back? Why, Faie?"

"*Nothing has changed. I can only protect you. I am powerless to help anyone else.*"

Celestine was sorely in need of sleep but every time her aching lids drooped and she fell into a doze, she found herself reliving the events of the last hours, watching in horror as the man she loved lurched toward her, a living puppet, moved by the will of the magus who had stolen his soul.

She sat in the dark in the music room, huddled in Henri's old robe de chambre, clutching Hervé's book. The soft, worn fabric still retained a hint of the scent of his body, and as she pulled it close about her, she found a little comfort in it. She did not want to go back to the room, her room, where he had died.

The physician had given Dame Elmire a sleeping draft to calm her. But Celestine had refused his potions. She needed to keep alert in case *he* returned.

Captain de Lanvaux had asked her, gently enough, "Why was the magus here? Why did he attack you?" and she had answered him, just as she had answered Jagu, that she believed his attack was in retribution for the Bel'Esstar affair.

"I've even had to lie to Captain de Lanvaux to shield you, dear Faie. And I owe him so much. He's stood by me and defended me. How can I tell him the truth?" In her exhausted state, she might so easily make a slip and reveal too much about her past. And then not even the captain would be able to save her from the Inquisition.

Although she feared that attending Henri's funeral would be more painful to endure than any torture the Inquisition could devise.

As the slow procession filed out of Saint Meriadec behind the Maistre's coffin, Celestine walked as if in a trance. Dame Elmire was too ill to attend, but Captain de Lanvaux stood at Celestine's side as the last sweet, sad strains of the choir of the Sisters of Charity floated out into the autumn air. Jagu was at the organ, and he had chosen to honor his teacher's memory by playing one of the Maistre's chorale preludes from the book that he had given Jagu at Saint Argantel's Seminary.

Celestine envied Jagu that he had a role to fulfill during the service; he could occupy his mind with changing organ stops and concentrate on his performance, rather than on the coffin that rested before the altar, beneath its simple wreath of lilies.

Crowds of people waited in the street outside in respectful silence under a cloudy sky.

I had no idea that the Maistre's music was so popular, Celestine thought dazedly. She was glad that she had hidden her face beneath a black voile veil; she was sure that as she passed by, the onlookers were whispering and nudging one another.

"So tragic . . . so young . . ."

Captain de Lanvaux had ensured that the Maistre's death was reported in all the journals as being from a sudden and devastating apoplexy, brought on by overwork.

"If the true reason were given . . ." he had begun, and Celestine had understood.

A sharp breeze had begun to blow from the river, stirring the tops of the cypresses and yew that lined the walled cemetery. The mourners had begun to drift away, but Celestine still stood with Jagu and the captain beside her at the grave.

"You killed him!" The voice was a woman's, throbbing with bitter accusation.

Celestine stopped as a tall, elegantly black-clad figure forced her way through the crowd of mourners, one finger pointed directly at her. She recognized Aurélie, dark eyes flashing with fury in a white-powdered face. Behind her, she saw Gauzia, muffled in a hooded cape, staring, yet for once saying nothing.

"You, Demoiselle Celestine. You who dared to call yourself Celestine de Joyeuse."

"Diva," said Captain de Lanvaux sternly, "this is not the stage of the Opera House."

But Aurélie came on, spitting venom. "You put a spell on him. You worked some kind of glamour on my Henri. You stole him away from me!"

Celestine shrank back against the captain. She had no idea how to defend herself against these unkind words.

"An apoplexy? At his age? I say you fed him some love potion, and *poisoned* him."

"These are serious accusations, Madame Carnelian," said the captain sternly. "If you had truly loved Maistre de Joyeuse, then you would show more respect. A great number of people cherished him and his music. This service has been held to honor his memory. You should keep that in mind."

Aurélie stared at Captain de Lanvaux, her reddened lips gaping open. She seemed in shock. Perhaps no one had dared to speak so forthrightly to her before, Celestine thought, stunned by the attack.

Gauzia still said nothing.

"Your singing career is over. No one will employ you now. That, at least, I can assure you. Come, Gauzia."

Gauzia shot Celestine a silent, reproving look, then turned and followed Aurélie out of the cemetery.

Jagu waited for Celestine. He looked around him at the familiar music room in which they had rehearsed so often together. The Maistre's desk lay just as he had left it, score paper open with scrawled notes of a half-finished composition, a phrase left hanging, incomplete . . .

It would never be finished now.

Jagu kept seeing echoes of past days: the Maistre looking up from the keyboard with his quick, easy smile; the Maistre listening to him play before correcting the errors, not interrupting every other note with a criticism like his other teachers at the Conservatoire . . .

The room was steeped in memories.

You taught me well, Maistre. I'll never forget you. Every time I play your music . . .

Jagu felt the ache of tears pressing at the back of his eyes again. But the time for mourning was over. He wanted to bring the magus to justice. And there were questions that had been tormenting him since Bel'Esstar that needed answering if they were ever to track down the murderer.

"Jagu." Celestine appeared. She looked so frail and wan in her plain mourning dress that he wondered if it was not too soon to approach her.

This was not going to be easy.

"H—how are you?" he asked, then wished he had bitten his tongue; how was she going to answer such a foolish question? "And Dame Elmire?" he said hurriedly.

"She's still not well enough to leave her bed." Celestine closed the door behind her. "Is there any news?" she said, coming closer to him. "About the magus?"

"That's why I've come. There's no one else in the house, is there?"

"Only old Francinette, and she's still as deaf as ever."

Jagu took in a deep breath. "Celestine. That day in the Basilica. I saw what happened. Others didn't. But I saw that you were . . . different. I saw the shield that you wove around the prince and princess."

"You must have been dreaming." Her expression was closed.

"Listen. I'm not about to betray you to the Inquisition. You acted to save the princess's life."

"How?" She spoke flatly. "How did you see?"

"It's ever since the magus set his mark on me." He rolled back his cuff and turned his wrist over; the magus's sigil could only faintly be distinguished, even in daylight, like a faint scar silvering his skin. "Ever since that day, I see things that others don't. It's like a sixth sense."

She extended one fingertip very slowly and touched the mark. Every move that she made was slow, as if she were sleepwalking. She looked up into his eyes. "Can he still control you, Jagu? He put his mark on you."

"It . . . it burns when he is near. That's how I knew. Both here and in Bel'Esstar."

"Does it still burn?"

"No. He must be far away."

"And if he were to die, would it disappear?"

"That's what Père Judicael told me."

Her fingers were still touching his skin; they stood, heads close together, locked in this strange, new understanding.

"I wish you had shown me sooner," she said.

"Let me share your secret. I swear to you I will never betray you." His voice trembled in his desire to convince her of his sincerity. "I care too much about you to let anyone harm you."

Her eyes searched his. Blank, empty of any hint of emotion, she seemed like a shell of the girl he loved.

"My father," she said, still speaking without expression, "left me a book. It is no ordinary book. It is a grimoire, containing some of the most closely guarded secrets of his profession."

"So your father was—"

"An alchymist, executed by the Inquisition for practicing the

Forbidden Arts. He was a good man, Jagu. But his partner and mentor, Kaspar Linnaius, escaped arrest and stole many of my father's secrets."

Jagu looked at her in amazement. "You're an alchymist's daughter? And you're working for the Commanderie?"

"You promised me, Jagu, you promised—"

"And I will keep your secret, Celestine." She had honored him by telling the truth, a truth that no one else knew. "But you must promise me also that you will never risk your life by using your father's grimoire. For if Inquisitor Visant discovers your true identity, he won't hesitate to bring you to trial—and destroy you, just as he destroyed your father. He is a ruthless, driven man. Not even the captain could save you." He waited, watching her face intently, praying that she would do as he asked.

"The book is all I have left of my father." For a moment he caught a glimpse of the alchymist's orphaned child, vulnerable and bewildered. She had lost her father, her mother, and now her lover.

"I understand," he said, more gently. "Of course you want to preserve it as a memento. But why join the Commanderie? You must hate the men who arrested and executed your father—and with good cause."

"I joined because I could think of no better way to hunt down Magus Kaspar Linnaius." The air of vulnerability had gone, replaced by a look of ruthlessness he had never seen before.

"Then, in our own ways, we joined for the same reasons. No wonder we make a good team."

Dame Elmire was dozing again; Celestine sat beside the old lady's bedside, her father's book on her lap, wishing that she could sleep so easily. A single night-light burned on the table, but Celestine had left the shutters open so that she could see the stars.

She still could not bring herself to return to her room. But she could not bear to leave his house just yet. She knew that once she made up her mind to leave, she would never return.

"*Why did you tell him your secret?*" The Faie was gazing at her from the cover of the book, her soulful eyes as bright as the winter starlight outside.

"Why?" Celestine had had plenty of time to wonder if she had been rash to confide in Jagu. "Because Jagu has as much reason as I to hate the Magus. And because . . . I trust him."

"*But how far can you trust him? Every man has his price.*"

"I would trust Jagu with my life. He's a good man."

"Who's there?" murmured the old lady. "I thought I heard voices . . ."

"It's only me, Dame Elmire," said Celestine, leaning forward to squeeze her wrinkled hand in reassurance.

"Isn't Henri back yet from the Opera House? He's late again . . ."

Celestine hesitated. Better to preserve the illusion, rather than distress the old lady with the unhappy truth. "No," she said softly, "he won't be back . . . till later."

CHAPTER 35

Celestine and Sister Katell stood side by side, gazing out at the grey waters of the bay. A sea breeze, tinged with brine, tousled Celestine's hair and stirred Katell's white linen veil.

"Four years," said Celestine, staring into the misted horizon. "And yet here it seems as if nothing has changed. Sister Kinnie is still making simples in the Infirmary, Sister Noyale is still as strict as ever in her choir training . . ."

"Well, excuse me!" said Katell crossly. "Sister Katell is now in charge of teaching the Skylarks to read and write. And a mouthy, mischievous bunch of little brats they are too. I'm sure we were never so ill behaved."

Celestine almost felt herself smiling. "I can't think of anyone better suited to teach them their manners than you."

"And you missed Saint Azilia's Day again. You promised me," said Katell severely.

Celestine could not meet her eyes. "I'm not sure," she said indistinctly, "that I'll ever be able to sing again."

"Dear Celestine." Katell wrapped her long arms around her, hugging her against her lean frame. If anything, she had become wirier and taller since they had last met. "Is that what *he* would have wanted? You were his inspiration. If you don't sing the music that he wrote for you, it'll be like . . . like losing your last connection with him."

Henri's music, unbidden, had begun to sing softly in her mind.

Where is my spring-moon lover? And that radiant melody, which he had written especially for her, now had a bitter resonance, tainted by the knowledge that there would be no more.

"I'm not yet ready," she said defensively, pulling away from Katell and setting off alone back along the shore.

Celestine gazed out of the guest room window. The moon was full, silvering the shore as the incoming tide washed away the footprints in the sand where she and Katell had walked earlier.

"It's time," she whispered into the night. "Katell was right. I must sing again."

By the moon's clear, fragile light, she returned to her packing. The prospect of returning to the bustle of Lutèce filled her with dread, yet as she mechanically folded her clothes and put them in her trunk, she had to admit to herself that much as she had appreciated the quiet of the convent, she had become increasingly restless as the weeks passed.

She placed *Lives of the Holy Saints* carefully between the top layers of linen, then took it out again, weighing it in her hands.

This ordinary-looking little volume was the cause of Henri's death.

"Why, Faie? Why did the magus want you and my father's book so desperately?"

A soft radiance illumined the austere room. The Faie emerged, gazing steadily at her with eyes as clear as spring rain.

"Who was he? Was he Kaspar Linnaius? Why won't you tell me?"

"He was the one who set me free."

Celestine had not expected such an answer. "But I thought my father was the one who—"

"That magus was little more than a boy then. He was not powerful enough to bind me. But that boy has become a man."

"And he called me Klervie. My real name. How could he have known . . ." Disjointed fragments of memory from her childhood in Karantec, long buried, began to surface. "Wait. Are you saying he was my father's apprentice?" There had been a dark-haired boy with green eyes who used to come to the cottage. Sometimes he brought scraps of fish for Mewen. "But all the magi at Karantec were executed. I read it in the Inquisition archives. No one survived. So how—"

"His master, Linnaius, stole me."

"He was Linnaius's apprentice?" Celestine hugged the book to her, overwhelmed by the sudden realization that Linnaius might have sent the soul-stealer to reclaim the Faie. "So it still comes back to Linnaius. And his apprentice, whom everyone believed dead, is very much alive."

"Alive?" echoed the Faie. *"After the injuries I inflicted on his hawk-familiar I doubt that either will have survived."* She spoke softly yet there was a ruthless edge to her words that made Celestine shiver; she knew now that the Faie's frail aura concealed a considerable and dangerous power.

"So he's no longer a threat to us?"

"I don't want to be in thrall again, Celestine, I want to stay with you." The Faie's aura bloomed in the darkness, caressing Celestine, surrounding her like an embrace. Celestine closed her eyes, relaxing in the calming warmth of her gentle light. "Yes," she murmured. "We've been through so much together. I couldn't bear to be separated from you now . . . you've become a part of me."

Ruaud de Lanvaux gazed down at the ring of office that the king had just presented to him. The last Angelstone hung on a gold chain around his neck over his robes of office. He longed to take the heavy embroidered garments off and put on his comfortable old uniform jacket again.

"May I be the first to offer my congratulations, Grand Maistre?" Celestine de Joyeuse stood waiting for him outside his rooms. A stab of bitter guilt pierced him as he remembered how he had accidentally crushed the soul-glass.

And crushed your hopes of happiness with the man you loved, Celestine. The possibility that it might have been too late to reunite de Joyeuse's soul and body anyway was nowhere near as consoling as it should have been.

"My dear girl, when did you return to Lutèce?" He had feared that the shock of losing Henri de Joyeuse might have driven her to retire to the convent for life.

"I've just arrived. When I heard your news, I had to come and see you." She smiled at him and it was a smile of genuine warmth, which gladdened his heart, driving away the lingering shadows of guilt. But as soon as they were alone together inside his study, her expression altered. "I have a request, Grand Maistre. I want to work as a Commanderie agent again. I want to track down the magus who murdered Henri and bring him to justice. Even if it means traveling deep into the heart of enemy territory to find him."

Ruaud saw a new look of resolve hardening her clear blue eyes. She had suffered a great loss but she seemed to have emerged more resilient than before. She would make a resourceful and courageous agent.

"Francia needs strong spirits like yours, Celestine. But you cannot undertake such a mission alone. You need a partner."

The Church of Saint Meriadec was shrouded in evening shadows, but a blaze of brilliant organ fanfares made the air tremble.

There was a driven, intense quality about the performance, almost as if the player had stood on the edge of the abyss and gazed into its darkest depths.

Celestine walked slowly toward the choir stalls where she had so often spent her days singing. The last organ notes died away and she looked up, knowing that she had positioned herself exactly where he could see her in his mirror.

"A word with you, Lieutenant de Rustéphan," she said. A moment or so later, he came hurtling down the little stairs—and then stopped, gazing at her.

"Is it really you, Celestine?" And then he hurried across to her. "I was afraid we'd lost you to Saint Azilia's for good."

"Oh, Jagu," she said, suddenly overwhelmed by emotion, "it's good to see you again." Yet neither she nor Jagu reached out to embrace each other; it was as if Henri de Joyeuse's ghost stood between them in the church where they had all made music together. "I have instructions here from the Grand Maistre." She held up the letter that had arrived by special courier. "It seems that we've been invited to give a concert in Mirom, at the Winter Palace."

"So we're to be partnered again?" he said. "We'd better start putting a program together."

"Who knows where we'll be asked to perform next?" she said lightly. "Maybe even at the Palace of Swanholm, in Tielen. I hear that Prince Eugene is having a fine concert room built there . . . close to the laboratories where his Royal Artificier works. What was his name, now? Oh yes, Kaspar Linnaius."

Their eyes met. "A pact, Jagu?" she said, holding out her hand. He gripped it between his own.

"This time we won't fail," he said. "We'll find this Magus—and we'll make him pay for his crimes."

CAST

The College of Thaumaturgy at Karantec

Klervie de Maunoir/Celestine de Joyeuse
Hervé de Maunoir, a young magus
Maela, his wife
Kaspar Linnaius, an elder magus
Rieuk Mordiern, a student magus
Goustan de Rhuys, another magus
Magister Gonery, principal of the college

The Seminary of Saint Argantel at Kemper

Jagu de Rustéphan, a pupil
Paol de Lannion, Kilian Guyomard, Emilion, fellow pupils
Abbé Houardon, headmaster
Père Magloire, librarian and archivist
Père Albin, Jagu's master

The Francian Commanderie

Ruaud de Lanvaux
Alain Friard
Grand Maistre Donatien

Lieutenant Konan
Père Laorans
Philippe Viaud
Père Blaize

THE CONVENT OF SAINT AZILIA

Abbess Ermengarde
Sister Kinnie
Sister Noyale, the choir mistress
Rozenne, Katell, Koulmia, Gauzia, Angelique, Celestine's fellow
    choristers

LUTÈCE

Henri de Joyeuse, the choir master
Dame Elmire Sorel, Henri's aunt
Aurélie Carnelian, diva

THE FRANCIAN INQUISITION

Inquisitor Alois Visant

ONDHESSAR

Imri Boldiszar
Lord Estael
Arkhan Sardion of Enhirre
Magus Aqil, Master of Poisons
Oranir, Aqil's apprentice

THE ROYAL HOUSE OF FRANCIA

King Gobain II
Queen Aliénor
Crown Prince Aubrey
Prince Enguerrand
Princess Adèle

ABOUT THE AUTHOR

SARAH ASH is the author of six previous fantasy novels: *Children of the Serpent Gate, Lord of Snow and Shadows, Prisoner of the Iron Tower, Moths to a Flame, Songspinners,* and *The Lost Child*. She also runs the library in a local primary school. Ash has two grown sons and lives in Beckenham, Kent, with her husband and their mad cat, Molly.